Cameron Cody stood at the window and watched the woman he intended to marry gather up her belongings and walk back to the beach house.

He refused to think about what her reaction would be when she discovered he was her new neighbor. Would she scream in frustration when she learned that she had fled Charlotte, North Carolina, and was hiding out in Jamaica for nothing?

As soon as he had gotten word that she intended to leave the country, he'd made plans to join her in paradise. And she might not know it yet, but her time for avoiding him had just run out. He was ready to make his move.

Cameron glanced around the home he had recently purchased, wanting to believe that luck was still on his side. Buying this house had been easy, but it was only the first move in gaining what he suspected would be the most valuable asset he possessed—Vanessa Steele.

BRENDA JACKSON

is a die "heart" romantic who married her childhood sweetheart and still proudly wears the "going steady" ring he gave her when she was fifteen. Because she's always believed in the power of love, Brenda's stories always have happy endings. In her real-life love story, Brenda and her husband of thirty-three years live in Jacksonville, Florida, and have two sons.

A *USA TODAY* bestselling author, Brenda divides her time between family, writing and working in management at a major insurance company. You may write Brenda at P.O. Box 28267, Jacksonville, Florida 32226, by e-mail at WriterBJackson@aol.com or visit her Web site at www.brendajackson.net.

riskyPLEASURES

BRENDA JACKSON

KIMANI
ROMANCE

To Gerald Jackson, Sr., the man who shows me
what true love is all about.

To all my readers who are participating in the
Madaris/Westmoreland/Steele Family
Reunion Cruise, 2007, this one is for you.

To my Heavenly Father, who gave me the gift to write.

Plans fail for lack of counsel,
but with many advisers they succeed.
Proverbs 15:22

 KIMANI PRESS™

ISBN-13: 978-0-373-86012-8
ISBN-10:   0-373-86012-9

RISKY PLEASURES

Copyright © 2007 by Brenda Streater Jackson

www.kimanipress.com

Printed in U.S.A.

Dear Reader,

Turn the air-conditioning up a notch and get the lemonade or iced tea ready because *Risky Pleasures* promises to be a scorcher.

Most of you know I enjoy writing sensuous love stories, the ones that give you a chance to escape into a world of fantasy. In Cameron and Vanessa's story I've set out to do just that, and I have to admit I turned up the heat a lot!

In *Risky Pleasures* there are two very different people who have one very important thing in common—an intense sexual attraction for each other.

Cameron's plan is long-term. He wants Vanessa for life, but doesn't think love has anything to do with it. For him, passion is merely a matter of possession. Vanessa's plan is short-term. She wants Cameron for a sex mate, but only for a few days. Like all my characters, my plan is to help these two discover that unforgettable days and nights of passion can be hazardous to the heart and can lead to a multitude of *risky pleasures*. The big question is, Are they up for the challenge?

I had fun writing this story and I hope you have just as much fun reading it.

Brenda Jackson

Prologue

"Take it from someone who almost found out the hard way, Van. Running away never solves anything."

Vanessa Steele shifted her gaze from the open suitcase to the woman standing in her doorway. Sienna Bradford had been her best friend since grade school, but it bothered Vanessa that at times Sienna thought she knew her better than she knew herself. Unfortunately, some times Sienna actually did.

"I am not running away." But not even Vanessa's short, gruff tone could convince anyone that she wasn't getting the hell out of Dodge because a certain man by the name of Cameron Cody was on his way to Charlotte, supposedly to spend some time visiting with her cousins.

"Then please explain what you're doing if you're not running away."

Vanessa sighed and tossed aside the blouse she was about to pack. "I'm leaving for Jamaica because Cheyenne called and asked if I would house-sit while the builders are putting in her pool. She hadn't planned on having to go to Italy for an unscheduled photo shoot," Vanessa said of her sister, an international model. "There's not a lot happening at work and a vacation in Jamaica is just what I need."

Sienna arched a brow. "And your leaving has nothing to do with Cameron coming to town?"

Vanessa nervously averted her gaze. "I wish I can say one has nothing to do with the other but that wouldn't be true and you and I both know it. Cheyenne's phone call gave me the out I need, and I'm taking it."

Sienna came farther into the room, forcing Vanessa to look at her. "What are you afraid of, Van? Why do you feel so much dislike and anger toward one man?"

"You of all people know why, Sienna. You know what Cameron tried to do to my family's business."

"Yes, but that was three years ago. And if your cousins have gotten over it and consider him a friend, why can't you?"

"I'll never consider that man a friend," Vanessa snapped.

"Then maybe you need to wonder why," Sienna replied smoothly. "There has to be a reason for your intense dislike of him."

Vanessa rolled her eyes. "There is, and I've told you what it is."

"I only know what you've convinced yourself it is."

Vanessa lifted a brow. "And what's that supposed to mean?"

"Only that I have eyes. I've been watching you and Cameron for a while now, especially at Morgan and Lena's wedding last month. What I saw between you wasn't animosity, but a buildup of sexual chemistry of the most potent and compelling kind. And I think the reason you don't like being around him is because, if given the chance, you'd want to have your way with him." Sienna grinned. "You'd probably jump his bones in a heartbeat."

"What!" Vanessa exclaimed, folding her arms

over her chest and giving her pregnant best friend an incredulous look. "How can you even think of anything so ridiculous?"

"Is it really so ridiculous, Vanessa? Think about it. He's the only man I know who has pushed your buttons since that guy you met in London."

"Well, yeah, that might be true, but he's pushing them the wrong way."

"And what if he starts pushing them the right way? What if one day you discover that Cameron isn't as bad as you think and that an affair with him is just what you need to take the edge off?"

Vanessa laughed. "I don't have an edge on."

"Yes, you do, and we both know it."

Vanessa walked over to her bedroom window and looked out. Yes, she had an edge on, all right. Not that she was counting, but it had been almost four years since that summer she'd spent in London with Harlan, a man she had fancied herself in love with. But Harlan couldn't hold a candle to Cameron Cody. As far as she was concerned, Cameron was the sexiest, most handsome man alive—which wasn't helping matters. It would be a lie to say she hadn't thought about doing him, because she had. A part of her saw it as the perfect way to get him out of her system. Right?

Wrong.

Another part of her saw it as dominance on his part, a sure victory for him. Eventually he'd take her over just as he'd enjoyed taking over corporations that suited his fancy. He had a reputation that made Genghis Khan look like a choirboy.

"Van?"

She turned back around to Sienna. "Are you suggesting that I engage in an affair with Cameron? Especially after what Harlan said?"

Sienna frowned and rubbed her stomach as she felt her baby kick. "Forget about what Harlan Shaw said. As far as I'm concerned, an affair with Cameron sounds like a good plan to me. You're twenty-six, old enough to know the score, and you and Cameron are spontaneous combustion just waiting to happen. I've never been around two more volatile individuals. And I'm not the only one who can feel the intensity, the passion, when the two of you are in the same room. Do us all a favor and finally do something about it."

Vanessa fought back the fear that ran through her at the mere thought of what would happen if she followed Sienna's suggestion. She would find herself at Cameron's mercy, become beholden to him—as she had to Harlan—and the thought of that filled her with disgust. On the other hand, the thought of sharing a bed with Cameron and finally letting go, putting aside her dislike of him to appease her overworked hormones, suddenly replaced the fear with red-hot pleasure. Wanton pleasure. It would be risky pleasure of the most intense type, the kind that would finally take the edge off. Her insides quivered at the very idea of Cameron giving her the best sex of her life. It was too much to think about. Downright scary.

She never wanted to be that vulnerable to a man. Especially not *that* man. There was so much about him she disliked. His chauvinistic, egoistical attitude was one a modern, liberated woman like herself couldn't stand or tolerate. Besides, there was her concern about just what kind of bed partner she would be. According to Harlan, she needed vast improvement in that area.

"Will it help matters if I promise to give it some thought while I'm relaxing on the beach in Jamaica?" Vanessa finally asked.

"You can't run forever. At some point you're going to have to stop running and do something about Cameron. It's obvious that he wants you, Van, and he comes across as a man who gets whatever he wants."

That was exactly what had her worried, Vanessa admitted silently. For some reason she had a feeling that Cameron's upcoming visit had a purpose, one that involved her. Maybe it was the way he had looked at her at the wedding, as if her time for avoiding him was up and that he was about to make his move. Unfortunately, it would be a wasted trip. When he arrived in Charlotte, she'd be long gone.

Chapter 1

This is paradise, Vanessa thought as she stood on the shore of the white-sand beach that overlooked the deep blue waters of the Caribbean Sea. Cheyenne's two-story home was located on a secluded cove in Montero Bay, on a private street with one other house.

Other than the pool workers, who arrived at nine and left by five, Vanessa was alone, except for the two days a week that the housekeeper showed up.

Cheyenne had already left for Italy by the time

Vanessa had arrived so her first days were spent unpacking and shopping.

This was day three and she had decided just to do nothing. Since weather reports had predicted it would be another scorcher of a late-July day, she stayed inside working crossword puzzles and sipping lemonade while reading a book she had picked up yesterday. Later that day, after the workers had left, she gathered up her large straw hat, her beach bag, which was stuffed with a bottle of wine and a glass, and a huge towel to head down to the beach.

When she reached what she considered a good spot, she casually glanced around. This stretch of private beach was shared only by whoever was living in the house next door and so far the place appeared empty. According to Helen, Cheyenne's housekeeper, the house had changed ownership several times, and rumor had it someone had recently purchased it.

Helen had gone on to say that a few years ago, the house had been owned by some gorgeous Italian jet-setting playboy by the name of Chardon Argentina. And if you went along with what everyone believed, a number of seductions had taken place in that house. It was even rumored that many of Hollywood's leading ladies had been overnight guests.

Vanessa shrugged as she spread the huge towel on the sand and sat down. She was glad she didn't believe everything she heard. Besides, what had happened in that house was not her business. After placing the huge straw hat on her head and situating the brim in such a way as to block what was left of the sun, she glanced toward the ocean, thinking she could definitely get used to this. She'd never had an entire beach to herself. She was glad that Cheyenne had invited her to stay.

She, Taylor and Cheyenne had always been close, but it was Vanessa who had decided to stick with the family business instead of pursuing other careers as her sisters had. She had returned home to Charlotte and the Steele Corporation after getting a grad degree from Tennessee State.

Taylor, who was twenty-four, had graduated from Georgetown with a degree in business and a grad degree in finance. After college, she'd moved to New York to work at a major bank as a wealth asset manager and was doing quite well for herself.

After obtaining a degree in communications from Boston University, Cheyenne, who was twenty-two, had taken a reporter position at a television station in Philly and in less than a year, her looks, personality and keen intelligence had gotten her a promotion to the position of anchorwoman on the morning news. That job was short-lived as she had suddenly realized she wanted to do something different and had become a model. Modeling meant a lot of traveling and living in some of the most beautiful and exotic places in the world. A year ago, Cheyenne had been doing a photo shoot in Jamaica when she'd stumbled across this particular house, fallen in love with it and purchased it.

Vanessa leaned back on her arms with her legs stretched out in front of her. She tilted her head back to enjoy the feel of the evening sun on her face, as well as the salty spray from the ocean on her cheeks and lips. She couldn't help wondering what was happening back in Charlotte. Had Cameron arrived yet? Had he discovered her gone? Was he upset about it? Why did she even care?

She was deep into her thoughts when a movement caught her eye, and she turned her head. In the distance, in front of the property next door, she could see a man standing close to shore. With the palm trees partially blocking her view, she couldn't make out his features, but she could tell he wore only a pair of swimming trunks. And he was overpoweringly male.

She sat up as her heart began pumping wildly in her chest, and she wondered what on earth was wrong with her. It wasn't as though she hadn't seen good-looking men before. So what was there about this tall, broad-shouldered, long-legged, fine-as-they-come brother whose aura was seeping out to her over stretches of sand? And what was there about him that seemed so oddly familiar?

Biting down on her lip, she fought against one particular ultra-sexy male image that tried forcing its way into her mind. She simply refused to go there. She would not let Cameron creep into her thoughts. Tilting her head, she refocused her attention as she continued to gaze at the man, not seeing as much as she would like due to the shade cast by the palm trees, the fading evening sun and the emergence of dusk.

Since this was a private beach she quickly assumed he was the owner of the house next door and wondered who he was. A celebrity perhaps? Was he married, single or in between lovers like she was?

A lump caught in her throat when the man eased

down his swimming trunks. It suddenly occurred to her that he was about to go swimming in the nude. Although their properties were separated only by a few palm trees, she wondered if he hadn't noticed her sitting here—if he had, evidently he didn't care.

She knew the decent thing to do was to ignore him, but she couldn't pull her gaze away. When he had completely removed the trunks, she held her breath and wished like hell that she had a pair of binoculars.

Reaching into her beach bag, she pulled out the bottle of wine and wineglass she had packed. By the time the man had dived into the ocean water she had not only poured a glassful but had quickly tossed back the contents, liking how the soothing liquid had flowed down her throat.

She decided to pour another glass, taking her eyes off the man for just a second. When she looked back, pausing with the wineglass halfway to her lips, he was gone. She sighed, wondering if she'd really seen him or if he'd been a mirage, a cruel trick of her imagination.

As she took a sip of her wine to calm her racing heart, a part of her knew that what she'd seen earlier had been the real thing.

* * *

Cameron Cody stood at the window and watched as the woman he intended to marry gathered up her belongings to walk back to the house where she would be staying for two weeks.

He didn't want to think what her reaction would be once she discovered he was her neighbor and that her flight from Charlotte had been for nothing. As soon as he had gotten word—thanks to her cousin and his loyal friend Morgan Steele—that she intended to leave the country for a few weeks to house-sit her sister's home in Jamaica, he had changed his plans. No big deal. Where she went, he intended to follow. Her time for avoiding him had run out. At thirty-five, he was no longer interested in playing games. He was ready to make his move.

When he was sure Vanessa was safely inside the house, he moved away from the window toward the wet bar to pour himself a drink. He glanced around the home he had recently purchased, wanting to believe that luck was still on his side. It had been easy enough to buy this house within a matter of hours, his first move to gain what he considered the most valuable asset of his life.

As he sipped his brandy, he recalled the exact

moment a little over three years ago when he had first laid eyes on Vanessa Steele. He had arrived at a very important Steele Corporation board meeting, one he'd assumed would give him total control of the Charlotte-based manufacturing company.

He had walked into the conference room, confident in his abilities and pretty damn positive that one of the Steeles would defect and throw their voting shares his way. After all, past experience had shown him that if offered the right price, family members had a tendency to prove that blood might be thicker than water but not thicker than the mighty dollar.

The Steeles had proved him wrong that day.

In less than an hour he had walked away after encountering the first defeat of his career as a corporate raider. But that afternoon hadn't been a complete waste, since he had sat across the table from the most beautiful woman he'd ever seen. He could admit now that he had focused his attention more on Vanessa Steele than on taking over her family's company.

The memory of that day would forever be etched in his mind. Something about Vanessa had immediately captured his attention. The moment he had gazed into her eyes he had suffered an instant jolt in his gut. He'd been mesmerized, awe-struck and captivated all at the same time. The other two Steele women had been just as good-looking, but it had been Vanessa who had caused his body and mind to react in all sorts of ways. Everything about her had turned him on, even when she had glared at him, which she'd spent most of her time doing.

During the years that followed, he and members of the Steele family had put the takeover attempt behind them. He was close friends with Vanessa's four older male cousins, especially Morgan, whom he considered one of his best friends. He even got along with her two sisters whenever their paths crossed. But Vanessa hung back, refusing to accept friendship or anything else from him.

She was different from the women he usually dated, since his taste ran to the tall, willowy, talk-only-if-you're-asked-to-speak kind. At five foot eight, she came up to his nose. He'd discovered that fact the one and only time he'd caught her unawares and had gotten up close. And instead of a willowy figure she had a feminine one, with a small waist and seductive curves to her hips. Whenever she passed, every male took notice. And then there was her face. It seemed the hairstyle she wore, short and flippy, was created just for her; it emphasized her ethereal facial features. Dark eyes, a voluptuously formed mouth, a chin imbued with intense stubbornness, and high cheekbones, compliments of her Cheyenne ancestry from her mother's side.

That day in the conference room he knew she had felt the intensity of his attention and hadn't liked it. That hadn't diminished his feelings for her, even though he'd known he should walk away and leave her alone. Ten years ago, at the age of twenty-five, he had learned one hard lesson when it came to matters of the heart. Stay clear of them. A woman who got too deep under a man's skin could ultimately become his downfall. Besides, he needed to use his time working deals and not pursuing resistant women.

But he had ignored the warning bells and now after three years of playing a no-win game, he was ready to pursue a relationship and come out a winner. Some would even go so far as to say that he'd taken drastic measures. All he said was that there came a time when a man had to do what a man had to do. Now he was finally going to do something about this chronic tug of desire that claimed his body each and every time he saw her or thought about her—which was all the time.

Today on the beach she had been wearing a wrap over her bathing suit, but she'd still looked good. He remembered the way the straps of the wrap had hung off her shoulders and how those graceful legs of hers moved when she walked. And when she had sat down and leaned back on her arms and stretched out her legs, he had gotten a nice view of her thigh, and even from a distance he had become so aroused that he'd had to jump into the ocean waters to cool off.

Cameron couldn't retract the smile that touched his lips. Experience had taught him a valuable lesson—if there was something you wanted, then you put all your efforts into getting it. You didn't wait for it to come to you or you'd never have it. And he was a man with a reputation for going after whatever it was he wanted. Hence, here he was, on this beautiful tropical island, going after Vanessa.

By this time tomorrow she would know that he was her neighbor. She would also know that for the remainder of her time on the island, he intended to seduce the hell out of her.

The last time he'd come up against the Steeles, he had failed. This time he would only be dealing with one. Vanessa. He wanted her and no matter what it took, he wouldn't fail at having her.

The ringing of his cell phone crashed its way into his thoughts. Annoyed at the interruption, he picked it up and flipped it open. "Yes, what is it?" he said gruffly.

"McMurray is trying to fight back."

Cameron recognized the caller's voice immediately. Xavier Kane was not only his right-hand man but also a good friend. The two had met at Harvard when Cameron was in business school and Xavier in law school. Though both had been loners, somehow they'd forged a bond that was still intact today. For years Cameron had tried to convince Xavier to come work for him, knowing it would only be a matter of time before his friend got tired of defending men who were guilty of white-collar crimes. Cameron had needed someone to have his back, someone he trusted implicitly, and X was that man. Now Xavier handled all the legal aspects of Cody Enterprises.

A faint smile touched Cameron's lips. "He can fight back, although it's rather late since Global Petroleum is now legally mine."

"Well, I just thought you should know that he

held a press conference today, and I don't have to tell you that he painted you as someone who won't have any sympathy or loyalty with the present workers when you clean house."

Cameron shook his head. "I bet while he was in front of the camera he didn't happen to mention how he messed up his employees' pension plan or how they were about to lose their jobs anyway at the rate he was going."

"Of course he didn't. His intent was to make you look bad. And when I called him to let him know we wouldn't hesitate to take him to court for slander, he made a threat."

Cameron raised a dark brow. "What kind of threat?"

"That you're going to regret the day you were ever born for taking his company away."

Cameron shook his head. "He brought that on himself."

"You and I both know he doesn't see things that way. And there's no telling what will happen when he finds out your connection to his company. After all this time he's evidently put behind him his bad deeds of yesteryear."

Cameron's face hardened. "He might have, but I haven't."

"Just be prepared, Cam. All hell's going to break loose when he discovers why you took his company away."

"How he handles things doesn't matter to me, X, and as far as I'm concerned, John McMurray is serving no purpose by causing problems now."

"Yes, but I've always told you that there's something about him that bothers me. It's like he's not working with a full deck most of the time. As a safety precaution I'm going to let Kurt know what's going on. I want to make sure his men know that McMurray is not allowed back on the premises. If he hasn't cleaned out his desk by now, we'll ship his things to him."

"I agree we should tell Kurt." Kurt Grainger, another college friend, headed up security for Cody Enterprises.

A few moments later, after hanging up the phone, Cameron banished John McMurray from his mind. The only thing he wanted occupying his mind were thoughts of a woman by the name of Vanessa Steele.

Chapter 2

"**W**hat neighbor?"

Vanessa tapped her foot impatiently on the ceramic tile floor. "I'm talking about the man who lives next door, Cheyenne," she said trying to hide her frustration. She had a harder time squashing the irritation she felt with herself for being so curious about the man's identity.

It was morning and the pool workers were ten minutes late already. She couldn't wait to gather her stuff and go back down to the beach in hopes that she would see the stranger again. For some reason he had played on her thoughts all night.

"I truly don't know anything about a man living next door," Cheyenne said convincingly. "That house has been up for sale for a while, but I hadn't heard anything of a new owner. It must have been rather recent."

After a brief pause, Cheyenne then asked, "Why are you interested in my new neighbor, Van?"

Vanessa frowned and searched her mind for a reason her sister would believe and decided to be honest. "I saw him yesterday. At least I caught a glimpse of him," she said, deciding not to tell Cheyenne about the man swimming in the nude. "And I liked what I saw."

"Umm, your hormones acting up, are they?" her sister asked in a teasing voice.

"You sound like Sienna, and no, my hormones are not acting up. It was the usual reaction a woman would have to a good-looking man."

"Then do something about it. Be neighborly and go over there, introduce yourself and welcome him to the neighborhood."

Vanessa's mouth quirked. Of the three of them Cheyenne had always been the most daring. "I can't do that."

"Sure you can. You're a liberated woman. You

don't have to wait for the man to make the first move. What are you afraid of?"

That was the same question Sienna had asked her about Cameron. "I'm not afraid of anything," she came back to say. She was wrong, though. She was afraid of something. Rejection. Thanks to Harlan Shaw.

"Well, my advice is, if you're interested, act on it."

"Goodbye, Cheyenne."

"Why do you always do that, Van? When someone tells you something you don't want to hear, you bow out in a hurry."

"You just answered your own question, Cheyenne," she said with a weak smile in her voice. "You're telling me something I really don't want to hear. Love you. Goodbye."

Vanessa hung up the phone.

A couple of hours later, Vanessa stood in her sister's kitchen with her back against the counter looking at the picnic basket she had placed on the table. It was her idea of a welcome-to-the-neighborhood gift and contained a bottle of spring water, a block of cheese she had picked up from the market two days ago, as well as a pack of crackers. Then there was the fruit she had added and for dessert, oatmeal raisin cookies she had baked.

Vanessa knew if either Taylor or Cheyenne was putting the basket together they would probably include a tablecloth, the proper eating utensils and enough food for two with the intent of joining him in a picnic instead of giving him everything he needed to enjoy on his own. To say both of her sisters were bold when it came to dating was an understatement. But then neither had encountered the likes of Harlan, the man responsible for rattling her self-confidence.

In fact, neither of her sisters nor her cousins had ever heard of him. The only person who'd known about him was Sienna. Vanessa had immediately been taken with Harlan's handsome features and smooth talk while vacationing for two weeks in London four years ago. He'd been a college professor from Los Angeles on a year's sabbatical doing research for a book he was writing.

She'd thought he was special, an intellectual genius. She'd also assumed that he had fallen in love with her, as she had with him, and that he would want to continue what they'd started once she returned to the States. Instead, on the last night they spent together, the one and only time they'd been intimate, he'd told her they were through. She hadn't been everything that he fully desired from a woman in bed. After the pain of his cruel words, she had made a decision not to let any man close enough to break her heart again. That was the main reason she kept a comfortable distance between herself and Cameron Cody. She would admit—but only to herself and only when she was in a good mood—that she was attracted to him, but her mother hadn't raised her to be a fool twice over.

So instead of being as bold as she wanted to be and inviting the man next door to picnic with her on the beach, she would do the neighborly thing and present him with a welcome basket and leave. She wouldn't even enter his home if he invited her inside. He was a stranger and she knew nothing about him. He could be married or some woman's fiancé. She had enough to keep her mind occupied over the next two weeks. She certainly didn't need a man around causing problems. All she had to do when she felt weak was to remember Harlan, although she had to admit Harlan's memory had a tendency to fade to black when Cameron was around.

She walked over to the basket, opened the lid and did a quick check to make sure she hadn't forgotten anything. She wondered what Mr. Neighbor would think when she appeared on his doorstep. She intended to meet the man then put him out of her thoughts once and for all.

Little Red Riding Hood.

That was the first thought that came to Cameron's mind when he glanced out his library window and saw the feminine figure coming up his walkway dressed in a red shorts set, a red straw hat and carrying a picnic basket. He pasted a smile on his lips. It seemed that Vanessa would be finding out his identity sooner than he had anticipated, but that was just as well.

He stood and pressed the intercom button on his desk and within minutes an elderly lady appeared. It seemed that Martha Pritchett came with the house, having been housekeeper to the previous four owners, over a period of fifteen years. She had been born and raised on the island and arrived early on Monday, Wednesday and Friday mornings. He really didn't need her that often and with little to do, she usually left by noon. But during the time she was there, he'd found her to be very efficient.

"Yes, Mr. Cody?"

"I'm about to get a visitor."

"And you want me to send them away," she said quickly, assuming what would be his position on unwelcome guests.

In most circumstances she wasn't far off the mark, but in this case, the last thing he wanted was Vanessa sent away. "No. I want you to do whatever it takes to encourage her to stay. I'm going upstairs to change and will be back down in a minute."

"Yes, sir."

"And in case it comes up in conversation, I prefer that you not give her my name."

If Martha found his request strange, her expression didn't show it. "All right."

With adrenaline of the strongest kind rushing through his veins, Cameron turned and left the room.

Vanessa stood, stretched and for the third time dismissed the idea of leaving before officially meeting her neighbor. She'd only rung his bell once when the door had been opened by an elderly lady with a huge smile who'd introduced herself as Martha.

Vanessa had given her the spiel of wanting to welcome her sister's new neighbor, and then, without batting an eye, the older woman had ushered her inside. That had been a little over five minutes ago. Explaining that the master of the house would be down shortly, she led Vanessa to the massive living room. A few moments later she had returned with a tray of hot tea and the most delicious teacakes Vanessa had ever eaten. Then she had excused herself.

Vanessa glanced around the room, admiring everything she saw and wondering if the decorating was the taste of the present owner or if, as in the case of Cheyenne's home, the furnishings had come with the house. Whichever the case, Vanessa was in awe of the furniture's rich design, as well as the cost of the paintings that hung on the walls. Being best friend to Sienna, who was an interior designer, had acquainted her with the different designs and style of furniture and it was plain to see everything in the house spoke of wealth.

And then there was this breathtaking view of the ocean through the large floor-to-ceiling window. She could stand there looking out at that view for hours, but she didn't have that much time to spare, she thought, glancing at her watch. The five-minute wait time had stretched to seven, and a part of her refused to be kept waiting any longer. Besides, each and every time she was reminded of what she had seen of her neighbor yesterday made goose bumps form on her arms.

What if he walked into the room wearing something as skimpy as the swimming trunks he'd had on yesterday? Or, worse yet, what if he was bold enough to walk into the room wearing nothing at all?

Vanessa felt her face flush at the thought and immediately decided maybe coming here hadn't been a good idea after all. She should have waited until their paths crossed on the beach or something. Sighing, she was about to turn around when she heard a deep husky voice behind her.

"Sorry to keep you waiting."

Vanessa went still. She knew that voice. She knew that sensual texture, that smooth timbre, that silky reverberation. Her throat immediately tightened around the gasp that formed in it. She felt heat flow up her arms as a tingling sensation swept through her at the same time that realization streamed all through her. It was highly unlikely that two men could produce that same sexy sound. It was a voice she'd always thought was meant to seduce, and it could only belong to one man.

She quickly turned around and her gaze clashed with dark eyes, the same dark eyes she often fantasized about at night in the privacy of her bedroom. Before she could utter his name in shock and disbelief, she watched as a small smile touched the corners of his lips right before he spoke.

"Hello, Vanessa. Welcome to my home."

"Your home?" Vanessa snapped the words as she fought the intense anger that was coursing through her, consuming every part of her body. If this was somebody's idea of a joke, she wasn't at all amused. She closed her eyes, hoping this was a bad dream. There was no way Cameron Cody could be here when he was supposed to be in Charlotte. But seconds later, when she reopened her eyes, he still stood across the room, staring at her. She could feel her blood pressure rise.

Her gaze swept over him. His head was clean-shaven, his eyes deep and dark. An angular jaw with a cleft in the chin completed an outrageously handsome face. This was the first time she'd seen him wearing anything other than a business suit or tux, but the jeans and pullover shirt looked good on him. He appeared tall, solid, rugged and impenetrable. And just as yesterday, when she had seen him from a distance, his mere presence denoted some sort of masculine power.

"Yes, my home," he said, breaking into her thoughts and stepping into the room.

She narrowed her eyes and placed her hands on her hips. "And just when did you buy it?"

"A few days ago," he replied in a low, controlled voice, a sharp contrast to hers. She was livid and her voice reflected her emotion.

"Please don't tell me that you bought this house when you found out I was coming here."

He shoved his hands into the pockets of his jeans and met her narrowed gaze. Instead of showing any sign of wilting under her angry stare, he simply said, "Okay, then I won't tell you."

Vanessa heard her own teeth gnashing and wondered if he heard it, as well. Angrily, she strode to the center of the room to stand in front of him. "Just who the hell do you think you are?"

"I prefer to know *your* thoughts instead, Vanessa. You tell me who *you* think I am."

She tried not to notice the sexy drawl in his voice when he'd said her name, or the intense look in his eyes. She threw her head back and tilted it at an angle. "I think you are the most ruthless, uncaring, callous, hard-nosed and unfeeling man that I know."

He nodded slowly and then said, "If you believe that, then it means you really don't know me very well, because I'm considerate, compassionate, loyal and passionate. I can prove it."

Of the four qualities he'd named the only one she could believe he had in his favor was passion. "I don't want you to prove anything. You being here and buying this house only show how far you'll go to get something you want, something you intend to possess. What is it about me that has become an obsession to you, Cameron? Is it because the Steele Corporation was the one company you couldn't get your cold, callous hands on and now you've decided to go after me for revenge?"

"My wanting you has nothing to do with revenge, Vanessa. It has everything to do with the intensity of my desire for you."

A part of Vanessa wished he hadn't said that one word, a word she'd been battling since meeting him. *Desire.* Cameron Cody wasn't a man a woman could ignore—at least not a woman with any degree of passion in her bones. There was something about him that grabbed you, snatched your attention the moment he walked into a room. It was something that went beyond just a handsome face and a well-built body. There was something perilous about him, something downright lethal. She was convinced that beneath his civilized side there was a part of him that could be downright ruthless, unrefined and plain old raw. Some women were drawn to such men, but she wasn't.

"I care nothing about the intensity of your desire for me," she finally said. "I just want to be left alone."

"I've left you alone long enough."

"Excuse me?"

"I said I've left you alone long enough," he drawled smoothly and in a **way that** had those same goose bumps reappearing on her arms. "I've given you more time than I've given anything I've ever wanted."

Fire flared in Vanessa's eyes. She couldn't believe the audacity of the man. "And should I feel grateful about that?"

Cameron moved a step closer. "It's not gratitude I want you to feel. Right now I want you to feel something else altogether."

Before she could blink, he stepped closer and pulled her into his arms. His mouth descended upon hers, snatching her next breath. For some reason that she didn't understand, instinctively her lips parted at the same time she felt strong hands wrap around her. Before she could register anything else, before she could regain total control of what was happening and stop it from going further, Cameron inserted his tongue into her mouth.

The moment she sampled his taste, just as bold and daring as the rest of him, she gasped. Then she moaned deep in her throat when her pulse rate escalated. Suddenly, she felt a spine-tingling sensation race through her body, along with an intense need to put all she had into this kiss.

The kiss was everything she'd hoped it would not be, the kind of kiss that drew her to him like a magnet. It was the kind of kiss that did more than give her a sampling of his taste. It was feeding her in a way she had never been fed before. His invasive tongue was doing things a male tongue had never done in her mouth before, making it an art. With other men, she had considered kissing a chore, something that was expected of you.

But Cameron was taking the art of French-kissing to a whole other level. It was downright scandalous, all the things he was doing. But a part of her didn't want him to stop. And he was getting her to join in the erotic byplay, something she had never done before.

She felt herself drowning in his sensuality, getting smothered in the passion. And she knew if she didn't put a stop to this madness now, he would claim a victory; the same way he did with anything else he went after. And she refused to become another one of his claimed possessions.

With more strength than she'd thought she had, she pushed herself out of his arms and inhaled deeply to regain control of her senses. She felt flustered and knew she probably looked it, as well. But to her way of thinking, he maintained a calm demeanor, looking totally in control, programmed and completely at ease. His coolness made her even angrier. It also proved what she'd said earlier. The man had no feelings.

"That should not have happened," she snapped.

"But it did, and it will again," he said with strong conviction in his voice. "We are two passionate individuals, Vanessa. The reason you didn't fight me off just now is because you've been aching to taste me just as long as I've been aching to taste you. And things won't stop there, sweetheart. They can only go further."

"No!"

"Yes. You can't fight me on this. Becoming mine is inevitable."

"Like hell!"

A small smile curved his wide mouth. "Actually it'll be more like heaven. That I promise you."

She took another step back. "Don't promise me anything, Cameron. Just stay away from me."

"Sorry, I can't do that."

Her mind registered his words but she refused to accept them. "I will fight you with every breath in my body."

"You do that. And at the same time I plan on claiming you with every breath in mine."

"You know nothing about me!"

"But I will. I intend to get to know everything about you, Vanessa. Count on it."

Knowing that continuing to exchange words with him was a complete waste of her time, she angrily moved around him to leave his home, pausing only to snatch her red straw hat off the table.

Chapter 3

"Mr. Cody, what do you want me to do with the basket that Ms. Steele brought?"

Cameron forced his gaze from the window where he watched an angry Vanessa make her way down his palm-tree-lined driveway toward the path that would lead her back to her place. To say she was highly upset with him would be an understatement.

He turned slowly, took a deep breath and let it out before asking, "Where is it?"

"I placed it on the kitchen table."

"Leave it there. I'll take care of it."

"Yes, sir." She turned to leave.

"And, Martha?"

She turned back to him. "Yes, sir?"

"If Vanessa Steele ever returns, whether I'm here or not, she is welcome."

He was certain that after overhearing his and Vanessa's conversation, his housekeeper probably thought that this would be the last place Vanessa would show her face again. However, if those were her thoughts, Martha was keeping them to herself. "Yes, sir," she said instead. "I'll make a point of remembering that." Then she left the room.

Moments later, curiosity drew Cameron to the kitchen to see exactly what Vanessa had put in his gift basket. Like a kid in a candy store he started pulling things out, smiling when he saw the oatmeal raisin cookies she was famous for, the ones he'd heard Morgan rave about so many times.

As he began putting everything back in the basket he saw that her intent was for him to have a picnic without her, since there was just enough of everything for one person to enjoy. That was thoughtful of her. But then, from what he'd learned of Vanessa, she was a rather thoughtful person, which was why she was involved in so many community projects. But, as he'd told her, there was a lot about her he didn't know, and since he intended to marry her relatively soon, he needed to continue his quest to get to know her.

Ten years ago he had vowed never to become involved in a relationship with even the remotest chance of becoming serious. He had made it a point to be totally honest with women he dated, to let them know up front that there were zero odds that the affair would go anywhere. He was very selective, preferring those women within his social circle. And there were certain things he just didn't do. He didn't invite them to functions that included his closest friends. And he never gave one free rein in his home. His home—and he had several— was his sanctuary, his private and personal domain. No woman had permission to invade his place. Until now. As he'd told Martha, Vanessa was welcome to his home at any time. If he was busy, he was to be interrupted; if he was asleep, he wanted to be awakened. It was important that he got his point across to Vanessa that she had become the most important thing in his life.

He leaned back against the counter, thinking about how she'd looked standing in the middle of his living room, as angry as any woman had a right to be. While she was standing there giving him what she saw as a much-deserved dressing down, he was giving her a dressing down of another type. He'd been wondering just what she had on beneath that cute pair of red linen shorts with the matching top. Some of the thoughts that had run through his mind had been outright scandalous. She hadn't been wearing a bra, he could tell that. But then her breasts were just the right size and shape not to need one. And when he had pulled her into his arms and kissed her, he had known the exact moment her nipples had hardened because he'd felt them press firmly against his chest.

After their kiss, when he'd finally released her lips, he couldn't help but recall how he'd left them moist and thoroughly kissed. And then there had been that deep, dark, desire-filled look in her eyes, just seconds before they turned fiery red and she began spouting off about him staying away from her. But, as he'd told her, that wouldn't happen.

He would admit her finding out he had bought this house just to be close to her threw a monkey wrench in things for a while, but he was determined not to give up. Eventually, she would get over it, especially when she saw he wasn't going away. He intended to use whatever means he found necessary to break down her defenses.

With that in mind he walked out of the kitchen and went to the nearest intercom to summon Martha.

"Yes, Mr. Cody?"

"I want a dozen red roses sent to Ms. Steele. And I want a bottle of wine delivered with the flowers. Have the card say, 'Thanks for the basket. I'd love to share its contents, as well as this wine, with you later today on the beach.'"

"Yes, sir."

Confident the older woman was capable of carrying out his wishes, he headed toward the study.

"Calm down, Vanessa, and stop yelling. I don't understand a word you're saying."

Vanessa inhaled deeply. Sienna was right. She *had* been yelling. Pausing, she rubbed her cell phone against her cheek to calm nerves that were already shot to hell. She couldn't believe it. She just couldn't believe it.

"Now do you want to start over and tell me what has you so upset?"

Sienna's voice—calm as you please—reminded her why she was so upset. "Cameron is here, Sienna."

"Here, where?"

Vanessa rolled her eyes. "Here in Jamaica. On this island. Living right next door. He had the audacity, the gall, to purchase the house next door. I am as pissed as any woman can get."

"I can tell. You're raising your voice again. Calm down. So, you're saying he found out you were skipping town and decided to follow you?"

"Yes, that's exactly what I'm saying. Just what am I supposed to do about that?"

"Make the most of it."

"Sienna!"

"Okay, considering how you feel about the man, I guess that wasn't a good answer."

"No it wasn't," Vanessa said, walking over to the refrigerator and grabbing one of Cheyenne's beers. "So come up with something else."

It was only after popping the top off the bottle that she remembered she didn't like beer. But what the hell, her day was a total waste now anyway. She took a swallow, straight from the bottle, and decided this particular brand wasn't so bad.

"Okay, but first I want to know how you found out he was there."

For the next fifteen minutes Vanessa filled Sienna in. It would have taken less time had Sienna not asked so many questions, especially when Vanessa told her about seeing Cameron go skinny-dipping.

"Well," Sienna said, sighing deeply. "You've

warned him to stay away from you and if he doesn't adhere to your request you can have him arrested as a stalker."

"Sienna!"

"Hey, I'm serious."

Vanessa rolled her eyes upward. "Cameron doesn't pose that kind of threat and you know it. He's merely being a pain in the ass."

"All right, then, let's cover one more time why he is such a pain in your rear end. The man is simply gorgeous, any woman can see that. Even I can and you know that I only have eyes for Dane. Cameron has money, plenty of it. And he has manners. He's refined, sophisticated, intelligent—"

"He's also in the business of taking people's companies away from them."

"Come on, Van. Are you going to hold what he tried doing to the Steele Corporation over his head forever? Business is business. You can't hate all the corporate raiders out there. Look at Ted Turner, another self-made millionaire who created more jobs than he took away. Corporate takeovers have become a way of life. Besides, look at the number of people who are benefiting from all those foundations Cameron has set up. He's on the cover of *Ebony* this month, by the way. You should pick up a copy and read the article. I did. I was impressed."

"Stay impressed. There's nothing that man can do that will impress me."

"It'll be your loss, and unfortunately another sister's gain. I bet there are a number of women out there who would love getting a piece of Cameron Cody right now."

"They're welcome to him!"

"At some point I believe I'm going to have to remind you that you said that."

Vanessa rubbed the bridge of her nose, wondering why she'd bothered calling Sienna anyway. For some reason her best friend could actually envision her and Cameron as a couple. How that was possible she didn't know. Vanessa couldn't blame Sienna's pregnancy for destroying her brain cells since Sienna had reached that conclusion long before she'd gotten pregnant.

She took another swallow of beer before saying. "Look, Sienna, talking to you is getting me nowhere. I called you for advice, not for you to take sides with the enemy."

"I'm not taking sides with the enemy. You are my very best friend and I love you. But I also think you're so full of dislike for Cameron that you aren't thinking straight. If you would put your dislike aside and sit down and analyze the situation, I think you would reach the conclusion that what he's doing is rather cute, as well as bold. I visited Cheyenne's place with you last summer so I know what that house next door looks like. Just think about it, Van. He went through all that trouble to buy that place just to be close to you. Why do you think he did that?"

"I already know why he did it. He told me. He wants me."

"And is that so bad?"

"Yes, it's bad because I refuse to become just another possession to him, one that he goes about obtaining just like his corporations. I refuse to let any man take me over that way."

"And what way would you want a man to take you over?"

Vanessa tipped the beer bottle up to her mouth and drank a large swallow again. It was only when her eyes started feeling heavy that she recalled another reason she had never liked beer. It had a tendency to make her feel sleepy. "I don't want to be taken over, Sienna."

"Okay, then, how about changing the strategy. You take over Cameron."

"What?"

"Think about it. Evidently he has this well-thought-out plan to win you over. What if you put yourself in position to be the one in charge?"

"In what way?"

"Any way you want. I have an idea what Cameron wants out of this pursuit. I see it in his eyes every time he looks at you. He definitely has the hots for you. And don't bother denying that you have the hots for him, as well. So, my question to you is this: What's wrong with an island fling? However, you'll be in charge, and you'll make the rules. Men like Cameron don't like following rules, especially if they're someone else's. But with you calling the shots, you'll be the one to decide what you want to do with him in the end, instead of the other way around."

Sienna's words reminded Vanessa of Harlan, and she was aware that her best friend knew they would. "Harlan Shaw screwed up your mind, Vanessa, but it's going to take a man like Cameron to screw it back on right. You can't see it so I won't waste my time saying it again. But I'm your best friend and I know what's going on in that head of yours. I also know what's going on in that body of yours. It's been almost four years since you've been with anyone. Cameron is available, he turns you on, so why not make the most of it?"

Vanessa glanced at the bottle and thought it must be the beer, because for one brief moment she was actually considering what Sienna had said. She shook her head, refusing to consider the suggestion.

"Look, Sienna, I'm feeling sleepy. I need to go lie down."

"Sleepy? Isn't it the middle of the day there?"

"Yes, but I just overindulged in a bottle of beer," she said, placing the empty bottle on the counter beside her.

"Okay, go to bed. But just think of how much more fun it would be if Cameron could join you there. Aren't you tired of sleeping alone? Aren't your inner muscles aching for a little hanky-panky?"

"Goodbye, Sienna," Vanessa said, not bothering to answer the questions.

"Goodbye, Van. Love you."

"Love you, too. But there are days I wished you weren't my best friend."

Even after Vanessa clicked off the line, she could still hear Sienna laughing.

Chapter 4

Hours later when Vanessa opened her eyes she glanced around her bedroom. The first thing she noticed was that the sun had gone down. Then as she pulled herself up in bed she felt those inner muscles Sienna had teased her about earlier. They were actually aching.

She quickly blamed it on the beer she'd drunk, which would also be the reason she'd conjured up that hot and heavy dream she'd had. In her dream she and Cameron had made love on the beach, under a beautiful blue sky. She had felt the soft sand beneath her back while he loomed over her, touching and tasting her everywhere before finally taking his place between her legs.

She quickly sucked in a deep breath, forcing the memory of the dream to the back of her mind. Getting out of bed, she walked over to the window and looked out toward the beach, watching how the waves hit the shore, how the seagulls flew overhead and how—

Her breath caught when she saw a lone figure jog by, invading her line of vision. Her achy inner muscles clenched when she recognized Cameron, wearing the skimpiest pair of jogging shorts she'd ever seen on a man. Her gaze followed him. Although she was still upset over what he'd pulled, she couldn't discount the fact that Cameron Cody had a great body to go along with his handsome face. She might be mad but she definitely wasn't blind. She could appreciate a nice piece of male flesh no matter what her anger level was.

Keeping her gaze focused on him as he ran at an even pace, she couldn't help but admire his muscular shoulders, broad chest, firm stomach, healthy thighs and strong legs. Those were the same legs that in her dream had wrapped around her thighs to hold her down when he entered her body over and over again.

And, as if her dream wasn't bad enough, there was the memory of the kiss they had shared earlier, so intense and more passionate than any kiss she'd ever experienced. He was a master kisser to whom every nerve and cell in her body had greedily responded.

Even now she could feel heat seeping through all parts of her body just thinking about it. His tongue had known just what it was supposed to do and had done it well. He had tumbled her resistance the same way the Berlin Wall had met its downfall. Whenever she thought of his mouth locked to hers, and the wicked and sensuous things he could do with that tongue, all those achy parts of her body acted up.

Vanessa forced herself to take a deep breath and then let it out. She felt so hot, her brow damp, that she wondered if the air conditioner was working. When the view of Cameron was lost among the thicket of palm trees, she moved away from the window, deciding to take a shower before going downstairs to meet with Helen before she left. Today was market day and there were a couple of items she wanted Helen to pick up. Beer being one of them.

As long as Cameron was her neighbor, Vanessa refused to share the private beach with him. If she had to remain inside for the rest of her stay in Jamaica, that would suit her just fine, because she would not give him the time of day…although certain parts of her body relentlessly pushed for her to do that and more.

Vanessa picked up the scent of the flowers the moment she walked down the stairs. She glanced across the room to see the huge vase of red roses on the living-room table.

"Where did those come from?" she asked Helen upon reaching the last stair.

Busy dusting, the housekeeper didn't pause or look up when she said, "They arrived a few hours ago. Aren't they pretty?"

Vanessa had to agree, although she really didn't want to, especially when she had an idea who sent them.

"They came with a bottle of wine."

Vanessa lifted a brow. "Wine?"

"Yes. I placed it on the kitchen table."

Vanessa walked over to the roses. They were simply gorgeous. The blooms were full, and the petals looked healthy and silky. Seeing the flowers reminded her of her father. His garden was full of flowers of all types, but especially roses.

She knew his death as a result of lung cancer was the reason she had been so gullible that summer she'd met Harlan. She had needed affection and unfortunately had looked for love in the wrong places and with the wrong man. She would not be making that same mistake again.

She pulled off the card and read it, confirming her suspicions. After everything she'd said, Cameron still had the nerve to invite her to a rendezvous on the beach later.

"I'm leaving in a few minutes, Ms. Steele. Is there anything you want me to pick up for you from the market?"

Vanessa glanced up at Helen. "Yes, there are a few things I need."

A few minutes later she had given Helen her list. Before the older woman could walk out the door she called out to her. "And, Helen?"

She turned. "Yes?"

"If you happen to see a copy of *Ebony* magazine on the rack, grab one for me, please."

"Yes, ma'am, I'll do that."

Once Helen had left, closing the door behind her, Vanessa shrugged her shoulders. Okay, so she was curious about the article on Cameron. But curiosity meant nothing. It would be a cold day in hell before another man got the best of her again.

Especially him.

"So, how are things going, Cameron?"

Cameron glanced around at what were fast becoming familiar surroundings as he talked on the phone to his friend Morgan Steele. "Vanessa knows I'm here," he said slowly after taking a sip of his wine.

"Umm, and how did she take it?"

"Like we both knew she would. Let's just say I'm not her favorite person right now."

Morgan's chuckle vibrated over the mobile phone. "I hate to tell you but you've never been her favorite person. You've always been her least-liked person."

Cameron couldn't help but smile. "Thanks, Morgan, for being so brutally honest."

"That's what friends are for."

After a brief pause and another sip of wine, Cameron said, "I want you to help me understand something, Morgan."

"Okay, I'll try."

"Why does Vanessa take my actions three years

ago as a personal affront? You and your brothers, as well as her sisters, were able to get over it. What's holding her back from doing the same? Is there something I'm missing here? Something you can share with me?"

"No, there's nothing I know about. The only reason I can come up with is the fact that the Steele Corporation was founded by my father and my uncle, Vanessa's father. And, as you know, her father died a few years ago. They were very close."

"You think she feels I was trying to take away his legacy?"

For a moment Morgan didn't respond and then he said, "At one time that thought did occur to me, but now I'm inclined to think there might be another reason altogether."

"And what reason is that?"

"Vanessa hasn't had a man she's ever gotten serious about, although I do recall her having a couple of boyfriends while she was in college. But there's never been anyone special, no one she's brought home for the family to meet. Now that I think of it, I believe her coldness toward you and men in general might be linked to what might have happened to her one summer."

Cameron paused with his wineglass halfway to

his lips. He felt the hairs on the back of his neck stand up. "What happened?"

"I don't really know. None of us do, although I'd bet my money that her best friend Sienna Bradford knows. Right after my uncle died, Vanessa took some time off from her job and went to Europe for a few weeks to get away. We were worried about her and thought the trip would be a good idea. Vanessa, Taylor and Cheyenne were close to their father and took his death hard, but I think Vanessa took it the hardest. Like her mom, she felt there was something they could have done to make him stop smoking years ago."

"A smoker will only quit when he's ready."

"I know that, but still, it was hard on her. The couple of times she called home from London she seemed to be doing okay, and I'd heard through the grapevine that she'd met someone, some guy who was also vacationing over there. I'd even heard from Cheyenne—or should I say overheard when she and Taylor were deep in conversation one day—that Vanessa fancied herself in love with him. But we all figured she only assumed it was love because she was going through a vulnerable period in her life, and she would come to her senses before doing anything stupid like bringing home a husband. Anyway, the next thing we know, she returns home and to this day she hasn't mentioned him. None of us even knows his name. The only thing I can figure is that she discovered the guy was playing her, and she cared more for him than he did for her. Most likely that's why she's keeping you at arm's length, to protect her heart. She's not sure she can trust you and probably feels that you're trying to take over her life."

In a way he was, Cameron silently agreed. That was definitely his intent. He wanted her life to become ingrained in his, but he didn't see that as a negative. He could only see positives, so why couldn't she?

"I suggest you use another approach," Morgan continued. "All of us discovered real early that strong-arm tactics don't work well for Vanessa. I've told you that before."

Morgan *had* told him that before, but Cameron was used to doing things his way. Now it seemed that his way wasn't working. "So what do you suggest?" he asked.

"You're going to have to revamp and do a sneak attack."

That comment had Cameron laughing. "Like the one you used with Lena?"

"Yeah, like the one I used with Lena. Laugh all you want but I got my woman, didn't I?"

"Need I remind you that it wasn't exactly smooth sailing for you, Morgan?"

"No, you don't have to remind me, but I was still able to make it work."

Cameron had to agree, since Morgan and Lena had been married a little over a month now. Morgan had also kicked off his campaign for a seat on the city council in Charlotte. "A sneak attack, huh?" he asked.

"Yes. A sneak attack. Let her think that whatever will happen between you two is only for the moment, nothing permanent. If you go into it promising tomorrows, she won't believe you. Women expect us to have commitment phobia, so let her think what you're proposing isn't for the long haul, although you know it really is. Vanessa won't consider a long-term relationship with a man, but she might be interested in a short-term affair if she was in control and calling the shots."

Cameron shook his head. Most of the women he knew would jump at the chance of having a permanent relationship with him, given the size of his bank account. "So you think if I use that approach it will work?"

"Yes. Try it and see. Let her assume it's nothing more than a fling and when it's over, you'll go your way and she'll go hers. Your job is to pull out the Cody charm and get her so taken with you that she won't want to go anywhere."

Cameron rubbed his chin as he pondered Morgan's advice. Then he said, "You do know this is your cousin's fate you're plotting, don't you?"

Morgan chuckled. "Yes, but my brothers and I trust you to do the right thing by her."

Cameron grinned. "Thanks for the vote of confidence."

"You're welcome. But if I'm wrong, Cameron, you'll have us to deal with. Understood?"

"Yes, Morgan. I understand completely."

Sitting down at the kitchen table, Vanessa resigned herself to the inevitable, taking the time to read the article on Cameron. Helen had put away the items she'd picked up at the market and had placed *Ebony* on the table in full view.

It didn't help matters that Cameron's picture— in living, vibrant color—was on the cover. Nor that the photographer's close-up sent a fluttery feeling all through her insides and had blood rushing through her veins. Cameron had been caught in a rare moment with a smile curving the corners of his lips. She would rather not admit that he looked so sexy that she had stared at the cover for too long before turning it facedown.

Vanessa sighed as she turned it faceup, and once again his picture sent tingly sensations all over her skin. One thing she'd discovered since that day three years ago was that Cameron was what fantasies were made of. She of all people should know, since he was a nightly invader into her dreams.

Deciding to get it over with, she opened the magazine and immediately flipped to page thirty-nine. Ignoring another picture of him—this one showing him entering the doors of one of the many corporations he'd taken away from someone—she began reading.

A short while later Vanessa pushed away from the table as she closed the magazine. Okay, she would be the first to admit it was a well-written article. As head of the public relations department at the Steele Corporation, she understood the importance of projecting a positive image, as well as a beneficial relationship with the public, and the article had definitely done that.

It showed a side of Cameron few probably got to see—his compassionate side. His philanthropic actions included establishing numerous foundations to help those less fortunate. Most of them Vanessa hadn't known about, but some, such as the Katrina Relief Fund, she was aware of; he had solicited her cousins' involvement in that particular project. Under Cameron's leadership and direction, several construction companies had rebuilt homes in New Orleans so the evacuees could return and reestablish their lives. According to the article, Cameron, acting as pilot, had gotten his private jet into the stricken city of New Orleans to provide aid and relief long before the federal government had arrived.

One thing the article hadn't focused on was how many companies Cody Enterprises had taken over in the past years, and how many people had lost their jobs because of those takeovers. There was no doubt in her mind that he was a man who liked being in total control, and he would handle any of his personal relationships the same way he handled his business.

Even when kissing her earlier today, he hadn't taken anything slowly. He had seen an opportunity and seized it. He had seen what he wanted and gone after it. With him there would be no compromise. It would be all or nothing, and only on his terms.

She walked around the house, pulling down the blinds. When she walked into the living room she couldn't help but stare at the roses. No doubt there was a purpose behind Cameron sending them. He probably assumed that this was the first step in breaking down her defenses, and that the next time he saw her she would be easier to bend his way. If that's what he thought, he definitely had another think coming.

She glanced out the window, realizing how much she'd missed spending any time on the beach today. Suddenly, the stubborn streak within her decided not to let Cameron's presence keep her from enjoying her time here. Tomorrow she would get up, pack a lunch and spend the day on the beach. She'd meant what she'd said when she'd told Cameron she wanted to be left alone.

Now she would see how good he was at following orders.

Chapter 5

The man wasn't good at following orders, Vanessa concluded the very next morning when she opened the front door to find Cameron standing there. Evidently he hadn't taken her seriously.

"What do you want, Cameron? I thought I told you to stay away from me," she said glaring at him.

"You did and I recall telling you that I wouldn't."

He leaned against the bamboo post, seemingly completely at ease. She watched him slip his hands into the pockets of his shorts and wished he hadn't done that. It drew her attention to what he was wearing—a muscle shirt and a pair of denim shorts that emphasized his masculine physique. She touched her stomach when her inner muscles became achy, and released a moan.

"Are you okay?"

Her glare deepened. "No, I'm not okay. I don't like being harassed."

"And you think that's what I'm doing? Harassing you?"

"Yes."

"Then I need to use another approach."

"What you need to do is turn around, go back to your place and leave me alone."

He shook his head. "I can't do that. We need to talk."

Vanessa rolled her eyes. "We have nothing to talk about since I have nothing to say to you."

"But I have something to say to you. I'd like to offer you a business proposition."

Her eyes widened slightly before returning to angry slits. "A business proposition?"

"Yes. One where you'll be in full control and calling all the shots."

Before Vanessa's mind could take in what he had said and dissect what he meant, he added, "I think

I need to clear something up right now, Vanessa, something you might have assumed. I'm not interested in a committed relationship…with anyone."

Now, that really threw her. Not that she was surprised he wasn't interested in a committed relationship, since most single men weren't. But it did leave her curious as to why he had been hot on her tail for the last three years. Or was it just as she'd thought? To him it had been a challenge, nothing more than a game he'd had every intention of winning.

Evidently he read the question in her eyes because he responded by saying, "The reason I've been pursuing you with such single-minded determination is that I think you're a very desirable woman and I want you. It's as simple as that."

She crossed her arms over her chest. Nothing with Cameron was ever simple. "So you bought a house just to be near me for a couple of weeks because you *want* me?"

"Yeah, and in a bad way. Three years' worth of wanting to be exact. I've dreamed of having you in my bed every night, and I figured it was time to turn my dreams into reality."

Although she wished it was otherwise, his words were having a naughty effect on her.

Sensations, warm and tingly, began flowing all through her veins, and the salty air from the nearby ocean was getting replaced with his scent, a pungent fragrance that was all man.

"It won't happen," she said with conviction.

"What won't happen?"

"Me, you, together that way."

"I think it will, because you're a very passionate woman, although it appears you keep all that passion hidden. I would love to tap into it."

Hidden passion that he wanted to tap into? She wondered what kind of alcohol he'd been drinking this morning. "Look, I have no idea what you're talking about." She decided not to tell him that she'd been told by one man just how passionless she was.

"Then let me break everything down for you. Let me make my offer. One that you can accept or reject."

"And if I reject it?"

"Then I promise to leave you alone for the remainder of your stay here as you've requested. In fact, I'll make arrangements to fly back to the States. But I'm hoping that you will accept it."

"And if I do?"

"If you do, I will take you on the sexual adventure of your life. Entertain old fantasies and create new ones. I plan to take us both over the edge, and when it's over, you'll go your way and I'll go mine, and I promise not to bother you again."

"Just like that?"

"Yes, just like that. My offer is that for the remainder of your days here, I will become your sex mate while we indulge in all sorts of wild and wicked play time."

Vanessa felt her stomach fluttering again. Now she wished she'd had a taste of whatever alcohol he had consumed that morning. She needed it. What he was proposing—although similar in nature to what Sienna had suggested—was crazy, absolutely ludicrous, outright insane. Still, his words refused to stop swimming around in her mind, and, as he stood there on her front porch in the sunlight, looking more handsome than any man had a right to look, she was tempted. Boy, was she tempted.

Pulling on her last bit of control, she said, "And what makes you think I want a sex mate?"

He took a step closer. "Your kiss. A man can tell a lot from a woman's kiss. Hunger, wariness, pain. I tasted all three. You want me as much as I want you. Being honest with yourself and admitting it is the first step. I can see it even now in your eyes, the heat, the yearning, the need."

He reached out and took her hand in his. Before she could pull it back, he rubbed his thumb across the underside of her wrist "Feel it here," he said of her pulse. "Your passion points. They're beating like crazy and drumming out a message you've ignored too long."

She pulled her hand back. "It's all in your mind," she said, then moistened her lips when they suddenly felt dry.

"I don't think so and I'm willing to prove you wrong."

Her eyes narrowed. "I don't want you proving anything."

"Don't you? Let's move on to your wariness. I tasted that, too. You want me, but you don't fully trust me. You're confused about where I'm coming from and, more importantly, where I'm going when it's over. I think I've made it clear what I want out of a relationship with you. And it's not wedding bells. But then I'm sure you feel the same way."

Before she could respond he continued, "And last but not least, I tasted pain, which is why you probably find it hard to trust me or any other man. But that's okay. I plan to take the pain away and replace it with pleasure of the most intense kind. After me you won't even remember your last fling."

Vanessa studied Cameron carefully. She gazed back into the intense eyes staring at her and felt another tug of her inner muscles. They were getting achier by the minute. Four years was a long time and her body was letting her know it. What Cameron had said wasn't helping matters. He wanted her for a sex mate. He wanted to tap into what he claimed was her hidden passion.

"Think about my proposition, Vanessa, and if you're interested in what I'm proposing, meet me on the beach at noon. Like I said, I'll let you set the parameters and call the shots. Turning over total control to anyone isn't easy for me, but I'll do it because I want you that bad. I'll take you on any terms."

She swallowed the tightness in her throat. "And what happens after you've had me? What if you get tired of me after the first time?" She couldn't forget that Harlan had done exactly that.

Cameron's soft chuckle caressed her skin. "Trust me, that's not possible. I doubt I'll be tired of you after the first thousand years. But how long the affair lasts will be up to you, and I promise to adhere to your time frame."

He took a step back. "Think about everything I've said and if you're interested, I'll see you on the beach at noon."

As Vanessa watched him walk away she knew she had to get a grip. Over the past three years the man had tilted her world, and now he was proposing to rock it in a way it had never been rocked before. She inhaled deeply, then let the breath out slowly. No, she told herself, the thought of a meaningless fling with Cameron was too much. She wouldn't even think about it.

She thought about it all morning. Pacing the confines of her sister's living room, she went through the pros and cons of Cameron's proposal, and it seemed the pros were tilting the scale.

If he had suggested such a thing five years ago, she would have told him just where he could go. But that would have been her pre-Harlan days, a time when she wanted to believe in romance and a forever kind of love.

She had grown up believing that two people could meet, fall in love and stay together for the rest of their lives, until death did them part. Her parents had done it, and so had her aunt and uncle. And when she had been looking at things through rose-colored glasses, she had wanted that same special love for herself.

But Harlan had taught her one vital lesson in

life, something she wouldn't ever forget: All that glittered wasn't gold. She was older and smarter now and didn't look through those rose-colored glasses anymore. After she'd thoroughly analyzed that summer in Europe, the one thing that stood out was how each day Harlan wanted to change her, mold her into the person he wanted by suggesting certain outfits for her to wear, foods that he preferred she eat and activities he'd rather they did. It was always what he wanted, without any consideration for what she wanted. It had always been about Harlan. He had controlled everything.

Even their lovemaking.

That night he hadn't asked for any suggestions or ideas. He'd done things his way, mainly for his own satisfaction. And if he thought she had failed in pleasing him, well, if the truth were known, he hadn't pleased her, either. But at the time she had fancied herself too much in love to care.

Now she did care.

After not having been intimate with a man since Harlan, the thought of a relationship with one just for sex should be a turnoff. But knowing the man involved was Cameron was quite the opposite. He turned her on. Besides, the dynamics of a man-woman relationship weren't what they used to be.

Men, she told herself, no longer courted you. They seduced you.

So what was wrong with seducing them back?

There would be no misunderstandings in their relationship. There would be a beginning and an end. And most importantly, it would be a way finally to get Cameron to leave her alone and a way finally to get the one thing her body needed. A man.

But not just any man.

It needed the man who'd so ruthlessly invaded her dreams, the man who could stare at her from across a room and make heat swell within her. The man who could start her pulse—her pleasure points—to beating in a way that sent blood racing through her veins.

And she would be the one in control.

That was the one thing that appealed to her. How would Cameron react once stripped of control? Once unable to call the shots? He would have a hard time of it, no doubt, but she would enjoy every single minute.

Every single inch of him.

She sighed deeply. Was she crazy to consider such a thing? Or was she crazy not to? She would be going into the affair with both eyes open, with no unrealistic expectations. There would be no future in the brief relationship they shared but at least her celibate days would come to an end. For the rest of her stay on this island, she would put out of her mind that Cameron Cody had to be the most insufferably irritating man she'd ever met and instead concentrate on how he was also the handsomest and sexiest. Being around him, looking into the darkness of his eyes, studying those intriguing lips and knowing what it would feel like being touched by those big, strong hands, being made love to with an intensity that took her breath away, was worth the risk.

For a short while she wouldn't feel guilty about being so incredibly attracted to him. She would take Sienna's advice and finally take her "edge off." And what better person to do it with than a man who was so utterly male? She and Cameron were spontaneous combustion just waiting to explode, just as Sienna claimed.

Besides, it was about time someone taught Cameron a lesson in humility. Not everything in life got played by his terms, his wants and his desires. People weren't like corporations; he couldn't just come in and take over their lives because they caught his eye for the moment.

A smile touched the corners of her lips. For the

second time in his life Cameron Cody was about to get outdone by a Steele. The first time her family had effectively shown him that family devotion was worth a lot more than his money. Now, with single-minded determination, she intended to show him that there were some things you just couldn't control. He was about to discover that all his management theories couldn't be applied to a personal relationship, not even a short-term one.

Whether Cameron realized it, he had met his match.

Chapter 6

It was high noon.

For Vanessa, the path leading from Cheyenne's home down to the beach had never seemed so long. She had changed from the sundress she'd been wearing earlier to a pair of shorts and matching top that were meant to capture Cameron's full attention, not that she didn't think she'd had it earlier when he had been standing on her doorstep.

She had seen the way his eyes had roamed over her. She had felt the heat in the gaze that had touched different parts of her body. At the time she'd been so taken aback by his proposal she had dismissed the intensity of his look.

In the future, when it came to him she wouldn't dismiss anything. She would keep her eyes and ears open, and, more than anything, she would keep her heart intact. She would not make the same mistake with him that she had with Harlan.

As soon as her bare feet touched the heated sand, another kind of heat quickly spread through her. Cameron had laid out a towel on the beach a safe distance from the water, and he had brought the basket she'd given him yesterday. But what caught her eye was the man himself.

He was shirtless, wearing only a pair of khaki shorts. Probably he had on his swimming trunks under the shorts, just like she was wearing her two-piece bathing suit under her outfit.

Regardless of the smell of the ocean water, she discovered the closer she got to him that his scent enveloped her. He was standing, looking out over the ocean with his back to her, but not for one minute did she think he wasn't aware of her approach. Her gaze traveled over him, appreciating the corded muscles of his back.

When she got within five feet of him, he slowly turned and her gaze automatically latched on to the bare, muscular contours of his chest and the sparse dark hairs covering it. Bringing her gaze back to his face, she watched the corners of his lips tilt in a slow, devastatingly handsome smile, the impact of which she could feel all the way to her womb. It was an intense tug that made her inner muscles clench.

"Thanks for coming," he said in a low, sexy voice that made her heart begin thumping and made goose bumps rise on her arm. "I'm going to make sure you don't regret your decision."

She came to a stop beside him. "We'll see, Cameron, but first we need to talk, to get a few things straight up-front. I want to make sure we understand each other completely."

He nodded. "All right. And after we talk I suggest we eat since it's lunchtime. Do you want to sit here to talk or do you want to walk along the beach?"

The thought of the two of them strolling along the beach together set up a romantic picture in her mind, and she didn't want to think romance. "We can sit and talk right here."

He nodded before taking her hand to assist her down on the huge towel. The moment their hands touched, she felt an electric current charge through her body and knew he felt it, as well. He sat down beside her. When one of his bare legs brushed against hers, her heartbeat quickened. The sexual chemistry between them was overpowering. Even if she had had on layers and layers of clothing, she still would have felt his touch. Every fiber of her body was attuned to him, but she was determined to dispel some of that high-voltage sexual tension that gripped them, made her forget about talking and want only to lie on this towel with him, naked, instead.

"So what are your rules?"

His words interrupted her thoughts and she glanced over at him. Even sitting there as casual as he wanted to be, he still looked dominating, far more powerful and commanding than she liked.

The sooner she told him just how things would be between them, the better. Then he could take her proposal or leave it. She was inclined to think he would leave it, because a part of her refused to believe he could put total control in her hands.

The next few minutes would tell.

"I want to share an affair with you, Cameron, for the remainder of the time I have left on the island. Twelve days to be exact. During that time I will forget my dislike of you, and I want you to forget your dislike of me."

"I don't dislike you. In fact I like you. A lot."

His words gave her pause, and it took a few

moments to regroup her thoughts. "Okay, maybe your feelings for me are not as intense as my feelings for you, but even you would admit we really don't get along."

"That was your choice. You turned me down each and every time I asked you out. You refused to get within ten feet of me."

Glancing down, Vanessa rubbed the bridge of her nose, wondering how they had strayed off the subject. She decided to use the opportunity to make him see that, unlike in the past, she wouldn't be putting distance between them now...not as long as she was in control.

"Forget about the past, Cameron, because I'm within ten feet of you now, aren't I? I'm sitting so close to you, I'm practically in your lap."

A naughty smile touched his lips when he said in a low voice, "If you want to ease over into my lap, I won't have a problem with it."

She rolled her eyes. "I'm sure you won't, but I need us to finish our discussion."

"All right."

"Like I said, we will put the past and our feelings behind us and start on that adventure you alluded to. But at the end of the twelve days, whatever we've shared will come to an end. No future. No promises. You will go your way and I will go mine, and if our paths cross again, which I'm sure they eventually will, given your close relationship with other members of my family, we will act as though nothing ever happened between us. There won't be any repeat or any suggestion of such a thing. When this affair ends, it's over. Totally and completely. Understood?"

He stared at her for a long moment but she refused to back down or wither under his gaze. She remained quiet and still while he considered her proposal.

Finally he spoke. "Yes, I understand but what happens if—"

When he stopped in midsentence she arched a brow and asked, "If what?"

"If we become addicted to each other. What if the intimacy is so good and we get so embodied into each other's systems that we don't want things to end? What if—"

Not wanting to hear any more, Vanessa reached out and pressed her fingers to his lips to silence his next words. She wished she hadn't when the tip of his tongue lightly flicked across her fingers.

The action made her gasp, nearly took her breath away. But for some reason she couldn't pull her hand back. She stared at him, felt those same inner muscles clench again at the heated lust forming in his eyes. Then she wondered if such a thing was possible. Could she possibly become sexually addicted to him? Or was he thinking too much of himself? There was no doubt in her mind that he probably could whip up some delicious sexual fantasies, but...an addiction? She shook her head. That couldn't and wouldn't happen.

She moistened her lips as she pulled her fingers away from his mouth, but not before his tongue flicked out for one more quick taste. She watched as he took that same tongue and licked his lips as if he had enjoyed the taste of her.

"It won't happen," she finally said, barely getting the words out. "I've never gotten addicted to anything in my life."

"Maybe the reason you've never gotten addicted is because you've never overindulged. For the next twelve days, with me, you will."

She saw something flicker in his eyes and for some reason she suddenly felt on her guard. "It doesn't matter. I won't get addicted."

She watched as his gaze dropped to her mouth and he said. "But if, when our affair is over you find you still want me, just let me know and I will make myself available. Anytime, anyplace and any position."

A wave of heated desire, larger than one of the waves forming out in the ocean, shot through her. Any position? Just what kind of fantasies had he conjured up for the next twelve days?

Vanessa had to struggle against the excitement that tried grabbing her in its clutches. He had painted one hell of a picture; the imagery was too sensual even for a graphic artist to try his hand at it. Someday, when this affair was over, she would wonder just how she got through it with all her senses intact.

Had she perhaps bitten off more than she could chew? But then she remembered that she would be the one in control. He couldn't do any more than she let him. She had the last word.

Struggling to regain power of her senses, she said, "Thanks for the offer but I don't intend to use it."

"That will be your choice, Vanessa, but it's out there if you change your mind."

"I won't."

He gave her a look that said, "we'll see." "And another thing, Vanessa, just so you don't accuse me of having an ulterior motive later, I might as well tell you that I've decided to make Charlotte my primary home."

His words shocked the hell out of her and she was grateful she was sitting down. It had been bad enough to endure his occasional trips to the city, but the thought of him setting up permanent residence in her hometown was too much.

"Why?" she snapped. "Why are you moving to Charlotte?"

"I happen to like the town. I own several homes, most of them in the areas where I have extensive business interests—Atlanta, Austin and Los Angeles—and of course, now this place here. But the home I recently purchased in Charlotte is where I intend to stay most of the time."

"Exactly where in Charlotte? What side of town?" she asked, clearly annoyed.

"The same subdivision where Morgan lives. I like the area and the homes there."

She nodded. So did she. It was a very beautiful area and the homes, all in the million-dollar range, were simply breathtaking. At least he would be living on the opposite side of town, quite a distance from her, so the chances of their paths crossing too many times were low enough not to worry about now.

"Well, I'm trusting you to stay on your side of town and I'll stay on mine," she said.

He smiled. "Don't worry. Charlotte is big enough for both of us," he said, standing.

She gazed up at him, hoping that it was.

"Now that we've come to an understanding about a number of things, do you want to go for a walk before we have lunch? Of course, the decision is yours," he said smoothly.

Walk? Vanessa thought, smiling humorlessly. *He wants to go for a walk?* She would have thought that a man like Cameron would immediately initiate his role as her sex mate by suggesting that they go to one of the houses and get it on. Was he trying to throw her off by using a different strategy?

She regarded him for a moment and was about to pull herself to her feet when he reached out his hand to her. His fingertips grazed her knuckles before his hand tightened around hers, effortlessly tugging her up. Trying to downplay the stirrings she felt between her thighs, she said in a tight voice, "A walk sounds like a good idea. It's a nice day out."

"Yes, it is."

He surprised her even more when he kept her hand tucked in his as they began strolling along the shoreline. She glanced up at him, and he looked at her and slanted a crooked smile before asking, "Is anything wrong?"

Nothing other than that I can actually feel my heart leaping in my chest, she thought. But instead she said, "No, nothing's wrong. But I would like to know something."

"What?"

"Who told you that I was coming here? Although I have an idea."

"Do you?"

"Yes."

"Umm, how would you like to go to dinner?"

She shook her head, knowing what he was trying to do. "You're trying to avoid my question."

"Am I?

"Yes."

He glanced sideways at her and gave her an easy grin. She had seen more smiles from him in the past few hours than she'd thought possible. "You're right. I am avoiding your question. But I won't reveal my sources."

"I think I know who it was."

He chuckled. "But you're not sure so leave it alone."

"I can't. I want to know who told you I was coming here."

"Why?"

"So I can deal with him."

Cameron chuckled. "Are you sure it's a he?"

She glanced over at him. "Pretty much."

"You're only guessing, Vanessa, and I'm not telling you. Now back to my earlier question of how you want to spend dinner?"

She wondered why he was asking. Did he have an idea? She decided to play her hunch. "I don't know. Any suggestions?"

"Yes. There's a concert tonight on the beach of the Half Moon Royal Villas. I think you might like it since I understand you enjoy reggae music."

Irritation stiffened her spine. Someone had again given him information about her. He evidently felt her displeasure and glanced down at her. "Why does it bother you that someone mentioned that to me?"

She stopped walking and turned to him. "Because that meant I was the topic of your conversation, and I'm not sure I like that."

Cameron stared at Vanessa, resisting the urge to pull her into his arms and kiss her. He wanted to indulge in the taste he'd sampled. Instead he said, "I think we need to clear the air about something. I've wanted you from the first moment I saw you, but I'm sure you know that already. And because I wanted you, I became fixated on knowing all there was about you, so I asked questions. Trust me, if my sources thought I was asking for the wrong reasons, they would not have told me anything."

"And you think wanting to know everything about me for the mere reason of sleeping with me is the right reason?"

Cameron smiled blandly. He had decided after talking to Morgan on the phone yesterday that he would modify his sneak-attack plan. When possible, he intended to be as honest as he could with her. Because of that, it would only be fair that she knew how much he'd wanted her initially.

"Yes, I think so. I'm a private person. I don't bring a lot of people into my life and I have established a certain standard for the women I date."

He saw the frown that appeared on Vanessa's face. Evidently she didn't like the thought of being grouped with the other women he dated. In the past he had always enjoyed a pretty healthy sex life, making sure no woman got close. But with Vanessa he had wanted more than a toss between the sheets. He had wanted a whole hell of a lot more and he still did.

"I saw my relationship with you as different," he said honestly. "With someone else it might not have mattered what was her favorite food, her taste in music or her favorite sports, but when it came to you, it mattered."

"Why?"

"Because, like I said earlier, and I've been saying now, I wanted you, and the depth of that want went beyond anything I've ever known. I've never been attracted to a woman this much before."

Vanessa shrugged. "It was probably the challenge. You didn't get the Steele Corporation so you decided to go after a Steele."

Cameron shook his head. "First you accuse me of seeking revenge. Now it's the thrill of a challenge. It's neither of the two. You're a very desirable woman, Vanessa. Why is it so hard for you to believe that?"

Morgan had mentioned something about the possibility of a man screwing up her life one summer a few years ago and since that time she hadn't dated much. Had the man done or said something to make her question her appeal, her femininity? If that was the case, he would make sure in the coming days that he did the opposite. The last thing Vanessa Steele needed to worry about was whether a man actually found her desirable.

"It's hard for me to believe because I know how men are. I have four older male cousins, remember."

"Yes, but three of them are happily married, so what's your point?"

She evidently took offense at his question. Her frown deepened. "My point is that while they're happy now, there was a time they dated frequently with no thought of settling down."

"And are you saying that women don't date frequently? I know some women who are just as bad as men when it comes to getting what they want, using whatever means possible."

She glared at him. "We aren't talking about women. We're talking about men."

Cameron raised a brow. "Are we? And why is that?"

Vanessa inclined her head to get a better look into Cameron's face and to keep the glare of the sun out of her eyes. "I don't know why that is and I would appreciate it if you didn't confuse me."

In that instant Cameron knew only one thing for sure: He had to kiss her. The way she had tilted her head back made her lips too accessible and he had a deep, compelling need to ravish them, kiss her crazy. Every nerve in his body was pushing him to do just that, so he leaned closer.

Evidently she picked up on his intent but didn't take a step back. Instead their gazes held, locked.

She tried clearing her throat lightly and said, "You never finished telling me about the plans for dinner."

"Dinner?"

"Yes. I think that's what we should be concentrating on."

His gaze moved from her eyes back onto her mouth. If she thought she could get him thinking about anything other than kissing her, she was wrong. Leaning closer, he said huskily, "The only thing I want to concentrate on, Vanessa, is your mouth."

"Cameron…" When his lips touched hers, his name became a shuddering breath from her mouth.

The last time they kissed he had tried zapping her of her senses, but this time he wanted to take things slow and tender. She parted her mouth beneath his and the moment she did so, he drank of her greedily but in a leisurely and unhurried way. He wanted every dip, swipe and lick of his tongue to solicit a reaction from her, a sensuous response. And if for one minute she thought she wouldn't get addicted to this, then he intended to prove otherwise. He had gotten addicted to her even before their first kiss. Her scent had been his downfall, but he could admit that her taste was doing a close second.

The kiss was incredible. It was heated and it made a tortured groan escape his throat when she began returning it, tangling her tongue with his, making an already heated situation even hotter.

He wrapped his arms around her, pulling her closer to fit into him. He felt her bare legs rub against his, felt the hardened tips of her breasts press against his bare chest, and he felt the hardness of his erection settle between her thighs. And when he heard her moan, blood rushed through his veins.

Cameron knew that if they didn't stop soon he would be tempted to lay her down on the beach, right here, and make love to her, to claim her as he wanted. He wanted to say to hell with a sneak attack. He wanted to operate on the got-to-have-you-now strategy but knew that he couldn't. Contrary to what she thought, he was fighting for long-term here and he intended to get it.

With that thought in mind, he drew back and heard her soft, breathless protest when he did so. He gazed down at her swollen lips, and the eyes that met his looked drugged in the most passionate way.

He knew he should say something, anything, or else he would be devouring her mouth once again. "I think the Tapas restaurant would be nice."

It took a second for her to comprehend that he had spoken. "For what?" she asked softly.

He smiled and wondered if she realized her arms were still wrapped around his neck and she was inching her lips closer to his.

"For dinner," he said throatily, deciding to inch his lips closer to hers, as well. "We can do dinner there and then do the concert. What do you think?"

Instead of answering him, she released a whimper the moment her lips touched his, reconnecting with his mouth again. As far as he was concerned, if they kept this up they could forgo dinner and just feast on each other; especially when he felt her taking the lead by wrapping her tongue around his.

He might work hard at making her addicted to this, but for him, things were even worse. For the past three years, Vanessa had been a fascination to him. Now she was fast becoming an obsession.

Chapter 7

It was a beautiful evening, Vanessa thought, as she leaned back against the headrest, feeling the wind off the ocean gently caress her face. She was in Cameron's convertible sports car as they made their way down the narrow beach road toward the restaurant where they would be having dinner.

She had to admit that her noontime meeting on the beach with him had gone well. After their walk they had returned to the towel and shared lunch. Their conversation had mostly been about the new addition to the Steele family, a beautiful little boy named Alden who had been born to Chance and Kylie, who had joined his teenage son and her teenage daughter together into an amazing blended family. They also talked about Morgan's bid for political office and how Cameron intended to be a part of Morgan's campaign staff. After they had finished eating, Cameron had walked her back to her place and, with nothing more than a peck on the cheek, he'd left.

"I never did thank you for the roses. They're beautiful," she said, finally breaking the silence surrounding them in the two-seater vehicle. "And the wine was a nice touch."

He gave a quick glance over at her. "You're more than welcome for both."

When silence settled between them again she decided to ask, "Is this car yours or is it a rental?"

"It's mine. I purchased it the first day I arrived, and I plan to keep it here on the island to use whenever I'm here. Do you like it?"

She smiled. "Yes, actually I do. Morgan bought a sports car for Lena as a wedding gift, but I'm sure you know that."

He chuckled. "Yes, I know. It's a nice set of wheels."

Vanessa nodded in agreement. "Lena said she'd

always wanted one, but had always stuck to purchasing something practical. Morgan decided to indulge her and she loves it."

"And he loves her."

Vanessa glanced over at Cameron. He sounded so sure of that, but then everyone was aware of how Morgan felt about his wife. He wasn't ashamed to wear his heart on his sleeve. Neither were Chance and Sebastian. They had been fortunate enough to meet women who were worth every ounce of their love, and since getting to know them and seeing what beautiful people Kylie, Lena and Jocelyn were, both inside and out, Vanessa understood why.

Deciding to keep the focus of the conversation on anyone but them, she said, "At what point do you think he fell in love with her?"

She had heard the story of how Morgan had been swept off his feet the moment Lena had walked into the ballroom at some charity function, but since Cameron and Morgan were close friends she wanted to hear his thoughts.

"According to Morgan, he fell for her the first time he saw her. Instant love. I understand it can happen that way sometimes."

"Do you really believe that?"

They had arrived at the restaurant and Cameron

noticed he was behind a few other cars waiting for valet parking. He turned to Vanessa, thinking that she had asked a good question and he wanted her to see the similarities between their situation and Morgan and Lena's.

"Yes. I believe a man can meet a woman and fall in love the moment he sets eyes on her." He could tell by the gentle lift of her brow that she was surprised by his response.

"That's interesting to hear you say that. Please elaborate."

He smiled. He'd figured she would want him to. "There's really nothing to elaborate on, Vanessa. Contrary to what some women think, all men aren't horrid."

"Women don't think *all* men are horrid."

"Maybe not all of you, but enough of you do to give some of us a bad rap. All it takes is for one man to mess up, and the masses of your gender assume the next one will do the same."

She straightened in her seat, her body going on the defensive as she frowned at him. "Are you saying if the roles were reversed that a man wouldn't be just as cautious? That a man wouldn't protect his heart from further pain?"

Cameron smiled weakly, remembering that he

was currently at that stage in his own life. Stacy McCann had definitely done a job on him when she'd claimed that although she loved him, she had to obey her father and marry a man who'd been born into wealth instead of considering marriage to Cameron—a man her father referred to as a "young punk with pipe dreams."

"No," he said. "All I'm saying is that at some point you have to move on and take another chance, risk all." At least to a certain degree.

He didn't utter those last words but he definitely believed them. He was certain he could not totally and completely give his heart to another woman ever again. But what he could do for Vanessa was to pledge her his undying devotion. While he hadn't felt love the moment he'd seen her, he'd felt an instant attraction, the kind he'd never before experienced. Vanessa might not have his love but she would have the next best thing.

"Dinner was wonderful, Cameron," Vanessa said as they sat in what she thought had to be one of the most exquisite restaurants on the island. In addition to the exceptional food and service, they'd been seated at a table with a breathtaking view of the ocean.

"I'm glad you enjoyed it," Cameron said, taking a sip of his wine. "It came highly recommended."

She didn't have to ask by whom since Chance and Kylie had come here on their honeymoon, and had raved about what a fantastic time they'd had. They had stayed at the Half Moon Royal Villas, where she and Cameron would be going later for the concert on the beach.

Feeling Cameron's eyes on her, she glanced across the table. The moment their gazes connected, a shimmering heat flowed all through her, pooling in the lower part of her body. Earlier, while they were eating and exchanging polite conversation, she had allowed herself to relax a little and let her guard down. Now, seeing the intense look in his eyes, she quickly pulled her guard back up.

His look was more than just intense, it was purposeful. The lighting of the restaurant played along his features, highlighting his angular jaw, cleft chin and sexy lower lip. Then there was something about the slickness of his bald head that gave him such a manly appeal. He looked so good in the tailored trousers and a white shirt that when she'd opened the door to him earlier, he had momentarily taken her breath away.

She continued to study his lower lip while she

gently traced the stem of her wineglass, thinking just what she would like to do with those lips. She'd never been a woman who felt comfortable making the first move, but she felt like doing so now. Besides, he was her sex mate and she was in full control and calling the shots. The big question was whether she was going to use that control. Could she ask him to make love to her as if it was nothing more than asking him to pass the butter?

She swallowed tightly, feeling the intense heat and awareness of the unbroken eye contact they were sharing. Why was she just now noticing things about him, things she hadn't taken time to notice before? Like the long lashes that covered his dark eyes, the pearly white teeth that seemed so perfect and straight, or the way he could never keep his fingers still for long. They were either holding something or drumming restlessly on the table.

"Ready to go?" he asked, his voice seemingly gentle.

"To the concert?"

"Yes. But if you prefer to call it an early night—"

"No," she said quickly, calling herself a coward. "I'm looking forward to the concert."

"All right."

She took another sip of her wine. Why couldn't she have told the truth? *Yes, I prefer calling it an early night, so we can go back to my place or yours and tumble between the sheets.* But she hadn't, and it wasn't a good idea for her to even think it.

Moments later, while they waited for their check, she decided to ask, "Have you moved into your place in Charlotte yet?"

The corners of his lips tipped into a smile. "No. That's the reason I was coming to Charlotte, to spend a few days getting settled."

"And you changed your plans to follow me here?"

"Yes."

Vanessa shook her head, still not sure what to make of that. "You'll have a lot to do when you get back."

"I'll manage."

Probably with hired help, she thought. Before she could think of another topic to keep the conversation going, the waiter returned with their check. She watched as Cameron signed off on the bill while thinking just how little she knew about him other than what she'd read in the newspaper or, more recently, in that magazine.

He was a high-school dropout who had gotten himself together to end up graduating cum laude from Harvard Business School. A self-made millionaire, he was one of the most successful men in the country.

She hadn't noticed that the waiter had gone, and she was still sitting there staring at Cameron. When she did realize it, she saw that he was staring back at her. For a moment she couldn't breathe and it felt as if her heart was pounding in her chest.

"Are you ready to leave now, Vanessa?"

Her gaze dropped to his mouth, and she saw it move, but for the life of her she had no idea what he'd said. Her mind, her thoughts, her entire body were centered on him and on how, just by looking at her, he could make a compelling need thicken inside of her.

"Vanessa?"

"Yes?"

A smile touched those full, irresistible lips. "I asked if you were ready to leave for the concert."

Sighing deeply, she nodded. She would go to the concert, but all she'd do was think about what would happen between them later.

Some women, Cameron thought, were meant to be made love to, day and night, twenty-four hours a day, seven days a week. Vanessa Steele was that kind of woman.

He was standing in line at the bar to get a refill on their drinks and couldn't help but stare at her. She was standing, leaning against a palm tree, listening to the music, her body swaying to the reggae beat.

He had been on edge all night, ever since picking her up. She had come to the door wearing a peasant blouse that hung off her shoulders and a matching skirt whose hem came to her ankles. And she had the cutest-looking sandals on her feet. He had been tempted to kiss her then and there and suggest they forgo dinner and the concert and go somewhere and make love.

But he hadn't made such a suggestion. Instead he had taken her hand and led her to his car, all the while knowing this would be one hot night for him in more ways than one.

The need for her was sharp and compelling. He wanted to touch her all over, kiss her all over, make love to her inside and out. Each thought intensified his need, his desire. Raw, primitive passion clawed at him. He could no longer hold it beneath the surface. It was there, forcing its way free, gripping him, slicing through him.

As if she felt the heat of his eyes on her, she

glanced in his direction and their gazes connected and then locked—something they'd done a lot tonight. At that moment a deep, intense sensation sent flames flaring through him and he knew he had to leave with her. Now.

"What would you like to have, sir?"

He blinked when he realized the bartender had asked him a question. He broke eye contact with Vanessa to glance at the man long enough to say, "Nothing."

The only thing he wanted to have was Vanessa. He turned to stride back to her, hoping that she would take his suggestion that they leave now.

Vanessa watched as Cameron began walking toward her, his eyes locked with hers. Even across the distance she felt his heat and read the intense look in his gaze. His shoulders looked massive and he appeared larger than life with every step he took. There was a profound sexiness about him. The way his pants fit his body had her mesmerized because she could tell when she glanced below his waist that he was aroused. From what? Just looking at her? Hidden fantasies in his mind?

She was glad that everyone else around them was caught up in the concert and didn't notice that she and Cameron were caught up only in each other. The closer he got the more she could feel her heart thundering, beating wildly in her chest. She no longer wondered how their night would end. He was painting a very clear picture.

"Our drinks?" she asked, when he finally reached her empty-handed.

"I think we need more than alcohol to cool off," he said huskily, reaching out and gently drawing her to him.

She met his heated gaze. "Do we?"

"Yes."

She then surprised Cameron by placing her arms around his neck, bringing her body up close to his. He knew there was no way she couldn't feel his erection, the intensity of his desire for her. Hell, she probably had noticed it when he was walking back toward her.

"And what do you think we need, Cameron Cody?" she asked, breaking into his thoughts.

The corners of his lips turned up slightly as he stared down at her. Then he leaned close to her ear and whispered, "I think we need to go someplace where we can be alone."

She gazed into his eyes for several long moments before saying softly, "I think you're right."

Chapter 8

"Would you like to see the progress that's been made on Cheyenne's pool, Cameron?"

No. Not really, Cameron thought as he leaned against the closed door. He dug his hands into the pockets of his trousers and watched as Vanessa crossed the room, her skirt twirling in fluid motion around her legs when she walked.

The ride from the concert had been the hardest drive he'd ever made. More than once he'd been tempted to pull to the side of the road, tug her into his arms and start something that he could handle a lot better in a bedroom. Right now the last thing he was interested in seeing was a swimming pool under construction.

"Cameron?"

When he hadn't answered, she turned and was looking at him with one beautifully arched eyebrow raised. He could tell she was nervous and that it would be to his advantage to do whatever it took to make her comfortable. And if that meant seeing her sister's pool then so be it.

Pulling his hands out of his pockets, he stepped a little farther into the room. "Yes, I'd like to see it." He then tilted his head in the general direction where he figured the pool to be and said, "Isn't it dark out back?"

"With the flip of a switch the area will become well lit."

Great. "All right, then, show me."

He followed as she led him through the living room where she opened a set of French doors. The scent of the ocean immediately filled their nostrils, but it was her scent that was driving him wild, and it had done so all evening.

When he followed her onto the patio, she flipped a switch and, true to her word the area lit up and he saw it—a huge cemented hole in the ground. "When I first arrived they were just digging it out," she was saying. "Now it's begun to take shape. Already I can tell it's going to be beautiful."

He shook his head and his mouth curled into a smile. "Pools aren't beautiful, Vanessa. People are beautiful."

Thinking they had wasted enough time already, he crossed the patio to where she was standing staring out at the pool. When he reached her he took her hand in his and turned her to him. His gaze took in the features of her face, moving from her dark eyes, her high cheekbones, her delicious-looking mouth and back to her eyes again. "*You* are beautiful," he said in a deep, husky voice.

She shook her head. "You're either seeing things or have bad eyesight."

"It's neither," he said, reaching out and gently looping his arms around her shoulders and taking a step closer, bringing their bodies right smack against each other. "I know beauty when I see it, Vanessa, and *you* are beautiful."

She sighed, and he knew she'd figured it would be a waste of time to argue with him, so she said, "Thank you."

"You're welcome."

At that moment a million scenarios began filling Cameron's mind, all of them fantasies or dreams in which she was a willing participant. His dreams were what had kept him going even when it seemed Vanessa's icy attitude toward him would never melt. Now he was ready to turn one of those dreams—didn't matter which one since there were many—into reality.

He decided to take things slow and dipped his head to brush a kiss across her lips. "I like tasting you," he said, watching her eyes darken.

"Do you?"

"Yes." He then dipped his head to kiss her again, this time gliding the tip of his tongue across the fullness of her mouth. "I do. You taste good. You smell good. And…you can do this to me," he said, slowly sliding his hands from her shoulders to her backside and pressing her against him so she would know exactly what he was talking about.

She arched into his erection, and his breath caught at such a bold move. "Are you sure *I* did this?" she asked in a whisper close to his ear.

A chuckle rumbled deep within his throat. "Baby, I'm positive you did it. I haven't thought of anything but making love to you all evening," he said, trailing kisses down her throat.

"Is that a fact?"

"Yes, definitely nonfiction." While one hand remained on her backside, the other gently caressed her back while he continued to taste her slowly, letting the tip of his tongue move to the underside of her ear.

"Cameron." Her voice was barely a whisper, but he could hear the deep desire in it.

"Yes?"

"Stop torturing me." She arched into him some more.

"You're the one in control, Vanessa. Just say the word."

"Take me."

She didn't have to say a single thing more. As far as he was concerned those two words said it all. He swept her into his arms and headed back into the house, pausing only long enough to adjust his hold on her so she could reach out and pull shut the French doors.

"Where to?" he asked, glancing down at her when he stood in the middle of the living room. Adrenaline was pouring through his veins at an alarming speed. He wanted her. Now. But he refused to allow their first time to be anywhere other than a bed. Later, all the others could be anytime, anyplace, any position, just as he'd said.

"The guest room is upstairs. First door on your right."

Before she had finished what she was saying, he was already moving in that direction. When he reached the room he gave the furnishings nothing more than a quick glance. His attention, however, was definitely drawn to the huge sleigh bed. It looked sturdy and that was good. He crossed the room and leaned down to place her on it and was surprised when she pulled him down on the bed with her, hungrily latching on to his mouth. He groaned deep in his chest when she slipped her tongue between his parted lips and knew her degree of need was just as high as his.

"Now, Cameron. I couldn't stand it if you waited." Her voice was filled with tension and desire and her words reflected a desperation that hit him below the gut.

In a tangle of ardent open-mouthed kisses and eager, frantic hands, he began removing her clothes, pulling the blouse over her head and sliding the skirt down her hips. He tossed her sandals aside and then she lay there, in full view, wearing nothing more than a white lace bra and a matching thong that barely covered her feminine mound.

Although the lingerie was fairly revealing, he wanted to see the real thing and reached out and unclasped her bra. Her breasts, in all their fine glory, were exposed to his eyes. He reached out and touched them, caressed them, then leaned over and took a hardened tip into his mouth, sucking relentlessly.

"Cameron…"

He pulled back to lower the thong down her thighs. She lifted her hips as he slowly slid the flimsy material down her legs. Tossing her thong aside, he reached out and touched her center. Finding it wet, he began stroking it, stirring up the scent of her in the room.

"Cameron…" she murmured his name again in a tortured groan. "Don't play with me. Just do it."

"If you're absolutely, positively sure that's what you want."

"I'm absolutely, positively sure," she moaned.

He stood back as his gaze moved all over her naked body, over her breasts, down to the core of her femininity then down the length of her gorgeous long legs, before inching back toward her center, the part of her that drew him. That's where he would get the ultimate, succulent taste he craved.

Unable to resist any longer, he quickly began removing his clothes while she watched him, feeling the heat of her eyes over him as he bared all. Her sexy scent now permeated the room, driving him crazy with the need to make love to her after three years of wanting her. He took the time to ease the condom he had taken from his wallet over his shaft before moving back toward the bed.

"I told you earlier that I liked your taste. Remember?"

She gazed at him through heavy-lidded eyes filled with desire. "Yes."

"Now I intend to show you just how much."

Vanessa gasped when his mouth took hers with heated possession, at the same time he moved his hand lower, past her stomach to settle right between her legs. He stroked her there again, ardently fondling the swollen bud of her womanhood.

"You're playing with me again," she accused in a breathless moan.

"Then let me try something else," he whispered in her ear.

Before she realized what he was about to do, he eased her back onto the fluffy bed coverings and began kissing a trail down her stomach. Every place his mouth touched made her skin feel sensitized. When he reached the spot between her inner thighs, he began placing heated kisses there.

Vanessa lifted her hips, barely able to tolerate the intense sensations overtaking her. Her need for modesty vanished, and she instinctively opened her legs when his mouth moved to the center of her.

She screamed his name at the first stroke of his tongue on her and her body quivered from the inside out when he began feasting on her hungrily, as if he'd been waiting a long time to do what he was doing. A strangled moan got caught in her throat and her hips rose off the bed when he stopped nibbling on her and began a tormenting lick.

"Cameron!"

She screamed his name again when her body exploded in one mind-bending, earth-shattering climax. By the time the sound echoed off the walls, he had leaned up to position his body over hers. The moment her trembling subsided, she looked up and gazed into his eyes.

"I've wanted you for so long," he whispered, his erection homing in on the heat of her like iron toward a magnet.

Still recovering from the effects of one hell of

an orgasm, Vanessa somehow found the strength to lift her hips, and the moment his hardened tip grazed her womanly core, he threw his head back and slid into her body. She wrapped her legs around him when he began moving back and forth inside her. With each thrust, her body was being navigated to a place it had never been before.

She might be the one in control, but he was the one plotting a course that was pushing her toward another skyrocketing experience. She had never known pleasure this intense, this extreme and forceful. It was as if his body knew just what position, what angle to take to hit that precise spot—her ultimate erogenous zone.

Each mind-blowing plunge was made to send her over the edge, and she felt her thighs quaking and her muscles spasming. When he bucked his body with an intensity that tested the endurance of the mattress springs, she felt her body explode at the same time his did.

"Vanessa!"

He hollered out her name, giving one last long, hard thrust into her body. She seemed to break into a million tiny pieces upon impact, never realizing something like this could be so powerful and earth-shattering. And then he was back at her mouth, kissing her with a hunger that was sending her body into an erotic spin all over again.

At that moment, the only thing she was totally aware of was that whether she wanted him to or not, Cameron Cody was rocking her world.

Neither wanted to move so they lay there, wrapped in each others' arms, their bodies connected, their limbs entwined for the longest time while their breathing returned to normal and their pounding heartbeats abated.

Sometime later, Cameron eased off Vanessa to look down at her. He was mesmerized, slightly shaken at what had taken place. He'd wanted her for so long, he wasn't surprised at the magnitude of his need, his craving, his desire. But what he hadn't counted on or expected was the intense degree of satisfaction and fulfillment he'd received.

Never before had any woman made him feel what he'd felt with her. If he had to describe it, he couldn't. No words could. Sensations he'd never before encountered had rammed through his body, overtaking his mind, as well. It was totally bizarre, impossible to comprehend and even a tad bit alarming that one single woman could make him feel that way.

But she had.

Somehow, Vanessa Steele had tunneled her way under his hardest covering, his most tightly sealed wrap, and was embedded under his skin. No woman had ever done this.

His gaze studied her face. Her eyes were closed and she was breathing evenly, but he knew she wasn't asleep. Like him, she was probably trying to get her mind and body in sync, which wasn't easy after what they had shared.

"You're one amazing woman," he said softly, truthfully, breaking into the quiet silence surrounding them.

He watched a smile touch her lips as she slowly opened her eyes to him. "Thank you. That was a wonderful thing to say."

He considered the look in her eyes. It was as if she was both surprised and relieved by his words. Why? Had someone once told her differently? An old lover perhaps? He pushed the thought aside, thinking if that was the case, the person evidently hadn't recognized true passion when he saw it. Besides, he didn't want to think of anyone else having shared something so special with her. That was all in the past. Whether she knew it or would accept it, she belonged to him now and that was all that mattered. He would always tell her how remarkable she was.

"It's true," he said, staring down into her face. From that first day he'd known she was a beautiful woman, but he hadn't known just how beautiful until now. She had that afterglow look, that aroused look in her eyes that said she could and would take him on again. Even now, after what they'd just shared, he still wanted to devour her, and he was certain she knew it because his erection had grown hard against her belly.

He leaned down, deciding that he wanted to play with her lips again, and began licking them from corner to corner. He liked the purr of pleasure that eased from her throat. He liked it even more when he felt her hand travel down his stomach to close over his shaft. He sucked in a deep breath and groaned when she began stroking him.

"Two can play your game, Mr. Cody," she whispered. Her hands were steady, her fingers confident, and he felt a rush of blood surge through his veins, especially the ones located where she had touched.

"You're playing with dynamite," he whispered, barely getting the words out when pleasure as raw as it could get shot all through him.

"Umm, I can believe that," she said softly, in a

sultry voice. "I'm still recovering from the after-shocks of the last explosion."

"Vanessa…"

Cameron said her name, whispered it from deep within his gut. He leaned down and kissed her, at the same time positioning his body over hers again. He slid into her, slowly, easily, and felt as if he was getting a piece of heaven. He groaned in pleasure as he continued to kiss her hungrily while slowly moving in and out of her body.

He felt on fire, scorched, and when her body began quivering beneath his, he literally went up in smoke. She called out his name, clenched his shaft with her inner muscles, pulling him deeper inside her, and he threw his head back and growled as he experienced yet another mind-blowing, body-ramming orgasm.

He had only one conscious thought: Just who was getting sexually addicted to whom?

Chapter 9

With her eyes still closed, barely released from sleep, Vanessa reached for the ringing telephone next to her bed. "Hello."

"So, who's my neighbor? Have you checked him out yet?"

Cheyenne's question jerked Vanessa out of her slumberous state and she immediately opened her eyes. Sunlight was pouring into the room and she could hear the shower running. Memories of last night came flooding back and a quick glance at the spot beside her in bed indicated tumbled sheets and an indentation where a man's body had been.

Cameron's body.

"Vanessa, hey, are you awake? I asked about my neighbor and if you'd had a chance to check him out yet."

Vanessa sighed, knowing there was no way she was going to tell her sister that not only had she checked him out, but she'd gone a step further and had slept with him, as well. "Yes, I'm awake, Cheyenne, and yes, I've checked him out."

"And?"

Vanessa rubbed a hand across her face. "And it's Cameron."

There was a pause. Then Cheyenne said, "Cameron? As in Cameron Cody?"

"Yes, as in Cameron Cody."

She could hear Cheyenne's soft chuckle and frowned. It always annoyed Vanessa that her two sisters had found Cameron's hot pursuit of her rather amusing. "So, I assume buying the house next door was a calculated move on his part after finding out you would be house-sitting for me for two weeks."

Vanessa sighed. If only her sister knew the whole story. "Yes, it was."

"Wow, that's really something for a man to want you that bad to go to those extremes. Why don't you put him out of his misery and go ahead and have an affair with him, Van?"

Vanessa couldn't help the smile that touched her lips. She doubted Cameron was in much misery this morning since they *were* having an affair. But it even went deeper than that. They were officially sex mates for the next eleven days. "I'll think about it."

"He's not going away. Determined men are like pimples. They keep reappearing."

"I'll keep that in mind."

"I don't understand why you don't like the guy. He's good-looking, sexy, wealthy and—"

"Goodbye, Cheyenne."

"Hey, don't you want my opinion?"

"Not really. Call Taylor and harass her." She then hung up the phone.

"It's not good to hang up on people."

Vanessa flicked her gaze in the direction of the deep male voice. Cameron was leaning against the bathroom door wearing only a towel wrapped around his waist. His body was glistening, still wet from his shower, and just as Cheyenne had said, he was good-looking, sexy…

She wondered how much he'd heard. "Cheyenne is used to me hanging up on her. We have that kind of relationship."

He took a few steps into the room and she had to struggle with the breath that was forcing its way through her lungs. The only thing worse than a good-looking Cameron was a half-naked good-looking Cameron. Although there was the towel, it didn't take much for her to visualize him wearing nothing at all, as he'd done most of last night. She had seen enough of him in the buff. Or had she? She then decided it hadn't been enough and that she would love seeing even more.

"And what kind of relationship is that?" he asked coming to sit on the edge of the bed beside her. He had a just-showered scent. His smell was fresh, manly.

"It's the kind where she expects me to hang up on her when she starts getting bossy, which she has a tendency to do. I'm the oldest and she's the youngest but sometimes I think she believes it's vice versa."

His sexy chuckle seemed to rumble off the walls in the room. "And what about your other sister? Taylor. The one living in New York."

Vanessa sat up in bed and braced her back

against the headboard. "Taylor likes keeping everyone out of her business, so she makes sure she doesn't get into anyone else's. She's the one we call the Quiet Storm."

He lifted a brow. "And why is that?"

"Because she doesn't have a lot to say. She's usually mild-mannered and easygoing. But if you piss her off, there's plenty of hell to pay."

"Oh, I see."

Cameron stared at her for a long moment and Vanessa began getting uncomfortable under his fixed gaze. "What?" she asked.

He smiled. "It just occurred to me that I hadn't kissed you good morning."

"Oh, were you supposed to?"

"Definitely."

And then he was inching his face closer to hers for a kiss. It was soft and gentle, but it didn't take long for it to turn into something desperate and hungry. When he finally lifted his mouth from hers, she kept her eyes on his lips and asked, "So what would you like to do today?"

The look and smile he gave her told her she hadn't needed to ask. "I'll let you think of something," he said.

A part of her felt that maybe she should send

him away, put distance between them to lessen the impact his mere presence was having on her. An idea formed in her mind; perhaps they should each do their own thing during the day and just come together at night. But she immediately squashed it. The thought of planning only their nights together seemed too calculated, nonspontaneous and such a waste of valuable time. There was that part of her that wanted him around both day and night, and they only had eleven days left. "Would you like to go shopping?" she asked.

He lifted a dark brow. "Shopping?"

"Yes. There're some wonderful shops in town."

He nodded. "All right, shopping it is. I need to go home and change but I'll be back within the hour. Unless you want to go back to sleep for a while to get some rest. We were up pretty late."

That was an understatement, she thought. They had been awake practically all night. She had used muscles she hadn't used in years, if ever. Those same achy muscles from yesterday were now aching for another reason.

"No, I'm fine. I don't need any more sleep."

"Okay," he said, standing slowly. "I'll see you in an hour."

Vanessa watched as he dropped the towel and

began dressing. Although seemingly unbothered by his nakedness, she was *getting* bothered by it. Her skin was beginning to feel tingly, and the memories of last night were beckoning for a repeat performance.

He was about to slip into his pants when she got up enough courage to act. "Cameron?"

He glanced over at her. "Yes."

"I don't need any more sleep, but there is something else I can use right now." She was certain the look in her eyes and the low pitch of her voice were a dead giveaway.

"And what's that?" he asked.

She sighed. He was deliberately making her spell things out for him. No problem. She could do that. "Come here and I'll show you," she said.

He slowly walked back over to the bed, and she leaned over toward him and kissed his bare stomach before reaching out and gliding her hands over his thick erection. "This," she said looking up at him, "is what I can use right now."

The smile that touched the corners of his lips sent all kinds of sensations throbbing through her, and when he stepped back and removed his shirt she knew that being a sex mate to this man was better than she had ever imagined. And the thought that he'd found her amazing in bed had boosted her confidence level sky-high.

The moment his knee touched the mattress she was reaching out to him, rubbing her naked body against his. And when he wrapped his arms around her and eased her down into the thickness of the bed coverings, she knew it would be late when they got to town to do any shopping. But then, some things just couldn't be hurried.

"So what do you think of this one?"

A surge of desire raced through Cameron as he sat in the chair at the dress shop surveying yet another outfit on Vanessa. It was hard to believe women did this sort of thing every time they purchased clothes. First, it took them forever to find exactly what they wanted on the rack, then they had to go into the dressing room to try it on and then come out wearing it to get someone's opinion. So far this was her sixth outfit. He had liked them all except for the one that had barely covered her thighs, definitely showing too much leg. He'd told her he hadn't liked the little black skirt, but she had smiled and placed it in her "to-buy" stack anyway.

He smiled when he thought of those legs of hers, the same ones that had wrapped around him tightly, locking him inside her body, clenching her muscles to draw everything out of him while they had—

"Cameron, I asked what you thought."

Her words reclaimed his attention. He tapped his fingers on his knee. This would be another one he didn't like. It showed too much breast. Hell, her twin globes were pouring out of it and the swath of light overhead was making it nearly impossible not to notice the hardened tips of her nipples pressing against the fabric. This dress would make a lot of women jealous. But it was the men he was worried about. Men would see her in this dress and immediately want to take her out of it.

"I don't like it," he finally said.

"Why?"

Last time, with the skirt, he hadn't given her a reason and she'd decided to purchase it anyway. Maybe if he told her why he didn't particularly care for this dress, she wouldn't buy it. "It shows too much cleavage. Your breasts are all but pouring out of it."

He then dragged his gaze over the rest of her and said, "The outfit leaves very little to the imagination. It's clinging to you like a second layer of skin. A man will look at you in that dress and immediately think of sex."

She glanced down at herself in the outfit. "You think so?"

"Hell, yeah."

She glanced back up, met his gaze and smiled. "In that case I think I'll take it."

Cameron immediately saw red and wondered if steam was coming out of his ears. Before he had a chance to say anything, she had darted back into the dressing room. She was lucky they were in a public place or he would be striding into that dressing room to teach her a lesson about tempting him.

He was about to settle back in his chair to wait for her to come out wearing yet another outfit when his cell phone rang. The caller ID indicated it was Xavier. "Yes, X, what's going on?"

"The main office at Global Petroleum was broken into last night. Security has been tight there for the past few days so we figure it might have been an inside job. A McMurray loyalist. We're discovering he had quite a few."

Cameron tightened his grip on the cell phone. "Was anything taken?"

"No, just a mess made with papers scattered all about. But a message was left for you, smeared on the wall."

Cameron rubbed the bridge of his nose. "What did it say?"

"Told you to give the company back to McMurray or you'll be sorry. Kurt told me to let you know that he's determined to find the person responsible."

Cameron nodded. There was no doubt in his mind that Kurt *would* find the person or die trying. "Okay, keep me posted."

"Do you want me to advise Kurt to let the local police know what's going on?"

"No, not yet. If we go to the authorities it will eventually get leaked to the papers. If the person is a McMurray loyalist then that's what they're counting on. Free publicity. I don't intend to oblige them."

"All right. I'll get back to you if anything else comes up."

Cameron clicked off the phone at the exact moment a rustling sound caught his attention. Glancing up, he saw the outfit Vanessa was now wearing. It had to be made of the flimsiest material ever created. He immediately came to his feet. "No. Hell no," he said, almost growling. "I don't like it."

He couldn't believe someone would design such

a thing for public wear. It was so thin he could even see she wasn't wearing any underwear. The dark area between her legs clearly showed that.

An innocent smile touched her lips. "What do you mean you don't like it?"

He crossed his arms over his chest. "Just what I said, Vanessa. I don't like it."

She placed her hands on her hips and he saw that the top part of the dress was just as transparent as the bottom. She might as well have been standing there naked. "In that case it's a good thing you don't have to wear it because I happen to like it," she said. "And I'm getting it."

She turned around to leave and he called out to her, annoyed. "I thought you wanted my opinions."

She turned back around. "I do."

Cameron frowned, puzzled. "Then please explain why the outfits that I don't like, you're buying anyway."

She smiled sweetly. "I want your opinion, Cameron, but that doesn't necessarily mean I'll take it. Those are all the outfits I intend to purchase today and I'll be back in a second." She slipped back into the dressing room.

Cameron couldn't stop the smile that curved his lips. It seemed some women were just born to be stubborn, and the one he intended to spend the rest of his life with was doubly obstinate.

He shook his head in despair. How could he have been so lucky?

Vanessa smiled at Cameron from across the table. They were sitting in one of those café-style restaurants that overlooked the bay while enjoying an early dinner. "I think we got a lot accomplished today."

He lifted a dark brow. "We?"

She dabbed her mouth with the corner of her napkin. "Yes. With your help I was able to pick out eight outfits that I think will enhance my wardrobe."

He rolled his eyes. "I didn't like half of them."

"Yes, but I liked them." *And you will too once you see me in them,* she thought. He had no idea she had bought the outfits with him in mind.

She placed her elbows on the table and supported her chin with her knuckles. "You're an only child, right?"

"Yes."

"It's unfortunate that you didn't have a sister, then you would understand how a woman's mind works."

"I don't need a sister to understand the workings of a woman's mind."

She gave him a quick smile. "It would have

helped. Then you would have realized you were approaching the situation all wrong in going after me. You're not a forever kind of guy, Cameron. And on top of that, you have controlling tendencies. You aren't the type of man a woman would consider getting involved with for the rest of her life. But you are fling material, which is why I decided to have an affair with you."

Cameron didn't like what he was hearing but decided not to contradict anything she said. She would find out how wrong she was when he had her just where he wanted her—when he had her good and addicted. "So, what's on the agenda for tonight?" he asked, placing his napkin down and leaning back in his chair. Anticipation of what was yet to come was already flowing through his blood stream.

"Umm, let's not plan anything. Let's go with spontaneous during our time together."

Cameron sighed. If he went with spontaneous she would be on this table, flat on her back with him on top of her, making out like there was no tomorrow. Sitting across from her and watching her eat and drink had been torturous. Each time she had taken a sip from her glass and he had seen how her perfectly shaped mouth had fit on the rim, he'd wished it was fitting that way on a certain part of him instead. And as if that wasn't bad enough, there had been the way her throat had moved when the liquid had flowed down it, making him wonder just how deep her throat was. Just the thought had given him an erection as hard as a nail.

"So, will spontaneous be all right with you, Cameron?"

He really didn't think she knew what she was asking, and he had no intention of telling her. "Spontaneous is fine with me."

"Good. You won't be sorry."

He lifted a brow. He knew he wouldn't be sorry and hoped like hell that she wouldn't be, either. But what she'd said did give him pause. "Why would you think I'd be sorry?"

Her face broke into a smile. "Because you come across as a man who prefers structure. I take it you like to think things through thoroughly before taking action."

She had him there. Rash decisions didn't sit well with him. But spontaneous with her was a no-brainer. He knew he wanted her and if given the opportunity to have her whenever and wherever, he would be a fool not to take it and run…to the nearest bedroom.

"Typically, I am that kind of guy, but I'm here

to enjoy myself, and for the next eleven days there aren't any limitations."

Not wanting to give her too much time to ponder what he'd said, he tilted his head toward the bar. "Would you like another drink?"

She glanced at her almost-empty glass. "No, I think I've had enough. But I would like to walk on the beach later tonight. Would you?"

He regarded her for a minute, thinking of the un-limited spontaneous possibilities. Then he nodded his head slowly and said, "Yes, I'd love to do that."

A smile curved her mouth and she murmured, "Great. I'm looking forward to later."

Chapter 10

Later could have come sooner, Cameron thought, as he walked barefoot along the beach. After their dinner date he had dropped Vanessa at home with the understanding they would meet on the beach after dark. When he'd asked if he needed to bring anything, she had simply smiled and said, "Just yourself."

So here he was with no specific plan in mind since spontaneous was the order of the evening. He looked past the palm trees toward her place and saw how well lit it was. Light spilled out, illuminating certain areas of the private beach.

"Cameron."

He turned toward the sound of his name and saw her standing next to a palm tree in a semi-lighted area. She was wearing the last outfit she had modeled for him. The one he had liked least. But seeing her in it now, the material as transparent as could be, had blood gushing through his veins.

As if mesmerized, he drifted toward her, his eyes never leaving her. With each step he took, his heart pounded out a heated rhythm and his teeth were clenched to stop the flood of sensations over-taking him.

Her outfit might have been provocative as hell, but it was her stance that was his undoing. She leaned against the tree, her legs braced apart in such a way that the flimsy material flowed all over her lush softness, her magnificent curves. Tantal-izing. Sexy. Seductive.

The latter had him entranced. Standing there in that outfit she was the epitome of sensual femininity. He could clearly see everything, the puckered tips of her shapely breasts, the flat stomach and small waist and the dark triangle between her legs. His mouth watered, his erection hardened and his breathing became a forced act.

The closer he got, the longer he looked into her passion-filled eyes, the more he wanted her.

The more he wanted spontaneous.

Every muscle in his body clenched with desire the moment he came to a stop in front of her. He reached out and, with a flick of his wrist, he unclasped the hooks on both her shoulders, and the dress slithered down her body and lay in a pool at her feet.

He whisked his eyes over her naked body and when, as if in a moment of nervousness, she lowered one of her hands to cover her center, he caught her wrist and moved her hand aside. She was his. And as far as he was concerned, what she was trying to hide was his. And he intended to have it. Now.

He took a step back and whipped his shirt over his head and with trembling, hot fingers he fumbled at his belt before jerking it free and tossing it aside. Then came his shorts. Anticipating what would happen tonight, he hadn't bothered with underwear.

Vanessa just stood looking at him, letting her gaze move from his face slowly down his body, stopping at his shaft.

It actually twitched under her direct perusal and he felt it harden even more right before her eyes. When she licked her lips, he released a tortured moan.

Instantly, she sank to her knees on the sand in front of him, and before he could draw his next breath, her hands closed over his erection just seconds before she took him into her mouth.

The impact of that sensual contact made his entire body shudder. She began stroking him all over with her tongue, then raking that same tongue across the sensitized tip, nibbling gently with her teeth before sucking deeply. He tangled his fingers in her hair, trying to tug her away one minute and then trying to hold her mouth hostage on him the next.

When he felt an explosion starting right there at the tip, he jerked back, and in one quick move he eased her down and positioned his body over hers. The moment she lifted her hips to him, he entered her in one smooth thrust, driving deep into her wetness.

She screamed his name at the same exact time he screamed hers, and it seemed every cell in his body fragmented as he was thrown into mind-boggling pleasure. Too late he realized that he hadn't used a condom just as he felt his body explode, releasing everything he had deep into her womb.

He held her there, her body locked to his, and

somehow, moments later, he found the strength to thrust deep into her again, and in no time felt himself succumbing, exploding once more.

This was rapture so pure, so unadulterated and perfect.

He knew it could only be this way with Vanessa.

"Would you like to watch a movie?" Cameron asked. "The previous owner left his DVD collection behind."

Vanessa glanced over at Cameron from across the kitchen and wondered if he was serious. After the rendezvous on the beach that had left them both naked and covered in sand, he had carried her to his place where they had used his outside shower. He had shampooed her hair and she had washed his back, then they had made love all over again, right there in the shower. Afterwards, he made her promise never to wear the outfit again and had given her one of his T-shirts to put on. They had decided they were hungry and now were in the kitchen.

"I'm going to have to pass on the movie, but I would like you to tell me who taught you how to cook."

He leaned back against the counter, holding a

cup of coffee in his hand. He had thrown together an omelet and biscuits. "My grandfather. After my grandmother died it was just the two of us."

She nodded. "Is he still living?"

He shook his head and she could see the sadness reflected in his deep-set eyes. "No, he died when I turned eighteen. Right before I entered college."

"The two of you were close. I can tell," she said softly. She could hear the special love in his voice.

She watched a smile touch his lips. "Yes, we were very close. He was the best."

She didn't say anything for the longest time until finally she admitted, "My dad was the best, too. He never had sons but it didn't matter to him. My mom, Taylor, Cheyenne and I were the apples of his eye and he always let us know it. I only wish…"

"What?"

"That I could have convinced him to stop smoking. He died of lung cancer, and a part of me wished I could have done something, hidden his cigarettes, anything."

"That wouldn't have helped, Vanessa. The person smoking is the one who has to want to stop. Your father would have continued to smoke until it was his decision to quit."

What Cameron was telling her was no different

from what her family and Sienna had told her. But when she remembered her father in his last days, how the cancer had left a robust man barely recognizable, a part of her still believed there was something she could have done.

Not wanting to discuss her father any longer, she decided to ask Cameron more about his childhood. In all the media releases she'd read on him, very little had been mentioned about it, except that he'd dropped out of school at sixteen.

"Was your grandfather your mom's father or your dad's?"

She watched him take a sip of his coffee before glancing over at her. "He was my father's father. My parents were killed in a fire at our apartment complex when I was six. My dad was able to get me out but when he went back in for my mother, the building collapsed."

Vanessa gasped and she immediately felt a tug on her heart. "Oh, how awful that must have been for you."

Cameron stared down into his coffee cup a long moment before finally lifting his head and meeting her gaze. "It was. And for the longest time, like you, I was on a guilt trip. I would often ask myself, What if Dad had gotten Mom out first? What if I had awakened and smelled the smoke first? What if I had convinced them to have a fire-escape plan like they had taught us in school? There were so many what-ifs, but I soon realized that none of them would bring my parents back."

Vanessa's heartstrings tugged tighter. She could just imagine the guilt that had consumed his young mind. "Is that when you went to live with your grandparents?" she asked.

"Yes, and they were great. It was as if they knew exactly what I needed." He chuckled. "My grandparents were pretty big on hugs. The warm and cuddly kind."

Vanessa smiled. She wondered how a man with such a warm and cuddly childhood with his grandparents could grow up to be the hard and controlled man that he was.

She opened her mouth to ask him another question when his cell phone rang. "Excuse me." He picked it up off the counter. "Yes, X."

Vanessa could tell from the expression on Cameron's face and the tenseness of his body that he didn't like whatever the person was telling him.

"Tell Kurt that I want this person found before he does any more damage." He snapped the phone shut.

"Trouble?"

Cameron jerked his head up and looked at her. "No, everything's fine."

"You're sure?"

"Positive."

She doubted he would tell her if things weren't fine and decided not to get upset by it. He really had no reason to share his business matters with her, since she certainly wouldn't be sharing any of the Steele business with him. "I've changed my mind."

The gaze holding hers was steady. "About what?"

"The movie. I'm not sleepy and I would love watching one if you still want to."

A small smile touched the corners of his lips. "Yes, I want to and I'll even let you choose something sappy."

Vanessa stood. "That's mighty generous of you, Mr. Cody."

He grinned. "Haven't you figured out by now that I'm a very generous person?"

"Need more tissue?"

Vanessa looked over at him with tear-filled eyes. "Sorry. I always cry whenever I watch this movie."

"Then why do you watch it?"

"Because it's a good movie."

"It's a tear-jerker."

She eased off the sofa to stand in front of him. "It's still a good movie. In fact, it's my favorite and has been since the first time I saw it when I was eight. I'm surprised you don't like it."

He shrugged. "It took Dorothy too long to find her way back to Kansas. As far as I'm concerned she wasn't too bright. She should have figured out a lot sooner there was no yellow brick road that would get her there."

Vanessa placed her hand on her hips, not liking his critique. "Do you have a favorite movie?"

"No."

"Not a one?"

"No, not a one. I like creating my own action," he said. With her standing right in front of him, her luscious scent was filling his lungs, and his T-shirt, which barely hit her at midthigh, was looking sexy as hell on her.

Not able to resist temptation any longer, he reached out and pulled her down into his lap. A naughty grin touched his lips. "In addition to creating my own action, I especially like taking part in my own love scenes."

And then he leaned over and kissed her.

Vanessa returned the kiss, doubting she would

ever tire of kissing him. She wrapped her arms around Cameron's neck and tasted him with the same hunger with which he was tasting her. Beneath her, his erection nudged her hip and his hand began tracing a path up her inner thigh.

Suddenly Cameron pulled both his mouth and hand away. "We need to talk," he said, resting his forehead against hers. "We need to discuss something I should have brought up earlier."

She kept her arms wrapped around his neck and met his gaze. "What?"

"I didn't use any protection when we made love on the beach tonight."

His words were like ice water thrown on her. No protection. How had she not realized? She'd never had sex with a man without using some type of protection. She'd been taking the Pill since her college days but when it came to sex these days, women had more to worry about than an unwanted pregnancy. There were serious health issues to consider.

"I'm safe, Vanessa. Don't worry about that," Cameron said as if reading her thoughts. "I get a physical every year."

"So do I," she quickly said, needing to reassure him, as well. "I'm safe, too."

He smiled and tightened his arms around her waist. "I know you are."

She was tempted to ask why he was so certain, but just the thought that he was sent a warm feeling through her.

"Now that we've covered that part, we need to discuss the other."

She lifted a brow. "What other?"

"The possibility of a pregnancy."

She shook her head. "That's not possible. I'm on the Pill."

He nodded slowly. "Anything is possible. The Pill isn't 100 percent guaranteed and if a child has been created, Vanessa, the agreement is off."

"What do you mean?"

"We agreed that once this affair ended we wouldn't be in contact with each other. But if you're pregnant that changes everything since I'd want to know about my child. Understood?"

She frowned, not liking the tone of voice he'd taken, and definitely not liking the way he was trying to take control of things. "I told you I'm on the Pill, so relax, Cameron. There won't be a baby."

"If there is—"

"Then I would let you know. But you're worrying for nothing."

He met her gaze for a long moment before standing with her in his arms. "Are you ready for bed?"

After that last conversation a part of her wanted to leave, to go back to Cheyenne's place and sleep in her own bed tonight. He had made her mad. But another part of her wanted to stay, to sleep cuddled under him and wake up with him in the morning. That was the part telling her to get over it.

She quickly made a decision and tightened her arms around his neck. "Yes, I'm ready."

Chapter 11

Four days later, Cameron leaned against the rail on his patio watching the sun rising over the ocean. Vanessa was upstairs, still asleep in his bed. He had slipped away momentarily to come downstairs to wait for a call he expected from Kurt…and also to think.

Although he had no intention of doing so, if he were to adhere to their agreement, he had only one week left to spend with Vanessa. And if he were to analyze their days together since becoming sex mates, he would be the first to admit that they had been some of the best days of his life. He smiled, thinking that a lot could be said for spontaneity.

There hadn't been too much they hadn't tried in the bedroom. But then the bedroom hadn't been the only place they'd made love. In fact, come to think of it, the only times they had actually made it to the bed was when it was time for them to retire for the night. Otherwise, spontaneous meant spontaneous.

Vanessa had seduction down to an art form, and he'd discovered the hard way—literally—that she was a woman of incredible talents. She had to be the most passionate human being on the face of the earth. Already his body was whirring with thoughts of what today would bring.

Although the sex was great, Cameron knew it wasn't the only reason he was enjoying every moment that he spent with Vanessa. Whether it was playing tennis, looking for seashells on the beach, swimming together, cooking, even shopping, everything with her was turning into an adventure.

They never talked about work but had shared their thoughts about the many charitable organizations they were both involved with. He had also discovered that she was a very compassionate person who gave her time to others generously.

When he'd told her about his involvement in Angel Flight, an organization in which CEOs volunteered their private jets to transport needy patients, she promised to propose it at the next Steele board meeting, now that the company was purchasing a private jet.

The ring of his cell phone interrupted his thoughts. He answered it. "Yeah, Kurt, what do you have for me?"

"An arrest has been made, Cameron."

He nodded, relieved. At first he'd tried not to get the authorities involved, but when there had been a third incident, he'd been left with no choice. For the next ten to fifteen minutes he listened while Kurt detailed how they had discovered the identity of the person responsible for vandalizing the offices of Global Petroleum on three separate occasions.

"Of course he won't admit McMurray put him up to anything," Kurt was saying. "But that's okay since the man was caught in full color on video. I'm going to make sure he does jail time for what he did, which will give him a chance to think about it."

Cameron nodded. "Good job, Kurt. The charges being brought against him will send a clear message to others that I mean business and I won't tolerate such behavior from any employee."

After ending the call with Kurt, Cameron leaned back against the rail and stared across the ocean. For some reason he had a gut feeling that this thing with McMurray was far from over. Bitter, John McMurray would continue to make problems or would hire others to do his dirty work for him.

Not wanting to think about McMurray anymore, Cameron switched his thoughts back to Vanessa. They had gone shopping again yesterday, this time for baby items. She was excited about the new addition to the Steele family, Chance's son, Alden. Cameron was grateful she hadn't asked for his opinion on anything since he couldn't recall the last time he'd been around a baby.

A baby.

He remembered his conversation of a few nights ago with Vanessa when they'd discussed the possibility of her being pregnant. Yesterday, while shopping for Chance and Kylie's baby, a part of him had wished that he and Vanessa had been shopping for their own child. He had never entertained any thoughts of sharing a child with a woman until now, but the more he thought about it, the more he liked the idea…with Vanessa.

He shook his head. First he needed to secure a strong relationship with the mother before he could even contemplate bringing a baby into the mix.

But he definitely was thinking about it.

"Okay, I'm stumped," Vanessa said, tossing aside the crossword puzzle she'd been working on for the past half hour. A few hours ago she and Cameron had made love upstairs in his bed and now they were stretched out beside each other by his pool in a double chaise lounge.

"Maybe I can help," Cameron said, glancing from the book he was reading. "What's the clue?"

Vanessa picked up the book. "It's a five-letter word for 'a fruit-loving bug.' The second letter is a *P*."

Cameron turned on his side and stretched his arm around her. "Aphid." He proceeded to spell it for her.

She stared at him, amazed. "And you knew the answer…just like that," she said, snapping her fingers for emphasis.

He shrugged. "No great mystery. I love science, always have."

Vanessa shook her head. He evidently loved math, as well, if the last two shopping trips were anything to go by. By the time they'd reached the cash register, he had totaled the purchases in his head, almost to the penny. She wondered…

She flipped on her side to face him. "Cameron?"

"Yes?"

Her heart began to race. It happened every time his sexy smile was directed at her. "It's plain to see that you're a very smart and intelligent man, and I don't believe you acquired those traits since reaching adulthood. So why did you drop out of high school?"

She watched what amounted to pain form in his eyes and he shifted on the lounger, seeming uncomfortable with her question. He lowered his arm from her shoulders. For the first time ever, Vanessa could feel him withdrawing from her. Though he seldom discussed his childhood, he had told her about his parents and how they'd died and about the grandparents who'd raised him. Why did this particular question bother him?

"I'm sorry if I asked you about something that's too personal, Cameron."

He glanced back at her and then, as if he had reached a decision about something, he pulled her back into his arms. "No, it's not too personal, at least not for you. I dropped out of school at sixteen because my grandfather lost his job. The company he had been employed with for over forty years deliberately laid him off less than a year before he was to retire so he couldn't receive any retirement benefits."

"Oh, how awful."

"Yes, it was. He was sixty-four and because of his age, there was no other place for him to go or anything else that he knew how to do. My grandfather wasn't the only person that particular company ruined that way. There were a number of others."

Vanessa sat up. She was angry. "But couldn't something be done about that company? Surely the government could have stepped in and—"

"The government did nothing," Cameron said, just as angry and very bitter. "There were no laws in place to protect workers against such tactics. And with no money coming in, I had to do something. I couldn't let my grandfather worry himself to death. His health hadn't been at its best as it was, and he was trying to make that final year."

"So you dropped out of school to help." It was a statement rather than a question.

"Yes. Gramps didn't want me to do it, neither

did my teachers, but there was nothing else to do. There was still a mortgage on the house and Gramps was still paying the medical bills my grandmother had left behind."

For a moment he didn't say anything then he added, "I'm just thankful for Mrs. Turner."

Vanessa raised a brow. "Mrs. Turner?"

"Yes. She was one of my teachers who thought I had a bright future ahead of me, so she volunteered to tutor me. When I turned eighteen I passed the GED and got my high-school diploma that way."

Vanessa nodded. She was thankful for someone like Mrs. Turner in Cameron's life, as well. "And what type of work did you do for those two years?"

"I worked at Myers Feed Store for a while, driving his truck, making deliveries, and then I went to work for Handover Construction Company. With the money I made I was able to keep food on the table for me and Gramps and buy his medication each month."

Vanessa knew from what he'd told her last week that his grandfather had died right before Cameron had entered college. That must have been a lonely time for him. "Thanks for sharing that with me, Cameron."

Instead of saying anything, he pulled her into his arms and just held her close.

"I can't believe you're taking time to call me," Sienna teased. "I thought Cameron was occupying most of your time these days. Don't tell me you've had enough of each other already."

Vanessa dropped down on her bed and glanced out the window. Down below she could see Cameron driving off, going to town to pick up the items they needed for dinner. Tonight they would get into the kitchen together. "No, we haven't had enough."

She thought about what she'd said then decided she couldn't really speak for Cameron and modified her reply. "At least I haven't had enough."

Sienna was the only person to whom Vanessa had admitted that she and Cameron were having an affair. To Cheyenne, who called periodically, she hadn't said anything, deciding to let her sister keep guessing, although Vanessa was pretty sure Cheyenne knew the score.

"How many more days?" Sienna asked her.

"Seven."

"Then what happens?"

"Then Cameron returns to Charlotte. I'll be

leaving a day or two afterward when Cheyenne returns."

"What's after that?"

Vanessa rolled her eyes. "Sienna, why are you asking me that? I told you that nothing happens after that. Cameron will go his way and I'll go mine. This was an island fling and nothing more."

"And what if you fall in love with him?"

Vanessa shook her head stubbornly. "Won't happen. You of all people know that I've learned— the hard way, I might add—how to keep my emotions in check."

"But why would you want to if the right person came along? You know that I wasn't ready for Dane when we first met. Talk about night and day. He was the rich kid and I was the one whose parents had more issues than *The New York Times* had newspapers. I tried to fight his interest, tried convincing him of all the reasons we were wrong for each other. Then I finally talked him into letting me be his bedmate for a night, thinking that would definitely get us out of each other's systems. You of all people know that didn't work."

"Yes, but you and Dane were meant to be together, I've always told you that. I never knew why you were fighting it and fighting him."

"The same way I don't understand why you're fighting Cameron. Okay, he can be a control freak at times, he likes being in charge, the master of his game. But even you said he's been letting you call the shots, allowing you to take control, so that means at least he's flexible. And can you honestly say that after spending a week with him, he's still the monster you always thought him to be?"

Vanessa remained quiet for a moment as she pondered Sienna's question. She thought about the time she and Cameron had spent together, all the fun they'd had. Then she said, "No, I don't think he's a monster."

Sienna must have heard the tiny catch in her voice because her friend didn't say anything for a while, until she asked, "Are you okay, Vanessa?"

"No, I'm not okay," she confirmed with a bit of gloom in her tone. "But I will be. It's just that…"

"What?"

"Nothing. I knew what I was getting into."

"Are you sure about that?"

Despite all the misgivings she was suddenly feeling, Vanessa refused to give in to the racing of her heart and summoned every ounce of her common sense. No, she told herself, what she was feeling was nothing other than good old-fashioned lust. "Yes, Sienna, I'm sure."

Vanessa held out her hand to Cameron. "The sharp knife."

He carefully placed the item she had requested into her hand and then watched as she expertly removed the bone and skin from the four chicken breast halves before tossing the meat into the slow cooker.

"Bell pepper."

He scooped up the bell pepper strips that he'd cut and tossed them in the pot to join the chicken.

"Now the can of pepper-jack cheese soup and the chunky salsa mixture."

Before handing those items to her, he eased closer to her while she stood at the kitchen counter. "My mouth is watering already."

His closeness and the low chuckle that rumbled close to her ear actually made her shiver. Even after a week her body still reacted whenever he was near. "Then I expect you to have a clean plate later," she said, placing the lid on the cooker and setting it to cook on low for six hours. "This is what I call easy and tasty."

"I can certainly see that."

Considering her mind had been elsewhere all day, ever since talking to Sienna, Vanessa had wanted to prepare something that didn't take a lot of thought, and this was the first thing that had come to mind. It was one of the first dishes she had prepared in her home economics class in high school and she had served it to her family, or anyone else who wanted to eat it, for three nights in a row.

"So it's going to take six hours?" Cameron asked, easing still closer to her.

She smiled, already knowing where his mind was going. "Yes, just about."

"Would you like to go swimming while we wait?"

"Sure. Why not? But I didn't bring a bathing suit over here with me."

Cameron's smile nearly sizzled her insides. "Who said anything about you needing a bathing suit? Let's be daring."

Vanessa chuckled. "If I recall, you've already been daring. I was sitting on the beach that day you decided to bare all before diving into the ocean."

He leaned over and touched her lips with his. "I saw you and even from a distance, I got turned on and needed to take a quick dip to cool off."

"You expect me to believe that?"

He took her hand in his. "Yes, because it's true.

Haven't these past days we've spent together proved it?"

To Vanessa's way of thinking, these past days they'd spent together proved how quickly she had succumbed to his charm. What bothered her most was knowing that sooner or later she would have to start withdrawing. Their time together was now a clock slowly ticking away, and every second, minute or hour counted…until the end.

The end.

She inhaled deeply and instinctively snuggled closer to him, and he wrapped his arms completely around her. They'd had a lot of these types of moments, usually after making love when there were no words left to say and he would just hold her. Making the decision to have an island fling with him had been hard, but now what would be even harder was walking away knowing there would not be a repeat. This was all they would have.

"Yes, I'll go skinny-dipping with you, Cameron," she finally said, turning in his arms and looking up to meet his gaze. "But I won't walk out of this house down to the beach naked," she added. "I'm going to need something to wear."

A smooth grin curled the corners of Cameron's mouth. "Will one of my T-shirts do?"

She couldn't help but laugh, recalling how many times she had walked around in his T-shirts and how very little they covered. She remembered one night in particular when, in one of her seductive moods, she had seduced him while wearing his L.A. Lakers T-shirt. He had practically ripped the thing off before taking her right here on the kitchen table.

"If that's the best you can do, then yes, one of your T-shirts will do," she decided to say, trying to block the memories of that particular night from her mind.

"You know where they are."

A grin tugged at her lips. "Yes, I do, don't I?" She pulled herself out of his arms. "I'll be back in a second."

Vanessa was halfway up the stairs when she glanced back over her shoulder. Cameron was standing in the doorway separating the kitchen from the living room. His hands were braced on either side of the arch and his stance was as sexy as sexy could get. At that moment she wished she had a camera to capture that pose on film so she could take out the photo on those lonely nights after she returned to Charlotte.

She quickly turned back around and made it up the rest of the stairs. Damn, she didn't need this now, especially not when she was trying hard to keep what they were sharing in perspective. And she definitely hadn't counted on it.

Cameron Cody was truly beginning to grow on her. Even worse, he was slowly but surely getting under her skin in a way she hadn't thought possible.

Chapter 12

Cameron heard Vanessa return even before her bare feet touched the last step. He glanced up and tried not to stare. But he couldn't help himself. The woman did wonders for his T-shirts.

It was his opinion that her body was outright and unreservedly perfect, and as she walked toward him, putting those long gorgeous legs out in front of her, his blood raced, literally pounding through every part of him. His gaze traveled all over her. This particular shirt—the one promoting his construction company—seemed shorter than the rest. The cotton fabric clung to her full breasts and curvy hips.

When she finally reached the bottom step she slowly twirled around with her hands on her hips. "So, what do you think?" she asked as a smile twitched her lips.

He groaned inwardly. What he really thought was that now was a good time to kiss that lush mouth of hers, or better yet, to whisk her into his arms and take her back upstairs. Everything about her, every sensuous detail, was wreaking havoc on his control, his ability to think straight, his ability to resist emotions he'd never encountered before.

"I think," he said, taking a step forward, "that you are the most beautiful woman I've ever met, whether you're wearing an outfit I personally don't like, my T-shirt or nothing at all. You are simply stunning."

A warm tingle started in Vanessa's breasts and moved lower, toward her midsection. The dark, tense eyes staring down at her seemed both serious and deeply enthralled. She bit her lower lip, trying not to let his words affect her so, and found it difficult. They *had* affected her.

She took a deep breath and glanced down at him. The only thing covering his body was a pair of outlandishly sexy swim trunks that left nothing to her imagination. They seemed like a second layer of skin and clearly emphasized the fact that he wanted her. Her heartbeat sped up at the thought of what would happen once they got down to the beach.

"I'm taking a large blanket and a bottle of body cream."

Vanessa hitched a brow. "Body cream?"

He smiled. "Yes, I want to rub it all over you after we take a swim."

A tremble ran through her body. She had a feeling that wasn't all he intended to do.

Vanessa lay on her stomach on the thick blanket with the sand as a cushion. She closed her eyes at the feel of Cameron's hands moving slowly, lightly over her shoulder, gently massaging the slope of her back and the curve of her neck. The cream he was rubbing into her skin smelled of tropical fruits, and his calloused fingers were working magic as he caressed her skin.

She released a long sigh when he rubbed more of the cream onto her back, tenderly kneading her muscles, working out her aches and pains at the same time he caused a different type of throbbing in her body.

"What are you thinking about?" he asked in an

almost-whisper, leaning down close to her ear. He was on his knees straddling her butt. She could feel his nearness, his heat, and the way his hands were touching her, moving down her back, the rear of her thighs and then her behind was sending all kinds of sensations through her body.

"Umm, I'm thinking about how good your hands feel on me," she said, almost in a purr. "I've never gotten this much attention from a man before."

"And is that good or bad?"

She paused, thinking about his question, before she answered. "Before this trip, I would have thought it was bad. But now I can't help but think it's all good. I can't imagine another man touching me this way, making me feel this way, and—"

She never finished what she was about to say. Cameron had gently turned her over and rubbed some of the cream onto her chest. He began rubbing it into her skin, caressing her breasts in a circular motion around the nipples while they hardened at his touch.

After smearing more cream onto her body, his fingers moved lower to her stomach and with the tip of his finger he drew rings around her navel, sending a rush of sexual pleasure through every pore on her body. A part of her wanted to reach out and cover her feminine mound from his gaze, but she couldn't. Besides, it would be a waste of time. She might be the one in control, but Cameron had a way of using anything she did to his advantage. She was beginning to see that he was smart in more ways than one.

"I didn't tell you everything there was to know about this particular cream, Vanessa," he said, his voice a low, sensuous timbre.

She let go of a shaky breath at the mere sound. "What didn't you tell me?" She looked up into his face. He was above her, straddling her body. Then he began lowering his head closer to hers. When he was just inches from her face he said, "The cream I've rubbed all over you is edible. Do you know what that means?"

Her gaze was locked with his and was filled with hunger, heat, and a hefty dose of arousal. Of course she knew what he meant, what he was alluding to, but she decided to play dumb. "No, what does that mean?" she asked innocently.

Bracing his hands on both sides of her head, he leaned down to within inches of her lips. "It means, Vanessa Steele, that tonight, under the beauty of this Jamaican moon, you will become my treat."

"Your treat?" she asked, her voice barely audible against the waves rushing toward the shore.

"Yes, but first this…"

And then he leaned closer, captured her lips and kissed her as though she was everything he had ever wanted, everything he had ever needed, and that kissing her was his lifeline for the next minute, hour, day. His mouth was feeding on hers with a hunger that made her whimper.

He slowly pulled his mouth away, and she immediately felt the loss of his lips on hers.

"Did I tell you that mango is my favorite fruit and this cream has plenty of mango in it?"

"Mango?"

"Yes. There's also a pinch of pineapple and avocado. Real tasty fruits. Exotic fruits. Fruits with mouthwatering flavor."

He picked up the bottle of cream and with his hands he smeared a trail of it from the tips of her breasts down to her stomach. When he came to her feminine mound with its smooth bikini wax, he stared at it for a moment before taking his hand and fully coating it with the fruity cream. It was like piling whipped cream on top of a hot fudge sundae.

"Cameron?"

"Yes?"

"What are you doing?"

"Fulfilling one of my fantasies. And I might as well confess right now that there's nothing spontaneous about this. This is something I've been thinking about for quite some time. And when we do part, Vanessa, I plan to take the taste of you with me. I want it embedded so deeply in my tongue that it becomes a permanent part of my taste buds. I want the scent of you to inflame my nostrils for all eternity."

"But we agreed—"

"I know what we agreed, Vanessa. This is an island fling and I will keep my word. But that doesn't mean I shouldn't remember what I consider to be some of the most special days I've ever had with a woman who has more passion in her little finger than some women have in their entire body. I won't do anything intentionally to look you up when we return to Charlotte, but as I told you in the beginning, I want to make love so good that you'll want to look me up."

"I won't," she said stubbornly, frowning.

"Then I really have my work cut out for me over the next six days, don't I?" he said softly, with a confidence she heard. His nostrils flared slightly when he continued. "You are in my system, and all these days of loving you only implanted you deeper. And before we separate, I'm going to make sure that I'm as entrenched within you as you are within me."

Vanessa glanced away, breaking eye contact as she looked out at the ocean. It was dark, and somewhere in the distance she could see the lights from a huge ship, probably a cruise liner. She was grateful they couldn't be seen from that far out at sea.

She breathed in deeply, wondering if she could become addicted to Cameron. Could he become an itch she would need to have scratched at some point? She shook her head, refusing to believe it. People engaged in affairs all the time and walked away. But the big question was this: Could she really and truly walk away from his loving? Endless passion, earth-shattering orgasms, an easy camaraderie with a man who made her feel desirable?

Yes, she could do it, because, although she had gotten to know Cameron a lot better than before, there were still some things about him that she wouldn't be able to tolerate. Such as his need to control and to be in control.

She turned back to look at him when she heard him removing his shorts. She watched almost spellbound as he slowly slid the garment down his legs, then she blinked, thinking that tonight his erection looked larger than usual. Was that possible?

A warm, hot tingle began in her midsection and quickly spread to the area between her legs when he slowly eased back to her, settling on his knees in the middle of her opened thighs.

"I'm going to lick you all over, starting here." He lifted her hips and placed her legs on his shoulders, bringing her feminine mound level to his. "Enjoy, sweetheart, because I certainly intend to."

Vanessa gasped at the first touch of Cameron's tongue on her sensitive flesh. Each stroke of his tongue was methodical, focused, greedy. He was giving her his undivided attention and it took everything she had not to scream out.

The intimate kiss might have started out as a late-night treat for him, but it was an entirely different thing to her. Each sensuous nibble was taking her to a place she had never been before, a place where only the two of them belonged. She didn't want to question the rightness of her thoughts, she just knew they were so.

The more he loved her in this most cherished way, the more sensations consumed her, taking over her mind and body. Her heart beat faster and her breathing became difficult. When the rumble of a scream was close to pouring forth from her throat, she bit down on her lips to hold it back. Her fingers dug into Cameron's shoulders, holding his mouth in place.

But the sensations became too much to bear. She tightened her grip on his shoulders even more and drew in a deep breath before letting it out by screaming his name when an orgasm hit.

"Cameron!"

The moment she called out his name he pulled his mouth from her and moved his body in place over hers. Then in one smooth and swift thrust, he entered her, going deep. "Wrap your legs around my waist," he whispered in her ear, and as soon as she did so, locking their bodies, he began thrusting in and out of her with the speed of a whip.

Her entire body clenched tightly, pulling everything she could out of him. She could tell he was fighting against an orgasm, trying to make it last, but she wanted more and she wanted it now.

Using her teeth she bit gently into his shoulder, then soothed the mark with her tongue. She felt him shudder, felt his body get harder inside hers and heard him moan close to her ear.

And then she felt it happen as he thrust into her hard. For the second time that night she didn't want to question the feeling of oneness with this man, the feeling that he could become her entire world, and that she was haphazardly tumbling into his.

She didn't want to think about anything, especially not the fact they had only six days left after tonight. The only thing she wanted to think about was how he was making her feel. This instant. This moment.

Vanessa knew that no matter what, after this time with Cameron, her life would never be the same.

Chapter 13

Cameron's eyes opened slowly during the predawn hours. Something had awakened him. He reached out to pull Vanessa closer into his arms and came up empty-handed. All that was there, other than the slight indentation on the pillow where her head had lain, was her scent, an arousing fragrance that had become such an innate part of his life.

He gazed around the room and saw the open patio door. Evidently she hadn't been able to sleep. For a long while, neither had he. It was hard as hell to accept that their twelve days were over and that today at noon he would be flying out, returning to the States.

He tightened his fists at his sides, damning their agreement. There was no way she could deny that their time together had been special, especially the last six days. They had taken early-morning walks on the beach, picnics on the bay, and had made love under the moonlight in a number of places. He would miss her like hell when he left and he hoped and prayed each day that she would realize they were meant to be together.

A shiver passed through him at the thought of the separation they faced. What if, when she returned to Charlotte, she had no problem in keeping her end of the agreement and would not want to see him again? What if their time together meant more to him than it did to her? What if his entire plan backfired and he wasn't any closer to having her as a part of his life than he had been before taking Morgan's advice?

He pulled himself up in bed, suddenly thinking about all the things he'd never wanted from a woman before, but now had to have from Vanessa. He'd thought he wanted possession, wanted to make her a part of his life without any deep emotional attachment or binding commitment. After all, he was a man who didn't do emotional attachments. But now he wanted it all. He wanted her.

He loved her.

He sucked in a deep, shaky breath with that admission. It was one he had thought he would never make again after Stacy. But Vanessa had proven him wrong. She had brought out in him something no woman had done in over ten years—his desire to love unconditionally. She had broken down his defenses and made the twisted reason he'd wanted her in his life into something he hadn't counted on. Love.

He had always wanted Vanessa but hadn't realized or accepted that he also loved her.

Now he did, and what the hell was he supposed to do about it? He slowly slid back down in the bed. One thing he would not do was let her have her way and turn her back on what they could have together. His heart was at stake, and he was determined that, in the end, she would love him as much as he loved her.

He heard the sliding of the patio door and lowered his eyelids, pretending sleep. He wasn't ready to admit his feelings to Vanessa just yet. Not until he had another workable plan.

Through half-closed eyes he watched as she dropped her robe and eased her naked body into bed beside him. She cuddled close, skin to skin, and lowered her head to his chest. Then, moments later she glanced up, placed a kiss on his lips and whispered, "I'm going to miss you when you leave, Cameron Cody. A hell of a lot more than I should."

He didn't say anything since he knew she assumed he was asleep and her words hadn't been meant for him to hear. But those words sent every cell in his body vibrating. If she was fighting any feelings for him and was pretty close to the edge, he intended to push her over. He would try and be patient, but he wouldn't let her send him out of sight and out of mind.

When she cuddled back in his arms to reclaim sleep, a smile curved his lips. There were some risks worth taking, and no matter what it took, he intended to convince Vanessa of that.

"Are you sure you don't want to go to the airstrip with me?"

Vanessa shook her head as she watched Cameron get dressed. They had awakened that morning and made love. Then they had gone downstairs and, as they'd done on a number of other mornings, they had prepared breakfast together. Afterwards, they had come back upstairs to make love again. Now she was sitting up in bed half-naked and he was putting on his shirt and pants. A limo would be arriving in less than an hour to take him to the airport where his private jet would return him to the States.

"No, I think it's best if we say our goodbyes here," she said.

He glanced up and looked at her and then he slowly walked over to the bed and pulled her into his arms. "What we shared was special, Vanessa. I'm going to miss it and I'm going to miss you. Why can't we—"

She quickly reached out and placed her fingers to his lips. "Don't, Cameron. You promised. All this was supposed to be was an island fling. We both agreed. Flings aren't meant to last."

Taking a deep breath, Cameron fought back the words he wanted to say. He would let her have things her way for now, but once she set her feet back on American soil he would intensify his plan.

"Regardless, I meant what I said. If your days or nights become lonely and you find you still want me, just let me know and I will make myself available to you. Anytime, anyplace and any position."

A small tremble rippled down Vanessa's spine at Cameron's offer. A part of her was tempted, but she held on to her resolve. Cameron had been wonderful these past few weeks only because he had allowed himself to put his guard down. He had been stripped of his control. Back in the States it would be business as usual, and he would go back to being the kind of man she did not want in her life. The kind of person who got what he wanted regardless of how he went about getting it. Ruthless, powerful, demanding. Those were three things she could not accept in any man.

But still…she would miss him. She would miss everything they had shared. For a little while he had stripped away her inhibitions, robbed her of her common sense and had filled her days and nights with more pleasure than any one woman had a right to receive.

"Vanessa."

She met his gaze, saw the deep longing there and knew what he wanted. She shook her head. "You'll miss your plane."

He smiled. The smile where the corners of his lips tilted so sexily, the one that sent tingly sensations all through her. "I can't miss the plane since I own it," he said huskily. "And I can't leave here without being with you again."

He kissed her then, a hot, open-mouthed kiss

that was filled with more passion than Vanessa thought she could handle. She would never get tired of savoring the taste of him. It was the kind of kiss that stirred everything inside her to life once again, that activated a dull, throbbing ache right between her legs.

"Cameron."

He gently eased her down on the bed, while running his hands up her legs, her thighs and finding that very spot that ached for him. Instead of clamping her legs together to stop him, she parted them and he slipped his finger inside her. Her response to his intimate touch was immediate, and she released a moan of need from deep within her throat.

How could she still crave this when she had made love in two weeks more times than in her entire life? How could his touch alone make an insufferable longing erupt deep within her? Those questions were obliterated from her mind, squashed by the sensations that began taking over.

Intense pleasure suffused her entire body as his fingers worked their magic on her, and then shock wave after delicious shock wave consumed her. She literally gasped at the magnitude. Her body trembled and she clutched him, held tightly to his shoulder as an orgasm rammed into her.

He held her for long moments, waiting for the aftershocks to cease, to ease from her body. Then he slowly released her and stepped back, and she watched as he began removing his clothes. He took a condom from his nightstand and put it on.

Vanessa could tell from the intense look in Cameron's eyes that even with the time restraints this wouldn't be a quickie. He intended to leave her with something she would remember for a long time. He was determined to get her addicted to him.

A rainbow of emotions arced through her. Resentment. Inflexibility. Stubbornness. But all three were overshadowed by desire, a need that was deeply intense within her, even after what she'd just shared with him.

When he came back to the bed, gloriously naked, she pushed all those unwanted emotions aside. Instead she wanted to concentrate on this one last time. Rising up, she eagerly went into his arms, kissing him with the same hunger and intensity with which he had kissed her earlier.

Later, after he left, she would question her sanity, drum up all that common sense that he had blown to pieces. She would go back to being her own person, a confident woman who didn't want or need a man in her life.

The tiny hot flames licking her body made any more coherent thoughts impossible. And when Cameron broke their kiss and eased her down in bed, she wrapped her arms around his neck, needing to hold on to him for just a little while longer.

The look in his eyes made her breathless, and when he positioned his body over hers and continued to look at her she could feel her body surrendering to him. To his wants and his desires.

When he entered her, she moaned at the impact and wrapped her legs around his waist. The way he made love to her, thrusting in and out, was making her delirious and she held on, needing as much as he was giving. She felt the muscles in his back straining with each powerful thrust.

And just when she felt the earth move, he leaned toward her and dipped the tip of his tongue into the corners of her mouth, licking her as though she was a taste he had to have.

At that moment the earth didn't just move, it exploded, and she felt herself being blasted to a place Cameron had never taken her before. She screamed his name until her throat seemed raw and still the sensations kept ramming her, nonstop. She was slightly taken aback by the intensity of her passion, the force of her need, and when he followed her over, when that same explosion tore into him, she tightened her hold on him, lifted her hips and locked him in place.

And then she felt it, that affinity she had never felt before with a man, a special oneness. And no matter how much she tried fighting the feeling, it wouldn't go away.

She was forced to admit that if she hadn't gotten addicted, she was pretty close to it.

Vanessa kept running down the beach, along the shore. Cameron was probably back in the States now, back on Charlotte's soil, and she needed to run.

She kept jogging, mindless of the exhaustion that had seeped into her bones. She wanted to be tired so she could sleep tonight, so the dreams wouldn't come. It would be bad enough when she reached out and found the place beside her empty.

She had stood at his upstairs bedroom window and looked down below to watch him leave. Right before he got into the car, he glanced up, knowing she would be there. He had stared at her for a long moment before lifting his hand. She had expected a wave but instead he had blown her a kiss.

That single action had gotten under her skin, and for the rest of the day all rational thoughts had been reduced to a mess of emotions.

So, for now, she kept running to release that wild, reckless streak that Cameron had encouraged. She was determined to be all right and to put her island fling behind her. Cheyenne had called. The photo shoot had ended and she was on her way home. That meant in a day or so Vanessa would be free to leave this island that would always hold so many special memories.

She kept running, feeling her muscles ache, feeling the heaviness of her heart, but she refused to acknowledge the pain, the anxiety, the deep, intense need Cameron had so effortlessly fulfilled. She had begun missing him the moment he had gotten into the car that had taken him away. He had left his door key with her and also his car key, both generously offered for her use.

Vanessa inhaled deeply as she continued to jog. She had taken a chance. She had trodden on dangerous grounds. She had indulged in a very special kind of risky pleasure. But she didn't have any regrets. What she and Cameron had shared was priceless and the memories would be endless.

When she returned to work on Monday it would be business as usual. That's the way she wanted it and that's the way she intended it to be.

Chapter 14

"Welcome back, Vanessa."

Vanessa glanced up to find her four cousins standing in the doorway to her office. She smiled. "Thanks, guys. It's good to be back."

"And you really want us to believe that you prefer being here over Jamaica?" Donovan, the youngest of the Steele brothers, asked.

She chuckled. "Hey, I didn't admit that but you know what they say. There's no place like home."

Referring to that quote from *The Wizard of Oz* made her think of Cameron and the night they had watched that particular movie together.

"Vanessa?"

She was jerked from her thoughts. She glanced over at Chance. "Yes?"

"I asked if you wanted to come to dinner on Sunday. We're having a small dinner party to celebrate the baby's arrival."

She smiled. "I'd love to come." She wondered if Cameron had been invited, as well, but decided not to ask.

"And mark your calendar for Friday night, two weeks from now," Morgan said.

She raised a brow while grabbing the calendar on her desk. "What's going on that night?"

"I'm hosting a party to officially kick off my campaign. The election is in three months."

Vanessa nodded. She didn't have to wonder if Cameron would be attending that event. He was committed to Morgan's campaign. She sighed deeply and after penciling in the date on her calendar she smiled up at Morgan. "Consider it done. Do you need me to do anything?"

"Ask my campaign manager," he said, nodding over at Donovan. "Or I could send you to Cameron since he's the second in command."

Vanessa frowned at Morgan. "No, that's okay.

I'm sure Donovan can tell me anything I need to know."

She saw the quirking of Morgan's lips and knew it was business as usual between them. He was still trying to shove Cameron down her throat. Well, little did he know, Cameron had already been there. She flushed at the memory.

"Vanessa, are you okay?"

She drew a deep breath and glanced over at Sebastian. "Yes, Bas, why do you ask?"

"You seem preoccupied about something."

If only you knew. "I'm not preoccupied, just a little overwhelmed with the amount of work piled high on my desk."

"Well, bring your thoughts off Jamaica. We have a lot of work to do this week. We need to call a press conference later today."

Vanessa raised a brow. "Why?"

With irritation in his voice, Chance informed her, "An article appeared in this morning's paper that we would be laying off over two hundred employees due to outsourcing."

Vanessa shook her head. "I can't believe someone has started that rumor again."

"Well, they have, and now we need to work on damage control both with our employees and the community. Although I do find it really strange it's started up again only since Morgan is seeking public office. It wouldn't surprise me if someone is trying to play dirty politics."

Vanessa nodded. She thought the same thing. It was her job to make sure the Steele Corporation maintained a positive image, and the sooner she got back into her job, the less time she would have to think about Cameron.

"What time is the press conference?" she asked Chance.

"At noon."

"All right, how about if we meet in an hour so you can go over some things with me?"

"That's a good idea. We'll leave so you can get settled."

"Thanks."

When her cousins walked out of her office, closing the door behind them, she leaned back in her chair, grateful she had plenty to do to keep her mind occupied. The last thing she needed was to dwell on the memories of the past two weeks.

"I saw the press conference on television the other day. I think it went well, Vanessa," Sienna said as she sat across from her best friend at lunch.

"Thanks, I can't believe we're still tackling that issue but all it takes is a rumor to make people panic when it comes to their livelihood," Vanessa responded. The two women were grabbing a quick bite at the Racetrack Café, a popular restaurant in town and one they frequented often.

Moments later Vanessa smiled over at her friend. "I can't get over just how pregnant you look. I've only been gone for two weeks and your stomach has grown tremendously."

Sienna chuckled. "To hear Dane tell it, I'm still not showing much, although I can't get into any of my clothes. Heck, I'm five months already, but the doctors told me the baby will probably be small. But then Dane was a preemie when he was born."

The smile left Vanessa's face. "Are you worried the baby might come early?"

"Not really, but if it does, I'll be getting the best medical care. Dane's mother tried to insist that we use Dr. Tucker, but Dane and I told her we were perfectly satisfied with the doctor I'm using. Needless to say, she wasn't happy about it, thinks I'm to blame and hasn't said too much to me since. She doesn't know how close I finally came to telling her off."

Vanessa frowned. The rift between Sienna and

her mother-in-law was an ongoing one that had started when Sienna and Dane had first begun dating. Sienna was not the woman Mrs. Bradford had wanted for her son. Dane had been born into a rather wealthy family, while Sienna was what Mrs. Bradford considered a "nobody."

Vanessa clearly recalled how a little over three years ago, Sienna and Dane's marriage had seemed doomed, headed for divorce, until a snowstorm had left them stranded together at their cabin in the mountains. The forced togetherness had given them a chance to talk, to analyze what had gone wrong in the marriage and to decide that they still loved each other enough to stay together and make things work. Now they were doing just fine and would continue to do so as long as they kept Dane's interfering parents out of their business.

After the waiter had delivered their meals and left, Sienna glanced over at Vanessa. "Well, are you going to tell me what went down in Jamaica between you and Cameron Cody?"

Vanessa glanced at Sienna over the rim of her glass of iced tea. After taking a sip, she said, "Come on Sienna, you know what a couple do when they're involved in an affair. Ours was no different and it was fun and enjoyable while it lasted."

"And you think it's over?"

"I know it's over. Cameron and I were very clear on the terms," Vanessa said. She hoped, for both their sakes, that he honored the agreement as he'd promised. But then she had no reason to think he wouldn't given that she'd been back in Charlotte for almost a week and he hadn't tried contacting her.

It would have been easy for him to do so. Her office was down the hall from Morgan's so it would have been relatively simple for him to drop by and visit Morgan and find a reason to seek her out. She didn't want to admit it, but she was a little disappointed that he hadn't.

"I take it the sex was good."

Vanessa blinked when memories assailed her mind. The sex wasn't just good, it was amazing. She couldn't help but think of all the satisfaction she had gotten from Cameron that she hadn't gotten from Harlan. Cameron had been a thoughtful, caring and unselfish lover.

"Well?"

Vanessa was pulled out of her thoughts. She glanced across the table and saw a silly-looking grin on Sienna's face, as if she'd been privy to her thoughts. Gosh, she hoped not! She cleared her throat. "Well, what?"

"Was the sex good? I happen to think it must have been."

Vanessa raised a brow. "Why would you think that?"

"Because you seem more at ease, relaxed, less tense. I can tell you've taken the edge off. And I have a feeling I should be thanking Cameron for that."

Vanessa didn't want to admit it but Sienna *did* have Cameron to thank for it. An affair with him had been just what she'd needed and just what she'd known it would be. Unforgettable. Since returning to Charlotte she hadn't been able to sleep a single night without reliving those moments in her dreams.

"Don't look now, but he's here."

Vanessa's stomach suddenly clenched. "Who's here?"

"Your lover boy. Cameron Cody. He just walked in with another man and the waiter is leading them over to a table near the wall. I don't think he's seen us."

Thank God for that, Vanessa immediately thought, fighting the thousands of butterflies that had been released in her stomach. Maybe they could finish eating and leave before he did notice them.

"Oops. He glanced over this way and saw us."

Sienna's words weren't what Vanessa had wanted to hear. "Then let's pretend we haven't seen him."

Sienna smiled. "Too late. I looked right in his face."

Vanessa picked up her tea glass with somewhat shaky fingers. "Fine, then I'll be the one to pretend."

"Too late again. He's coming over this way."

"Great! That's all I need."

Sienna lifted a brow. "If you keep acting this way, I'm going to think you're in need of something else. Are you getting your edge back on again?"

Vanessa hadn't thought Sienna's comment the least bit funny and was about to tell her so when she saw a shadow cross their table. She swallowed as she glanced up into the darkest, sexiest eyes that had ever been given to a man. And at that moment she remembered how those same eyes got even darker just moments before he—

"Sienna. Vanessa."

Cameron's greeting broke into Vanessa's thought, just at the right time. "Hello, Cameron," both she and Sienna said at the same time. Vanessa couldn't help but take in the sight of him. He was standing beside their table, dressed in a designer business suit, seeming completely at ease in the sexy stance she liked so well, his feet planted apart as if he was ready to take on anybody, especially her. And he would do it in such a way that would leave her totally breathless if not totally wrenched from never-ending orgasms.

"I saw the two of you and wanted to come over and say hello," he said to both while fixing his gaze directly on Vanessa.

Vanessa cleared her throat. "That was kind of you," she responded.

He nodded slightly and then said, "Well, I'll let the two of you get back to your meal. I'm dining with my attorney."

"Thanks for dropping by and saying hello," Sienna said smiling.

"It was totally my pleasure," he assured them.

Vanessa caught on to that one word. *Pleasure.* The man was the king of it. He could deliver it like nobody's business.

"It was good seeing both of you."

"Same here," Sienna said.

Vanessa, who was trying to recover from a flash of one particular memory that had taken place in Cheyenne's shower, merely nodded.

He turned and walked off. When Sienna was sure he wasn't in hearing range she asked, "Am I to assume you no longer dislike him as much as you used to?"

Vanessa shrugged as she bit a French fry. "He's all right."

"That's not what I asked you, Van."

Vanessa frowned. Sienna wanted things spelled out for her. "Yes, you can assume that. But…"

"But what?"

"Cameron Cody is still Cameron Cody. He just happens to handle things differently in the bedroom than he does in the boardroom. I've seen him in action in both, Sienna."

"And the way he carries himself in the boardroom is the one you can't get over, isn't it?"

"Should I be able to? It showed me what I can expect after the touching, kissing and the deep thrusts. You still have a man who likes being in control. A man whose actions can actually destroy a person's livelihood when they find themselves out of a job."

"Didn't you read that article in *Ebony?* Although there tends to be some changes whenever a new management team comes on the scene, from what I gather, Cameron actually looks out for the employees of any company he acquires. In fact, the benefits package he brings is usually better than the one it replaces. He ends up being a blessing in disguise."

A blessing in disguise. Now that was a different way to look at him, Vanessa thought. And although he had been exactly that to her in the bedroom by literally destroying Harlan's claim that she was not worth a damn in bed, she could not imagine him being thought of that way in the boardroom.

"Well, it no longer matters what I think of Cameron," she finally said, wiping the corner of her mouth with her napkin and fighting the urge to tilt her head, ever so slightly, and look over to where he was sitting. The tension that had invaded her stomach moments earlier was now a warm, melting feeling of longing that was seeping right to her center. It was a part of her that knew Cameron by name.

"Well, I hate to be the one to tell you this, Van, but Cameron still wants you. Evidently he didn't get enough in Jamaica."

Sienna's words sent heat pouring through her. She swallowed deeply. "What makes you think that?"

"The way he was looking at you. He was talking to both of us, but he was looking at you, with that I-want-you-in-my-bed look. I recognized it since I've seen it in Dane's eyes plenty of times."

"Well, he might as well get it out of his eyes," Vanessa said with irritation in her voice. "We made an agreement and I expect him to keep it. We reached a clear understanding before he returned to the States. What we shared in Jamaica ended in Jamaica."

"And you actually believe that?"

Vanessa couldn't fight it anymore. She gave in to the urge and took a quick glance across the room to where Cameron sat. Automatically, as if he'd been expecting her to look, their gazes caught, locked, held. She felt something. A hypnotic connection that was having a strange effect on her. From across the room she could feel his gaze. It was an intimate caress, touching her everywhere, leaving no part of her body without contact. And she could smell his scent. It was as if they were still out there on the beach and his scent, all manly, robust and sexy, mingled with the salty ocean air.

"Vanessa?"

She drew in a deep breath, forcing her gaze to return to Sienna. She found her friend studying her intently. "Yes?"

"Why are you fighting it? Why are you still fighting Cameron?"

Vanessa's hand tightened on the glass of tea she picked up. She needed a sip to cool off. Instead she took a long swallow. "I don't want to be just another thing that he controls," she managed to say moments later.

"And that's all you think you would be to him?"

"Yes."

"Well, you might not want my two cents but I happen to think you're wrong. I believe, if given the chance, Cameron could be the best thing ever to happen to you, and how he conducts business has nothing to do with you."

A part of Vanessa wished that was true, but still, she couldn't separate the parts of the man. She didn't want to know there were two parts of him, one she liked and one she didn't. She wanted to like the whole man. "Can we talk about something else now?" she quietly asked.

Sienna nodded as she leaned back in her chair. "Okay, what do you want to talk about?"

"How about names for your baby? Have you come up with any more since the last time we talked?"

Vanessa needed this, a change in subjects. It would help her ignore the sensations flowing through her. As she sat and listened to Sienna, she fought the urge to look at Cameron one more time. It wasn't easy.

* * *

"Who's the woman, Cam?"

Cameron didn't have to ask what woman X was referring to. "The one in the green pantsuit is Vanessa, Morgan's cousin, and the other woman is her best friend, Sienna Bradford."

Xavier nodded. He studied his friend over the rim of his wineglass. "And what's going on with you and Ms. Steele?"

Cameron lifted a brow. "What makes you think something is going on?"

Xavier chuckled. "Mainly that you can't seem to keep your eyes off her, and I've never known you to be that attentive to any woman."

Cameron placed his fork down by his plate and leaned back in his chair to meet X's curious gaze. "Vanessa isn't just *any* woman."

"She isn't?"

"No."

"Then who is she?"

Cameron glanced back over to where Vanessa was sitting, wishing she would look over at him again, feel everything he was feeling, want everything he was wanting. When time ticked by and she didn't look his way, he finally returned his attention to X to answer his question.

"Vanessa is the woman I intend to marry."

Cameron thought that the shocked look on Xavier's face was priceless. "Marry?"

"Yes."

Xavier shook his head, chuckling. "Does she know that?"

"She doesn't have a clue. Vanessa has no idea that she will be the most important merger of my life."

Chapter 15

"Alden looks so much like you that he could be your son," Kylie Steele leaned over and whispered to Vanessa as she stood holding the newest member of the Steele family.

Vanessa grinned. "Only because people always said Chance and I favored each other. For a long time all my friends at school thought he was my big brother instead of my cousin."

She looked back down at the baby she held in her arms. "He's simply gorgeous, Kylie, and I can see him being a heartbreaker just like his uncle Donovan when he grows up."

"Gosh, I hope not." Kylie laughed. "There's the doorbell. Another guest has arrived. I'll be back in a minute."

"Wait! You want me to hold him until you get back? I know nothing about babies."

Kylie grinned. "You'll be fine, but if you start feeling an anxiety attack coming on, Chance is right across the room talking to Bas and his parents, and I'm sure Tiffany or Marcus will be coming in off the patio at any time. They enjoy taking care of their baby brother."

Before Vanessa could say anything else, Kylie was gone. She glanced down at Alden, almost tempted to cross the room and hand him over to his father, but then she couldn't help but be taken in by those dreamy dark eyes staring back at her. Yeah, this kid would grow up to be a heartbreaker. He was such an adorable baby.

She'd never given any thought to having a child of her own, at least not that she could recall. At some point she probably had, most likely during her childhood years when she'd played with dolls. After that, all she'd ever wanted to do was grow up and work alongside her father, uncle and cousins at the family corporation.

She would admit that after meeting Harlan and

assuming she had fallen head over heels in love, the idea of having a baby might have slipped into her thoughts for one fleeting moment, but that was about it.

And then there was that time, just a few weeks ago in Jamaica when Cameron had brought up the possibility of a baby after they had carelessly made love on the beach without any protection. She was certain she was fine, but he evidently didn't trust the potency of the Pill. As she gazed down into Alden's beautiful face, although she didn't want to she could imagine holding another baby, *her* baby. He would look just like his father with dark eyes, a deep cleft in his chin…

She sucked in deeply, wondering why she was even going there. Why was she imagining Cameron as her baby's daddy? He should be the last person that she would envision in that role.

Suddenly her pulse kicked up a notch and she quickly glanced around. Most of the people Chance and Kylie had invited to their dinner party were family members and close friends. She'd overheard Donovan mention to Bas earlier that Cameron had left Charlotte a few days ago to check on problems he was having at his company in Texas; he wasn't expected back for another week or so. Upon hearing that news, she had immediately let her guard down and relaxed, thinking she didn't have to worry about seeing him here tonight.

But now…

She recalled Kylie had gone to the door and she turned toward the foyer. Her breath caught. Cameron was standing there, leaning in the doorway, staring at her. Under his intense gaze she felt tense, exposed, taut, and she turned around, intending to leave the room. But before she could take a step, Cameron was there, standing behind her.

"Vanessa."

His voice, deep and husky, made goose bumps rise on her skin, and she could feel the heat of him standing so close. She knew it would be rude to walk off now, so she was forced to turn around to face him.

"Cameron."

The moment her gaze locked on his face, up close and personal, she felt her heartbeat kick up another notch. This was the face she had awakened to each morning in Jamaica. This was the man whose body had cuddled so close to hers at night. The man who could make her scream out at a mind-blowing orgasm—anytime, anyplace and in practically any position.

She felt her cheeks flush at all the memories that

flashed through her mind. She dragged in a deep breath and forced herself to speak. "I thought you were out of town."

"I flew back for a few days then I'll be leaving again."

She nodded. "Is everything all right? I understand you left town because you were having problems at one of your companies."

"Yes, there was the matter of a small explosion I had to deal with."

Vanessa gasped. "An explosion?"

"Yes."

"Was anyone hurt? Was there much damage?"

"Luckily no one was hurt and the damage was minimal. I gather whoever set it didn't intend to hurt anyone, they merely wanted to make a point."

Vanessa raised a brow. "A point?"

"Yes, to me."

Vanessa was about to ask what he meant by that when Kylie walked up. "I guess you thought I had deserted you, Vanessa, but I wanted to check on everything in the kitchen. Jocelyn's sister Leah is a sweetheart for volunteering to come to Charlotte and prepare such a feast for everyone. She's a fantastic cook." She then reached out to relieve Vanessa of Alden.

"Yes, I heard that she was," Vanessa said, gently placing the baby into his mother's arms.

"Dinner will be ready in a few minutes so the two of you can continue to enjoy yourselves until then," Kylie said, smiling at the both of them before walking off to join her husband who was talking to one of their neighbors.

Vanessa knew there was no reason she should feel nervous about being with Cameron. She certainly knew him well enough. Just thinking of all the things they had done together was downright scandalous. And she knew that although they were here together, neither one of them had actually broken their agreement. She couldn't blame him for his relationship with her family and it would be unfair to do so. Today they were victims of circumstances, and it would not be right to expect him to stay away from various functions and events just because she might be there.

"How have you been, Vanessa?"

She looked into his face but tried not to gaze directly into his eyes. "I've been fine. What about you?"

"I've been doing okay. Did your sister return to Jamaica in time to finish overseeing the construction of her pool?"

"Yes. I talked with her a few days ago and the pool's almost completed. They're putting water in it next week."

She suddenly felt tense and swallowed deeply, then she flicked her tongue out to wet her lips. When she saw Cameron's gaze latch on to the movement of her tongue, her stomach clenched and intense heat settled right smack between her thighs.

She inhaled deeply. The more they stood here talking to each other, the more they were playing a game of self-torture, wanting something neither could have again. It was time to move on. "Well, I think I'll go talk to Sienna for a while. It was good seeing you again."

And without giving him a chance to say anything, she quickly walked off.

Later that night, after her shower, Vanessa slipped between the cool, crisp sheets. She stared up at the ceiling, her mind consumed with thoughts of the time she had spent this evening at Chance and Kylie's home.

There was no way she could deny there was still a very strong attraction between her and Cameron. In fact, it was possibly even stronger than before. How else did she expect her body to react when it came within ten feet of the man who had indulged it, made love to it?

It seemed that no matter where she had gone in Chance and Kylie's home, all she had to do was turn around and Cameron was there, staring at her with those deep, dark eyes of his, though always keeping his distance. That hadn't stopped her body from desiring him, though, from wanting him and from needing to indulge in the forbidden just one more time with him.

She flipped on her stomach and buried her face in the pillow. How could she even consider such a thing? She had risked an affair with him before and she was paying dearly, mainly because he had brought her body back to life. He had made her aware of places on her body that could stir feelings within her from a mere touch.

His touch.

She shook her head, determined to get under control these hot emotions she was experiencing so that when she saw him again she could handle herself in a totally professional manner. Any other reaction toward Cameron was unacceptable.

She jumped when the phone on the nightstand rang. It was her landline. Most people called her on her cell phone; few had her home number.

Glancing at the caller ID, she smiled. It was Taylor. Neither Cheyenne nor Taylor had made it to the dinner party tonight. It was unusual for either to miss a family function of any kind. Chance indicated both had called with their regrets. Cheyenne had come down with a stomach virus and Taylor was knee-deep in trying to work out a large business deal for a very influential client.

Vanessa quickly picked up the phone. "Okay, Taylor, it's not my birthday, and there's no such thing as Sister's Day, so why do I deserve the honor of a phone call?"

She could hear Taylor laughing on the other end of the line. It wasn't that Taylor never called, she just didn't call as often as Cheyenne. But lately even Cheyenne's calls didn't come as often as they used to. And there were times she couldn't be reached at all. Donovan had once teased her about leading a double life, which was something Cheyenne hadn't thought amusing at the time. She had simply explained that as a model she would often frequent countries with poor cell service.

"Don't mess with me, girl," Taylor said. "I shouldn't be calling now. I still have tons of work to do on this deal I'm trying to close for my client."

"It's that big?"

"Bigger. With the commission alone I'll be able to buy that place I've been eyeing for a while in D.C. The one that's right on the Potomac."

Vanessa smiled. Taylor had fallen in love with the nation's capital when she'd lived there while attending Georgetown University. At the time, she'd had an apartment in Virginia, but had always had dreams of returning one day and buying a place right in the heart of D.C., preferably on the water.

"Hey, I'm not mad at you. Go for it," Vanessa said, knowing what a workaholic her sister could be at times.

"Speaking of going for it, I talked to Cheyenne earlier and she told me that you and Cameron finally hooked up."

Vanessa frowned. Cheyenne had a big mouth. And she didn't know the full details of what had transpired between her and Cameron those two weeks. Since Vanessa hadn't told her youngest sister anything, she'd evidently drawn her own conclusions. "Cameron and I have not 'hooked up.'"

"Sorry. I was just going by what Cheyenne said."

"And you of all people should know better than that. He bought the house next to Cheyenne's in Jamaica, so he was there at the same time I was. No big deal."

"Sure, if you say so," Taylor said chuckling. "You know I'm not one to get in anyone's business, Van."

"Please, don't start now."

"I won't, but I wasn't born yesterday. I know the man wants you. Now, whether or not he's finally gotten you is your business. But I think he's cool and handsome and everything you need."

"And just what is it that you think I need?"

"The same thing most women need. A good man in your life. A man to hold you close at night, keep the demons away, be there when the going gets tough."

"And you think Cameron would do all those things?"

"I don't know why he wouldn't. He seems like the type of guy who takes his obligations seriously. You could do a whole lot worse."

Vanessa fought the urge to tell her sister that at one time she had. And "worse" was a man by the name of Harlan Shaw. Before Harlan there had been Dr. Derek Peterson. She'd met Derek at a party right after returning to Charlotte from college. She had liked Derek and had quickly accepted his date, although her cousins had warned of his reputation.

Derek had come to pick her up one Saturday night and they hadn't been out of her driveway five seconds before the good doctor began growing hands. They were hands he intended to use on her at every traffic light and stop sign. The words, *No, Behave yourself,* and *Keep your hands to yourself,* had fallen on deaf ears. By the time they'd reached the restaurant she had taken as much as she intended. As soon as he came around to open the door for her, she had kneed him in the groin so mercilessly, that the restaurant manager had thought they needed to call an ambulance. An embarrassed Derek had assured everyone that he was okay before literally crawling back into his car and leaving her stranded. She had called her cousins to come get her, and to this day there was still bad blood between them and Derek.

"Vanessa?"

She remembered she still had her sister on the line. "Yes?"

"Think about what I've said about Cameron and I promise that will be the last time you hear anything from me on the subject."

"I'd appreciate that."

"Touchy, touchy."

"Only when people get into my business. I

can't wait until you get a love interest so I can get into yours."

"Is Cameron a love interest, Van?"

Before Vanessa could utter the denial on her lips, Taylor giggled and said, "That's okay. You don't have to tell me anything. It's your business. So tell me, how is Sienna doing?"

Vanessa was glad for the change in subjects. The mere mention of Cameron had ignited a throbbing between her thighs and that wasn't good, especially since she would be sleeping in her bed alone tonight. But later, she would have her dreams.

"Yes, X, I'm flying back to Texas tomorrow. I returned to Charlotte because there was a function I couldn't miss attending." *And a person I couldn't miss seeing.* "Arrange a private meeting between me and McMurray. What he's paying his thugs to do has to stop," Cameron said angrily, rubbing a hand down his face. "It's time for him to know who I am, why I took his company away and why I intend to keep it, no matter what he does."

Hours later, a tense Cameron couldn't sleep. His restlessness had nothing to do with his ongoing problems with McMurray, but with a certain young woman by the name of Vanessa Steele.

He had needed to see her again. He had needed to know that that same potent chemistry he'd felt all during their time together in Jamaica was stronger than ever.

She was fighting him. He could feel it every time their eyes met. He knew he was gambling, but he had to believe their island affair meant more than just sex to her, just as it meant more to him. She might not be able to put it all together now, but eventually she would. Although he would keep their agreement, he intended to be at every function that she attended if he could. His flights back and forth to Texas were becoming a nuisance, costing him valuable time; time he should be using to get on the good side of a certain woman.

That was why his ongoing problems with McMurray were unacceptable and had tried his patience for the last time. For some reason the man believed that if he kept up his dirty work Cameron would eventually throw in the towel and sell the company back to him.

McMurray couldn't be more wrong.

John McMurray sat at the conference table beside his attorney with his arms crossed over his chest and fixed Cameron with a mean, level stare.

"I have no idea what you're talking about, Cody, and you don't have any proof, so don't waste your time accusing me of anything."

Cameron sat at the head of the table, with Xavier Kane on one side and Kurt Grainger on the other. "But we do have proof, McMurray, which is why one of your men is behind bars now."

McMurray's attorney touched his client's elbow, cautioning him from saying anything more. He then spoke on his client's behalf. "Again, Mr. Cody, contrary to whatever proof you think you might have, my client is innocent, which means you are mistaken."

A smile split Cameron's face. "Then ask your client if the name Samuel Myers means anything to him?"

The attorney didn't have to ask McMurray anything. The nervousness that darted into McMurray's eyes was a dead giveaway. However, the attorney said, "My client doesn't know a Samuel Myers."

Cameron leaned forward. "Myers says differently. Let's cut the bullshit. Frankly, I'm getting fed up with this entire ordeal. Your client lost his company."

"You took it from me!" McMurray yelled out in anger.

Cameron nodded. "Yes, I took it from you and do you know why?"

When neither McMurray nor his attorney responded, Cameron said, "Because you don't deserve to have a company, McMurray, and how you solicit loyalty in a few of your employees is beyond me. But then, for the right price, anyone can be bought."

"Are you accusing my client of bribery?"

"Yes, for starters. Does the name Fred Cody ring a bell?"

John McMurray's face twisted with more anger. "I wish you would stop throwing out the names of people I don't know. Judging by the surname I can only assume he's some relative of yours."

Cameron shot the man another forced smile. "Yes, he was my grandfather. He had worked for your company for over forty years, and right before he was to retire—less than a year before, in fact—you had him fired. That was almost twenty years ago."

"Twenty years ago! You're getting back at me for something I did twenty years ago? Hell, I was in my late thirties. Whatever I did then was because I was following my father's orders. What else was I to do?"

"Have a conscience. That year you released six men from your employment, men who had given Global Petroleum their blood, sweat and tears, yet you fired them without any compensation or benefits. And when they tried banding together to take your company to court, you and your father paid people to harass them and their families, scaring them to the point where they wouldn't fight the big corporation that had done them wrong. They barely had money to eat and live on, and you and your father made it impossible for them to afford to fight you any longer by deliberately dragging things out in court."

"If we fired them, then there had to be a reason for it," McMurray snapped.

"Oh, you had a reason all right. You and your old man didn't want to give them what they deserved after working for you all those years. But now I will. For the first five years, any profit I make from Global Petroleum will go to those men and their families. Of the six, four are still living, almost impoverished. So as you can see, McMurray, I'm trying to right a wrong that you and your family did."

Cameron nodded to Xavier who slid a manila envelope over to McMurray and his attorney. "I suggest the two of you read those documents, ponder them," Cameron said. "If I'm forced to expose them, I will. I have sworn affidavits from Samuel Myers, as well as from the woman who was your father's secretary, Hannah Crosby. Ms. Crosby claims she was paid to falsify documents, and Samuel Myers has confessed to being one of your father's henchmen. He's provided us a list of all the bad deeds that your father paid him to do. If you're willing to have the press dig into history and dishonor your family's name, then go ahead, keep doing what you're doing, in other words, basically the same tricks your father pulled years ago."

Cameron leaned over the table and his smile was gone. Instead his face was a mask of pure anger. "The only difference is, your henchmen don't bother me, McMurray, and I'm not going anywhere. Do you and your family a favor, accept your loss and take an early retirement. Otherwise, you leave me no choice but to send a copy of what's in that envelope to every newspaper in Texas."

McMurray jumped out of his chair, almost knocking it over. "You won't get away with this, Cody."

"I already have. You don't own Global Petroleum anymore. I do. Accept it. And let me give you a friendly word of warning. If there are any more mishaps to *my* company that I trace back to you, instead of spending your remaining days in retirement, I'll going to see to it that you rot in jail. Count on it."

An angry John McMurray stalked out of the conference room with his attorney—who'd taken the time to grab the envelope off the table—following right on his heels.

Xavier shook his head and glanced over at Cameron. "That man is bad news."

Kurt nodded in agreement.

Cameron released a deep breath as he leaned back in his chair. He had a feeling they hadn't seen or heard the last of John McMurray.

Chapter 16

Cameron walked into the kick-off party for Morgan's campaign with two purposes in mind. He wanted to show his support for his friend and he needed to see a certain woman again.

It had been two weeks since he'd last seen Vanessa at the small gathering in Chance's home and now he was in a bad way. And no matter what it took, he was going to make sure she was in a bad way, too, by the time the night was over.

"Cameron, it's good to see you."

He smiled when he was approached by Jocelyn

Mason Steele. She was the woman he had chosen to run his construction company based in Charlotte. Already nearly one hundred people were on payroll, with several lucrative projects lined up to keep them busy.

He leaned over and gave her a peck on the cheek. "You look beautiful as usual. Where's that husband of yours?"

She grinned. "Bas is around here somewhere. I think he's trying to dodge his old girlfriend," she said teasingly.

Cameron glanced around. The party was being held on the main floor of the Steele Building and decorative streamers and red, white and blue balloons were everywhere. "Cassandra Tisdale is here?" he asked.

"Yes, Cassandra and the entire Tisdale family. Time will tell if she's here to throw her support to Morgan or to be nosey. But then, we really don't care. Since throwing his hat into the ring, Morgan has received numerous financial backers even if the Tisdales decide to support Roger Chadwick."

Cameron nodded. He knew the story. The Tisdales had wanted Morgan to marry a member of their family by the name of Jamie Hollis, a senator's daughter. When Morgan had refused and told them in no uncertain terms that he would be marrying the woman he loved, namely Lena Spears, that hadn't sat too well with them…until Morgan had taken matters into his own hands and made sure Cassandra and her cousin Jamie knew that he meant business. He'd warned if they continued spreading gossip about him and Lena, he would start spreading some of his own about them.

"The buffet table is set up on the other side of the room and there's plenty to eat," Jocelyn told him.

"Thanks, but I'm going to let Morgan and Lena know I'm here before I start mingling."

A few minutes later he found them, talking to Vanessa and another man. He frowned. Was the man her date? His stomach clenched at the possibility. There was only one way to find out. Without wasting any time he approached the two couples.

Lena was the first to see him and turned and smiled radiantly. Not for the first time he thought Morgan had struck a gold mine with this woman. A Queen Latifah look-alike, she looked gorgeous in her mint-green pantsuit. Whoever thought Lena Spears would not complement Morgan was sadly mistaken.

"Cameron, I'm glad you could make it," Lena said, reaching out and giving him a hug. "I understand you've been out of town a lot."

"Yes, I have." He then shook hands with Morgan. "Seems like a nice turnout."

"It is," Morgan said. He turned to Vanessa. "Cam, you already know Vanessa."

"Yes. How are you tonight, Vanessa?"

He picked up on the unevenness of her breathing when she responded in a soft voice, "I'm fine, Cameron. And you?"

"I'm fine, as well." He glanced over at the man standing by her side. Too close, as far as he was concerned.

"And this," Morgan was saying, "is Reverend David Carrington. He recently moved to town to become the new pastor of the Redeem Baptist Church."

The man might be a minister, but there was no wedding band on his finger, Cameron noted, so anything was possible. But not with *his* woman. "Nice meeting you, Reverend. I'm going to have to visit your church one of these Sundays."

Reverend Carrington smiled. "Please do. In fact, I plan on having a blazing sermon this coming Sunday."

Cameron nodded. His mind was not on the good man's Sunday sermon. Instead he was trying to come up with a way to get Vanessa alone without breaking their agreement, even if only for a few minutes.

"Oops, I left my speech upstairs on my desk," Morgan said, looking apologetic.

"I can go get it for you," Lena quickly volunteered.

"No," Morgan said just as quickly while settling his arms around her waist. "I need you to stay down here with me and greet our guests. Vanessa can catch the elevator and get it for me."

Vanessa looked surprised. "I can?"

"Yes, you don't mind, do you?"

Vanessa sighed. What could she say? Of course she didn't mind. Besides, it would give her a chance to escape Cameron's presence. She had seen him the moment he had walked into the room. It was as if she had radar and it had homed right in on him. He was impeccably dressed in a dark suit and looked as though he had just stepped off the cover of *GQ*. Her equilibrium hadn't been the same since he'd arrived. Weeks of nonstop dreaming about the man was taking its toll. Standing so close to him, breathing in his manly scent, was definitely too much.

"Of course I don't mind. I'll be back in a second," she said, turning to walk off.

"Thanks. And take Cameron with you."

She swirled back around. "What? Why do I need to take Cameron with me?"

"Because Derek Peterson is here. Surprised the hell out of us."

At the swift elbow he received in his side from Lena, Morgan glanced over at the Reverend and said apologetically, "Sorry about that. What I meant to say is that he surprised the *heck* out of us, since he dislikes the Steeles so much."

"Who's Derek Peterson?" Cameron asked curiously.

Morgan wanted to paint the true picture of the man, but out of respect for Reverend Carrington again, he merely said, "Let's just say he's a not-so-nice person who has it in for Vanessa."

She frowned. "He doesn't have it in for me, Morgan."

Morgan chuckled. "Yes, he does. You almost crippled the man."

Vanessa rolled her eyes. "That was almost six years ago."

Morgan smiled. "Doesn't matter. There are some things a man doesn't forget and almost losing his balls—"

He cleared his throat and glanced over at the

Reverend again. "I mean, almost losing his *jewels* is one of them."

Reverend Carrington tried to hide his grin. "Please point this gentleman out to me. I definitely need to invite him to church on Sunday."

"If you think it will help," Morgan said, more than happy to oblige.

"The Word always helps," was the minister's response.

"Then I say go for it," Morgan replied. "And you can kill—or save—two birds with one stone since he's standing over there by the punch bowl talking to Cassandra Tisdale. I think she's a person who will need to hear your sermon on Sunday, as well."

Reverend Carrington nodded. "My sermon will be for everyone, so I'm looking forward to seeing your face in the congregation on Sunday, too, Mr. Steele." He then walked off to where Derek and Cassandra were standing with their heads together.

"I'm going upstairs now," Vanessa said, turning to walk off.

"Now that I've heard about this Derek guy, I think I'll go with you after all." Cameron followed in step beside her. He owed Morgan for this. Chances were Morgan hadn't left his speech on his desk upstairs. Cameron had a feeling it was right in his friend's pocket.

He and Vanessa didn't say anything as they walked toward the bank of elevators. They slowed their steps when they heard loud, angry voices coming from behind a closed door, Vanessa chuckled.

Cameron glanced over at her. "What's so funny?"

"From the sound of things, Sienna has finally gotten fed up and is giving her mother-in-law hell. It's about time."

They rounded a corner to the elevators. Luckily, one opened right away. The moment they stepped in and it closed behind them, Cameron could feel the heat. He moved to the far side of one wall and she moved to the other.

"I'm sorry that Morgan put you on the spot like that, Cameron. I really didn't need an escort."

He glanced over at her. "I don't mind."

He averted his eyes from her so he wouldn't be tempted to close the distance between them, take her into his arms and kiss her. She looked so good in her red dress that showed just what a gorgeous pair of legs she had. And it didn't take much to remember how those legs could wrap around him, holding him tight inside her and—

"How's that problem going with your business in Texas?" she asked, looking everywhere but at him.

He released a deep sigh, glad for her interruption into his thoughts. "I'm hoping it's been resolved. Time will tell."

She nodded and turned to stare at the wall again. Moments later he couldn't fight it any longer and looked at her. Gosh, he loved her. And he wanted her. Here. Now. Right this second. As if she read his thoughts, she slowly turned toward him.

The moment their gazes connected, sexual tension seemed to crackle in the air between them. He saw the deep look of desire in her eyes and took a step toward her at the exact moment the elevator came to a jolting stop.

That seemed to snap her to her senses and she took a step back. "We need to get off now."

He'd had enough. He refused to torture himself any longer. "I personally think what we need to do is go somewhere and make love."

He watched her eyes darken even more, confirming she was thinking the same thing but was still fighting it.

"What about our agreement?" she asked softly when the elevator door opened and she backed up slowly, stepping off.

A smile touched his lips as he followed her. "I won't tell anyone that we broke it if you don't."

She stopped walking. He waited for her to say something, to respond. It seemed like forever before she asked quietly, "You promise?"

His mind was muddled and at the moment he didn't understand the question. "I promise what?"

"Not to tell anyone that we broke our agreement?" she whispered.

His smile deepened and took a step toward her. "I'll promise you anything."

She inhaled deeply and glanced down at her watch. "Morgan is expecting us to return with his speech."

At that moment, Cameron's cell phone rang. He pulled it out of his pocket and answered. "Yes?"

After a brief pause, he said, "No, we hadn't made it to your office yet. No problem, I'll tell her."

He clicked off the line and put the phone back in his jacket pocket. "That was Morgan. He didn't leave the speech on his desk after all. It was in his pocket."

Vanessa frowned. "Umm, now, isn't that amazing. Seems like perfect timing."

Cameron nodded. "Yes, it does, doesn't it?"

"We were set up," she said.

"Looks that way."

"And you're not upset about it?"

His low chuckle sent soft shivers all through her body. "Not in the least. Are you?"

"I should be."

He nodded. "But *are* you?"

"No." She glanced around. "While we're up here I might as well show you my office. You've never seen it before."

"No, I haven't."

"All right, it's this way, right down the hall from Morgan's."

They walked side by side and all Vanessa could think about was that he was here, and they were alone, hot and horny. Thanks to him she knew what horniness felt like; she'd been suffering from it for weeks.

When they got to her office door she pulled a key out of her small purse, but her hands were shaking so hard she couldn't fit the key in the lock.

"Let me help," he said, sliding a hand around her to the door. When he opened it, she quickly stepped inside and he followed, closing the door behind them. And relocking it.

He didn't even glance around. Instead he snaked out his hand and captured her wrist and pulled her to him. The moment he did so, it seemed something between them broke loose, and he went for her mouth at the same moment she went for his.

Spontaneity.

He'd missed it. He wanted it. Now.

He picked her up and swirled around, placing her back against the closed door while their mouths were still locked. Hungry, they devoured each other like starved, crazed addicts. He broke the connection just long enough to flip her dress up and push her silk panties down. With one hand he unzipped his pants, pulled out his shaft, and before either could take another breath, he thrust into her.

"Cameron!"

She screamed his name and just that quickly, an explosion went off inside her, sending shivers of pleasure all through her body. But he kept going, demanding that she come again. She did and with her legs wrapped tightly around him, and the way her fingers were digging into his shoulders, he could tell that this orgasm was just as powerful as the first.

"Don't stop, Cameron. Please, don't stop," she whispered frantically, kissing his face all over.

Little did she know he couldn't stop now even if he wanted to. Not even if the building were to catch on fire. They were burning to a crisp right now anyway. He kept thrusting into her, nonstop, fast, hard, needing her, needing the connection with the woman he loved.

When he felt it, the sensation started in his toes and slowly worked its way up to his shaft. Vibrations, shock waves. It was an orgasm so powerful, it tore into him. He threw his head back to the point that his veins nearly burst in his neck. But he didn't feel any pain. He felt only ecstasy. Pleasure. Vanessa.

Breathing once again, he buried his head on her chest, between her breasts. He could die at this moment and he'd go happy, satisfied, feeling total completeness.

When the shivers stopped, he pulled back, but he did not pull out of her. He kept her pinned against the door while he was still inside her. He met her gaze and said softly, "Please don't say this shouldn't have happened."

She licked her lips before asking, barely with enough breath to speak, "Can I think it?"

He shook his head. "No."

She nodded. "You did say, anytime, anyplace and…any position."

A smile touched his lips. "Yes, I did."

"And I see that you meant it."

"Every word."

Vanessa felt him growing hard inside her again

and tightened her legs around his waist to keep him locked to her. "Some people might be wondering where we've disappeared to."

"Let them wonder. I'm sure Morgan will tell them something believable."

She nodded again. "I hope so because I haven't gotten enough of you yet."

"And I haven't gotten enough of you, either."

And then he leaned forward and captured her lips at the exact moment he thrust deeper inside her. Once, twice. Again and again.

The heat was on again and he planned to take it to the limit.

Chapter 17

"Woman, you're killing me," Cameron said through clenched teeth. They were at his house, in his bedroom, and Vanessa was on top of him, riding him like crazy. He clutched the bedspread and balled it in his fist. The woman was amazing, simply amazing. He had thought that same thing in Jamaica but now, on American soil, he was doubly sure of it.

After leaving her office they had finally gone back downstairs to join the party, barely hearing the last of Morgan's speech. Then they had quickly said their goodbyes, not caring that after having been missing from the party for over an hour, they were making a grand escape.

She had followed him home and they had barely made it inside the door before they were at it again. This time she was in control. First they had made love on the floor in his living room until their strength was depleted. And then he had carried her upstairs to his bedroom, where he had undressed her properly before making love to her again.

They had fallen asleep, but she had awakened him—less than ten minutes ago—saying she needed to ride him, and he had flipped on his back, happy to oblige. Now he was looking death in the face. The woman was going to kill him.

"I won't kill you if you stop holding back. I made it clear what I want."

Yes, she had. For some reason she enjoyed the feel of him exploding inside her, shooting his semen all the way to her womb. The moment he did so, she would clench her inner muscles and pull everything out of him, as if his release was something she had to have.

"Damn, you're really asking for it this time," he warned, barely able to get the words out.

"Good, now let go and give me what I want, Cameron. Now!"

"You better hope those pills you're on do their job tonight. If not, this is a baby in the making," he muttered just seconds before his body bucked and he exploded, giving her just what she wanted.

As if his orgasm had lit her sensuous torch, she climaxed, as well, clenching him more deeply while calling out his name. Knowing she needed this from him, he gently flipped her on her back without breaking contact, taking control and riding her. This was crazy. This was madness. This was making up for weeks of going without her in his bed—something he never wanted to do again.

After they came again, simultaneously, he lay against her, breathing hard but thinking how great life was. He was a man in love and he had the woman he wanted in his bed. Now if he could only convince her to become a forever part of his life, as well.

"Sneaking out on me, Vanessa?"

Vanessa swirled around, holding her shoes to her chest. "I thought you were asleep, Cameron. It's time for me to leave."

He glanced to the window. It was daybreak. In essence she had spent the night. He moved to get out of bed. "Let me slip on something and walk you to your car."

"No. Please don't. I'm fine."

He stayed put, seeing the look of uncertainty in her eyes. Did she regret what had happened last night? There was only one way to find out. "When will I see you again?"

He watched her nervously lick her lips, and his stomach clenched when he recalled just what she had done to him with those same lips and tongue last night. He also noticed she was backing up slowly toward the door. "I'll call you."

"When?"

She shrugged. "I don't know. I hadn't counted on this."

He figured now was not a good time to tell her that he had. A part of him had wanted to believe she still desired him and the attraction between them was just as strong and hot as it had been in Jamaica. What had happened last night had proven him right.

He knew he couldn't be completely honest with her anymore. He stood. "Can I give you something to think about?"

"Yes, what?"

"I love you."

She closed her eyes and her shoes dropped to the floor. The sound made her snatch her eyes open and she dropped to her knees to pick her shoes up. Without looking at him she gathered them in her arms and said, "This is getting complicated. I have to go."

He took a few steps toward her. "What's so complicated about me loving you?"

She looked at him as she stood up. "Because I'm not sure how I feel about you."

He reached out and pulled her to him again, making her drop her shoes for a second time. He picked her up in his arms and moved to sit on the bed with her cradled in his lap. His teeth caught her earlobe before he whispered huskily, "Don't you? I'm betting my money that you love me, too."

She pulled back and stared down at him. "Why do you think that? Because we enjoy great sex together? A lot of people enjoy great sex, Cameron."

He shook his head. "We're not talking about a lot of people. We're talking about *us*. And we share more than great sex. You're everything I want in a woman, Vanessa. You're compassionate, honest, trustworthy and—"

"But I'm having doubts about you, Cameron. You take people's companies away. What you do affects their lives. I read an article on the Internet a few weeks ago about what you did to that company in Texas, Global Petroleum, and how the people resent you for taking it over and that's why you're having problems there."

Cameron moved her off his lap and stood, somewhat irritated and trying like hell to hold on to his temper. "You can't believe everything you read, especially not off the Internet, Vanessa, and particularly not off that particular site. John McMurray had that site up and running for a while mainly to discredit me."

"But—"

"But you have to trust me. I know what I'm doing."

"But I don't. My family could have been in the same boat that Global is in now had you succeeded in taking over the Steele Corporation."

"No, the circumstances are different, Vanessa."

"I don't think that they are."

Cameron inhaled deeply. He loved this woman with all his heart and soul but more than anything, he wanted her to believe in him and trust him completely. "I'm leaving for Texas tomorrow and will probably be gone for a week or two. When I get back, let's have dinner and talk.

There are a few things I think we need to clear up, okay?"

She slowly nodded and then stood and slipped into her shoes. "I have to go. If I don't see you or talk to you before you leave, I hope you have a safe trip."

And then she was gone, hurrying out of the bedroom and down the stairs to leave his home.

"So, Vanessa, how do you think things went at the party the other night?"

She glanced up from the document she was reading to see Morgan in the doorway of her office, a silly grin on his face. He knew better than anyone that she had missed most of the party while she was in this very office playing hanky-panky with Cameron.

Even now the memories were still vivid. She wished she had gone to church on Sunday to hear Reverend Carrington's sermon. She glared over at her cousin. "I have a bone to pick with you, Morgan."

He smiled. "What kind of bone?"

"Not a juicy rib-eye, that's for sure. I don't like being set up."

"And you think you were set up?"

"Yes."

"Umm, I don't recall you complaining about it

that night when you came back downstairs. In fact, you looked rather giddy. Like the cat who'd gotten the canary."

"That's not the point."

"Then what is the point?"

She inhaled deeply and decided to use another approach. "What is it with Cameron? Other guys have tried dating me, and you, Bas, Donovan and Chance have always been overly cautious, checking them out to make sure they don't intend to run off with the family china. Yet, Cameron is a man known to take over companies and it seems like the four of you, especially you, Morgan, are all but handing me to him on a silver platter. Hell, let's forget about silver, let's even try a gold platter."

"We like Cameron. He had a rough life with the way he lost his parents, yet he made it. He's a survivor."

"But look at what he's doing to those companies," she implored.

Morgan rolled his eyes. "Name one company where the employees haven't benefited from Cameron's takeover."

"What about that one in Texas? Global Petroleum."

"That's personal for Cameron."

Vanessa arched a brow. "And how is it personal?"

"He had a score to settle with the owner."

"And for that reason he took over an entire company? What about the employees?"

"Like I said, they will end up in better shape. A lot better than Cam's grandfather did over twenty years ago."

Vanessa frowned. "What about Cam's grandfather?"

Morgan came into her office and closed the door behind him. "You know about him?"

She shrugged. "Only what Cameron shared with me. I know he was fired from his job of forty years less than a year from retirement, and he lost all his benefits."

"And did Cam tell you the name of the company responsible?"

"If he did, I don't remember. Why?"

"Because Global Petroleum is the same company that fired not only Cam's grandfather but five other men who were about to retire. None of them had a grandson like Cam who was willing to drop out of school to help make ends meet. Two of the men died within the first five years, the others still living are destitute. They're old men, in their late eighties. One is in his nineties. Cam took over Global Petroleum not only for revenge, but he's taking the company's first five years of profits to give to those remaining four men so that they can live out the rest of their lives without wanting for anything. All the profits will be split among the survivors and their families."

Vanessa leaned back in her chair, amazed. "He's actually doing that?"

"Yes. And in my book that's a pretty nice gesture for a guy you think is nothing more than a jerk."

"I never said he was a jerk. I just never understood him, until now."

Morgan shook his head. "And you still don't understand him, Vanessa. The man loves you. That's why I don't worry about what may or may not be happening between the two of you. One thing I've discovered since becoming Cam's friend is that true friendships are important to him, and because of it, he picks his friends carefully. And the reason he loves you is that he truly believes you're more than worthy of his love."

Morgan crossed his arms over his chest and met her gaze. "The big question of the hour is whether you're going to prove him right or wrong."

* * *

That night, after taking her shower, Vanessa slipped into bed with Morgan's words from earlier that day on her mind.

"...*And the reason he loves you is that he truly believes you're more than worthy of his love.*"

She shook her head. If Cameron did think at one time that she was worthy of his love, chances were that after what she'd said to him their last morning together he didn't feel that way now. She had told him that she doubted him, and now he probably wouldn't want to see her.

She sighed deeply, knowing she would go stark raving crazy if she had to wait another week before he returned to Charlotte to find out. She quickly reached across the bed for the phone.

A sleepy feminine voice answered after three rings. "Hello, Lena, how are you? May I speak with Morgan for a minute?"

It took another minute for him to get on the phone. "Vanessa, it's almost midnight. What is it that can't wait until you see me at the office in the morning?"

"I hope to be on my way to Texas by then."

"What are you talking about?"

"I'm going to Austin and I need Cameron's address. Hold on, let me grab a pen."

A few minutes later, she ended her call with Morgan. She believed she was worthy of Cameron's love. Now she had to make sure he still believed it, as well.

Chapter 18

"Cam?"

Cameron glanced up from the papers he'd been reading and saw both Xavier and Kurt standing in the doorway to his office. It was late afternoon and the three of them were working at his Austin home. So far, since his meeting with McMurray a few weeks ago, things had been running smoothly at Global Petroleum and he hoped they continued to do so.

"I thought the two of you were leaving to pick up dinner."

Kurt cleared his throat. "We were, but you got a visitor."

Cameron frowned, wondering who it could be. Very few people knew about the small ranch-style home he had inherited from his grandfather. He had to assume his visitor was one of the neighbors. Lately, more than one had come forth offering to buy his house mainly to get the land, which consisted of over ten acres. "Tell whoever it is that I'm busy."

"I don't think you want us to do that," Xavier said with a smirk on his face.

"Why not?" Cameron asked, not understanding just what was wrong with his two friends.

Kurt grinned. "Maybe you ought to see for yourself and then I think you'll understand."

"Fine," Cameron said angrily, tossing the report on his desk. He stood. "Where's this person?"

"In your living room."

Cameron left the office with Xavier and Kurt right on his heels. He'd taken a few steps and then turned around with an arched brow. "Just what the hell has gotten into you two?"

Kurt gave a sly chuckle. "Ask us that after seeing your visitor."

Cameron frowned, thinking he really didn't have time for this.

He walked into the living room and stopped dead in his tracks. The first thought that came into his mind was that he *did* have time for this. Vanessa was standing in the middle of his living room wearing that black skirt he didn't like, the one she had purchased in Jamaica. His throat went dry and his gaze traveled the full length of her, up and down her legs, her thighs… Speaking of her thighs, the skirt barely covered them.

Their gazes connected. He felt the heat. It didn't matter why she had come, all he cared about was that the woman he loved was here in his place, invading his space, affecting the very air he was breathing.

"Now you understand what we meant, Cam?"

He blinked, suddenly remembering Xavier and Kurt. He quickly turned to them. "Leave!"

Kurt, being the smart-ass, said, "Are you sure? She could be an enemy. Maybe we ought to search her first."

"Touch her and I'll have to kill you," he said through clenched teeth. "Leave and don't come back."

Xavier raised a curious brow. "I thought we had a lot of work to do. You said we'd be working well into the night."

"Out!"

He watched the two men make a beeline for the door, and, as soon as the door shut behind them, Cameron turned his attention back to his visitor.

He took a couple of steps forward. "I never liked that skirt on you."

Vanessa met his heated gaze and said, "Then take it off me. But I need to warn you it's the only thing I have to wear."

He frowned. "You wore that all the way from Charlotte?"

She shook her head. "No, but I did wear it from the hotel in downtown Austin. I had that full-length raincoat over it," she said, indicating the yellow slicker tossed across a chair. "A lot of people stared since the sun was shining outside."

He released a deep sigh. "Thank God for that."

"For what? That the sun was shining outside?"

"No, for that full-length raincoat."

She nodded. "Aren't you going to ask why I'm here?"

He shook his head as he crossed the distance of the room to stand in front of her. "You can tell me later. Right now I can only concentrate on one thing."

"And what are you concentrating on?"

"Taking that damn skirt off of you."

Vanessa's body reacted instantly to Cameron's

words. Blood rushed through her veins, every cell seemed sensitive. The tips of her nipples beneath her top tightened and a warm pool settled between her thighs. He was the only man who had the ability to do this to her. With just words and an intense look, he could put an achy need within her so compelling and deep that she knew of only one way to soothe it.

"Don't concentrate too hard," she heard herself saying.

He didn't.

The next instant Cameron reached out and with a flick of his wrist he undid the fastener at her waist and the skirt dropped to her feet. Just that easy. Just that quick. She was left wearing her top and a silky strap of barely nothing that was meant to cover her feminine mound. He thought it wasn't doing a very good job and he licked his lips in anticipation of tasting her. Without wasting any time, he removed her top and then got down on his knees and eased her thong down her legs.

He inhaled deeply, taking in her scent, and then he dipped his head and tasted her, right in the juncture of her thighs.

"Cameron."

He sucked in a deep breath when he rose to his

feet. Every muscle in his body ached for her. God, he wanted her. He wanted to make love to her all day and all night. And he didn't intend to waste any time.

He swept her into his arms and strode quickly to the bedroom where he placed her on his bed. He drew back to remove his own clothes but she caught hold of his collar and pulled him back to her and began nipping at his bottom lip, licking it from corner to corner with the tip of her tongue.

Sensations within him intensified, making his need for her monumental, nearly insane. He was so fully aware of this woman—his woman—and he intended to leave his imprint all over her. He pulled back again and this time he swiftly removed his clothes, then rejoined her on the bed. He wanted to erase whatever doubts she had about him. He wanted to fill her with his love, so much that it would spread to her own heart. He had enough for both of them.

"Cameron."

When she opened her arms, he went into them, and when she captured his mouth, he surrendered all. Something akin to desperation swept through him, and he ran his hands everywhere on her body, needing the feel of her beneath his palms and fingers.

A distant part of his brain told him to take things

slowly, but he couldn't. He needed this session to be fast and quick, deep and hard, and he needed it now. He eased his body into place over hers and entered her, and the moment she arched against him, he felt a climax coming on. But he held it back, needing the connection a little while longer.

It was a challenge when every cell in his body was electrified, every pore open to sensations he felt only when he was inside her. And when he felt her own orgasm rip through her, his heartbeat accelerated and his pulse kicked up another notch. He was too far gone to hold on any longer and when the world seemed to explode all around them, he felt it. It seemed the bed rocked, the ground shook, the lights in the ceiling began falling....

"What the hell!"

He jerked up. He was not imagining things. He pushed Vanessa out of the way before a layer of plaster fell down on her.

"Cameron, what's going on?"

Instead of answering her, he snatched her wrist and handed her his shirt as he quickly slipped into his pants. "Hurry up and put it on so we can get the hell out of here."

It didn't take long for him to figure out that someone was outside firing explosives into his home with the use of a handheld missile launcher. He dropped to the floor and pulled Vanessa down with him when all the walls seemed to start tumbling down.

When they crawled to the living room the place was in shambles, and he jerked her head down as a missile flew past her head. He cursed. The damn thing had barely missed her. He knew whoever was on the outside expected him run out through either the front or the back entrance, thinking that they had him cornered.

"Cameron, what's going on? What are we going to do?" Vanessa whispered.

He glanced down at her. She didn't deserve to be involved in this. The person on the other side of that door had a beef with him and not her. He needed to get them to the part of the house that he knew was safe. The storm cellar his grandfather had built right after Hurricane Gilbert.

He glanced down at her. "I need you to trust me, Vanessa," he said meeting her gaze and gently rubbing her cheek. "I'm going to get us out of here."

She nodded. "I do trust you, Cameron, and I love you. That's why I came all the way to Texas. I couldn't wait to tell you."

Her words touched him and he wanted to kiss

her, but time was not on their side. He needed to get them out of there. They made it to the kitchen and he pushed open the cellar door. It had been years since he'd been down there but this would be their refuge until help arrived. Someone had to have alerted the authorities by now that his ranch had become a war zone.

He led Vanessa down the stairs and except for a little dust and a few spiderwebs here and there, the place was okay. He took them as far back into the cellar as he could and then pulled her into his arms. This was a waiting game and he only hoped whoever was out there would eventually assume he had succeeded in what he came to do and haul ass.

In the meantime…

He turned Vanessa to him and leaned down and kissed her, needing the taste of her, the assurance she was all right and they were together. She wrapped her arms around him and held him tight.

Cameron wasn't sure how long they huddled down there before he heard someone call his name. He placed his fingers to Vanessa's lips, not yet certain whether the person beyond the cellar door was friend or foe.

A smile touched his lips when his name was called

out again and he recognized Xavier's voice. "Stay put for a second while I let him know we're down here."

Vanessa watched as Cameron raced up the wooden stairs and responded to his friend's call through the door.

"Stand back, Cam!"

He did and then she saw the head of a huge ax slice through the door frame before it was kicked in. And then those two men stood there, the ones who had let her into Cameron's house earlier. The expressions on their faces showed they were relieved to see he was okay, but they were mad as hell.

Cameron turned, opened his arms to her and she raced across the cement floor and up the stairs to him. And when he gathered her into his arms, she knew that everything would be all right.

Later that night, back in her hotel room, Vanessa cuddled close to Cameron in bed. "I'm sorry about your home, Cameron."

When Xavier and Kurt had pulled them out of the cellar and they'd had a chance to see the damage, her heart had ached for him. But then that same heart had filled with anger that someone had wanted to do that much harm to the man she loved. He was not intended to survive the attack.

"I was thinking of rebuilding anyway. I've received a number of offers to sell but couldn't bring myself to part with it. That land is where I spent some of the happiest days with my grandfather and I needed that link."

Vanessa nodded, then frowned. "Well, at least they caught those guys."

"Yes, and they're spilling their guts. I can't believe John McMurray would go that far. The man is truly demented." McMurray's arrest had made national news. The shame that had been brought on his family had come from his hands and not Cameron's.

"And how on earth were they able to get those types of weapons? Something like that could probably shoot a plane out the sky."

"It can, which is why in most states they're outlawed. I'm just glad that Kurt brought Xavier back here to get his car and saw what was happening."

Vanessa nodded. She was, too.

Cameron glanced down at her. "Did you mean what you said earlier, just before we made it to the cellar? That part about loving me?"

She smiled. "Yes, I meant every word. You're not only my sex mate, you're my soul mate, as well. I do love you, Cameron."

"And I love you. Does this mean you'd consider marrying me?"

She grinned. "Yes, if you ask."

He turned toward her in bed, took her hand in his and gazed deep into her eyes. "Vanessa Steele, will you marry me? For better or for worse? Will you be my soul mate and my sex mate? The mother of my children? My best friend? My—"

She placed her finger to his lips. "Cameron Cody, I will be your everything."

He leaned closer, and, right before he captured her lips with his, he whispered huskily, "You already are. You were definitely one risky pleasure worth taking."

* * * * *

Sexual Healing

"Are you okay?"

Leah Mason glanced up at the man walking beside her and a faint smile touched her lips. "Yes, Reese, I'm okay."

She sighed inwardly. No matter how many times he asked her that, her answer would always be the same. But deep down she knew it was a lie. What could be okay about a twenty-three-year-old woman who couldn't let the man she loved touch her—at least anything beyond a kiss?

"Did you enjoy yourself?"

They had reached the front door to his home, and she stopped and turned to him. "Yes, I did."

That was not entirely true, either. They had been visiting his family and because no one knew the full story of why she had mysteriously left Newton Grove five years before, breaking Reese's heart, his family resented the fact he had started seeing her again. She knew they were worried that she would up and leave and break his heart a second time.

"When we get inside I want you to talk to me, baby."

He opened the door, and when they walked into the foyer, he reached out and took hold of her hand and led her to the living room. When they sat down on the sofa he turned to her, tightened his hold on her hand and said in a low tone, "Now tell me what's up, Leah. And don't deny something is bothering you because I can feel it."

Leah sighed deeply. Not for the first time she wondered why she was blessed with having such a wonderful man in her life. He had always been so attuned to her every thought, want and hurt. And he had tried so hard to take the hurt away.

It had been six months since he had learned the truth of what had happened to her that fateful night, what had driven her to flee from her

family and the man she loved. Since then she and
Reese had agreed to take things slowly, rebuilding their relationship one day at a time and giving her time to put behind her what Neil
Grunthall had done.

Reese had been patient, understanding and
more supportive than any man had a right to be.
But still, after all this time, she hadn't been able
to get beyond being a victim of rape.

He scooted closer beside her on the sofa, continued to hold her hand and looked deep into her eyes.
They sat so close their thighs were touching and she
began feeling butterflies go off in her stomach, the
first sign of anxiety from a man being too close.

Inwardly, she fought the feeling that tried to intensify and glanced down at their joined hands for
strength. She told herself that he wasn't an ordinary
man. He was Reese, the man she had fallen in love
with at seventeen, the man she had given her vir-
ginity to just months before her eighteenth birthday
and the man she had planned to marry, and they'd
have all the babies he wanted to give her.

He was the also the man who had secretly built
his house for her, to give to her as a wedding gift.
She hadn't known about the house when she'd fled
town. At the time it would not have mattered. All

she'd been able to think of that night was her humiliation, shame, hurt and disgrace.

Neil, who had seen Reese as his enemy, had raped Leah as a way not only to get back at Reese, but also at Leah's father for firing him. She had felt that her father and Reese were the last two people she could have gone to with the truth. There was no doubt in her mind that they would have killed Neil with their bare hands, and she couldn't risk that. So she had run away without telling anyone what had happened. She hadn't even confided in her sister Jocelyn.

Jocelyn.

She smiled when she thought of the older sister she was finally getting closer to. Jocelyn was twenty-seven to her twenty-three. But even with the mere four-year difference in their ages, they had never been close. Jocelyn had always been "Daddy's" girl, while Leah had been "Mommy's" girl. Their mother had died when Leah had turned thirteen. That had been the worst period of her life. She had felt so alone. No one seemed to know how badly she was hurting and a part of her had been convinced that no one had cared.

The only thing she had looked forward to was finishing school and leaving Newton Grove…at least that had been the only thing until Reese and his family had moved to town in her junior year of high school. He had been employed by her father's construction company. It was during that time that Reese became the focus of her life, her entire universe and the only one she held dear. And Neil had brutally destroyed all of that in one horrible night.

"Leah?"

She glanced up, met the intensity in Reese's dark eyes. She actually felt it. And she felt something else. Desire. She could feel his passion like a gentle caress to certain parts of her body and although she wanted to respond, a part of her mind would not let her. For some reason, she had a mental block that refused to let Reese tap into what was behind her fears. If only she was strong enough to let go, but she wasn't. Even after resuming counseling sessions with a therapist, she hadn't been able to move forward with that part of her life.

"I'm fine, Reese, really," she said at last. "But it hurts to know how your family feels about me now, when before we were so close. And it hurts even more to know their present feelings are justified."

"But they don't know everything, Leah. They don't know what happened to make you run away that night," he said softly, gently squeezing her hand.

"I know and I can't get upset with them for how they feel about me. I'm sure they're wondering why you're even seeing me again, spending so much time with me."

"What I do is my business, Leah, and my family knows that."

"Yes, but I still can't help but feel bad for them. They don't know the entire story. They're worried that I will hurt you again."

"But you won't. You promised you would stay in Newton Grove and not return to California, and that we would work things out, and we will."

She felt the tears coming and blinked a few times to keep them at bay. "Will we, Reese? It's been six months and although I'm comfortable with us kissing, I can't seem to get beyond that and that's not fair to you. I know you, Reese, just as you know me. You want me. You want to sleep with me and make love to me the way any man would want to with the woman he loves. But I just can't get beyond certain things."

"But you will. I truly believe that. We will continue to take things one day at a time, Leah, and no matter what anyone thinks or how long it takes, you and I are in this for the long haul. We're going to work through this. I truly believe that."

His words gave her some of the strength she needed. Because he believed, she wanted to believe. He was good at feeding her hope and she clung to him. His expectations for them, his belief in their future was what had kept her in Newton Grove when Jocelyn had moved to Charlotte a few months ago after getting married. There was no one here for Leah other than Reese. He was the reason she had remained here instead of returning to California where she had tried to start a new life.

And he was the reason she had opened a café in town, right next door to his warehouse. It was there that he built his furniture. Reese had a gift when it came to carpentry—connecting his hands to wood. Her father had left him money in his will. The small sum was enough for Reese to start up his own business.

Leah had made a hefty sum from the sale of her share of the construction company her family had owned. Together, she and Reese had purchased this piece of real estate that had been perfect for both of their needs. It gave her the space she needed to start her restaurant, yet it was comforting to know Reese worked in the building right next door.

They were now a twosome and did practically

everything together. He usually got to the warehouse before she arrived at work, and each morning he would be her first customer before she officially opened. They would sit and talk over coffee and pancakes before her two staff members arrived. And he always dropped in for lunch and then at the end of both of their work days—around three in the afternoon—he would come in and sit while she closed up for the day. Then they would either go to his place or hers for something to eat. Occasionally, they would dine somewhere in town.

She could not ignore the cold stares she got from all the young women who just couldn't understand why the town's most eligible bachelor preferred hanging on to the woman who had broken his heart instead of moving on to someone else.

Leah sighed, deciding not to think about that any longer. She glanced around. Reese had built this house for her years ago, but when she had left town he'd felt hurt and betrayed. Eventually he'd sold it to Jocelyn. Jocelyn had sold it back to him when she'd gotten married to Sebastian Steele and moved away.

A part of Leah knew that the reason Reese had wanted the house back was because he was hoping that one day the two of them would live in it as man

and wife and raise the family they'd always wanted. He had so many high hopes for them.

"So why did you bring me here tonight, Reese?"
she couldn't help asking as she continued to glance
around.

"I wanted you to see the changes I've made to
the place, especially the basement. And I want
your opinion about a few things I'm doing to the
windows."

She nodded and smiled as she stood. "Okay, let
me see what you've done."

A couple of hours later he had taken her home
and they were strolling up the walkway to her door.
He stood back while she unlocked the door. She
knew she didn't have to ask him if he wanted to
come inside for a minute because she knew he did.
As always, he would kiss her good-night; it was
the closest he was able to get to her.

"I really like the changes you made to your
house, Reese," she said to break the still quietness
of the night.

"It's *our* house, Leah. Always remember that,"
he said, unlocking the door for her.

As soon as she closed the door behind him, he
touched her hand and she turned to him. This was
a part of their relationship they both looked

forward to, the only physical part she felt comfortable with. She always knew that no matter how intense the kiss became, Reese would pull back before things got too out of hand. She admired his ability to stay in control. His control gave her the chance—even if only for a little while—to let go and indulge in at least one facet of her fantasies.

She gazed into his face thinking as she always did that at twenty-eight he was a handsome man. Tall, broad-shouldered, dark ebony eyes and skin the color of semi-sweet chocolate. She felt his hands move to her waist and instead of feeling panicky, she felt heat fill her insides.

"Good night, Leah." His voice was deep and husky.

"Good night, Reese."

And the moment she said the words, he lowered his head and gently captured her mouth with his and she let go, sliding her own hands around his waist.

She closed her eyes when their lips touched. The kiss reminded her of better times when she had been sexually free and uninhibited. Their tongues mingled, dueled, tangled.

He made a sound deep within his throat. She heard it and was totally aware he had gotten aroused. She could feel him pressed against her stomach. But she wasn't afraid of it because in the back of her mind a part of her needed this kiss from Reese as much she needed air to breathe.

Slowly, he pulled away and she sensed things were getting too heated. She glanced up at him and he smiled. It was a slow, warm smile that touched her all over. Then he reached out and tilted her face up and leaned down and brushed a kiss across her lips one more time.

"Dream about me tonight, sweetheart."

She smiled. "I always do, Reese. I love you so much."

"And I love you, too, Leah."

And then he was pulling her into his arms, holding her close and she felt it and knew he felt it, too. The need to assure each other of their feelings, their love and the knowledge that what others didn't understand, they did. What had happened that night five years ago was something they would deal with and work through. Together.

Moments later he took a step. "Don't forget that tomorrow I'm leaving for Memphis to pick up supplies. I won't be back until noon."

She nodded. She had forgotten. "Thanks for reminding me."

And then giving her one last caress across her

lips, he turned and left. And as always, she felt an intense surge of loss with his leaving.

Leah glanced around her restaurant. It was small but just what she wanted and needed. Already, she and Reese had discussed the possibility of expanding and she was glad there would be no problem doing so.

Since opening a few months ago for breakfast and lunch, she had begun getting a steady flow of customers. Because the buildings she and Reese had purchased were right off the interstate, truckers stopped by and she had discussed with Reese the possibility of expanding her hours to include dinner.

"Leah, you have a call."

She turned around and smiled over at Marie. A single mother who had recently moved to town, Marie had become a godsend. The hours at the restaurant afforded Marie time to get her two little boys to the bus stop in the morning and to be there to pick them up in the afternoon. "Thanks, Marie, I'll take it in my office."

Leah quickly walked in the back to her office, wondering if it was Jocelyn calling. Although her sister had moved to Charlotte, they made a point of talking a few times a week. She was happy for Jocelyn. Her sister had found the man of her dreams and was happily married to one of the infamous Steele brothers, Sebastian.

She smiled as she picked up the phone. "Hello."

"Leah, this is Daniel."

Leah raised her brow wondering why Reese's brother would be calling her. "Yes, Daniel, what is it?"

"It's about Reese. He asked me to call you. He was involved in an accident on his way back to town and—"

"An accident!" Panic raced through Leah's body. "What happened? Is he okay? Where is he?"

"Yes, he's okay, just bruised up some. We're at the hospital. Some trucker fell asleep at the wheel and plowed into him. I understand from the state troopers that things could have been much worse, especially if Reese hadn't been familiar with the roads and hadn't been able to retain control of his truck. Otherwise, there's no way he would have been able to stop the vehicle from going over a cliff."

Leah closed her eyes, imagining such a thing happening when she remembered the mountainous roads between Newton Grove and Memphis with all those sharp curves. She began shaking. "Where is he, Daniel? I need to come to him. I need to—"

"You really don't need to do anything. The only reason I'm calling is because he asked me to."

She paused, hearing the cold bitterness in Reese's brother's voice. At that moment, anger suddenly tore into her, but she wouldn't give in to it. There was a lot about her and Reese's relationship that Daniel didn't know. "And I appreciate you calling, but I really need to know what hospital he was taken to." She needed to see Reese, talk to him and make sure he was all right.

"There's no need for you to come here. The doctor has fixed him up and has given me the okay to take him home and that's what I'm doing. You can call and talk to him later. 'Bye."

Leah heard the click in her ear and for the longest time just stood there and stared at the phone. If anyone thought she wasn't going to find Reese and see for herself that he was all right then they had another think coming.

She pulled the apron over her head as she grabbed her purse and headed for the door. It would be closing time in an hour or so and Marie could do it for her. At the moment, the one and only thing on her mind was getting to Reese.

* * *

Leah pulled into Reese's yard at the same time Daniel did, and she barely gave her car a chance to stop before she jumped out of it. As soon as Reese opened the door to Daniel's truck to get out, she was there. And as if he understood, he pulled her into his arms and held her close to him.

A part of her wanted to cry. She'd seen the scratches on his face, the cut on his forehead and the slightly bruised eye. She thanked God because things could have been a lot worse. She could have lost him.

She pulled back and placed her hands on his shoulders and studied his features. Even banged-up he was the most handsome man she knew. And because she needed to know that he was totally okay, she moved closer to him and, on tiptoe and ignoring his brother's presence, covered his mouth with hers. She gave a sigh of relief, then one of pleasure, when he began kissing her back, accepting the invasion of her tongue as he continued to kiss her and she kissed him, over and over.

In the distance, she heard Daniel clear his throat and she and Reese reluctantly parted. She glanced over and saw the frown that covered Daniel's. "If the two of you don't mind, I have to get back to work. I'd like to get Reese settled before I go. The doctor gave him some pain pills and said for him to lie down and rest," he said.

She heard the underlying message in Daniel's words. He would take care of his brother and wanted her gone. But she had news for Daniel Singleton. She wasn't going anyplace.

"You can go on back to work, Daniel. I'll handle things from here. I'll take care of Reese."

Daniel narrowed his eyes at her, and she knew he wanted to say something, probably something smart, but he decided to hold his tongue in front of Reese. She felt his anger. Daniel was only eighteen months younger than Reese and the two of them had always been close. He saw her as the woman who had hurt his brother deeply.

"I'll be okay, Danny. I need you to go and assure Mom that I'm all right. Let her know that Leah is here with me and that I'll be fine."

Leah could feel the tension between the two men and it nearly broke her heart to know she was the cause of it. Daniel stared at Reese for the longest time before finally nodding. Getting back into his truck he glanced through the window at them one last time before pulling off. Leah then turned her attention back to Reese. Taking his hand in hers, she said warmly, "Come on. Let's go inside so I can get you settled in bed."

Less than an hour later, Reese had showered, put on his pajamas, eaten the chicken noodle soup Leah had prepared, taken his medication and was out like a light. Leah thought that even asleep he looked sexy.

She stood at the foot of the bed and smiled down at the man she loved with all her heart. She didn't want to think about what could have happened, but thanked God for what hadn't happened.

She glanced down at herself, deciding she needed to take a shower, as well, but knew she didn't have any clothes to change into. She also knew she wouldn't be leaving Reese alone tonight so she made a quick decision. He had a drawer full of T-shirts; she would shower then slip into one and then wash and dry the clothes she was wearing for tomorrow.

Knowing Reese would be sleeping for a while, she crossed the room and opened several drawers before locating the one where he kept his T-shirts nicely folded. She found one that advertised Singleton's Handcrafted Furniture that she knew would work. She checked on him one last time before leaving the room to use the shower in the guest room.

A half hour later she had showered, put on Reese's T-shirt—it came to midthigh—and sat curled up in a chair by his bed, watching him as he continued to sleep. It was just turning dusk when she stood to stretch her muscles and decided to give Jocelyn a call to let her know about Reese. Tiptoeing out of the room she went into the living room and picked up the phone.

Moments later she heard her sister's voice on the line. "Hello?"

"Jocelyn? This is Leah."

Jocelyn knew something was wrong the moment she heard the strain in her sister's voice. "Leah? What's wrong?"

Hearing Jocelyn ask that question opened a flood gate of fears for Leah, fears of what she could have lost. In no time she was pouring out everything to her sister while trying to keep her voice composed. Near the end, she lost her battle not to cry and ended up sobbing. "What if he'd been killed, Jocelyn? What if I had lost him?"

"But you didn't," was her sister's calming words. "Reese is okay."

Despite Jocelyn's efforts to reassure her of

that over and over, Leah's stomach still trembled at the thought of how he could have been taken away from her.

"Look, Leah, while Reese is sleeping, you should get some rest yourself. You're wound up pretty tight and you need to clear your mind of everything for a while."

Leah nodded, knowing Jocelyn was right. "Okay. I do need to rest my mind and thanks for listening. How are things going in Charlotte?"

For the next ten minutes Leah listened while Jocelyn told her how she had adjusted to being Sebastian's wife and what a loving family he had. His parents, brothers and cousins had accepted her with open arms and, although she missed everyone in Newton Grove, she loved her life with Bas living in Charlotte.

After ending the call Leah decided to telephone Reese's mother and brother to let them know he was doing okay. She hung up the phone minutes later thinking they actually seemed appreciative for the information she had provided to them. She then threw her jeans and top into the washing machine with plans to dry them later. She noticed the time was seven o'clock as she made her way around the house, locking everything up for the night.

As she passed through several rooms, the thought that Reese had built this house with his own hands and just for her made her chest swell with love for him. Jocelyn had finally told her how he had worked for their father's construction company in the day and then at night and on weekends he had built this home for her. At the time, she hadn't known of Reese's special gift because he had meant to surprise her with the home on their wedding day.

While she mused about the house, she decided to use the guest room that was closest to Reese's room. She wanted to be close enough to be able to hear him if he woke up in the night and called for her. As she settled down in the bed, she lay flat on her back and looked up at the ceiling. She willed herself to close her eyes for just a little while.

For a moment, a really brief moment, she wanted to pretend that she and Reese were married and living in this house together, and that he was in the shower and in a few moments he would be joining her in the bed.

That pleasant thought was on her mind when sleep finally overtook her a few moments later.

Reese heard the sound of a woman calling out to him in a panicked and frantic voice. Leah's voice. His eyes popped open and he forced them into focus. Then he heard the sound again.

"Reese! No! Don't go!"

Jumping up he glanced around the room, remembering where he was and why Leah was in his home. When he heard her cry out a third time he raced out of the room, following the sound. Had she had a nightmare? Was she reliving that night with Neil Grunthall?

He entered the guest room to find her thrashing about in the bed. Not wanting to frighten her, he knew he had to be careful how he approached her to pull her from the throes of the tortured sleep she was enduring. Wanting her to know it was him and not Neil, he began talking to her in a gentle voice.

"Leah, it's Reese. You're okay, sweetheart. You're with me and you're okay."

He watched as her eyes flew open and she jerked upright in bed and glanced over at him. He saw the haunted look in her eyes and it almost broke his heart. He quickly moved to her, sat on the edge of the bed and gathered her into his arms.

"It's okay, baby. It's okay."

"Reese," she said sobbing, wrapping her arms around his neck as if she would never let him go. "I thought I had lost you. I dreamed that I saw your truck go over the edge of that mountain. Oh, Reese, it was awful."

It then dawned on Reese that her nightmare had nothing to do with Neil but with him and what had happened to him earlier that day. He gently stroked her back and held her. "I'm fine, Leah. I'm safe and I'm here with you now."

"But I saw it," she said, still sobbing.

"It was only a bad dream, baby. I'm alive and here with you. Look at me."

She slowly released him to look at him. He saw the reddened eyes, the tear-strained cheeks and the quivering lips. He brushed a kiss across those lips and then said gently. "See. I'm here."

"But I could have lost you," she said in a low, trembling voice. "I could have lost you, Reese."

He heard the gut-wrenching torment in her voice and didn't know what to say; so instead he did what came instinctively. He pulled her closer into his arms and he kissed her.

Passion such as he hadn't felt in a long time poured out of him as he put everything that was him into that kiss. Tonight he felt connected to Leah in a way he hadn't felt in a long time...nearly five long years. He tried remaining in control and fought the need coursing all through his body, but she was returning the kiss, stroke for stroke, mating her tongue with his as frantically and as desperately as he was mating his with hers. If being aroused could kill then he was a dead man, because he was aroused to the nth degree. His desire was potent; it felt vital to his survival, his mental and physical endurance.

He gave in when she pulled him down on the bed with her as they continued to kiss, and when she instinctively wrapped her body around his, that desperate need he'd felt earlier was clawing in him, taking everything he possessed to keep his control and sanity.

And suddenly, when he felt Leah's hand on him, sliding up his thigh and then settling on his crotch, stroking his erection through the material of his pajama bottoms, he broke off the kiss and pulled back. He knew she was not acting rationally and was reacting to the bad dream she'd had. The last thing he wanted to do was give in to his needs and take advantage of what she was going through.

"No, Leah," he said, pulling her hand away from him. "We have to stop."

"No, Reese," she said, looking at him with tortured eyes. "We have to finish. I need to know you're okay in my own way. I need to know that I didn't lose you."

"But you didn't lose me, baby. I'm okay and—"

"No! I have to do this! Please, let me. Take your bottoms off for me. Please."

He heard the desperate plea in her voice and saw the tortured look in her eyes. He lifted his hips and removed his pajama bottoms and tossed them aside and before he could make a move to do anything else, she had pushed him back in the bed and was straddling him.

He sucked in a deep breath, trying not to notice how the T-shirt she was wearing had ridden up nearly to her waist, giving him a delectable view of her nakedness, especially of her feminine mound. He sucked in an even deeper breath when she took hold of his erection and began stroking it before shifting her body to bear down on him, lowering her own body to his. "Leah! Wait!"

She stubbornly shook her head, letting him know there was no waiting. She wanted to be a part of him now. She needed the connection. He needed the connection, as well, but willed his body to remain still and to let her have her way with him.

He discovered moments later that remaining still wouldn't be easy when she eased all the way down on him, slowly, while staring deep into his eyes. Her body was tight, and at one point it was like making love to a virgin all over again. But she refused to stop and as she continued to sink deeper, he felt her inner muscles clench him.

"Leah!"

He called her name when she began easing up and down on him, slowly at first and then in a faster rhythm. She was tearing at his sanity, his hold of his senses and his control. The look he saw in her eyes was stunned, filled with a profound need, and the movements she made on top of him reflected that. When he saw that lying still was no longer an option, he nearly lifted his hips off the bed to thrust upward into her at the same time as she surged downward, riveting their bodies to the hilt. Each time they touched, her stomach, pelvis and thighs rubbing against his, a gnawing ache that had been within him since the last time they'd made love almost five years ago was being soothed. And when she increased her pace, pistoning her downward and upward strokes to a degree that was as intense as it could get, his hips continued to surge up, making each thrust that much deeper, more meaningful, unforgettable.

Reese closed his eyes when he heard her scream

out his name, and he drove himself deep inside her
as he locked his legs around her. He might have
hell to pay later, but he needed this. He needed her.
A coil of need tightened inside him and then
snapped when his own climax exploded in a ball
of gigantic sensations that ripped through every
part of his body. He screamed out her name, and
at the same time he felt all the love any one man
could have for a single woman emanating from
deep within him. Emotions he'd held back for
almost five years tore from him.

"Reese."

His name was whispered from Leah's lips in a
hoarse, enervated breath before her exhausted
body collapsed on top of him.

Reese shifted his body in bed and pulled the
covers over his head as his dreams got more
intense. He had dreamed that he and Leah had
made love several times and she had been in
control by taking the on-top position. His body felt
hard at the thought, and in sleep he grabbed the
extra pillow in the bed and sank his face into it.

His eyes flew open when he inhaled the scent.
Leah's scent.

He jerked up in bed and glanced around, suddenly realizing it hadn't been a dream. He and Leah had actually made love in this very bed.

And now she was gone.

Hell!

Jumping out of bed he slipped into his pajama bottoms, wondering where to search for Leah first. He could imagine the setback what they'd done would cause. He had to find her, apologize for losing control and—

"Going to a fire, Reese?"

He jerked around. She was standing in the doorway holding folded laundry in her hands. And she looked…at peace.

He blinked. It might have been his mind playing games on him, so he had to be sure. He inhaled deeply as he slowly walked over to her, not really knowing what to expect when he got close.

He came to a stop in front of her and searched her face before asking softly. "You okay, baby?"

She nodded as a small smile touched her lips. "Yes, Reese, I'm fine. I had washed my clothes earlier and thought I would dry them while you were…"

"Forget about the clothes, Leah. How do you feel?" he asked with deep concern in his voice.

She glanced down at the floor before lifting her

head to meet his gaze again. Then to his surprise, the corners of her lips tilted into a smile. "Mainly sore."

For a quick moment he was startled by her words, and then he released a relieved sigh before taking a step closer to her. "You wanted it," he said in a low husky voice, not taking his eyes off her as he remembered that they really had made love several times.

He watched as her smile widened. "Yes, and if I recall correctly, I even took it. The nerve of me being so bold."

He grinned. "Yes, the nerve of you."

Then moments later the amusement vanished and was replaced with concern. "Other than being sore, how do you feel, Leah?"

This time it was Leah who took a step forward and in a surprising move she wrapped her arms around his neck. "Other than sore, I feel wonderful. Reborn. Rejuvenated. I feel like a woman who has been given her life back, Reese. I had to be shocked into it. The thought of losing you, not sharing my love for you in a physical way again, made anything Neil had done to me no longer central in my life. To me, what's important is moving ahead with you, sharing my love and my life with you, for better or worse. Good times or bad. I love you. I want to marry you. I want to have your babies. And," she said in a softer voice. "I want to get your family together and tell them the truth. I couldn't stand it if they opposed our marriage."

He took the clothes out of her hand and gathered her to him. "You don't have to tell them anything, Leah. All they need to know is that I love you."

"But I want to tell them. I have to. Your mother and brother deserve to know the truth. And I want them to know what a wonderful man you are to have stuck by me for these six months, to have gotten me through some pretty difficult times. You are truly a special man, Reese Singleton."

And then she was on tiptoe kissing him with all the intensity of a woman in love. Reese swept her into his arms and carried her to the bed. A quiver of love and happiness flowed through her because she knew that once again she would receive sexual healing of the purest form in the arms of the man she loved.

Two weeks later, Reese swept his wife of just a few hours into his arms to carry her over the threshold of the house they would share. The wedding had been private, with only family and close friends. That's the way they had wanted it.

He placed Leah on her feet and closed the door behind them. She smiled up at him, looking beautiful, totally radiant in her light-blue pantsuit. She had been a beautiful bride.

"Jocelyn looks happy, doesn't she?" Leah asked, smiling up at him. "Sebastian is good for her."

And then she took a step and wrapped her arms around his neck. "And you, Reese Singleton, are good for me. And I love you."

He pulled her tighter into his arms. "And I love you, too, Leah Mason Singleton."

She smiled, liking the sound of her new name. She looked into his eyes. "It might be too early even to think about something like this, but I want a baby. Your baby. If it's a boy I want to name him after you and if it's a girl, I want to name her after my mother. I felt her presence today, Reese. Hers and Dad's. They are happy for me. They are happy for us. And your mom and Danny are happy for us, as well."

And she truly believed they were. Since she had tearfully told them the truth, they had been so supportive of her and Reese. And every day she was building a better relationship with his family.

"I want a baby, too," Reese said, pulling her closer to him. "Are you happy?"

She smiled. "I'm very happy." She glanced at

her watch. They would drive to Memphis and spend the night, and the next morning they would fly to Hawaii to begin their honeymoon. "Do we have time?" she asked him grinning.

He knew what she was asking. Ever since that night they had made love again, it was as if they were making up for lost time. Her fears had been destroyed by his love. He swept her back into his arms. "Baby, for that we'll make time."

She wrapped her arms around his neck as he started for the bedroom. "There's a lot that can be said for sexual healing, don't you think?"

He looked down into her eyes. "Yes, but then what we share is a powerful force because no matter what, in the end true love will conquer all."

He leaned down and kissed her. Unhurriedly. They had the rest of their lives together. Forever.

Some promises were just made to be broken...

Other
People's Business

Debut author

PAMELA YAYE

Stylist Autumn Nicholson looked like the kind of uppity,
city girl L. J. Saunders had sworn off. And Autumn wasn't
interested in casual flings, especially with a luscious hunk
who'd soon be leaving. But fate, well-meaning meddling
friends and a sizzling, sensual attraction all have other plans....

*Available the first week of April
wherever books are sold.*

KIMANI™
ROMANCE

www.kimanipress.com　　KPPY0150407

What happens when Prince Charming arrives...
but the shoe doesn't fit?

THE GLASS SLIPPER PROJECT

Bestselling author
DARA GIRARD

Strapped for cash, Isabella Duvall is forced to sell the
family mansion. But when Alex Carlton wants to buy it,
her three sisters devise a plan to capture the handsome
bachelor's heart and keep their home in the family.
The question is...which of the Duvall sisters will
become the queen of Carlton's castle?

*Available the first week of April
wherever books are sold.*

KIMANI™
ROMANCE

What a sister's gotta do!

At First
SIGHT

Favorite author

Tamara Sneed

Forced to live together to get their inheritance,
the Sibley sisters clash fiercely. But when financier
Kendra and TV megastar Quinn both set their sights on
wealthy Graham Forbes—sweet, shy Jamie's secret crush—
Jamie unleashes her inner diva.

*Available the first week of April
wherever books are sold.*

Sometimes love is beyond your control...

Bestselling author

ROCHELLE ALERS

The twelfth novel in her bestselling Hideaway series...

Stranger in My Arms

Orphaned at birth and shuttled between foster homes as a child, CIA agent Merrick Grayslake doesn't let anyone get close to him—until he meets Alexandra Cole. But the desire they share could put them at the greatest risk of all....

"Fans of the romantic suspense of Iris Johansen, Linda Howard and Catherine Coulter will enjoy this first installment of the Hideaway Sons and Brothers trilogy, part of the continuing saga of the Hideaway Legacy."
—*Library Journal*

Coming the first week of April
wherever books are sold.

ARABESQUE®

www.kimanipress.com

Bestselling author

ADRIENNE ELLIS REEVES

SACRED GROUND

An inspirational romance

Gabriel Bell has just inherited fifteen acres and a house
from a great-grandfather he never knew existed—but the
will is anything but straightforward. What is the treasured
destiny that he has only three months to find? And what
does the intriguing Makima Gray have to do with it?

Coming the first week of April
wherever books are sold.

ARABESQUE®

www.kimanipress.com

KPAER0090407

A searing and unforgettable novel about secrets,
betrayals…and the consequences of one's own choices.

Acclaimed author

Phillip Thomas Duck

Apple
Brown
Betty

With her brother Shammond having turned into a career
criminal and her family life in shambles, Cydney Williams
leaves her hometown of Asbury behind to build a new life.
But she soon discovers that the ties that bind us can also
define us.

**"His writing is emotional and touching, while at
the same time dramatic and powerful."**
—*Rawsistaz Reviewers* on
PLAYING WITH DESTINY

*Coming the first week of April,
wherever books are sold.*

sepia™

Visit us at www.kimanipress.com KPPTD0410407

"A relationship built within the church is a concept
not too often touched upon and it made for a nice
change of reading."
—*Rawsistaz Reviewers*

CAN I GET
an Amen
AGAIN

JANICE SIMS • KIM LOUISE
NATALIE DUNBAR
NATHASHA BROOKS-HARRIS

Follow-up to the ever-popular
CAN I GET AN AMEN...

The sisters of Red Oaks Christian Fellowship Church
are at it again—this time there are some new members of
the church looking for love and some spiritual healing...

Coming the first week of April
wherever books are sold.

ARABESQUE®

www.kimanipress.com

KPCIGAAA0670407

Seething with rage

Molly was half wild with excitement. She adored dancing, and she had the best dress in the world, and she was crazy about Rushing River Inn, and her silver slippers on her small slim feet were the perfect finish for her outfit.

But half of Molly — the invisible half — was seething with rage.

Con was taking Anne.

LAST DANCE

CAROLINE B. COONEY

SCHOLASTIC INC.
New York Toronto London Auckland Sydney

No part of this publication may be reproduced in whole or in part, or stored in a retrieval system, or transmitted in any form or by any means, electronic, mechanical, photocopying, recording, or otherwise, without written permission of the publisher. For information regarding permission, write to Scholastic Inc., 730 Broadway, New York, NY 10003.

ISBN 0-590-45785-3

12 11 10 9 8 7 6 5 4 3 2   2 3 4 5 6 7/9

Printed in the U.S.A.   01

Prologue

The Last Dance.

It celebrated the final day of the school year.

The following morning, there would be no classes where the five girls would run into their friends and compare notes. No more exams — but no more lunchroom talks, either; no hellos to shout in the halls; and no more rides to share going home.

It was the end of school, and the beginning of summer.

Next year they would be seniors.

Five girls stared into their mirrors.

Would this be a dance of love? A dance to begin on?

Or would it be a dance of loneliness? A dance to end on?

Two of the girls wished upon a star. One styled her hair a second time. One shrugged. And one of them picked up her telephone, called her date, and said, "Forget it. We're not going."

Chapter 1

Just friends.

Kip thought it was possibly the worst phrase in the English language. Yes, Mike had said, if you want to go to the Last Dance, I'll go with you, but we're just friends, remember. It's not a date.

Kip remembered. Clearly.

"Just friends," she muttered to herself as she fixed her hair. "Yuck. Boys don't look at you until you're thirteen. Then for the next two years they make gagging noises and jab each other in the ribs whenever they see a female person. When they're sixteen, they show off like insane cave men. At seventeen they take a quick plunge into dating — like swimming off the coast of Antarctica. Six months later they leap back to the shore of all boys' company and want to be *just friends*."

Kip ran to the door of her bedroom, stuck her head down the hall, and yelled to her four brothers, "I'm against it! Just you behave better when you're old enough to date! Do not, repeat not, be *just friends*."

Only one of her brothers was home, and he was young enough to have been put to bed already, so nobody took her advice. It was Kip's experience that nobody ever took her advice anyhow.

She had agonized over what to wear to the Last Dance. It was being held at the Rushing River Inn, at the foot of Mount Snow, a resort that featured an elegant ballroom and a vast screened verandah overlooking the ski lifts. Rushing River had a swimming pool, tennis courts, restaurant, game rooms, stables, croquet courts, and trails for cross-country skiing in winter and hiking in summer.

Supposedly the high school group was restricted to the ballroom, verandah, and terrace.

Kip was very grateful not to be in charge of this dance, as she had been of the Autumn Leaves Dance. She would stake two years allowance that the restrictions were going to be broken quickly and often.

What do you wear to a dance that will be chilly with air conditioning inside and hot with June mugginess outside? What do you wear if you might be sitting on the stone steps or leaning against a tree — but you also want to be perfect for flirting by candlelight near the grand piano?

Kip had bought a blouse of filmy white, with a lacy camisole under it, and a tea-length skirt of hot pink with splashes of yellow and violet. It was one very loud pattern. Half of the time Kip stared into the full-length mirror and decided she looked absolutely smashing, and the other half of the time she decided she was an embarrassment to the fashion world. She had fixed her hair with three very thin velvet ribbons of the same gaudy colors, their long delicate ends trailing over her thick brown hair and down over her bare shoulders. The back, but not the front, of the blouse was very low cut. Kip liked herself better from behind and kept turning to stare at herself over her shoulder.

Oh, Mike, Mike.

They had had such a good time for ten weeks. Ten precious weeks that worked out just the way Kip had hoped they would: laughter and love and kisses and talk and time together.

Then it was baseball season. "See you later," said Mike, and it turned out he didn't mean later that afternoon, or even later that week, but later in the year, when baseball was over. Kip went to all the varsity games, huddled in a blanket when it was still cold, and perspired in the sun when it was not. Baseball was too slow for Kip; every game seemed to last a dusty lifetime. And Mike never even looked her way, whether he was on the bench or pitching. I don't know the secret of life, Kip thought glumly, but that little round white ball with its little white stitches has sure got some answers.

Friends.

Okay, they would go to the Last Dance and be friends.

After all, Kip had close to seventeen years of experience at this "we're just friends" stuff. It wasn't as if she was a beginner at being "just friends."

Tomorrow, summer vacation would begin.

Kip had her first full-time job: waitressing at a fish house.

If when she came home smelling of fried flounder and tartar sauce, she knew that after her shower, Mike would take her out, it would all be bearable. But she had her doubts. Mike had his first full-time job coming up, too, and it wasn't in Westerly: he'd be driving every day to Lynnwood to work on a construction site. And he was, Kip thought gloomily, just as excited about his summer job as he had been about baseball.

Please, please, don't let this really be our last dance, Kip Elliott thought. I want to dance with Mike forever!

The L word.

It was what all the girls wanted to hear.

But, oh, it was a scary word, that L word, and rare was the boy who was willing to use it.

Anne Stephens, trembling with fear, sat waiting for Con to come and get her. Con wasn't about to use the old L word, that was for sure, but he was taking her, and he had promised over and over not to leave her. Not for one dance, not for one soda, not for one minute.

She was only going because Con said she had to. It would be good for her, he explained. She would get tough. She had to face everybody sometime, and it might as well be now.

Anne agreed only because there was no school the next day. She would not have to see anybody again until September 5, if she chose.

Last year, on September 5, she and Con started junior year as the most loved couple: the most beautiful girl and the handsomest boy, the brightest, funniest, most popular pair in the entire high school. Ah, but that was last year. And this was the *last dance*.

But it was Anne's first. First in many months.

Okay, stay calm, Anne told herself. Either kids will ask about it or they won't; either they'll be nice or they won't. You can't control it.

But what will I say? she asked herself for the thousandth time. When they say, "Where've you been since January, Anne?" do I say, "Oh, off having a baby." When they say. "What did you name the baby?" do I say, "Whoever adopts it gets to name it?"

Anne had held the baby for ten minutes. It was a little girl, so tiny she had a hard time believing that's what a baby was. She had thought they were much more substantial. She kissed its tiny bald head, and her tears fell gently on its red wrinkled skin and Anne thought, I can't give her away! I have to take care of her, and feed her, and see her grow, and —

And give this miniature daughter no father, no family, no home, no future?

And for herself, Anne — no high school diploma, no husband, no home, no future?

Anne was given a little paper to read about the parents who were going to adopt her baby. (She always thought of it as "her baby," not as Con's, because Con was so horrified by the whole thing you would have thought Anne had become an alligator hunter, not a mother.) The parents were over thirty, they were both college graduates, the mother (Mother? thought Anne. That's what *I* am. *The mother.* How impossible!) planned to stop working and stay home with the baby she had been dreaming of for over ten years.

It had not been a dream for Anne.

It had been a nightmare.

But it was over now. She was slim again, which was apparently what mattered most to everybody else, and her parents and her grandmother were practically normal with her, and it was time to get back into the swing. Con was taking her to the Last Dance.

Anne thought it was an absolutely horrid name. Who could have thought of such a thing? Why not Summer Prom or The June Fling? Last Dance sounded all too prophetic.

It was a hot evening. Windows were open to catch any slight breeze. She heard a car two blocks away, and the downshifting of the motor, and the slam of the door.

No, no, I can't do this, thought Anne Stephens. But nothing showed on her face. It stayed perfectly lovely and calm in the mirror in her hand, as if the face belonged to somebody else.

But it was her grandmother who flung open the screen door and came in the house. In the shadow of the living room, Anne stared at the grandmother who had been so disappointed in her. "Anne, darling, you look so lovely," said her grandmother, hugging her.

But it wasn't the same hug as last year's. They were all slightly afraid of her: because she had become a mother? A woman? Or because she had not been, after all, the child they thought they knew so well?

Con would greet her with the same hug: nervous, quick, moving back before she could take any comfort from it. Anne's life and body had changed so much in the last months and his not at all. He was still a reckless crazy teenage boy, who had to pay a fortune for car insurance and whose chief pleasure was his sound equipment: the stereo, the compact discs, the videos.

"You look beautiful, Anne," he would say

next, in his husky, sexy voice. It was the one thing that had never come into question: her beauty. But she didn't care how she looked. She wanted him to say, ". . . and I love you, Anne." He was exactly her height, so that their eyes always locked and their lips always met. Con was dark, with an athlete's build and a perfect smile, with hair as thick as her own, but almost black, as hers was almost gold. His profile should have been on some antique coin, with that long nose and that up-lifted chin.

He wanted to take her to the Last Dance.

But he was so distant from her! So nervous with her! Sometimes she thought it was just because (just?) of their baby . . . but sometimes Anne though he had another girl-friend, one who had not gotten heavy, or presented difficulties, or made him feel guilty. Sometimes Anne pictured this other girl-friend and felt sick, and full of rage, and full of fear. And sometimes she didn't care, either.

Oh, if Con would only say "I love you."

But that L word was scary.

And nobody scared quicker or more thoroughly than Conrad Winters.

Anne Stephens moved quickly to the phone. She could not go through with it. Con was not enough support. She dialed his number fast, before he could leave his house and get to his car, and when he answered she said, "Don't come, Con. I don't want to go to the dance."

* * *

Beth Rose had chosen a summery dress in soft flowery colors, and the thick infuriating red hair that had been the bane of her life for so many years had finally become a joy, and now it hung in heavy ringlets from a long narrow comb that gave her a mane like a wild horse. She loved the contrast of her strong firm hair with her fragile papery dress. She was in a dancing mood. All week, music had run in her head: music to dance by, music to flirt by, music to laugh by . . . but mostly . . . and always . . . music to adore Gary by.

Oh, what had life been before Gary?

Pallid, dull, repetitive.

And now?

Well, first it was scary. Yes, Beth Rose would have to put scary ahead of romantic. Because you couldn't count on Gary. He never said you *could* count on him — in fact he stressed that you *couldn't* — and Gary didn't lie. He *wasn't* reliable. And that was scary.

But if he showed up — oh, then it was romantic!

Beth Rose considered herself the most stodgy of personalities. She was the sort of person who would always stay for clean-up, and never skip the middle of boring books, and always, always pay her library fines. She had also been, until Gary, a wallflower. Last year, at another dance, Gary said, smiling, "Well, a flower anyway," and kissed her. Now when Beth Rose stood by a wall, she felt she was not a wallflower, but truly a rose, because to be with Gary was to be special.

She even got along better with her parents because of Gary. The new pleasure of being popular made it easy to laugh when they nagged, and Beth Rose discovered something astonishing: If she laughed, her mother and father laughed! Life at home had moved from a sour lane to a sweet one.

The only snag was that Gary did not have what you might call an attentive nature. Sometimes he helped in his father's restaurant, sometimes he got interested in school, sometimes he worked in the drama production, and sometimes he was fixing his car. And sometimes, with about equal emphasis, he wandered over to Beth Rose's and took her out. Gary never saw anything wrong with this: He felt life was perfect — a dose of mechanics, a dollop of girlfriend, a smidgen of studying, and a speck of work.

It was Beth Rose who felt the proportions were off. She would have liked to see ninety percent girlfriend and ten percent other. She said that to Gary once. Gary said, "You're kidding," and laughed and kissed her and they went on to a movie and shared popcorn. It never crossed Gary's mind that no, she was not kidding.

The L word.

Beth Rose and Anne had discussed that L word at length. Gary was definitely not in love with Beth Rose. He liked her fine, but

he also liked everything else under the sun
fine. It was useless even to ask Gary if he
loved her because he would have said, "Sure,"
and then he would have said, "You wanna
borrow my Dad's motorcycle and helmets and
we'll go up to Mount Snow? You wanna ride
the ski lift in summer? It's pretty. I love it."

Beth Rose did not want to be loved the
same amount as a ski lift in summer.

Her mother came into the room, where she
was fixing her dark red hair for the second
time. "You be nice to Anne, now, Brose."

A year ago Beth Rose would have tensed
and gotten upset. Now she just laughed.
"Mother, I've been nicer to Anne than anybody, including Con. It's my Aunt Madge she
went to live with, right?"

Mrs. Chapman shook her head. "I still
don't see why she couldn't stay at home."

"Because our town sends pregnant unwed
teenagers to a special high school in Lynnwood, and Anne didn't want to go. She was
crying twenty-four hours a day, Mother."

Beth Rose took the comb out of her hair
and tossed her head violently, and now the
curls sprawled all over her head like a garden of red poppies. Sometimes Beth Rose
thought the best thing about this excellent
year was not even Gary, but her new friendships with Anne and with Emily, girls in the
junior class who never even knew her name
before — never spoke to her because they
never noticed her — and now each was on
the phone with her at least once a day, talk-

ing boys, and life, and boys, and parents, and boys. (Emily and Beth Rose liked to start and end all conversations with boys.)

Mrs. Chapman said, "I don't want you out late, dear."

"Okay."

That means no later than one A.M., dear."

"Okay."

"That means leaving the dance shortly after midnight, dear."

"Mother, I know! My middle name is Cinderella. Gary knows. He's been taking me out all year! We've got the rules down!" Beth Rose laughed, surrendered her wild hair to the elements, hugged her mother, and dashed downstairs to leap into the car with Gary.

She could never wait for him to come inside. She was always ready early, always halfway on the date before Gary was even halfway to her house. She always ran out and jumped into the front and slid over the seat, and Gary would be laughing at her exuberance, and she would kiss him hard and he would just sit there, letting her, and then he would back out of the driveway.

This time she didn't do any of that.

This was the Last Dance.

And Beth Rose wanted Gary to do it *right*.

Molly was schizophrenic.

She was half wild with excitement. She adored dancing, and she had the best dress in the world, and she was crazy about Rushing River Inn, and her silver slippers on her small slim feet were the perfect finish for her outfit. Her dress was very short, very purple, with one lightning strip of glitter; her stockings were lace, her belt a silver chain with a dangling silver sun and stars, and her matching earings reached to her shoulders. When she danced, she rang like tiny bells.

But half of Molly — the invisible half — was seething with rage.

Con was taking Anne.

Talk about blackmail. It wasn't Con's fault Anne hadn't been careful. Anne should have known better. And if Anne was such a dork she had to leave town and go live with somebody until she had the baby, because she wouldn't have an abortion, well, that was Anne's problem. Con, perfect Con, should not be subjected to such a thing, and she, Molly, had seen to it that from January to the first of June he wasn't.

Molly had been laughter and fun, lightness and giggles.

She never asked anything of him; they never talked of anything serious, and gradually Con had stopped calling or visiting Anne. Anne was fat, anyway, and repulsive. And of course every time he had to visit her, Con was reminded of what happened, and Molly felt this was unfair. Somebody as wonderful as Con should not have to feel any guilt because Anne was dumb. Certainly she, Molly, would never be that dumb.

So here they were at the Last Dance, the pay-off socially for the whole long winter and

the whole wet dismal spring, and who was
Con taking?

Anne.

It was enough to make you spit.

Molly pounded her silver heels on the floor,
and it was no dance — it was a tantrum.

But she blamed nothing on Con, and she
blamed nothing on herself.

It was Anne Stephens' fault, and if precious, elegant little Anne thought she could
just waltz back to Westerly and take Con
and her social position back up as if nothing
had happened, well, precious Anne was
wrong.

Molly was keeping Con, and that was that.

Molly smiled into the mirror.

The mirror said nothing.

Molly's smile said it all.

Emily was shaking so hard she could
barely find the telephone, let alone dial. Oh,
for a phone with memory that would accom-
plish these tasks for her! What if Matt had
already left? What if he was on his way?
What would she do then?

"Oh, Matt!" she cried out, when he did
answer. "Oh, Matt, don't come. Forget it.
We're not going."

"Not going? But Em, I thought you were
so excited about this dance. We bought that
dress, and — "

"And Mother and Dad are splitting up
tonight, Matt. Right now. This minute.
They've been throwing things at each other

for hours and screaming horrible accusations, and Mother is packing a suitcase and shoving her things in her car, and she says I have to go with her, and we're leaving *now*."

Emily did not know why she was weeping so much. Her parents had no more use for her than they did for each other, and it was only since she began dating Matt that they saw anything good in their daughter at all. Matt was so wonderful they figured Emily must have something invisible going for her that they had not yet spotted.

It terrified her to think of moving away with her mother. She could manage a different high school, even if it was her senior year — her precious senior year — that would be lost. She could leave behind the familiar neighbors and rooms and garden and kitchen. But the only thing that had saved the Edmundson family this long was the fact that the rambling multilevel house permitted them to live quite separately. Emily knew she could not live in a three-room apartment in Lynnwood with her mother. They would be at each other's throats. They could not pull it off. Emily had managed never to fight her parents the way they fought each other, and she could not bear to start now. The thought of the wars to come, once she and her mother were jammed in next to each other and could not be apart, was enough to make her feel ill.

"So let them split," Matt said. "You and I

are going to a dance. I've never been to Rushing River Inn, and I plan to throw you in the swimming pool. So be prepared. You'll know when I'm going to do it because first I'll unpin your corsage and set it in a safe, dry place. The money I paid for these flowers, I'm not getting them drowned in chlorine."

His voice was as goofy as his grin, all spread all over the place, silly and sane at the same time. Oh, how Emily loved Matt! She took a deep, shaky breath and tried not to break down. "Matt, you don't understand. Mother is in the hall screaming at me to get in her car, and Dad is on the landing, screaming at me to stay put."

Her parents' voices terrified her. Screaming at *each other* she had gotten used to. But screaming at *her* was new, and she wanted to hide from them, under the bed or in the closet, like a baby.

"M&M, I understand perfectly," said Matt, who had begun calling her for her favorite candy, and also because her name (Em) and his initial (M) were M&M. "And who cares? You're sixteen, soon to be seventeen. Old. Very, very old and mature. And we're going to a dance, because kids like us spend all our time doing fun things. I have four new tapes, and my mother bought the neatest new snack — looks kind of like mouse droppings, but it really tastes pretty good. I'm bringing it to eat in the car so we can keep up our strength, and you'll like it."

17

Matt had a mind filled with thoughts. Emily visualized the inside of Matt's head as a clothes dryer with a glass door: thoughts tumbling like drying jeans and socks, with no relationship to each other except they were all crammed into the dryer together. You had to concentrate to follow Matt, and tonight she could not think.

Emily's parents appeared in her bedroom door.

The door framed them, like a picture, perhaps a twentieth anniversary picture — not that they planned to have or celebrate one. Her mother said fiercely, "Emily, the car." It sounded as if she were introducing them.

Her father yelled much louder, "Emily, you're not going anywhere."

Matt said in her ear, "I heard that. They sound a little irritable. Listen, M&M, be happy, it's finally going to happen, this divorce you've been worried about for so long. We'll stay out all night, and when we get back at dawn, they will have split."

"But Matt," she protested. The tears had begun, and she did not know what to do about them. Emily generally choked when she cried and couldn't talk. Anyway, she couldn't tell Matt anything now because her parents were listening.

"If you do not come with me to Lynnwood right now, young woman," her mother said, "as far as I am concerned you do not need to come at all."

Emily clung to the phone like a life raft. Her own mother was giving her one chance — just one — now or never. Come or I don't love you?

Her parents, unable to look at each other any more, because they were so angry and feeling so violent, glared at her instead. Her father bellowed, "You go with that woman, and I'm changing the locks, and you're not coming back here. And that's that."

"Just stay calm and come with me," Matt said in her ear.

Stay calm?

What — was he out of his mind? Stay calm? And if she went with Matt, she would have neither mother nor father; Matt couldn't bring her home after the dance because she woudn't have one!

Emily wanted time to think.

She wanted to talk with her counselor in school and maybe her music teacher, who was very understanding even though Emily was a poor saxophone player at best. Then she wanted to talk with Matt's grandfather, who was the most wonderful person on earth, and definitely with Beth Rose, who had become such a good friend this year. Emily figured she had at least a month of heavy-duty consulting to do before she could make this decision. And they were giving her one minute.

Why, oh why, couldn't she have a *nice* family? Why couldn't she be like Kip, with that horde of terrific little brothers, and that cozy mother who loved to give parties, and that father who seemed to do nothing but laugh and hug all the time?

Matt said, "Lemme talk to 'em."

Oh, *yes*. He would be a buffer: like the wall around a castle. She could put him and the telephone between herself and her parents' fury. Emily said, looking at neither parent, but holding the phone in their direction, "Matt would like to talk to you." Let them fight over who got to do that as well.

Her mother took the phone and slammed it back down, hanging up on Matt. "Get in the car, Emily, we're leaving."

They loved each other once, Emily thought, or they wouldn't have gotten married. How did this happen? How —

Her mother grabbed her wrist. Hard enough to hurt.

And Emily said softly, "Mother, I'm going to the Last Dance with Matt. I'll telephone you and let you know what I decide about living with you or Dad."

Her father said, "It won't be me you live with, young lady, if on the night I need you most, you go traipsing off with that loopy jerky kid."

She almost fell for it — his needing her — but the truth was that Mr. Edmundson seldom needed anything except his television set, and if he needed her, it was only to bring his food from the microwave in the kitchen to the TV in the family room.

Family room, she thought.

Some family.

Sobbing, she jerked her wrist free. She tried to run out of the room, but her father blocked the door. She shoved him away and ran down the stairs and out of the house. She would call Matt from the neighbors' — wait for him around the corner — figure out what to do later!

Her parents were yelling at her, and their terrible voices followed Emily across the lawn. She fled farther than she thought she would. She could not stop running, but crossed backyards, and stopped, panting behind a stranger's garage.

Emily Edmundson thought — What have I done?

It won't be a Last Dance!

It'll be a Last Home, Last Family, Last Mother and Father.

Inside the house, the phone rang again.

It was Matt.

Mrs. Edmundson said harshly, "She's coming with me, Matt, and not going to the dance. Do not drive down here." And she hung up hard enough to damage the phone.

Chapter 2

"You came," Anne said.

Con just looked at her. She would never get used to the silence of that look: not by one quiver of his heavy eyebrows did Con give away what he was thinking. "Yes," he said, and nothing more. She stood in the hot dark living room and he in the hall, lit by the lowering sun and cooled by the breeze from the screen door. Anne thought they might stand that way for hours: heat and emotion turning them to statues.

But Con said, "Let's go, kid. I not only paid for the tickets but also for the chance to win a VCR. We have to get our questionnaires and start filling them out."

He had started calling her "kid" when she got back from the hospital. She liked to believe she was still a kid, but inside she felt old, old, old. Brighten up, Anne told herself, you're a high school junior off to a dance, not an old crone beaten down by decades of misery!

She did not take a single step toward Con. He would have to walk to her. And he did, grinning his old careless grin. He caught at her waist without getting panicky, half danced her to the porch, and even kissed her.

He opened the door of his car for her. For a moment she thought she saw a baby seat in the back, but the weird vision vanished instantly, and she shivered. How long would her life be haunted by the baby she had given up?

Con had given nothing up. But they could not talk — once again they could not talk — of what Anne had endured that he was not part of.

Con said, "I filled yours out for you. Everybody else did them in school."

Anne had no idea what he was talking about.

"For each ticket," Con explained, "they gave you a questionnaire — boring stuff like what's your middle name, where were you born, what do you collect, where have you traveled, and what have you done lately. They're going to make up a quiz for us to do at the dance, using the interesting answers we came up with. We have to run around the ballroom, asking the other kids questions until we have it filled out, and the first person to get it all filled out wins the VCR."

Anne tightened up. What have you done lately? Would people be asking her that? Would they come up and say, "Anne, are you the one on this list who just had a baby?"

Con touched her knee very lightly. "Don't worry," he said, "all your answers came out fine."

"And did you know everything about me?"

Con grinned. "What I didn't know, I made up," he said.

"I won't know my own life when it's time to fill in the blanks," Anne protested. But she was beginning to laugh. Perhaps she would have fun after all. Perhaps Con's relaxed air would infect her, and the mountain winds would blow away her nerves.

"If you don't know, I'll tell you," Con said. "I have all the answers."

Gary sat in the car waiting for Beth Rose. He liked the occasional dance because he rather enjoyed dressing up and going somewhere special. Tonight he was wearing possibly the reddest pants in the entire world. They were cotton, and slightly baggy, and so red that people were going to complain all during the dance. Even in the dark, his pants were going to blind the eyes. He had already thought of wisemouth retorts for a variety of possible remarks about his red pants. His shirt was ivory, with a few narrow horizontal stripes — also red — and he was carrying a jacket, in case Beth Rose gave him a hard time, but that was not usually her style.

Beth Rose was undemanding. His own family did a good deal of yelling, but if Beth Rose ever raised her voice, Gary had not heard her. Whatever he felt like doing, Beth

Rose generally felt like doing, too. She always seemed to be in a good humor, and most of all, she was always glad to see him. It was kind of nice, to drive up to a house and know, for absolute sure, that the person living there would fling herself on you with delight.

But when he was not with her, Gary rarely thought about Beth Rose. Gary's mind landed on one thing and stayed there, so that if he was fixing his car, he was not also dreaming of a date that night. He was simply fixing the car.

When Beth Rose did not dance out of the house and leap into his car, he was mildly surprised, but figured she was still brushing her hair or something, so he waited longer. The sunset was beautiful, and he stared into it, watching the distant clouds change colors.

Beth Rose still didn't come.

With a vague sense that he might have the wrong night, Gary got out of the car and wandered up to the house.

"Beth Rose?" he called, poking his head inside the screen. "You coming or do I have the wrong night?"

She had been watching him steadily through the slats of the blinds. Now she sat up on the couch and heaved a sigh. It's very simple, Beth Rose told herself. You just stop being in love with the guy. The only thing you can say for Gary is, he's *here*. He's not in love; he's hardly even awake.

Six months of dating according to Gary's standards.

Which were low.

Which said a date came when Gary felt like it and consisted of what Gary wanted to do. When he remembered.

Maybe this really should be the last dance, Beth Rose thought. Maybe it's time for me to say goodbye and find a boy who puts me first.

She tried to imagine such a boy, but she could think only of Gary, whom she still adored as much as she had the first night.

Gary walked on into the living room, saw her on the couch, and grinned at her. Beth Rose's heart flipflopped, in spite of the strict orders she gave it not to. With two steps Gary crossed the room and dropped like a very tall stone onto the couch next to her. The sofa didn't break, but it definitely bent. Gary tipped backward, resting his feet on the wall and his head on her lap. "So? We're dancing here?"

"No, we're dancing at Rushing River." Normally she would have bent her head to kiss him, but tonight she sat there as if nobody lay in her lap at all.

Gary said, "Why didn't you come out to the car?"

"Because I wanted you to come in here."

Gary touched her freckled nose with his fingertip. "Got your wish, then, lady." He grinned at her again, drawing a smile over her lips until she smiled back. "I see I have to play caveman if we're going to get to the dance in time to win that VCR." He sat up fast, turned, slid a hand beneath her, and scooped Beth Rose into his arms as if she were the pillow on the couch.

"I don't know that I would call this cave-man behavior," Beth Rose said. "As I recall, cavemen drag their girls by the hair."

Gary laughed. "Next year," he promised, and carried her to the door. She arched her back and tried to kiss him, but he tilted his chin back teasingly and wouldn't let her.

And I call him unromantic, Beth Rose thought, leaning back in his arms and start-ing to laugh.

When she leaned back, her thick red mane of hair caught in the middle hinges of the front door. Gary stepped back slightly to free her hair and her dance slippers whacked the doorknob. Gary turned to the side to fit her through that way and got the hem of her skirt under his shoe.

Beth Rose was laughing hard enough to shake them both.

Gary's face turned red.

"Keep blushing," Beth Rose teased. "We need a match with your trousers if we're really going to be color-coordinated."

Gary attempted a frontal attack on the door.

"Aaah," yelled Beth Rose, "you can't go that way — my hair isn't going with you!"

Gary swore under his breath.

"What did you say, Gary darling?" Beth Rose was giggling insanely. She said, "I guess we'll dance here after all. At least my feet won't get tired."

"The trouble with romance," Gary said very irritably, "is it's so easy to look like a jerk."

"But Gary," Beth Rose told him, "you're the handsomest jerk in town."

"Oh, good," Gary said. "I feel better now."

Kip and Mike Robinson were the fourth couple to arrive at Rushing River Inn. "You're always so efficient," Mike said, smiling. But she could tell that it annoyed him, to be early instead of with the crowd.

Kip could never figure out what other people were doing with their time that they could drift in an hour or two hours later than an event began. If a dance started at eight, Kip was there at eight, and not two minutes later.

It was perfectly clear that the Last Dance wasn't even going to think about beginning before ten. How — *how* — were she and Mike going to manage all that time without a bunch of friends to help spread the burden?

Pretending to circle around and check out the ballroom of Rushing River Inn, Kip swirled until her bare back faced Mike, and she tossed her head slightly so the pink and violet and yellow ribbons would tangle in her thick brown hair and he would untangle them.

Mike said, "Well, we can start filling in these questionnaires. Course there's nobody here yet to ask." He began studying the questions to see if he already knew any of the answers.

Kip finished her circle and faced him. She knew she was graceful and pretty tonight, and now, in the dim light of the ballroom, she knew that the wild colors of her skirt were the right choice: the darkness softened them, and yet the vividness remained. Mike either hadn't noticed or didn't intend to. It *is* the last dance, she thought. We have just come as friends, and Mike is afraid if he says one nice thing, he'll tip the balance, and I'll fling myself on him, and he'll have to cope with it.

Kip wanted to cry.

She thought, if I cry, Mike will freak out.

Girls didn't mind their emotions all over the place; boys couldn't stand it. Kip often thought that a girl's tears were like a broken egg in the palm of the boy's hand: all he wanted to do was shout "Yucky!" and wipe it away.

She could not cry; she could not be a slippery, slimy, broken mess that Mike would despise.

If I'm not going to think about Mike, what am I going to think about? Kip asked herself. She stared around the room for help and noticed the questionnaire for the VCR prize which she gripped in her left hand. The hand that wanted to be holding Mike's.

Kip was immediately aware that the distribution of these questionnaires was not well organized. They were going to run into snags. Frowning slightly, she said, "Now if they would just — "

Mike stopped her instantly. "Kip, it's *their* problem," he said. "Give it a rest, okay?"

Kip quivered inside. Mike's voice was sharp, irritated. And it was also embarrassed, as if he had known Kip would do something like this and wished she would behave better.

There's really only one thing I'm terrific at, Kip thought. Organizing. I can juggle twenty balls and never drop one. I'm not glamorous, or a great singer, or a brilliant student, or even anybody's very best friend. I'm just good at being in charge.

For the first time, Kip understood that what Mike did *not* want in a girlfriend was the one thing she was good at.

The air-conditioning in the ballroom was very strong. She was chilled, and being chilled depressed her.

"Some of these questions are really fascinating," Mike said in surprise. "I have absolutely no idea who any of them could be. Listen, Kip. Who was born in Beverly Hills? Who is sixteen and has moved twenty-eight times? Who at this dance has shaken hands with the President of the United States?"

Kip stared blindly at the questions. She could not even read them. Five minutes into the Last Dance, and she was teary and tense. Oh, Mike, Mike, why don't you love me like you did? Even as she thought this, she knew it was just an old song. How diminishing to have the very same problem as people in songs. Kip wanted to be so special they would need a new song just for her unusual situation.

"Who is the only person at the dance who doesn't like chocolate?" Mike read on. "Who at this dance has a pet peacock?"

A pet peacock? Kip thought. How bizarre. Who *does*? She said, "Mike, I'm freezing. Let's go out on the verandah. We'll be able to watch everybody driving up, and I'll stay warm."

"Oh, you just want to supervise the arrivals," Mike said rudely. He went back to the quiz and didn't take a step toward the doors. "Who was born on an ocean liner?" Mike read. He had a smile stuck on his face, as if he'd left the smile there by accident and would come back for it.

But it was Kip herself who had been born on the ocean liner. It made quite a story, and it was one her mother loved to tell, and her father hated remembering. In all the dozens of stories she and Mike had shared, that one somehow had never come up. She and Mike talked so much about the present, about their own lives and their own thoughts, that they had never considered going back sixteen years to their births.

He'll question every person at the dance to find out, Kip realized, but he won't think of asking me: he's bored by me. He figures he knows all there is to know about Kip Elliott.

Kip watched the band set up. She didn't want a band; she wanted a DJ. Half the time the band couldn't play the pieces you wanted, or they played some dumb arrangement of their own that just made you tense, because you wanted it to be like the recording.

"Oh, what's the point, Mike?" she said tiredly. "We already have a VCR. I don't even want to win."

"I do," Mike said. "Get organized and win and give me the VCR, okay?" He grinned at her and walked away.

Walked away!

Kip stared at her departing boyfriend. He had had another growth spurt. His pants were slightly too short and his shirt stretched too taut over his shoulders. Another time she would have loved thinking about how tall and muscular he was these days, but tonight she was just furious because his clothes didn't fit, and he was turning his back on her.

I'd rather get organized and give you a long walk off a short dock, Kip thought.

He was her first boyfriend, and what Kip could not get over was the idea that he *had* gotten over it.

What on earth had happened to those crazily joyous first weeks? When he spent the whole day after school at her house? And had dinner with them? Did homework with her and practically had to be chased out with a broom by Kip's mother? And then the instant he got home had to telephone to tell her all the things he had thought about during the drive back?

"Come on," Mike said irritably. "You said you wanted to go outside, so let's go."

Kip walked after him, and he held the glass door for her, and they walked into the hot night. Mountain breezes made it pleasant, and there was no view to compare with this one. Mike appeared to be enjoying the scenery. Kip could remember a time when she was the only scenery Mike wanted to gaze upon.

Where had he gone — that Mike who loved her?

Did he miss the love himself?

Did he even remember it?

Kip remembered every minute, as if she had a tactile diary that recorded each kiss and touch and caress.

She made one final try. Stepping up close to him, touching his shoulder, using her flirty voice, she said, "Actually, Michael, the dancer who did one of those things on the questionnaire is none other than that sexy exciting woman — tah-dah! — Kip Elliott!"

And Mike, her Mike, who once thought she was the most fascinating human being on the face of his earth, said, "Aw come on, Kip, you've never done anything interesting."

Matt's family specialty was not spicy food, nor downhill skiing, nor Trivial Pursuit. It was advice.

"All right," his mother said instantly. "All right, you must drive straight down there. Go directly to Emily's house, and tell her we want her to live with us."

"Absolutely not!" Matt's father shouted. He was six feet tall, and Mrs. O'Connor was five eleven, but she rose higher than her husband because she was wearing heels and had puffy hair. "Don't listen to your mother, Matthew. We will not interfere with the Edmundson situation. That was her mother you spoke to, and we can't run around making things worse. Emily has to stay with her own family, that's what families are for."

Matt, as usual in his family, now had two absolutely opposite views of what to do. To interfere, or not to interfere, that is the question, Matt thought. He knew Emily would want him to interfere, but —

"Impossible!" Matt's grandfather shouted. He was the tallest of them, at six four, and his voice got louder with every passing year. "Her own family just broke up. The girl *needs* you, Matthew, what are you hanging around for?"

Matthew, at five ten, was the family shrimp. He had to look up to all of them, which annoyed him. With all those great tall genes, how come he wasn't six six?

"Change your clothes, Matthew," his mother said. "That tuxedo is too dressy. Obviously you're not going to the dance. First drive to their house, and get the address of Mrs. Edmundson's new apartment from

Emily's father, and then drive to Lynnwood and collect Emily."

Matthew was not wearing a tuxedo, just a summer jacket, but it didn't seem like the right moment to give his mother a lesson in men's fashions.

"Absolutely not the way to do it!" Matt's father shouted. "Matt will stay right here and wait for Emily to telephone him."

Matt stuck an arm between them all and fished around on the kitchen counter for the first available set of car keys.

"I don't believe in waiting," Matt's grandfather said, leaning down to yell in Matt's ear. "Nothing comes to him who waits except more time to wait in. Patience is *not* a virtue. Hit the road, Matthew."

Matt thought this would be an excellent time to get extra gas money from his grandfather, but he was wrong. One word about wanting cash and the entire focus of the O'Connor shouting changed. "Why haven't you saved more?" his grandfather demanded sternly. "What's the matter with you anyway, don't you have any backbone?"

"Yes," Matt said, "I just don't have any money."

"I think it's a disgrace that when your girlfriend needs you, all you can think about is money," his mother said, looking shocked.

"Mom, I'm going to get her right now, okay, it's just that a full tank of gas is a safer way to look for somebody."

His father said, "All right, Matthew.

Here's a ten. Now you phone us as soon as you find out anything, do *not* invite Emily to stay here, encourage her to make peace with her parents, and stay out of the whole thing."

"How can he stay out of it when he's going down to interfere?" Matt's mother asked. "You're spoiling him, always handing him money."

Matt said, "Anyway, her parents aren't nice. That's all there is to it. You guys are very sheltered here. You think other people are nice. Well, some of them aren't, and Mr. and Mrs. Edmundson are two of the least nice people I know."

"Nonsense," his grandfather said. "How could a fine girl like that come from two rotten people? Of course her parents are fine people. Just going through a rough moment, that's all."

Matt curled the ten in his hand, backed away from his clamoring family, and said, "No, they're crummy people. All Emily's moments with them are rough."

Anne gazed out the car window.

Mount Snow was green now in the middle of June: green in that thick shimmering emerald color, before the heat of summer has sunburned the leaves. The trees met in the middle of the road above Con's car, and they whipped through a tunnel of branches and leaves. Rushing River ran fast, tumbling over rocks and through ravines, and Con drove close to the edge of the road, while Anne stared down into the rocks and looked for deer.

The sun was lowering in the sky. Purple and gold and rose-red layers of clouds drifted and shifted. The mountain leaped up out of the hills and towered above them, blocking the sun completely, so that the road was suddenly dark and cold, and Anne shivered.

Con said, "You feel okay?"

"I'm fine. Just shivered because the sun went behind the mountain."

Con drove a little faster. She had a sense that Con was driving away from something instead of toward the dance.

They pulled in the gate at Rushing River Inn. Split rail fences edged the lane like dark brown embroidery, and blue iris bloomed in clumps. Rushing River Inn was a vast white clapboard resort with towers, circular glass porches, and roses climbing the walls. Con drove around back where the parking lots were hidden by rows of thick hemlock hedges. The flower gardens for which the Inn was famous were in splendid bloom, and Anne gasped and smiled when she saw them. The rear of the Inn had been modernized, with glass walls replacing the old wrap-around porches. There was a breathtaking view of Mount Snow. From the outside the glass reflected the mountain many times and the viewer seemed to be encircled with its majesty.

It was hot, and Con glanced at the immense outdoor swimming pool that lay below the terraces. Off bounds for the dance. Con was sorry. He would much rather go swimming than dancing.

He took Anne's arm and thought things were going rather well.

Then Molly got out of the car opposite his.

Anne knew instantly that it was Molly Con had been seeing while she was off having his baby. She knew by the smirk on Molly's face and the involuntary tightening of his grip on her arm; she knew because she could actually feel his pulse race, and see him lick his lips.

I still care, she thought.

And instead of wanting to weep because of it, she wanted to shout with joy.

I care! I care! she wanted to yell. I didn't die inside! I didn't curl up and go away! I'm still here, and I still care, and I can still love!

Con pretended not to have seen Molly.

Molly, wearing a remarkably short, aggressively purple dress, simply stood there watching the couple. Con was stiff as a board, turning neither to his left nor his right, but trying to move blindly ahead to a safety zone in the Inn.

Anne stopped walking. "Why, hello, Molly," she said graciously. "I haven't seen you in months. How are you?" She had never seen a more horrible dress. The fabric was cheap and clingy, and the color was not Molly's. Actually, it probably wasn't anybody's color, but definitely not Molly's. And anyone wider than a pencil would look heavy in it.

Oooh, goodie, thought Anne gleefully. I can still be catty and everything! And here I thought I was going to be a shriveled-up, depressed old hag for ever and ever.

Con examined the motionless ski lift hanging over the grassy green cut on the mountainside.

Molly said, "Oh, *I'm* fine, Anne. But how are *you*?"

If he actually loves Molly, Anne Stephens thought, he has no taste, and I despise him. Anne made an instant, and possibly very stupid, decision. "I'm excellent, thank you. That's a very interesting dress you have on, Molly. Where did you manage to find it?" Anne began walking again, and Con fell in step with her.

He was looking at her with a mixture of nervousness and breathlessness that could only mean one thing: he was ready to confess his sins to her.

Happiness left as quickly as it had come. No, Con. No, no, no, no, no, don't tell me anything! Let's pretend Molly is just some dumb girl in a dumber dress. Don't tell me you went out with her, and definitely don't tell me you did anything more than that.

Anne said, "Oooh, look, there's Kip and Mike! And there's Beth Rose just getting here with Gary! Oh, I just can't wait to see everybody again. Con, you were absolutely right, absolutely, this was the right thing, we're going to have a great evening."

Con blinked.

Gary yelled, "Hey, Winters!"

Con saluted him.

Anne said, "Doesn't Beth Rose look lovely?"

Con rarely noticed Beth Rose, and he found her hard to notice now. He wanted to stand up on Mount Snow and try to figure this all out from a mile away. Where it was safe. Anne dragged him to the door where she hugged Beth Rose, who hugged her back. Con wanted to look over his shoulder and see if Molly was walking right behind them. But then if she was, it was really the last thing he wanted to know anyway, so he stared straight ahead and tried to think of something complimentary to say to Beth Rose.

Gary, who hadn't seen Anne since she left town to live with Beth Rose's Aunt Madge, surprised them all by giving Anne a hug and a kiss and a grin. "Anne," he said, "you look radiant enough to light candles."

"She what?" repeated Con. "What did you say?"

"That was on the cover of some four-inch-thick paperback romance Beth Rose was reading. I memorized it for a suitable occasion. It was pretty good, wasn't it? Did you like it, Anne? Want to hear it again?"

They all laughed. Con laughed extra loud, to drown out Molly's distinctive footsteps which he could now identify.

"The point is," said Beth Rose, "you're supposed to say it to *me*."

"Oh, shucks!" said Gary. "Blew it again.

Oh, well." He offered his right arm to his date, and his left arm to Anne, and walked into the ballroom with two girls. Con leaped after them, in case Molly tried to take his empty arm herself. "You don't have to walk that close, Con," said Beth Rose over her shoulder. "You don't need to protect my ankles from enemies."

"Sorry," mumbled Con, and he fell back.

Gary said something, and both Anne and Beth Rose giggled and gave him half a hug: a right-handed hug from Anne and a left-handed hug from Beth.

Gary always made the girls laugh. Con didn't know how Gary did it. He could make Molly laugh, but he had the feeling that Molly had planned to laugh anyhow; it wasn't him doing it. As for Anne, he had made her laugh maybe twice in the last six months. He tried to forget that he had not visited her many more times than that either.

We'll stick to Gary and Beth Rose like SuperGlue, he decided. In case Molly decides to have a showdown. He could smell Molly's perfume and hear her dress swishing faintly and the violent tap of her sharp high heels.

Anne said, "Here's your VCR chance, Con."

The very first question his eyes fell on said, "Whose middle name is Elmer?"

It was Molly's middle name. So much for winning the VCR. If Con filled in that blank it would prove he had gotten to know Molly. "Let's go out on the verandah and watch the sunset," Con suggested. He could see Mike Robinson out there, and Mike was always good for sports stories. Crowds were safe.

"Watch the sunset?" Gary repeated. "Boy, you and I have got our romantic lines down now, Con. You should have seen me calling for Beth Rose tonight. I was amazing. She wants romance and did I ever hand it to her. Especially the way I got grease all over her hair from the hinges of the door and had to cut away one of her curls. See the bald spot there? That is a romantically derived bald spot Beth Rose has." Con led the way, and the four of them emerged on the terrace next to Kip and Mike Robinson.

"There is not a bald spot!" Beth Rose cried.

Gary nodded solemnly. "Your mother and I didn't tell you because we were afraid you wouldn't come to the dance. But it's pretty bad. Keep your head turned away from the sun so it won't shine."

Mike and Kip were laughing.

Beth Rose said, "Anne, is there a bald spot?"

Anne did a long and serious search of the thick curls. "Beth Rose," she said, "I want you to stay very, very calm."

Beth Rose closed her eyes. She said, "Gary, if there is a bald spot, I am hiring Kip's four brothers to do away with you."

Kip said, giggling, "They have been complaining that their allowances are awfully low. I think you could get them cheap, Beth Rose."

Anne was truly happy for the first time in months. She was with friends, and she was laughing, and the sun was warm. It was not, after all, the last dance. It was the first, and it would be beautiful. "Beth Rose," she told her friend, "your hair is so thick that mice could camp out and be safe. If you have a bald spot, it is the width of pine needle."

Beth Rose muttered, "You had to mention mice. I hate mice." She ran her hands through her hair searching for mice, until they all laughed and began telling her the mice were hiding out a little to the left, and down — yes — there they were! Quick, grab them!

And Molly watched, and heard, and hated.

Chapter 3

Emily's feet were narrow and already tan from the first weekends at the beach. Her beach sandals had two wide straps, but the dancing sandals she was wearing this Saturday night had one thin silver strap. Her tan lines were like pale shadows of the silver strap. She was wearing pink polish on her toes, darker than the pink on her fingernails, and now she had grass stains on her sandals.

If I run much more, she thought, I'll tear the straps. These shoes aren't strong. She had bought the shoes very inexpensively, thinking of them as shoes for a single night. Now she wondered if these were going to be her only shoes for a long time to come.

She was shaking all over.

They screamed at me, she thought. They felt like killing me. How can I live with either one of them? What am I going to do now?

She came out through a backyard, crossed another set of gardens, and emerged on Maplewood Lane. Going through people's yards, she was still pretty close to her own house. By car, however, this would take a half mile of maneuvering. It would never occur to her parents to look for her on Maplewood.

Fighting tears, she thought it would never occur to her parents to look for her at all. They didn't really want her. She stood next to a lilac bush, its blooms spent, its thicket-like growth protecting her from half the street. She thought, That scene in my bedroom — it worked out the way they wanted it to! Now they can blame *me* instead of each other. Now it's *my* fault that I don't have a parent or a home. After all, I'm the one who ran off instead of being reasonable and choosing one of them.

She stared at the houses on Maplewood. Colonial in style, they had all been built about twenty years before, and now the trees and shrubs were thick and full. There were no sidewalks, because nobody expected to walk anywhere. She felt very obvious and very stupid, strolling along Maplewood in her silver sandals. And now that I'm here, Emily thought, what do I do?

Someday I will live in a real city. Chicago or New York. And when I walk, I will walk with a million other walkers, and I will not feel dumb because sidewalks will be my life. I will blend in with crowds, not hunch around pretending to be a maple tree.

Her dress was pastel green and rather long, only four or five inches above her ankles. It was dotted with silver knots and a silver rope was loosely tied a little below her waist. She didn't normally care for pastels, because to Emily they looked faded-pale rather than on-purpose-pale, and she felt the dull colors faded her, too. But Matt had gone with her to buy the dress, and he loved the tiny silver knots all over the fabric and didn't appear to notice the dull green beneath them. She bought the dress for him.

She walked to the end of Maplewood, forgetting there was no outlet. At the turn-around, there was nothing to do but walk in a circle around the circle and head toward the other end of Maplewood.

Who on Maplewood did she know well enough to ask if she could use their phone and call Matt to come get her?

I could just go up to a stranger's house, she thought, telling herself to be brave and poised. Tell them my predicament. Ask to use the phone. But it was a toll call. And she had not stopped for her purse. There'd be so many explanations. And how many people, after all, did Emily want to tell this to? "Pardon me, may I use your phone, my parents threw me out, and I need a ride to a dance." It sounded at best as if Emily was not playing with a full deck.

Somebody peered at her from a side window.

How stupid she must look! A summer dancing dress, silver slippers, no purse, no companion, no destination. Everybody on

Maplewood would know everybody else. They would know she wasn't a burglar; not the type. But they would wonder what a high school girl was doing wandering up and down a dead-end street. A dead-end person, no doubt?

All the old familiar feelings of worthlessness swept back over Emily Edmundson. Back before Matt: back when feeling faceless and personality-free were everyday feelings for her. It was remarkable what confidence could do for you. She got the same grades, she spoke in the same voice, she had the same hair; but the girl she had been six months ago was a zero. Matt gave her confidence, shoring her up like dikes around Holland. Only the week before, Emily had thought that if anything happened between her and Matt, she would still be the new Emily: the confident strong Emily.

But now with her home vanished like dishwater down the drain — without even a purse full of identification to prove who she was, and what she did — Emily felt worthless.

She could not seem to get enough air into her lungs.

The only word that seemed to move around in her head was *Matt, Matt*, and it spun like clothes in the dryer of her mind, flipping, rotating, dashing itself against the spinning metal sides of her skull, until she had a terrible headache.

Two houses from the end of Maplewood, she stopped walking. If she came out on

North Street, she would be walking on the street her mother would take driving to Lynnwood. Could she bear seeing her mother? Emily's mother had not been kidding when she said come now, or don't come. *Don't come?* Could any mother really mean that? Yes, Emily Edmundson thought, mine meant it.

Emily wanted to be at the dance, where the kids she knew were laughing and being silly and hugging hello and kissing good-bye. She wanted to be with Matt, whose family style was loud constant talk and advice and half crazy companionship of all ages.

Someone came out of the house next to her and said, "Is it — Emily Edmundson? Emily? Are you all right?"

The girls giggled on the terrace and the boys talked sports. Mike and Con stood as close together as dates, and Kip and Anne exchanged glances and decided not to comment on how eagerly, how quickly, their boys moved into a safety zone of other boys. They studied the questionnaires, laughing. Kip started to tell them that she was the one born on an ocean liner, but decided not to. She wanted them to ask her! And then she would tell them the long crazy ridiculous story, with all the details her mother always put in. She knew the story by heart.

Anne said, "There's nothing here about the L word."

Beth Rose laughed. "That's because not a single boy in all Westerly High has ever used the L word."

Kip said, "We should give away VCRs. That's our whole problem. We aren't offering a big enough prize! If we said to our dates, use the L word and you get a VCR, then we'd have a chance!"

They managed to laugh at everything they said, an impenetrable trio. They did not know that it made the boys nervous, the way they became a solid unit, and they did not know that Molly was aching to be a fourth in their group. They would never have asked Molly to be with them. Anne because of her new knowledge; Beth Rose because she had seen Molly at her worst many times; and Kip because she had always despised Molly.

Molly didn't buy candy bars when the school band was raising money for new uniforms. Molly wouldn't take an hour to sell school pins when the basketball team was raising money for summer basketball camp scholarships. Molly wouldn't sign the petition to get the student parking lot resurfaced. She wouldn't even raise her hand to vote during student government meetings because she skipped them and went shopping instead.

Neither Kip nor Beth Rose knew that Con had spent many an evening with Molly, because Con at least had enough brain to sneak through that relationship, and Molly at least had enough brain not to demand more from

Con. So the only person who knew, incredibly, was the last person Con wanted to have know: Anne, herself.

Behind the girls, Molly stood burning.

She had never really had a female friend. She had never really been able to stand in a huddle like that and giggle with girls. They're just jealous of me because I always have boys, she thought. They make a wall of their pretty expensive dresses to keep me out because they're jealous of me.

Molly decided to start the problems between Anne and Con by seeing to it that Anne was a nuisance to Con. When Anne set her purse down on a chair, Molly waited a few minutes until everybody was distracted and then she simply took the purse and moved it across the ballroom and slid another girl's lacy white sweater over it. Anne was the kind of girl who traveled with everything she owned: from little Kleenex packs to extra pens; from two lipstick shades to an out-of-date school ID. Anne's purse was something she turned to constantly the way Molly herself turned to a boy: oh, dear me, Molly would cry, I forgot to bring any money! Oh, Jimmy, can you buy me a soda? And Jimmy always would. Or Roddy, or Paul, or Jared, or whoever Molly was seeing at the time. Anne had never seen anybody except Con; she knew nothing. She was a fool.

Molly slid near the group again. Any time now Anne would have to have her purse for something, and it would be gone, and she would make Con search for it, and Con hated things like that. While Con poked hopelessly, trying to locate it, going back to the car for it, hearing Anne whine about it, she, Molly, would look at Con in sympathy.

And he would look back, and wish he was with her instead of Anne.

From the large assortment of cars in the O'Connor driveway and yard, Matt chose the old station wagon. It went through gas like fire through a forest, but it had a great radio, and it was the only car with air-conditioning. He put on his seat belt, turned the radio up nice and loud, and set off. One good thing about old station wagons: they were built for power. Touch that accelerator, and you're in the next state. Emily liked the wagon because of the radio and because she was always getting exhausted on one of Matt's drives (he liked to say they were going for a "little drive" and come back four hours later) and she could sleep in the back. He loved driving a car with her asleep. It made him feel trusted.

Matt took the turnpike to Emily's, which he didn't usually do: too many state police around. Plus it was boring. Straight roads, nothing happening. Matt liked narrow curving roads, on cliff edges, with steep inclines, because Emily always screamed, "Matt! Don't drive off the edge!" and then

Matt could always answer, "Oh, M&M, you spoil all the fun. I was really looking forward to an air drive."

He decided he would just cruise slowly past the Edmundson home, first, see if any bodies were in the yard, if moving vans were pulling away, that kind of thing.

He had forgotten to put snacks in the car after all. Well, he had the extra ten from his father; he would stop off with M&M at the Dairy Queen and — oh, no! he'd forgotten — they were actually on their way to a dance. He looked nervously down to see if he'd dressed properly, and he had, so that was all right. He glanced in the mirror to see if he'd run a brush through his straight dark hair, and he had, so that was all right, too.

He decided not to take exit 67, which would take him through four traffic lights on the way to her house, but exit 66, so that he could cut through the industrial park and on up to her house the other way.

Matt swung left, then right, and thought about Emily living with them. He really could not imagine such a thing. The whole idea of a girl in his house — other than his mother — was something he could not even get a grip on. On the other hand — Emily living with her mother was impossible, because Mrs. Edmundson didn't even like Emily. Matt always felt that Mrs. Edmundson had had someone else in mind entirely when she gave birth to that baby girl and felt cheated that the girl was Emily.

Matt didn't feel cheated.

He adored Emily.

He thought once Mr. Edmundson calmed down, Emily should live with him. Emily's dad was an okay person as long as Emily's mother wasn't around. He could be funny and affectionate. It was just that the last several months had been such hell for them that the funniness and love were submerged in the separation fights.

Matt thought he would convince Emily to go back to her father's place after the dance, and he was pretty sure he could talk Mr. Edmundson into this, too.

Now the problem was to locate her.

Matt turned down North Street. Only a few blocks to go.

It was Christopher Vann.

Few people had made bigger fools of themselves than Christopher had at last autumn's big dance when he went with Molly. He'd gotten so drunk he got into a fight with the band and had to be forcibly removed by the police. Emily and Matt had gotten to the dance very late and missed the entire scene, but of course they had heard every detail over and over from Kip and Mike, Beth Rose and Gary. Everybody thought it served Molly right, but not many people stopped to wonder about Chrstopher.

Christopher had been a shining star when he graduated and went on to an Ivy League school, but something happened between

Westerly and college. Nobody really knew what, because Christopher confided in nobody and went out with girls who wouldn't care what his problems might be as long as he paid for the evening and the evening was fun.

Emily barely knew him: he was two years older than she, and when he was a junior, she was a freshman and definitely in her prime wallflower years. When she was in ninth grade, had she spoken aloud even once to a boy? Ninth grade had been a little like having her jaw wired: when she saw boys, Emily's mouth clamped shut and neither words nor smiles came out.

So turning to see who was speaking to her, she was amazed to see Christopher at all and terribly pleased that he knew her name and had recognized her. Christopher had lost that extra weight he'd been carrying the fall before and was looking very tan and fit again. "Why, Christopher," she said, "you look great! How are you? I'm so glad to see you."

"What are you doing wandering around Maplewood?" Christopher asked, laughing a little. He had a sophisticated smile — not at all like Matt's goofy grin.

"Just taking a walk," she said. She could not decide what to tell Christopher, if anything. "You're so tan for mid-June, Christopher! What are you doing these days?" she managed to say.

"I'm the lifeguard at the pool at Rushing

River Inn. It's a great job. I just sit there and soak up the sun. Every now and then I teach a little swimming to some kids. Nothing ever happens. I listen to a lot of radio." Emily did not know that her breathless tension looked to Christopher like a girl panting to be in his arms. She did not understand the grin that was sliding over his lips and the thoughts that he was having.

"And next fall?" said Emily.

"Next fall, I'm going to Central State," he said. Emily was glad that somebody's life was working out after all. It did not occur to her that Christopher might be bitter about going to an ordinary school or about having lost a year.

His smile was so smooth. It reassured her. Maplewood Lane was a road for happy families: you could tell by the shady trees and the neat trim around the white houses and the wonderful smell of steak being barbecued a few houses away. Emily didn't stop to think that her own street looked and smelled exactly the same.

Maplewood Lane seemed to Emily a sign that all would be well before long. The sun had not yet set, the air was warm, her parents would calm down, and Matt would show up.

Resting on these hopes, Emily said, "Actually, I'm halfway running away from home."

Emily tended to believe that other people were trustworthy. She tended to think that a nice smile meant a nice person, and that someone who had problems of his own would understand and care about hers. She said, "Oh, Christopher, it's my parents. I love my father, but he's been so awful lately because he's so mad at my mother, and now she's moving out, which is a blessing, but she says I have to live with her or she'll never speak to me again, and my father said if I even go with her for a minute I can't live with him either, and I . . . I just ran off." At the last minute she did not confide that her mother and father both had been ready to smack her. The vision came back, horrifying her all over again, and she thought, Matt, oh, Matt, come for me! The sick feeling hit her stomach again, and Emily put a hand over her mouth, feeling nauseated.

"Great dress to run in," Christopher observed, taking a fold of the material between his fingers. "I love these little silver knots!" He released the skirt, with its excess fabric, and ran his fingers very lightly over the knots of silver thread. He followed the seam of the dress up the sides and over to the silver heart necklace with its short silver chain. "You planning to camp out here on Maplewood in this dress?"

Emily stepped back. She could not deal with this on top of all her other problems. She wanted to step farther back, but it seemed rude.

Christopher's smile stayed just the same, as if he were a photograph and not a person.

"And practical running shoes, too, Emily. I admire your choice."

Imagine being nervous of somebody I know perfectly well when we're standing in the front yard on Maplewood Lane, and ten other houses are watching us. I just don't have enough experience, she thought. "I'm on my way to a dance," she explained, forgetting that she did not know Christopher perfectly well — she did not know him at all.

Christopher tilted his head. "Without a man in your life? Allow me."

Emily struggled to paste a smile on her face to show him it was nice of him to be gallant. "Well, my boyfriend was coming for me, but my mother hung up on him, and if he does drive down here, he won't know where to find me, and I'm not really sure what to do." She took a breath before asking if she could make a toll call on his phone, and Christopher said, "So where's the dance? At the high school again?" Christopher shook his head slightly. "I was a little out of it that time, but as I recall the theme was pumpkins. I laughed so hard."

Emily said uncomfortably, "Actually the dance is at Rushing River Inn."

"No kidding?" Christopher took her arm and guided her toward his front door.

"If I could use your phone and call the O'Connors," Emily said hesitantly, "then I could probably straighten this out."

"Nah, I'll just take you there. He'll show

up. Don't worry. Just let me get my license and my car keys. You think I'm dressed up enough for a dance?"

Christopher — asking if he was dressed up enough? Although he certainly did look good in a shirt and jeans, most of the boys would wear a jacket and tie. But he'll only be dropping me off, she thought, so what difference does it make? She said, "Christopher, if I could just use your phone? And if you don't mind, the bathroom, too — I — um — it's been — "

But Christopher did not head for the door to his house. He opened the car door instead. It was a beautiful scarlet sports car and even as he led her to it he smiled at the car, adoring it, and himself in it. Emily wanted to rip her arm free and race across the grass and —

What is the matter with me? Emily thought. Am I such a jerk that the only solution I have to anything is racing around backyards? I cannot spend my whole life coping by running away!

Her stomach hurt so much now she felt as if they should go to the clinic, not the dance.

"I love to crash parties," Christopher said, with the same smooth smile. "You'll be my ticket, Emily." And he linked his arm in hers, securely, like a chain.

It was not that Anne needed anything, it was just the female habit of checking to be sure her purse was where she had left it.

"What's the matter? Con asked, watching her."

"My purse. It's gone."

"Got to be right there," Con said.

"It isn't. Con, I know I set it on this chair."

"You must not have," Con said tiredly. "Because the chair is empty."

"Which purse was it?" Beth Rose asked. "That big white straw one?"

"No. The big pink leather bag." Anne kept turning, as if the purse must be lying at an angle to her vision, and if she just found the right place to stand, she would spot it. Molly hid a grin.

"What did you bring it for anyway?" Con asked irritably. "You never need any of that stuff you're always hauling around."

Molly loved how everybody reacted on cue. Even Gary, who usually leaped to help any damsel in distress, didn't leap this time. Beth Rose, if she carried a purse at all, carried tiny cloth ones on long shoulder straps so that the purse dangled, hardly noticed. Tonight Beth Rose had a tiny clutch bag in silver fabric with sparkles. Molly saw how Gary looked with satisfaction at his girlfriend, who didn't lug suitcases around and then lose them and embarrass him.

Beth Rose said, "Well, maybe you left it in the car, Anne. Con, why don't you go look in the car for her?"

Con glared at Beth Rose and then controlled himself and said, "I don't think she —

"I didn't leave it in the car. I distinctly remember putting it on the chair," Anne said. "Somebody must have taken it."

Con heaved a sigh. An enormous sigh, out of all proportion to the problem. A sigh that implied that Peace in the Middle East rested upon Con's shoulders. Now Beth Rose glared at Con, and Gary muttered to Beth Rose to take it easy, and Mike looked at the sunset and whispered to himself alone, "Girls."

Molly was happy.

The pool was shaped in an L, with the smaller end very shallow for kids to wade in safely. Along one side were beds of flowers, mostly scarlet geraniums, with a very narrow strip of cement between them and the pool to prevent leaves and mulch from actually getting in the water.

It was hot outdoors, but nothing really had started indoors. Nobody felt like dancing, mostly because nobody else had started dancing, and nobody felt like eating, because they weren't hungry yet, and half the girls were on diets anyway. They held their questionnaires and didn't ask anybody anything, because it just seemed dumb, and faked. So they wandered out of doors and made a few remarks about how lovely Mount Snow was, and then they wandered down near the pool and gazed at the water and wished they were in bathing suits instead of dancing clothes, so they could go swimming and cool off.

Mr. Martin, who was an assistant manager of the resort, was a big bearded man with an enormous belly. He was wearing a very nice suit with a bright paisley vest and a solid color tie that picked up the gaudiest color in the paisley vest. Indoors, with the air-conditioning, he was very comfortable. Outdoors, in the heat, he began perspiring by the bucketful and became crabby.

"Lee!" he yelled at one of his waiters.

Lee was seventeen, and had graduated that very Saturday afternoon from Lynnwood High. All sensible Lynnwood High grads were off partying in Lynnwood this very minute, but Lee unfortunately had to work. Lee was not in a good mood, and all these happy Westerly kids made him very, very irritable. He didn't think much of Westerly anyhow, especially since Westerly had beaten Lynnwood in every single sport Lee was in this year: wrestling, track, and tennis. It was Lee's belief that Westerly boys paid off the referees. He had just learned, moreover, that his roommate for freshman year at Central State was going to be a Westerly person. He kept looking at this bunch, at their old "Last Dance" and wondering which of these dorks was going to live with him. He had read over their little quiz and seriously considered adding the question, "Which one of you will be Lee Hamilton's roommate, and are you worthy of this honor?" but he knew Mr. Martin would kill him, which did not seem an auspicious way to begin his summer.

"Yes, Mr. Martin?" he said.

"Lee, go down to the swimming pool and

tell those kids the pool is off limits for them tonight. They reserved the ballroom, the screened verandah, and the terrace and that's that. The swimming pool is for overnight guests and anyway, we don't have a lifeguard on tonight, so nobody can be down there. Keep those teenagers up here where they belong. That's your job, Lee; don't screw up."

Lee rather liked the idea of yelling at Westerly kids. He stomped down the gravel path and immediately recognized Gary Anthony, who had trounced him in every wrestling match they had ever had. Great, Lee thought. "Okay, everybody," he said loudly, trying to sound like Authority, "the pool is off limits, and I've got to ask you to stay up on the terrace if you want to be outdoors."

The "everybody" he addressed did not even look his way.

Lee raised his voice and repeated the order.

The only thing that happened was that a girl in a very short purple dress asked him if he had been born on an ocean liner. Lee stared at her. She grinned right back, very flirty, and said, "Come on, now, cooperate, I want to win the VCR, don't you? I don't even recognize you! You must not be a junior, huh? Where's your quiz? Have you gotten any answers yet?"

Lee said, "I'm a waiter."

The girl laughed. "No, really, do you have any answers?"

Lee said, "Just that you're not supposed

to be down at the pool. You want to help me round up all your friends and herd them toward the terrace?"

The girl laughed again. She said, "No, really, tell me."

Lee hoped for the sake of Westerly High that this girl did not represent the typical I.Q. He walked around her and aimed for Gary. He figured if he could get Gary headed for the terrace, maybe he could get the rest of them.

Molly was enraged.

Her expertise was boys. She rarely winked at one who didn't wink right back, and a smile from Molly always meant a smile from the boy. Who was this kid, anyway? Well, whoever he was, she didn't like him. He was cute, too. Not very tall, which was too bad, because Molly preferred height in a boy, but very muscular. Like a wrestler. Of all the boys here, he was the one she would most like to see in bathing trunks.

She thought briefly of shoving him in the pool. Being soaked would take away a little of his snobbery and reveal a little of his body, too. He'd have to peel off that jacket then, wouldn't he?

Beth Rose and Gary and Anne and Con were tiptoeing along the narrow stone strip between the geraniums and the deep end of the pool. Kip and Mike Robinson had taken off their shoes and were sitting on the edge, dangling their feet in the water. Two couples were dancing on the cement, to the music from a radio one of them had brought. It was like a separate dance; the popular kids were having their own down there while the ordinary kids were up in the ballroom.

Molly watched Con. Anne was in front of him, and his hand went to her waist, to guide or to caress, Molly could not tell.

The purse thing had worked nicely. It took them fifteen minutes to find it, and Con didn't believe Anne when she claimed she hadn't put it there. Con was now making an effort to be nice to Anne: an effort which, if Molly knew Con, he could not keep up very long. Con liked things to go smoothly or not at all.

I know how to handle Con! Molly thought. I deserve Con. He ought to be mine. It's my waist his hand should be on!

Anne turned slightly just as she got to the end of the geraniums and faced Con. She pursed her lips as if to kiss him, but Con didn't lean forward to kiss Anne. He concentrated — or pretended to — on his balance.

Balance? Molly Nelmes thought. Balance. Or lack of it?

For the third time the unknown wrestler/waiter ordered everybody away from the pool.

Molly slid between the two dancing couples and up behind Gary and Beth Rose, Kip and Mike, and Anne and Con.

Chapter 4

Matt slowed down slightly. He didn't come this way often and he was afraid of missing the turn to Emily's house. His heart was beating harder, and he was laughing at himself. "What are you, a knight in shining armor?" he teased himself. "You think M&M's going to be standing in the driveway in her green dress with the silver knots, her arms held out, so you can sweep her away to safety?"

It was exactly what he was thinking.

He loved the whole idea.

He and Emily had saved a life six months before and the afterglow of doing that had stayed with them both a long time. Now the idea of protecting Emily, of being the one she waited for to give her a better life, was another glow. Matt was grinning, alone in the car, happy about the whole idea.

He adored Emily.

Plus, he was slightly superstitious. They had met by such an accident — both of them showing up at a student convention neither of them much wanted to attend — both sitting down with a sigh where there happened to be empty seats. Then finding each other there, and never even knowing what the convention was about afterward: just talking, talking, talking, as if there would never be enough time to share all the thoughts they wanted to share. Matt truly loved Emily.

He slowed down, squinting into the glare of the sunset, trying to read the street signs.

Out of Maplewood shot a bright red Corvette. A beautiful, very expensive car. Normally Matt checked out cars very carefully, because he loved them, and his happiest days were when his latest car magazines arrived in the mail. But this time his eye happened to fall upon the driver and the passenger.

At the same time the driver accelerated right into Matt's path, he leaned over to kiss his girl.

And the girl was Emily.

The dark was soft and comfortable. Anne felt safe. If only the whole evening could stay like this: dusk, where you could still see each other, but not clearly. She didn't want to go back to the strong harsh lights of the terrace, and she didn't want to take her questionnaire and be forced to walk from person to person, grinning like an idiot and demanding to know who had been born on an ocean liner.

The whole thing with the purse upset her.

Con's mouth had been tense with annoyance, but Anne couldn't rest until she had that pocketbook back, and she couldn't help it. She just hated it that life handed out these nothing little predicaments that proceeded to ruin the important things.

And so when Con's hand went around her waist, she loved it: she wanted it to happen again. That touch was a whisper of what had once been between them. And what could surely be again! The reality of the last several months faded. The softness of dusk made her romantic again.

The pressure on her waist increased. She followed the pressure as if this were a dance and Con wanted to move in a different direction across the floor. But she was still on the pool edge, and she said nervously, "Con?"

His hand gave her a tremendous shove.

"Con!" Anne screamed. There was nothing to clutch but air. Anne catapulted right into the water.

There wasn't much time to think, but if she was going to get soaked, so was Con! Oh, that traitor, that manipulator! Letting her think in the dusk that they loved each other after all! That skunk! He couldn't even come right out and say he didn't want to be there with her! The coward! He had to knock her purposely into the pool! What had she done to deserve this? One misplaced purse? Well, she had had a baby! Did he think the last nine months had been exactly a bed of roses for her? How dare he?—How —

Anne's fingers closed around his jacket.

She yanked him right along with her. She heard him yelp, like a puppy, and then she hit the water. My hair! she thought, underwater. My dress! My makeup!

Oh, she would kill him! Here he was in the water right next to her. Well, she would just drown him, since the location was so convenient. "Con," she sputtered, coming up first, "Con Winters, you're dead."

Lee Hamilton could not believe the girl was pulling him into the water with her. He tried to hang onto something, but there weren't any handy rails or posts, and he went right over. What a way to celebrate his high school graduation: all these Westerly High kids would laugh at him, and then he'd lose his job, and then his parents would kill him, and. . . .

Lee took a deep breath full of chlorined water, choked, surfaced, spit water like a whale spouting — and the girl proceeded to try to drown him. Lee rarely opened his eyes underwater because the chlorine gave him eyeburn, but this was obviously not the time to be blind, so he glared at her underwater and tried to shake his fist. Underwater it was slow motion. Her yellow hair swirled around like a mermaid's. Even underwater with a crazy person trying to drown him, he was struck with how beautiful the girl was.

They came up together and he bellowed, "You tried to drown me!" and she yelled "I thought you were somebody else!" and Lee screamed, "What's the matter with you, are you insane?" and the kids who were safe and dry up on the pool edge laughed like hyenas, which he might have expected anybody from Westerly to do, and she said, "Con pushed me in!"

"I did not," Con said, "I wasn't even next to you. You *fell* in."

Oh, the treachery of him! Anne tread water. The boy she had pulled in with her swam away from her. Anne, furious, humiliated, and soaked, swam out to the middle of the pool and kept right on yelling at Con. "You cockroach!" she screamed. "All I've been through because of you, and the first thing you do is push me in the water! Conrad Winters, I hate you! You are the scum on the pond!"

"There's no scum in there," Molly said gleefully. "In fact, you're turning blue from the chlorine, Anne. Your hair is a weird color."

Lee swam to the edge of the pool to climb out. Gary, grinning, knelt in a puddle of water at the pool rim and was reaching out a hand to help Lee out. Lee took it gratefully. Anything was better than being in the same body of water with this crazy beauty queen. But Lee was to learn that this was not a reliable crowd. Gary, being Gary, didn't pull Lee out, but let himself be pulled in instead.

Gary's full weight landed right on Lee and they both sank like stones in the water.

Gary came up laughing, which was his style.

Lee came up homicidal, which was a new one for him.

The rest of the girls, screaming and giggling, ran back toward the bushes so they wouldn't get shoved or yanked in.

Beth Rose hated wet hair. When she got married, she would never wash her hair when her husband was home, because she didn't want anybody to see what she looked like with wet hair. So far she had managed never to go swimming with Gary, just sit on the sand. She was certainly not going to start swimming with him at this dance either. Poor Anne, soaked like that. Of course, Anne still looked perfect. Beth Rose backed into the flower garden, where lovely teak benches sat in convenient corners. Not only would she be safely dry here, she would be forgotten. There were times when wallflower status was best of all.

"I hate you, Con," Anne said in a grim, teeth-gritting whisper.

Con was trying not to laugh. "Now, Anne, let's not get excited. You just lost your balance. Swim over, I'll give you a hand up." He knelt by the pool.

"Better not," advised all the boys. "She's gonna drown you for sure, Con."

They laughed hysterically. The kids indoors, hearing gales of laughter from down at the pool, came pouring out of the ball-room and running down the path to join the fun.

Mr. Martin ran after them, his stomach jiggling like a summer Santa, shouting, "No, no, no, no, no!" Dozens of teenagers converged around the pool, and two boys immediately kicked their shoes off, preparing to jump feet first on top of Lee and Gary. The three in the pool were treading water. Gary was laughing, Lee was trying to laugh, and Anne thought she might never laugh again.

"I hope you realize I've just lost my job," Lee said wearily.

"I'm sorry," Anne said. "I was trying to be sure that Con lost his life." She still thought it would be nice if something long-term and painful happened to Con at that moment.

"She isn't usually like this," Gary told Lee. Gary was having a fine time. He had been hot anyway, and now he was nice and cool. Not so good for his shoes, but there was a price to pleasure. "Anne's usually a very nice person, Lee," Gary explained. "I think she probably doesn't care to go swimming in a dress, that's all."

Several of the newest arrivals suggested the possibility of simply removing dresses all around.

Molly said, "Gary, where did you buy those red pants from? The whole pool is turning red around you."

Gary floated, lifting each leg like scissors, sending little pink waves out over the pool.

Mr. Martin barely managed to stay upright as he catapulted down the gravel path, stomach first. It really was time to go on a diet. Next week. Right now he needed strength to cope with the kids. The resort should have a policy of refusing admission to anyone older than fourteen and younger than twenty. Mr. Martin yelled, "Lee! You started this! You are finished! You are dead!"

Lee rolled his eyes to the black night, and then let himself sink like a stone, and hung under the surface of the water blowing bubbles.

Kip giggled. She and Mike used to do stuff like that, all the time. Now she practically needed a form in triplicate to get him to phone.

Mr. Martin's voice was going after only a few sentences. Hoarsely, he bellowed, "The rest of you kids go back to the ballroom or this dance is over!"

Nothing happened.

Kip sighed. She could organize the whole thing and get this straightened out in a heartbeat. She could make Anne feel better, save Lee's job, calm Mr. Martin down, get the quiz off the ground, and herd all these teenagers back to the ballroom. And if she did . . . Mike Robinson would be angry with her . . . tell her he was tired of the way she had to run everything . . . and did she remember they were here as "just friends"?

Kip stared at Mike, trying to decide what he was to her. Was it worth it to submerge her real personality — worth it to pretend she wasn't good at being in charge? If she did hang onto Mike, all she would have was a boy who wanted her to be different than she really was.

I am special, Kip thought. And I want a boy who agrees with that. I want to be like Beth Rose and have Gary. I want a boy who will stick with me through thick and thin. I want everybody to see me and think of two: like Pammy and Jimmy or Sue and Jason.

Well, if I find that special boy, it won't be here. Everybody at this dance arrived in pairs.

Kip shrugged.

She turned to the knot of kids, knowing even as she did so that this was the end of her relationship with Mike Robinson. "Up the hill," she said firmly, escorting Pammy and Jason to the steps first and nudging Sue and Jimmy after them. "Your first clue," she called out, "is that the person who was born on the ocean liner is one of this bunch! That narrows it down. Now move along. The band is doing requests. Sue, go be a pain and ask them for something they won't know. George, you and Caitlin make sure everybody has a pencil. There's a box of them by the front door, but nobody remembered to take one. Come on, George, you love doing stuff like this. Now, Caitlin, grab Kimberly and Pete over there as you're going. Dance those two on up to the dance floor."

It always amazed Mike that anybody obeyed Kip; he thought she sounded like a first grade teacher making her kiddies line up to use the water fountain. But it worked for Kip, and people liked her in spite of the fact that she was yelling at them. He, Mike, did not like it at all. Mike pulled back into the shadows before Kip gave him an assignment, too.

He really would rather be playing baseball.

The thing with baseball was, you knew the skills you had to have. And you were with boys, and you understood them. Not that Kip was a mystery: in fact, she made everything all too plain most of the time. It was just that boys were easier. Mike was terribly grateful to be a boy.

And not terribly interested in having a girl.

Kip had made too much of it, that was the thing. He wanted a girlfriend some of the time, but Kip wanted a boyfriend all of the time.

Mike truly didn't remember the evenings he'd hardly been able to tear himself away from the Elliott household. He didn't remember lying in bed wanting Kip's voice so much he had to call her three times in one evening.

The thing was over, and that was all.

Mike had no memories to call upon: he had not stored up a single moment.

Gary called out to the manager, "Hey,

listen, it's my fault, and I'm really sorry, you know? See, Lee here and I used to wrestle on different teams, and I got all excited when he was standing near the edge of the water and I just shoved him in." Gary vaulted out of the pool without assistance. All the girls paused to enjoy this athletic maneuver.

He would have pulled Anne up after him, but she swam away. So instead he gave Lee a hand. This time he didn't let go, but pulled Lee out and pretended to dust him off. A reddish puddle began to form around Gary's ankles.

"Are you bleeding?" Beth Rose asked nervously from behind a tall stand of flowers.

"Yes," said Gary, "it's fatal. You *dye* of it," he added, and they all groaned at this pitiful attempt at a pun.

Anne's rage had worn off. Now she was just soaked and shivering. She refused to be near Con, so she was trying to pull herself out of the pool on the opposite side. There was no ladder there, and she was exhausted and could not quite haul herself out of the water.

Con walked toward her. Molly got in his way and said, "Clumsy little thing, isn't she? In *everything*." Molly rolled her eyes suggestively.

Con walked around her, but even that tiny moment had been too long. Lee had already circled the pool and yanked Anne up.

Soaked; her yellow hair plastered to her, and her pale pink dress another skin, she was absolutely stunning. Con wanted to shout, I'm sorry, I'm sorry, oh, Anne, let's —

But he hated scenes.

Anne wiped the water from her face as if she had been crying, and Lee realized, surprised, that indeed she was crying, and crying hard.

"I'm sorry," she whispered. "I'm really sorry."

Lee was shaken. "It's all right," he said, patting her stupidly. Where did you pat a person to calm her down? "Don't worry about it."

The wet beauty queen looked at him sadly, and Lee was shaken again. This was a girl with a lot more to worry about than ruined dancing slippers.

Now only the original handful of kids were still by the pool. Kip was herding the rest in the sliding glass doors to the ballroom. They could hear her shouting out, "All right now, pairs break up! No going back to the person you came with until you have the answers to five questions. That's right, five! Any five answers and you can find your date again!"

They obeyed her like army privates a sergeant. The low buzz of chatter turned to a roar of questions and answers.

The last thing they could hear clearly was somebody saying, "Look at question number eleven. Somebody here hates chocolate. Now that's weird. Who would even admit it?"

The glass doors slid shut, containing the noise and the dance.

Anne blended her tears into the pool water with the back of her hand.

Mr. Martin said, "Oh, well, just one of those things, I suppose. You three wet ones, go into the cabana and dry off. Okay, Lee, you still have a job."

Anne stood very stiffly. Come tell me you love me, Con, she thought. If there was ever a moment to use the L word, it's now.

Kip bounded down the path, having got the dance squared away, ready to take on the task of drying Gary, Lee, and Anne. All the rest but Mike turned to thank her. "I like you, kid," Mr. Martin said. "You want a job for the summer? What's your name? You've got style. I admire style. I pay for style."

Nobody had ever said of Kip that she had style. What a wonderful word! Not that she was good at pushing people around; not that she was good at organizing; not that she had to be in charge, or die.

She had *style*.

She turned to see what Mike thought, but Michael Robinson was standing behind Con Winters, his head bent next to Molly Nelmes, and they were talking to each other. Kip looked to see if at least Beth Rose had heard, but Beth Rose was giggling over Gary's bleeding pants. Anne and Con were like statues frozen in a game of tag.

Had nobody heard that lovely compliment?

Was there no one to share it with?

What good was a terrific compliment if you had to repeat it yourself in order to be appreciated?

Kip's chin came up high enough to make swallowing hard. Slipping into the cabana, Kip took a huge white towel from the pile behind the desk and brought it out to Anne, who was trembling in the evening breeze. The boy she had yanked into the pool thanked her for Anne's sake. "Shall I get a towel for you, too?" Kip asked.

The boy grinned. Another nice grin. Kind of like Mike's. Probably hid another selfish personality, too. The boy said, "No, thanks, I saw where you got it. I'll get my own, no need to put you out."

Gary said, "I came in red pants, and I'm going to leave in pink. Look at this, all my dye is on the pavement. Hey, Kip, throw me a towel, too! I'm going to turn it red for them." He walked wide-legged toward Anne and Lee, dripping pinkly all the way.

Gary glanced back over his shoulder. Beth Rose had not followed. He could see her hovering by the bushes. In the dark he could not tell what she was thinking, or what she wanted. But then Beth Rose rarely said what she wanted anyway. You had to guess, which Gary found difficult. He would in some ways have preferred Kip, who all but made you out a list.

Con sighed and tagged after Gary. He was

going to get blamed for the water thing, too. Okay, he *was* to blame for the baby. But he hadn't pushed Anne! He would never do a thing like that! She was just clumsy and awkward. Although she was invariably graceful. For a moment Con wondered . . . and remembered that Anne had called him names in front of all their classmates. *Cockroach!*

I stuck by you, he thought, conveniently forgetting that he had stuck much closer to Molly.

He took a deep breath. Okay, he would be mature about all this. It was what his parents told him to do all day long. Furious, humiliated, and resentful — but trying to look casual — Con decided to hug Anne.

Anne walked away from him.

Con grit his teeth and walked after her.

Anne walked farther away.

Con didn't move again. Let her sob into her towel! He could not stand any more of this female-ness!

He stood, wondering how to extricate himself from this mess, when his friend Gary rescued him once again. Gary said, "Hey, Con, dance with Beth Rose for me till we get dried off, okay? And get our quizzes all filled out. I want that VCR!"

Con saluted, grateful for the assignment. He didn't have to follow Anne, and he didn't have to worry about Molly making a move either. He could just be Beth Rose's escort. "Come on, Beth," he said. He thought that if anybody in the ballroom teased him for being called a cockroach by his girlfriend he would break their bones. And enjoy doing it.

The resort's cabana included not just hot showers and dressing rooms, but a couple of clothes dryers and a nice selection of hair dryers. Kip convinced the boys and Anne to wrap up in the huge white towels while she tossed their clothes in a dryer. She put Anne's at low heat in one dryer so wrinkles wouldn't set in the fragile fabric, and the boys' suits in the second dryer. Lee and Gary paraded in front of their small but appreciative audience with the towels around their waists, chests thrown forward, arguing about whose muscles and whose tan were superior.

"Gary wins," Lee said mournfully. "And to think I've graduated and will never have another chance."

"There's all summer," Gary pointed out. "I'm in a fighting mood. Water does that to me. While everybody else dances, you and I can wrestle."

"No," Anne said, "don't wrestle. Let's all calm down." She didn't feel well; her insides felt all mushy. She looked at these boys and tried to imagine herself saying chummily, "See, I just had a baby, and I'm not all the way on my feet, yet." Oh, yes, a perfect opening line for everyday chat at a dance.

She wanted Con here wrapping this hot towel around her, drying her hair, telling her not to worry, telling her he was sorry. This was the dance that she had dreaded, and he had insisted she *had* to go to, then he started the evening off by shoving her into the water?

Lee, knowing nothing of Anne's background, kept on talking about wrestling. He seemed to think Anne would love to watch a good wrestling match here in the cabana — give her a little something to enjoy while she dried her hair.

Should Kip tell Lee that Anne was weepy because her darling Con, the father of her baby, had once again proved a rather weak limb to go out on?

But holding the dryer to Anne's hair, running her fingers through the golden strands to separate them and fluff them, Kip realized how attractive Lee was. Maybe *this* is the boy for Anne, Kip Elliott thought. Maybe it's time Anne admits that Con is handsome but worthless. This Lee fellow — he's not as handsome, and he's probably not worth *much* — but he's definitely worth *more*. Maybe I should bring them together, the way I bring all other things together.

Kip said, "Here, Lee, you do Anne's hair while I check on how the clothes are drying."

She shoved the blow dryer in his hand and wrapped his fingers around it.

Lee was very startled. He had no idea how to be a hairdresser, and it wasn't exactly a career he yearned for either. He held the dryer as if it was burning his palm, and hoped that Anne's hair would dry very, very fast. "Did you two come alone?" he asked the girls. "Or are you both with Gary?"

Gary laughed a little.

"*All* the girls are with me," Gary said. "I have quite a fan club in Westerly. They see me dripping pink dye on the floor and they go berserk."

"No, really," Lee said. "I want to know."

"Anne's date washed out," Kip said. "Melted in the heat, faded in the sun."

"My makeup is ruined," Anne said.

"No, you look perfect," Lee told her.

And of course she did, Kip thought. That was the thing with Anne; it was very deceiving. When a person always looked perfect, you figured her life went in perfect lines, too. Now Kip without her makeup was hardly even visible. Kip didn't even like her four little brothers, let alone the rest of the world, to see her before she had her mascara on.

That was the trouble with my relationship with Mike, Kip thought. He adored my family: all the noise and all the brothers and all the places we were always going. He liked the crowd of it, because he could bring along his brothers and sisters, and we could be this gang of happy people.

But he didn't actually like me.

Gary said, "Okay, dumbo, here's how it works."

For one horrible moment, both Anne and Kip looked up, thinking Gary was talking to them and about to explain to these female dumbos how life worked. But of course Gary was just telling Lee that Anne was with Con and Kip was with Mike. The girls laughed. "What?" Gary said, not hearing anything funny.

"You," Anne said, poking him gently. "You're always funny. And what's more, you do have a fan club. I'm in it."

"And I'll organize it," Kip said.

They all laughed.

The cabana was very warm, and very humid. Gary watched his less than red pants through the glass of the dryer. Kip's hair turned to brown frizz and Anne's hair, of course, lay smooth and silken on her shoulders. Her dress came out fine, but her slippers were ruined for good.

"Oh, well," Anne said, "I always dance barefoot anyway."

There was a funny little silence.

Kip thought, And who's going to dance with you tonight, Anne?

Anne thought, And who's going to dance with me tonight?

Gary thought, I wouldn't be in Con's shoes for anything. Afraid Anne would start to cry, Gary said, "Well, Anne, my fan, may I have the pleasure of escorting you back to the dance? I am damp but honest."

Anne did start to cry, but she smiled through her tears, and Gary pretended he didn't see them. Anne bowed to him, and he bowed back, offering his arm. Together they walked out of the cabana.

The pink and white striped awning over the door fluttered in an evening breeze.

Lee figured he couldn't go wrong by imitating Gary. He turned to the pretty girl with the fluffy brown hair and the perky laugh and said, "Well, Kip, lady with style, may I have the pleasure of escorting *you* back to your dance?"

Kip giggled, pleased beyond measure that after all there *was* somebody who had heard Mr. Martin's compliment.

"You could even stay to waltz with me," she said, taking his hand as if she actually meant to waltz.

Lee panicked. He could not dance at all, let alone waltz. He had no sense of rhythm. Half the kids you saw dancing fast dances looked fantastic, and the other half looked ridiculous, as if they had all come down with a twitching disease. Lee knew he was of the twitching disease sort. But waltz? A dance with steps? Horrible thought.

"I've never danced in my life," Lee said.

"In your *life*?" Kip repeated.

"In fact, I'm not sure I've ever *seen* anybody waltz," Lee admitted.

"You haven't lived," Kip told him, and she proceeded to teach Lee to waltz. "All you have to do is count to three," she said, "and move your feet in a little triangle. You sort of chase your own feet. Like this."

Lee had heard that there was a follower and a leader in every dance couple, but since he had never tried it, he had no idea what it really meant. Kip simply guided his feet by holding his back and his hand.

He actually felt graceful! Kip swirled in the tiny space; her dress swirling after them, its folds of wild color catching between Lee's legs as he moved, and then sliding back against Kip. How feminine she felt!

He got the hang of it far quicker than he had ever thought, and he didn't feel like a jerk at all. He bent his head, and his face brushed her hair slightly, and a whiff of her perfume came to him, and Lee lost the beat.

"You're a natural, Lee. Maybe tonight you and I will waltz again." She sighed and let go of him and stood in front of the mirror running her fingers through her hair. She sighed a second time, as if the hair were hopeless. Lee said, "It looks really nice."

She laughed. "Yeah, well, at least it's dark out."

"Guess I'd better wait on a few tables, huh?" he said. "While you waltz away the evening."

They walked out of the cabana.

The stars and a half moon were out.

Lee stuck his elbow toward the girl, and to his delight, she tucked her arm in it.

Pretty nice.

I am Cinderella, Kip thought, her hand tucked in Lee's arm. I go back to the ballroom and I'm alone. Mike will have found a group, and be asking quiz questions. He'll shy away from me. If I decide to catch up to Mike now, I'll have to follow him like a puppy. Lee was mumbling something about waltzes. She managed a smile. Just call me Kip, the girl who can always smile, she thought sadly. "I don't think this band is going to do any waltzes, Lee."

"Well, you claim to be an organizer. Organize it. I'm counting on you now, Kip. Don't let me down."

They smiled at each other, but Kip thought, *Don't let you down?* Don't make me laugh. All boys let *me* down.

If I organized a waltz, you wouldn't be there.

And Mike would vanish quicker than a tan in winter.

Chapter 5

Matt O'Connor was burning with fury and confusion.

Who was this boy he had never heard of, never seen, and yet was a close enough friend for Matt's girl to go to him instead of waiting for Matt?

Emily's family caved in, her parents tried to strike her, her home vanished — and she had *somebody else* to go with?

Go where?

He was the one with tickets to the Last Dance.

He was the one who had picked out that green dress.

Look at that car, just look at it! That was the car of a show-off with money. A handsome guy, too. Kept turning to smile at Emily. He liked Emily. Why would he like Emily unless he had a lot of encouragement?

Matt could not think straight.

He was sure he was Emily's first and only boyfriend.

He was sure the only other boys in her life just happened to sit near her in school.

But he was wrong.

Here was someone his own age that she turned to without waiting for him to come.

You knew I would come! he thought. You knew I would never abandon you! But half an hour later you're in somebody else's car, getting comfort from somebody else. And he's doing a great job, it looks like. You don't miss me. Look at you, all snuggly in that bucket seat.

Jealousy, an emotion Matt O'Connor had never experienced and never known he was capable of, made him so angry he wanted to drive right into the rear end of that sports car. Smash through the bumper, smash through the chrome. He followed them. They were much too absorbed in each other to look behind even once.

"Only one person at the Last Dance hates chocolate," Pammy read out loud. "Okay!" she yelled at the top of her lungs. "Admit it, whoever you are! Who here hates chocolate? Don't keep us in suspense."

Her date Jimmy said, "Ssssshh, Pammy. If they yell out the answer, then everybody knows. The point is to win the VCR and we don't want everybody to know."

"But this is important," Pammy said. "I mean, chocolate is my life. Next to you, of course, Jimmy. I need to know what weirdo in this room doesn't love chocolate."

Pammy and Jimmy were the classic couple: they lived in the same condo, and had been going to school on the same bus since kindergarten, and dating since seventh grade. Pammy was petite and sharp angled and quick, darting here and there. Jimmy was pudgy and slow and funny and always seemed a little confused. They adored each other.

The dance began in earnest. The band was playing a tortured version of a current hit, and the kids had divided into roughly equal thirds: one-third were holding their hands over their ears criticizing the band, one-third were happily dancing and bumping into everybody else, and the last third were filling out questionnaires and screaming over the music. Beth Rose said, "Well, I'd like to know what person here has shaken hands with the President of the United States."

She had acquired a second escort. Con on her left had been joined by Mike on her right. It was so odd to be with two boys, neither one of whom had brought her. She didn't feel popular, though. She felt used.

Jimmy stared at the questions and in his thick way could not imagine how to find out anything. His lips moved as he worked his way down the page only to discover that nothing about him, Jimmy, had been written up as a question. He and Pammy were not off to a running start.

I want Gary, Beth Rose thought. Admit it, girl, you adore him, you've got it bad.

But she had come down with the disease of love, while Gary was simply a carrier. She thought that probably Gary would never catch love himself!

"Let's find Kip," Jimmy said. "She's so organized, she's probably finished her quiz by now. We can just copy her answers."

Mike Robinson groaned. "You can't find Kip," he said. "She's off organizing the clothes and the hair drying."

"Oh, poor Kip," Pammy said, sympathetically. "She always ends up with the work instead of the fun."

"Don't feel sorry for Kip," Mike said. "Feel sorry for me. Kip loves doing that stuff. I'm the one who's stranded." He tapped his chest with his fist, trying to look forlorn. Beth Rose did not fall for it.

"You're not stranded," Molly Nelmes said, snuggling up to Mike. "I'm here."

Beth Rose hoped that Mike would say "Yuck!" and brush her away like spaghetti sauce on a white sweater. But no, Mike seemed pleased and when Molly took his hand, he let her, and even if Beth Rose was a judge, applied a little pressure of his own when Molly squeezed his hand.

Molly didn't want Mike; she wanted Con; but most of all, she wanted a man, and Mike would do for the moment. Mike cooperated fully, and Beth Rose began to dislike him. Why did Kip always get the short end of the stick? If anybody ever *earned* a boyfriend, Kip did.

Con didn't take his eyes off Molly. Molly's body fit into the curves of Mike's slouch, and Molly entwined her arms with Mike's, and penciled an answer in Mike's quiz instead of her own. Mike and Molly began dancing at the same time they wrote on the quiz. It was very sensuous: not really dancing, just winding around each other — testing — seeing what might be there.

And Con was jealous.

Oh, it was enough to make anybody lose faith in romance.

Beth Rose had gotten close to Anne this year because it was Beth's Aunt Madge who gave Anne a home.

The night Con proposed, he and Anne had been in Anne's kitchen, and her family was out, and it was late in the evening, and Con kept trying to find something interesting to watch on the tiny countertop black-and-white television. Anne kept trying to get him to admit that they really did have a serious problem. But in the end he had asked her to marry him — changing the channels all the way through the cable dials four times before he found enough courage. Then he hung onto the dial and stood on the far side of the room and looked at the wallpaper beyond the TV.

Anne told Beth Rose, "He forced himself to ask me. That was the horrible part. We loved each other, but asking me to marry him was a horror show worse than anything we saw in an R-rated movie."

"Would you have said yes if Con sounded like he really wanted to get married?" Beth Rose had asked.

"No. Oh, no," Anne said. "We have another whole year of high school yet, and then college. Do you know what the divorce statistics are for two seventeen-year-olds getting married? Whew! No, Beth, but I wanted him to *want* to!"

"Some people rise to the occasion," Beth Rose told Anne firmly. "Maybe he would have been a fine husband and a fine father."

Beth Rose was now standing in a ballroom with Con, and Con couldn't even bring himself to hold a hair dryer to Anne's hair, let alone earn a living and diaper a baby. He was, in fact, wishing he could be dancing in Mike Robinson's place with Molly.

And yet Beth Rose liked Con. He was weak minded, but she thought he might outgrow it. She did not believe, however, that he would outgrow it any time soon.

She couldn't bring herself to get mad at him. "I have one answer for you, Con." She tapped her quiz. "It's me."

He had forgotten her, and when she spoke he seemed to pause and ask himself who this red-headed girl was. "Let's see," he said, trying to work up some interest in what Beth Rose could have done. "Are you the one who's been trying to finish knitting the same sweater for six years?"

Beth Rose managed to laugh. What poor girl had written *that* as the only interesting thing about her? "I'm the one with the collection of toy fire engines."

Con was astonished. "You? But — that's such a boy kind of thing to do!"

Beth Rose laughed. "The first nine were originally my grandfather's collection. I inherited it, and I just kept adding to it. I have some with real engines, some that wind up and some that are just desk decorations. One of them has carved wooden horses to pull it and another one has six metal horses pulling the water pumper. I have almost forty fire engines now. The Smithsonian wrote to me last year and asked if they could buy one of them because there isn't another like it. It was a childhood toy of President Theodore Roosevelt."

Con was much more amazed that it was Beth Rose with the collection than that the collection existed.

"You and Anne will have to come see it one day," Beth Rose offered. There was much more to tell about the collection. She waited for Con to ask her what answer she gave the Smithsonian.

But he was looking at Molly.

And Molly knew it.

Pammy and Caitlin and their dates converged on Con and Beth Rose. "We heard you muttering over here," Caitlin said. "Don't deny it. You have an answer. Now what is it? Admit it."

Beth Rose teased them. "I'll give you one chance. If you ask me the wrong question, you're out of luck and you'll never get the VCR."

Caitlin wailed, "Oh, no! Okay, let me guess. Are you the person here who's been trying to finish knitting the same sweater for six years?"

Con laughed out loud. "That's what I thought, Caitlin. It's a good guess but it's way off the mark."

A good guess? Beth Rose Chapman thought.

Tears rose hot and painful in her eyes.

She knew suddenly that they would all assume that.

Anne Stephens clung to Gary's arm. He made an excellent escort. He had a basic kindness that never deserted him. And yet, Anne would never have dated Gary. He was too removed. "Drifty" was Anne's word. Gary never settled on anything — from an athletic team to a girl.

And I still think Con will settle? Anne asked herself. Con, who shoves me into the water on our first appearance in public together.

The Last Dance.

I guess it is.

Gary said, "You look lovely, Anne. I kind of wish you had been willing to come back up here soaked. The way that dress was then, you'd have been the hit of the dance."

She thanked him, wondering what kind of

explanation Con would give her. If he had come up with one.

She thought of their daughter: their thirty-two-day-old daughter.

Gary opened the huge glass door into the ballroom. It was quite dark, so that kids working on their quizzes were hunched in little groups under the few wall lights, and the rest danced lazily to a slow number. Nobody looked at Anne. She had not realized she had been holding her breath until she let it all out in a long slow controlled puff.

Thirty-two-days-old, Anne thought. What does she weigh? Does she have any hair yet? Does she smile into her mother's face? But I'm her mother! It's my face she should smile up at!

Gary propelled Anne straight across the room, past preppy Caitlin and her date, and Pammy and Jimmy burbling around like toddlers in a bunch of grown-ups.

Beth Rose was standing stiffly near Con. Molly and Mike were attached like sticky tape on Con's other side.

Anne held tightly onto Gary's arm.

Kip had an iron will.

Or so Mike liked to tell her.

"You're not even human, let alone female," he liked to tease her. "You're made of iron."

Kip got to the door first, opened it herself, and held it for Lee. He said thank you, but Kip did not hear it. Across the room her eyes found Mike. He was wrapped around Molly like gift ribbon.

She thought of the evening ahead, without a date. That was a scene she had played enough. She had few choices here. She could beg Mike to dance with her. She could get into her Organizer, but Nevertheless-a-Wallflower-Nobody-Wants role. Or she could just throw in the towel and go home.

"You stopped walking," Lee said.

"I don't have anywhere to walk to," Kip said.

Ahead of them, Gary took Anne to Con like a package he couldn't deliver fast enough.

Lee said, "Which one is your boyfriend?"

"I don't think I have a boyfriend. If you mean the male person I used to date who told me he would come to this dance only if I remembered that we are friends, just friends, nothing but friends, that male person is the one who is currently mating with the girl in the purple dress."

Lee howled with laughter. "They're not quite mating, yet," he said.

"Give them thirty seconds," Kip said.

Lee said, "Give them a lifetime. I don't think you need that guy any more than you need a hole in the head."

"Yes, but what am I going to do now? This is a dance. I don't have a partner."

"What do you mean by that?" Lee demanded. "Didn't you just teach me how to waltz? Did you think it was a robot down there counting to three?"

Kip said, "Yes, but you have to work, Lee." This one is another Gary, she thought, taking on charity cases by the hour. Well, I'm not going to be anybody's charity case. She said, "Thanks, Lee. You're very nice and I'm grateful. But I'll have a good time anyhow. Don't worry about me."

She kissed him and he kissed her back.

Kip had no way of knowing that Lee had never had a girlfriend, never kissed a girl on the lips, never had a date. He had always been too shy, too unsure of himself, too awkward to ask a girl to go out with him.

She could not know that Lee found girls like Anne — beautiful though she might be —annoying. He disliked anybody who had to be led around, escorted, given aid like a wounded animal in the road. He felt overwhelmed by bouncy bubbly creatures like Pammy who attached themselves to boys for each waking minute. He was puzzled by girls like Beth Rose who expected you to mind read instead of just saying out loud what she wanted.

Lee had decided to stay out of the whole boy/girl scene. Who needed all those complications? If a date introduced anything into your life at all, Lee thought, it was just plain old trouble.

Kip's kiss had been on the cheek.

She smiled and walked away.

The white lacy blouse was cut very low in the back. Her shoulder blades made two faint shadows on her pale skin. The bright skirt swayed. It had a satiny lining, and even though the band was playing as loudly as any band could, Lee fancied he could hear the swishing as well as see it. He watched Kip walk right up to the group that included her boyfriend — or, as she put it, the male person with whom she had come — and manage to laugh and joke with her friends, pull out a questionnaire, and exchange a silly hug with another boy over an answer.

For the first time in his seventeen years Lee considered the possibility that maybe a girl could be worth complications.

Emily's family rule was seatbelts first. She had started life in a big white plastic baby seat, and moved on to the seatbelt of the middle backseat of the car, and only as a kindergartner graduate to the front seat and the big seatbelt. To Emily it was unthinkable to sit in a car without fastening a seatbelt.

Christopher's car had bucket seats, and as her hands located the straps and began locking them in, he did the same — but he fastened his seatbelt into her buckle and took her buckle out of her hand and pushed the metal tip into his fastener. They were overlapped now. Not tangled, but difficult to undo because they were angled backward.

Christopher said, "Same kids going to be at this dance who were at the last one?"

"Pretty much." She was very uneasy. I

shouldn't be in this car, she thought. She said, "My boyfriend Matt — I think I'd better call him. You know, why don't you . . . just . . . why don't you just take me back home, Christopher? Just go around the block."

Christopher looked amused. "I'm your neighbor," he said. "What are you getting worked up about, Emily?"

She flushed. A boy who lived only a few blocks away from her was thoughtfully driving her to a dance. A resort where he worked every day, where all her friends would be.

Christopher smiled at her. "I can't drive you home, Emily. Your parents don't want you there. You and I will dance the night away instead."

It was important not to be rude. Smiling back, Emily said, "Actually I'll be with Matt all evening. I mean, it's nice of you to drive me over, but — I tell you what, Christopher, why don't we stop at this drug store, and I'll call Matt on the pay phone."

"You have a dime?" Christopher asked, still smiling. There was something wrong with the smile. It was too smooth.

"Uh. No. No, I don't. Could you lend me a dime?"

"No," Christopher said, still smiling, "I couldn't." He drove past the pay phone, and his right hand came down and stroked the seat belts, as if to check that Emily was securely fastened down. Matt did that all the time, and it made Emily feel so safe and special. But this was different. This was as if Emily were his prisoner, and he was checking the ropes.

Emily stared out the window. They passed a little group of shops, one of those patches of stores that crop up in suburban areas: shoe store, pharmacy, bank, Zip Mart, and law offices. The Zip Mart was open. It would always be open. She would be safe in there.

Safe? she thought. Safe?

Now Emily, aren't you getting a little dramatic? Nothing is happening.

Christopher said, "Got you all roped in, don't I?"

He patted the crossed seatbelts.

She tried to smile at him. After all, he was being extremely nice to her, going out of his way like this, ruining his Saturday evening. She must not be rude in return.

His same smooth smile came back. He seemed to have only the one smile: it didn't grow or shrink or change in quality: it was the smile of a store mannequin.

Emily wanted to rip open the car door and leap out onto the sidewalk and run, run, run.

I can't leap out of this car, she thought. I'll look so dumb! How will I ever face him again? What explanation will I give him when he stops the car and wants to know what I'm doing? Will I say, I don't like your smile, Christopher, so I decided to walk the eleven miles to Rushing River?

They came to a STOP sign and Christopher's smile turned to face her.

What an odd thought, Emily realized. She was thinking of the smile as something separate: as a thing. The thing looked at her.

For maybe half a block Christopher drove without once looking at the road: that smile fixed on Emily like a trap.

He's crazy, Emily thought.

Chapter 6

Con, too, had parents. Parents who had given him tremendous freedom very young, assuming he could handle it. Parents who had been very angry, disappointed, and heartsick to find the kind of freedom Con had chosen. Parents who said to him before the dance, "You haven't been in public with Anne since she left Westerly six months ago. You've got to help her and not let anybody say a word. If they do, flatten them. Put Anne first, do you hear?"

Gary transferred Anne to Con as if she were a package.

Con kissed the package lightly. "Are you all right?" he asked. Anne looked perfect to him, but then she always did. She had a smooth elegance that nothing, even unwed motherhood, had ruffled. He had made the mistake of saying that once to his own mother, who yelled at him until the house shook.

"Ruffled?" screamed his mother. "Ruffled,

Conrad, is a ridiculous word! The girl is terrified, do you understand that? *Terrified*! So visit her! Make her feel better!" But it terrified Con, too. And he had visited Molly instead, who made *him* feel better.

"Dry now, thanks." Anne managed a smile. She looked as if she belonged on the cover of *Seventeen*.

He wanted to run. "I'm sorry that happened. I didn't mean it to, really, Anne. I guess I must have knocked against you, but it wasn't on purpose, okay? I never would have done that." He had not been standing near Anne; it was not his fault she got wet; but this was the right thing — he had taken responsibility. Now they could get along. Con felt better.

Anne looked across the room at nothing in particular. She ran her hand over her glossy hair, as if checking to see if it really was dry. The chandelier over her head caught the golden highlights. Shadows fell beneath her eyes and changed her cheekbones. She was inexpressibly lovely.

"Con, you're very angry with me, or you wouldn't have shoved me in the pool. I wish we could talk it out, I wish you and I could resolve all this rage we're feeling, but I don't think it's possible after all."

Anne stared into space, seeing something he could not. Is she seeing the baby? he thought.

Con had never seen it . . . her. Con's parents had. His mother had wept.

Had Anne held the baby?

Con had never asked. He thought, I'm ready to talk. We've got to talk. I can handle it now.

But it was too late.

In her soft mellow voice Anne Stephens said, "Maybe you should just drive me home, Con. We'll stop pretending we can put it back together, and we'll go our separate ways."

"All right!" Pammy shouted. "Who here has skied in six countries, and why didn't you take me along?"

The whole dance broke up laughing.

Pammy yelled, "I am serious, guys. Somebody at Westerly High has skied in six countries. It says so right on this quiz. I demand to know why I was not aware of this, and why I was not offered a chance to go along."

Nobody admitted to being the person who had gone skiing in six countries. Nobody else knew who it was either. Gary said, "This VCR is going to be very, very hard to win if nobody admits doing anything."

"I can't even imagine what the six countries are!" Pammy went on. "The United States and Canada, okay, that's two. And I suppose this jet-setter has skied in Switzerland and Italy, that's four. But where else do they even have mountains?"

Beth Rose tried to see herself in a life where she not only went skiing, she flew to New Zealand or France to get there. Beth Rose had never even skied on Mount Snow. The thought of racing downhill made her ill.

Beth Rose had a feeling she was the boutique shopping, hot chocolate drinking variety of skier.

But who cared about quizzes and skis anyway? She wanted to dance. She wanted to be held by Gary, and feel his warmth, and hear his voice, and accept his kiss. She looked at Gary, hoping he would sense what she wanted. She hated begging for things. She felt about three years old, saying, Gary please can we dance, Gary, please can we do this, Gary, please can we do that?

But Gary was not tuned in. He was laughing at Pammy. "I personally went skiing in the Ural Mountains in Russia last year, and this year I plan to ski Japan."

Pammy pretended to beat upon Gary's chest with her fists. "You meanie," she said. "And I bet you're going to go and take Beth Rose, too, aren't you? When are you going to realize I'm your true love?"

"Aaaah, you just want a free flight to Japan," Gary said. "I'm onto your schemes, girl."

It was Gary they laughed with, Gary they flirted with — she, Beth Rose, was still the girl who probably couldn't even knit a sweater.

Beth Rose wanted to talk to a girlfriend. Anne and Emily would understand.

Very softly Gary said, "Bethie?"

He was behind her. He leaned over her shoulder, his slightly damp heavy cotton shirt pressing against her bare skin, and he whispered. She loved whispering. The privacy of it: knowing that Gary wanted to talk to her, and only her, and never mind Pammy and skiing abroad!

He almost never called her Bethie, either. She leaned back against him, overdosing on romance. Chandeliers sparkling, Anne and Con together again, Gary murmuring her name, love songs playing. . . .

"I'm already bored," Gary said. "You know what let's do? Let's walk up Two Cliffs Trail and see Mount Snow by night. Two Cliffs is my favorite picnic spot anyhow."

Beth Rose was crushed. She hated trails and outdoor things. She was always getting a blister or turning her ankle. And tonight she was wearing slippers, not sneakers. Plus, it was dark out! How did Gary expect to find his way through the woods at night? They were supposed to sit admiring a view? In the pitch dark? What if they missed the trail and fell off the cliff?

She wanted to dance!

She wanted to show off her dress, her style, and her figure. She wanted to lean on Gary and —

"Come on," Gary said. "Let's ditch all these kids. This whole quiz thing is getting to me. Pammy and her crowd are getting to me, and I don't want to get drawn into Con's problems either."

Startled, Beth Rose looked back at Con and Anne.

Oh, no, she groaned silently. A fight if I ever saw one.

Con and Anne were talking, but with their backs to each other. Anne was studying the wall, Con the floor. Anne had the posture of a damp dishrag and Con was as rigid as a telephone pole.

The Last Dance, Beth Rose thought ruefully. I've got to find out who named it. She's got second sight, whoever she is.

Lee swept.

Mopped.

Distributed potato chips and filled lemonade pitchers and added ice to the coolers.

And thought about girls.

He had not known how hard it could be to sweep, mop, and fill when you were thinking about girls.

Especially when the girl you were thinking about was getting pushed around by her so-called boyfriend.

And it was amazing how much work there was to be done out there in the ballroom where Kip was.

Women! Matt thought.

What am I following them for?

What do I care?

Let her do what she wants! Let her have eleven boyfriends! Let her dance with fifty-nine other boys. Let her —

The red Corvette ahead of him only half

stopped at the stop light before making a right turn on red. Arrest him, Matt thought grimly, there's never a cop around when you—

Emily stepped out of the car.

The car was still moving, and she simply opened her door and stepped out, gracefully not getting caught in the door as it swung back, not falling on the pavement as the car kept going, and not looking back at the car either.

The Corvette screeched to a full stop, and Matt, who had forgotten he was driving while he was staring at Emily's exit, nearly drove right through the sports car. The driver jumped out, equally furious at Emily and at Matt. "Hey! What's your problem, Emily?" the guy bellowed, and then immediately turned to scream at Matt, "You practically shoved into my rear end, buddy, watch where you're going."

Emily walked swiftly down the sidewalk without looking back.

Matt yelled, "I'll shove in your face, never mind your rear end!" He jumped out of his car and shouted, "Emily!"

Emily turned on the sidewalk, saw Matt in his old wagon about six inches away from Christopher in his shiny Corvette. How had this happened? Like someone watching a tennis match, Emily stared first at Matt and then at Christopher and back again. "Emily, don't do that," Matt said impatiently, "you look dorky. Come on, get in, what's happening?"

"Oh, Matt," Emily whispered, as she raced into the street to fling herself on top of him. The force of this banged Matt backward into the door handle.

Matt had never been hugged so hard. He thought she might crack his ribs but didn't say so. "What, were you kidnapping her or something?" he said to the handsome guy.

"Women," the guy muttered, who got into the red Corvette, stepped on the gas so hard the tires screamed on the pavement, and spun around the corner, going back the way he had come.

"Oh, Matt!" Emily cried, her face buried against him. "Matt, I've been so dumb. First I got in the car with this kid who offered me a ride — it's the boy Molly used to go with, Christopher Vann — and then I got all panic stricken. Over nothing, Matt! I'm so embarrassed. I don't know what scared me. I was trying to be polite, it's important to be polite, but I got more and more scared, and finally I just jumped out of the car. How did you find me? Were you following me? Oh, Matt, I adore you."

He stuffed Emily in the passenger side, hopped in the driver's seat and pulled over into the parking lot of a little doughnut shop.

Matt's family solved a great many problems with food. Matt felt that with a few jelly-filled doughnuts and orange juice to wash them down, he'd have it all under control. Then a nice kiss to finish off the snack and they'd be off for Rushing River, happy as could be.

But Emily's family, alone among all the families he knew, did not use food to solve difficulties. In fact, the Edmundsons rarely tried to solve difficulties at all. Emily didn't want a jelly-filled doughnut any more than she wanted Christopher Vann. She pushed it away, far enough that Matt was afraid it would fall behind the counter and nobody would get to eat it. That would never do. Matt rescued the doughnut and ate it himself. "Would you rather have a lemon-filled one?" he asked, trying to be sensitive.

"Matt!" Emily's whisper was a cry of pain. It frightened him, but he didn't know what to do about it. "Don't you understand?" she said desperately.

"No, I don't." This seemed to require an apology, so Matt apologized. "I'm sorry. You'll have to tell me, M&M."

"I was afraid of him."

"You said that. I just don't know what you were afraid of."

"But Matt, I don't know either! Maybe . . . maybe. . . ."

Matt squashed lemon filling all over his hand. "He didn't try . . ." Matt sputtered. "I'll kill him. I'll slice him into — "

"No, Matt, he didn't try a single thing. He didn't do a single thing. He didn't say a single thing. He was just *there* and *scary*."

Emily burst into tears.

The waitress turned from her other customers, coffee pot in one hand, and a frosted cruller in the other. "Everything's all right," Matt said to the waitress.

Emily cried harder. Matt patted her, but that was no more effective than a lemon-filled doughnut.

Matt considered his own family to be the most sensible people on earth. If only one of them were here right now, to say the right thing to Emily! But he was the only available O'Connor representative. He said slowly, "If your instinct said to be scared, I'm sure you were right to be scared."

He would never tell her he had suspected her of dating Christopher on the side. Some things were best never said aloud.

He wrapped the rest of the doughnut in its little square of waxed paper and convinced Emily to get back in the car with him. He thought briefly of driving the long distance back to his own house and having his mother take over on this one, but he decided the person Emily really needed was her very own mother. Surely a girl's mother would come through in a situation like this. Even Mrs. Edmundson would come through once Matt explained what had happened.

Matt went out the opposite entrance of the doughnut shop parking lot and drove the short distance back to the Edmundsons.

Molly loved this ballroom.

The chandeliers were breathtaking: seven of them altogether, with intricate crystal teardrops glistening like prisms in the sun. The floor was polished wood, the walls either glass — black now with the dark outdoors — or wallpapered in a pattern of pretend greenery: ferns and palms and ivies. But in several places, there was real greenery, identical to the paper, so that suddenly, there really was a fern frond in your face, and a big potted palm at your feet.

The band was at the center back, and a grand piano they weren't using was on the far side. Food was in another room, and kids drifted continuously from food to dance floor and back. As always, it was the girls who wanted to dance and the boys who wanted to eat.

But what Molly liked best of all was that the ballroom was shadowy.

Once, during a wild number that was all drum and screaming, they turned up the lights and added some flickering colors, and everybody loved that.

Now it was dark again, and Molly slid from fern to piano and listened.

"Come on, let's kiss and make up," Con said. "Let's dance, okay?"

Anne shook her head. Just once, just slightly.

Con's chin tipped up — just once, just slightly. He was getting mad. He said, "I'm sorry it happened. Let's not dwell on it."

"I have to know why you did it, Con."

"I *didn't* do it, Anne. I'm sick of this discussion. Let's dance, huh?"

"You did," she argued. "And I need to understand why. Do you hate me? Do you hate our baby? You haven't asked about her."

"Anne, she isn't ours any more. She got adopted. Let *them* worry about her."

Molly was tickled. She had taken quite a risk, shoving Anne into the water. If Con had realized she was doing it, she'd have dug her grave with him. But Anne didn't, and Con didn't, and nobody else did either.

Molly gave Con and Anne about another fifteen minutes to break up forever. Of course, he'd have to drive Anne home. Anne might be able to work him over going home. But Molly didn't think Anne would bother this time.

And then something happened to make Molly totally happy.

Kip — good old, organizing old, charitable old Kip — came across the room to rescue Anne. Well, Kip and Anne might not figure out what was going to happen next, but Molly sure knew, and she sure loved it. Con might hang in there with one girl he used to love, but Con would *never* stay when two girls were both trying to make him say he was sorry.

Lee Hamilton cleaned up a mess of spilled soda somebody had just reported over by the piano. He took a long time mopping. Some of the girls were really lovely, and he liked watching them dance.

Kip was standing with her so-called boyfriend. Why weren't they dancing? If he, Lee, were here with Kip, he would be dancing.

Her boyfriend said, "Listen, Kip. I'm not going to get involved. They want to run around the cliffs in the dark, that's their problem, not ours."

"Mike, you've got to stop them. Come on, you're a boy, make them stop."

Mike groaned and rolled his eyes. "Kip, nobody is going to *make* Con or Gary do anything, least of all me. You can make your little brothers obey you, and no doubt you can make your girlfriends obey you, and you can make your yearbook staff obey you. But you can't push Con and Gary around tonight, do you hear me? This is their dance, they bought tickets, and if they want to dance up on Two Cliffs with Anne and Beth Rose, so be it."

"But they could fall," Kip protested.

Mike said, "Kip, they don't want to die at seventeen. They don't want to get their bones broken and their lungs punctured. They'll be careful, okay? They'll watch what they're doing. So just leave it, okay?"

Kip glared at him. And then she whirled. If her boyfriend wouldn't stop Gary and Con, she would give it another try herself. Lee hadn't noticed the skirt before, but now he saw how full it was, and how it swished like a ballet dance when she spun around so angrily.

Mike caught Kip's arm and held it hard. Mike wasn't interested in dancing. He was just furious. "I am so sick of the way you interfere with everybody, Kip. It just so happens that I'd kind of like to walk up to Two Cliffs at night myself, and don't interfere with me, and don't come along. Got it?"

Kip flinched as if Mike had hit her. She actually turned her face away from those words and bit her lips. "Mike, please — "

Mike said, "Kip. Get lost."

He walked away.

Kip stood still.

Lee seriously considered taking his mop up on the cliff and giving Mike a little shove over the rockiest, highest part.

He might have, too, except that Mr. Martin appeared by his side. "Lee, we got more spilled food all over the verandah. Go sweep that up. Then we need more soda on the bar out on the terrace, and we're out of hot hors d'oeuvres at the snack bar there. Be sure to put out more chips while you're at it. Potato chips are cheap. Check the dip. Come on, Lee, move along."

Should he tell Mr. Martin what the boys were planning?

It didn't sound dangerous to Lee.

Besides, Lee wasn't at all sure that Two Cliffs was really the destination. Hadn't he dried Anne's hair himself? Hadn't he watched that beautiful redhead Beth Rose dance with his wrestling opponent Gary? Those were two gorgeous girls. If he, Lee, were wandering around in the dark with girls that lovely, it wouldn't be to see the profile of Two Cliffs in the dark.

As crowds do, this one shifted.

The quiz-oriented group around Pammy and Caitlin moved toward the piano and ferns that hid Molly. Gary, trying to convince Beth Rose to go with him on an All Night Hike, decided four might be fun and began looking for a couple with more get-up-and-go than Beth Rose. The dedicated dancers were really warmed up now and swinging all over the place. Sharp elbows and whirling skirts took up space the rest had to avoid.

Anne said, "Just take me home, okay?"

Con said, "Anne, I did not push you, okay?"

Gary said, "Just a walk, that's all, Beth Rose, and nobody's going to fall over the cliff edge, okay?"

Kip said loudly, "Maybe we should all get out our quizzes and work a little harder to find some of these answers."

Molly said, "Kip, nobody cares, okay?"

And Con said, "Hey, what are you up to, Gary? Did you say a walk up to Two Cliffs? That would be neat. In the dark? I love it! Let's go. Come on, Anne, let's go with them."

"Great," Anne said. "First you shove me in the pool, now you want to shove me off the cliff. It's called love."

Chapter 7

Kip hurt so much she wanted to double over and hold her side.

Nobody cares, Molly had said.

And nobody did.

Because nobody argued, nobody turned to comfort Kip, nobody put his arm around her.

Nobody even noticed.

She meant to find the bathroom — that ever-perfect place for a girl to run when she had problems, emotional or physical. A double hiding place — the room itself, and the cubicle if you really needed solitude.

But she turned down the wrong hall once outside the ballroom and when she flung open the door she thought would take her to the women's room, she found herself in a sort of kitchen. Nobody was cooking anything there; it seemed to be more of a storage area. Its stainless steel countertops gleamed, and its refrigerators were spotless. The tiles were tiny beige octagons, and the windows were high above the shelves.

And Lee Hamilton was pouring potato chips from enormous yellow cellophane bags into enormous wicker serving baskets.

He was glad to see her.

And Kip stayed for one reason only: there didn't seem to be anybody else at the Last Dance who was glad to see her.

Molly did not want Con hanging around Gary.

Gary had an amazing ability to calm people: Gary could hand out peace of mind the way a waiter could hand out pieces of chocolate cake. Somehow he would say the right thing to Anne, and Anne would laugh and the tension would lessen. Then Gary would say the right thing to Con, and Con would grin, and exchange a glance with Anne . . . and Con and Anne just might make up.

Well, Molly would not have that happen.

Molly would separate them somehow.

She listened to the crowd, and circled, and tried to come up with a solution.

Beth Rose said to Gary and Con, "But it's against the rules. We're not supposed to be anywhere but the ballroom, the terrace, and the screened verandah."

Gary grinned and chucked Beth Rose under the chin. "Yeah, but I'm bored with the ballroom, the terrace, and the screened verandah. I want to see the world, and I'm going to start with Two Cliffs at night."

"We don't have shoes for that kind of thing," Beth Rose said weakly.

Gary could not have been less interested in what sort of flimsy dance slippers the girls had on. He and Con just laughed and pressed through the dancers toward the glass doors and the mountain trails.

Oooh, good, Molly thought. Con's leaving without Anne!

Gary had a firm grip on Beth Rose, who would not, if Molly knew that wimpy girl, protest a second time. Con strode after Gary. Delight rose like carbonated bubbles inside Molly.

Con paused.

No, Molly thought, no, don't, Con, come on, don't.

Con Winters stretched out a hand Anne could not reach unless she took a step toward him. "Come on," he said pleadingly, as if he really wanted her. Con did not look at Gary, nor at the dancers, nor at Molly. He looked only at Anne, with little boys' eyes, wanting her company on his walk.

Molly grit her teeth. She had to stop this now, or they'd melt back into each other's arms.

Pammy unexpectedly said, "It's gotten chilly out. The wind is cool now. You need a jacket, Anne."

Good idea!

Molly slithered out of the crowd like a snake through rocks. She passed the ferns and the piano and found the chair where most of the girls had tossed their sweaters earlier when it was so hot they were gasping for

breath. Anne, whose mother and grandmother dressed her as if she were a tall
Barbie doll — eleven hundred matching outfits — didn't have just any old cotton sweater.
Oh, no. A beautiful shawl with dark wintry
colors, that nobody else would think of wearing in June, but that set off Anne's golden
hair perfectly, and turned her from a blonde
angel to a sultry princess.

Molly swept the shawl behind her back,
knotting it, and slid past the ferns again.
One potted fern — a great tall tropical thing
that reminded Molly of a hotel lobby in New
York City — sat in a tub of dark earth.
Molly tucked the shawl in back of the fern,
draped a few fronds over it, and the shawl
was invisible.

There.

Now Anne would whine that she couldn't
find her wrap. Con would be patient for — oh,
maybe a minute — and then Con would go
on without her and that would be that.

Lee perched on the stainless steel rim of
a vast center preparation table. He had very,
very long legs and the minute he sat down
he seemed slightly out of proportion. But Kip
wasn't sure. She kind of wanted to stand next
to him and see where his waist and each
knee and elbow folded; see if he was just
very long, or really out of whack.

Lee said, "I need your opinion."

Kip loved being asked for her opinion. And
this kid was serious, she could tell. A deep

wrinkle furrowed a brow that obviously had never wrinkled before. The wrinkle had a hard time staying there in such unfamiliar territory. Lee's face kept going back to a smooth cheery one and he had to struggle to force the frown to stay. She also had this truly weird desire to run her finger across the wrinkle. Especially in that little dip a little left of center. His forehead wrinkle was shaped exactly like a bracket you made to attach different paragraphs together: rounded at the ends, peaked in the middle.

Lee said, "See, this is unfamiliar territory to me."

Kip liked standing in front of him now. Their eyes were even. She had always thought that was the neatest thing about Anne and Con: their eyes were always even. It put them, literally, on the same wave length. Kip had always thought a boyfriend precisely her own height would be perfect. Well, she was wrong. Mike was her height and he was gone.

The L word.

He'd said it enough back in the winter.

Now he appeared to have forgotten even how to spell it, let alone use it.

"What territory?" Kip asked. She liked to know exactly what was happening; she could give him a better opinion if he gave her all the facts.

"Falling in love."

Kip tried looking at the boy from several angles to see if he was being a jerk, or pulling her leg, or entertaining himself at her expense or what. All she could see was that funny little frown. "Okay," she said cautiously. "Go on."

"What's it *feel* like?" Lee asked intensely, leaning way forward. He leaned almost into her face. If Kip had leaned forward the same number of inches, they would be kissing. She restrained herself, but it wasn't easy.

She said, even more cautiously, "Well, tell me how you feel, and I'll tell you what I think."

"I'm obsessed," Lee said. "I can't even sweep a floor without thinking about her."

Kip nodded, letting out a lungful of air in a very controlled fashion, as if she could control Mike that way, or The L Word, or at least herself. "Yup," she said, "that's part of it."

"You have fantasies that would make the girl abandon you before you've even met," Lee said.

"Oh, absolutely. Definitely. You're getting warm now."

"Warm!" Lee Hamilton said. "I'm burning up."

"I think you've got it," Kip said. "Sounds like love to me."

The big white station wagon made the familiar turn into Emily's own street. There was the red house on the corner, where even in the dark, the three boys were throwing a baseball. And then the two identical ranch houses. The tiny Cape Cod where Emily used to babysit. The empty lot. And then the next-door neighbors, where Mrs. James drove them all crazy practicing her piano, which even after years of lessons she could not play without a zillion errors — and then her own house.

The forsythia bushes her father had planted when they bought the house new — Emily'd been in nursery school — had grown into two immense balls of green. The weeping willow was forever dropping its thin whiplike branches all over the grass, so that the Edmundson household had a permanently littered look to it. The narrow porch, only three steps up and running the width of the house, had a row of hanging pots: impatiens mostly, flowering hot pink and orange in the shade of the porch.

I'm home, Emily thought, oh, I'm home!

She jumped out of the car and ran up the steps, so glad that her mother's car was still there, and her father's truck, so glad to know that it was going to be okay, they could —

Her mother stormed out of the house, flinging the screen door so hard that it actually snapped off the bottom hinge. A little piece of metal flew like shrapnel across the porch and into Emily's bare leg. "What are you doing here?" Emily's mother shouted. Emily shrank back.

Mr. Edmundson flung the screen door to hurl a duffel bag, a suitcase, and a lamp out past the porch and onto the grass. Matt, following Emily, stood dumbfounded when a lamp landed at his feet. He picked it up and tried to straighten out the squashed shade.

"Mother," Emily began, "this terrible thing happened. Or didn't happen, actually. You see—"

Mrs. Edmundson never even looked at her. "And furthermore," she yelled at her husband, "if you think I am putting up with the kind of servitude you expect—bring this, bring that, heat this, put ice cubes in that, wash this, mend that—well, you're wrong! I'm leaving!"

Mr. Edmundson threw a cardboard box after his wife. It was taped shut and didn't fall apart when it hit the grass slightly to the left of the lamp, but it made an ominous cracking sound.

"Get out of my sight, Emily," her mother said. "I am through with this whole family. You didn't want to come with me to start with, fine. I don't want anybody anyway." She began slinging the lamp, suitcase, and duffel into her car. Matt felt peculiar not helping, but he would have felt even more peculiar if he did help, so he just stood there, trying to blend in with the forsythia bushes.

Mr. Edmundson slammed the screen door shut, and now it hung sideways by its only remaining hinge. Then he slammed the solid wooden door and audibly locked it. Mrs. Edmundson flung herself into her car and switched on the motor.

She was much too angry to notice that

Matt had parked behind her. Matt leaped back into his wagon and reversed out of Mrs. Edmundson's way. She backed out violently and left a bigger patch of rubber in the road.

She had forgotten the cardboard box.

Emily on the porch and Matt on the grass stared at it, as if perhaps it contained some answers.

Mrs. Edmundson had evidently forgotten something else, too, because Mr. Edmundson opened the door and hurled a large black plastic garbage bag full of something soft and squashy out into the yard next to the box. Matt jumped out of the way, but he needn't have. What landed on his foot was almost weightless, as if perhaps it were a down sleeping bag.

Well, if it was, Matt thought, they won't be sharing it again in this lifetime!

"Daddy?" Emily said nervously, taking a step toward the door.

Her father said, "You made your choice, girl. Live with it."

He slammed the door and inside the house, he threw the lock.

Emily walked up to the door as if to knock, but instead of knocking she lay her cheek against the wood and cried softly.

The broken screen door was caught in the wind and knocked rythmically against her heels.

The door was not opened again.

* * *

"Now the real test question is, are you the only one feeling this way?" Kip asked. She was beginning to enjoy this weird conversation. "That's a very common problem with love. And, of course, you get to throw in heartache, heartburn, heartsickness, and insomnia."

Lee nodded several times. Kip found herself nodding with him, so that they formed a little duet, bobbing up and down. She forced herself to quit. Lee said, "This Mike is worth all that?"

"I don't think he's worth anything at this point," Kip said. "But that's the thing with true love. It doesn't matter whether the guy is worth it. You're stuck with it anyway."

"That doesn't sound very reasonable," Lee objected. "I like to think of you as a very reasonable person."

"Too reasonable," Kip said glumly. She had no idea what this kid Lee's purpose was and no idea why he had picked her to talk to, except that she was there. But Kip felt blue, and obviously Lee was frowning for the first time in his young life, so they might as well commiserate. She'd tell him her sad story, and he'd tell her his. They could shed a few tears together and maybe share that extra bag of potato chips.

Romance in a hotel kitchen.

Well, beggars couldn't be choosers.

Kip said, "So who is it you are obsessed with, and how long have you felt this way, and precisely what are her feelings about it?" How Mike would hate a sentence like that. I am not a list! he would storm at her. Don't make lists when you're talking to me!

Last year Kip had read at least ten books from the adult section of the library on how to improve yourself. She had read books which helped you develop a good attitude, or be tough, or be powerful, or wear the right colors, or find your own parachute.

She had found that the effect of each book was to make her feel wonderful the night she read it.

In the morning, of course, she would find out again, that she was still herself, Katharine "Kip" Elliott. What did those books really expect you to do? Turn yourself in for a new model?

Oh, sure, the books could tell you your life was very satisfying, your life was what you made of it, and your life and happiness did not depend on a boy, and it was true. Totally true.

But a boy was wonderful.

And those short weeks when Mike had loved her so much — oh, those weeks were perfect.

And gone.

Kip flirted with Lee because it was better than going back to the dance and admitting that this really, truly was her last dance with Mike.

But this guy Lee, he immediately put up three fingers to tick off as he answered each of her points.

He said, "One. You."
Kip nearly fell off the table.
"Two. Half an hour."
Kip's jaw sagged.
"Three. I don't know her feelings."

Anne Stephens had forgotten that she had even brought the paisley shawl. It was a typical clothing purchase in her family: her mother had seen it in an expensive shop, bought it for Anne, put it over her shoulders and said, "You'll wear this, you look perfect." Anne's mother was happy. And since Anne didn't much care, Anne took it along to the dance.

The only clothing Anne had picked out for herself was maternity clothing. Her mother and grandmother had not gone along on those little trips.

You thought I could come to this dance, and sort of dance off everything that had happened. I guess I thought so myself. I thought I would hop back into this life, the way Alice hopped through The Looking Glass into Wonderland.

I've hopped in. But I'm not there. I'm still partly with my baby.

Don't think, don't think, don't think, Anne cried silently. After all, when you were running around with Con making love in empty rooms, you got pretty darn good at not thinking. Not thinking was what you did best, Anne Stephens. So don't think now, either.

Con held out his hand to her. "Please," he said. "Please come."

Oh, his voice! Soft and deep and little boy. She had always submitted to that voice. Now suddenly Anne thought, Why do I want a *little* boy? Why don't I yearn for a grown-up? What flaw is in me that I want a *little* boy like Con?

She said, "All right, Con. I'm coming. Just let me run to the girls' room first."

Con was used to that anyhow. "Okay," he said, sighing, resigned.

Anne slipped past the crush of girls; ignored anybody asking her if she was the answer to any of the quiz questions; pretended not to see Molly, with Molly's hot eyes and Molly's bright jealous stare; and burst out of the crowded ballroom into a wide quiet hall with maroon carpeting and prints of Audubon birds on the walls. The women's room was lovely, with a sitting room in the front, complete with lounge in case you felt faint, a wash room, a lavatory room, and a place to change babies' diapers. The wallpaper was flocked, maroon against silver, patterns of weeping willows and dancing tropical birds, whose long tails drifted against the leaves of the weeping willows making a tapestry of curves.

Anne felt peaceful.

She looked at herself in the mirror.

She looked perfect.

It was amazing, she thought, how she who

was so imperfect had come into the world equipped with a perfect face, figure, and complexion. Even the gold hair that had been soaked and blown dry by some strange boy who laughed like a nut while drying it, now lay glossy and lovely, with its special swing, as if Anne moved only in slow motion.

The mirrors covered one wall. Behind her, the door opened and into the ladies' room came the back of a woman. How odd that she's coming in backward, Anne thought, starting to smile, and then she saw that the woman was pushing open the door with her back because with both arms, she was cradling a tiny child.

The mother never saw Anne.

She was completely fascinated by her own baby. "Tricia," crooned the mother.

Anne turned cold all over. It's my baby, she thought, it's my daughter! If I ask this woman about her Tricia, the woman will say, We just adopted her, she's thirty-two-days-old today, isn't she perfect?

Anne began to sob.

Her body did not sob with her: she kept the sobs in her chest, the technique she had learned when she first had to tell her parents about her pregnancy, and she was so afraid they would hear her crying herself to sleep every night. Her face stayed motionless. The tears came through. She followed the mother around the corner and into the cubbyhole with its high counter and tiny sink where the mother could change Tricia.

Anne had to ask.

Had to know.

Through stiff lips she muttered, "Your baby is lovely. How old is she?"

The mother kept a tight grip on the baby so she wouldn't roll off the counter and turned to smile at Anne. The mother said, "She's eleven weeks old. Isn't she wonderful? Isn't she perfect?"

"Yes," said Anne, and she went into a toilet cubicle and shut the door on herself. Get a grip on yourself, she thought. If you go around thinking every little baby in the world is yours, you're going to have a complete nervous breakdown, and they'll lock you up for six generations.

She thought, If only Con and I could have been that happy over our baby!

She thought, We would have to be ten years older to be happy. Finished with school, off to a good start, married.

She thought, It was impossible.

Oh Con, oh Con, I have to talk to you! I have to let all this pour out! I have to say a thousand things, whether they hurt you or not, whether they hurt me or not — I have to talk!

Perhaps a mountain trail in the dark was a good idea. Con would hold her arm and she would lean on him because of her silly shoes and they would talk softly in the privacy of the blackness of night.

She felt better already.

She could even smile.

She even managed a half a dance step when she left the women's room to rejoin Con.

Kip said, "So tell me your fantasies, Lee."

Lee had turned off the light in the kitchen. He mumbled, "I think they have to be demonstrated, not talked about."

Kip sad, "I don't think we know each other that well."

Lee said, "I don't think we know *anybody* that well!"

Kip said, "But why me? I mean, I had you all picked out for Anne if she and Con break up. Which they ought to **do**, if Con isn't going to grow up. Or Anne grow down."

"A person can't grow down," Lee said.

"Sure they can. I see it all the time. Half the boys in my school are incredibly immature. And Mike, he was very mature when we went together and very immature now that we're not."

"Oh, that kind of growing down," Lee said, and she could almost feel his grin. She thought, I've never seen his grin! I want lights on! I want to check this guy out. She thought, He has a crush on *me*? He's obsessed with *me*? It's *me* he thinks is terrific? You're kidding.

"Anyway," Lee said, "why would anybody want a girl like Anne? She's all weak-kneed and nervous. I don't want somebody to lean all over me. I'm not a tent pole, you know."

Kip's first reaction was to defend Anne to the last red blood cell, but this would have involved betraying Anne, so Kip decided to let it alone. Besides, it was pretty neat, to be considered superior to Anne. Kip would have said that such a girl didn't exist — and here was Lee Hamilton saying *she* was that girl!

"I like this conversation," Kip said. "I love to talk about me."

"Good," Lee said. "You talk about you, I'll talk about me, it'll be perfect."

In a crunch — a real, horrible, sickening crunch — you needed your girlfriends. Emily wanted Beth Rose and Anne.

Here was Matt — dear, goofy, crazy Matt, her Knight in Shining Armor — babbling along about the Last Dance and how they were late as usual. And of course they were — hours late. And she loved him, and how his tie was completely askew and how one corner of the button-down shirt buttoned down and the other corner bent upward, and she loved how he had run his fingers through his hair, leaving the left half smooth and attractive and the right half standing straight up.

But she didn't want Matt.

And she didn't want to go to a dance either.

She was so rattled by that strange scary ride with Christopher.

How could she trust her judgment, she

who hopped out of cars, and panicked over nothing, and got nauseated over the prospect of a dance?

Emily felt as if her skin had been peeled off, and nothing was holding her together any more: she was just a lot of nerve endings and bones lying loosely in the seat next to Matt, and if somebody touched her, all her pieces would scatter and all the king's horses and all the king's men couldn't put Emily together again.

Lee decided to kiss Kip.

He hadn't kissed anyone before, but he figured he had seen people kiss on TV probably twice a night since he was . . . oh, let's say he stopped watching Mr. Rogers when he was 5, so that made 12 years times 365 nights, well . . . probably there were 10 or 15 nights a year when he didn't see any TV, so call it 350 times 12 times 2 kisses meant he had witnessed 8,400 kisses.

Ought to be enough, Lee Hamilton thought, grinning in the darkness.

And it was.

Chapter 8

Con, Mike, and Gary made their plans.

They were a very attractive trio.

Con, like Anne, was perfect: body, profile, expression, clothes, all coming together in a relaxed fashion, rather like a model for designer jeans.

Mike was simply an all-around, decent looking kid: not too tall, not too thin, nice enough smile, easy laugh.

Gary was dark haired, fair skinned, mysterious, sexy, and distant.

They formed an impenetrable trio.

Anne walked back into the ballroom and stared at them. What was that military word for a groups of soldiers? A phalanx. Mike, Gary, and her Con were a phalanx.

How scary a group of one sex is to the opposite sex!

Anne grew uncertain.

In the dim light, with the rock music of the band pounding in her ears, she stood waiting for a signal from Con that he really did want her with him.

But she had waited too long.

"Let's go!" Gary said impatiently, and Mike nodded. Gary took a solid grip on Beth Rose, and Gary, Mike, and Beth Rose walked out into the night. Con took two steps after them, looked back, saw Anne, gestured sharply for her to follow him.

It was an order, that wave.

Come on, woman, you've kept me waiting long enough.

I've had it, Anne Stephens thought. He is a little boy. I am a woman. Enough already.

She shook her head. If Con wanted to be a grown-up, why then he'd come over and ask what she, Anne, wanted to do. If Con wanted to be a little boy, he'd run along after his pack of friends and toddle up the mountain.

Anne did not look back.

She did not see Molly laughing ecstatically, and then hiding her triumphant laughter. Molly slid out from behind the potted ferns and said softly, "I'm dying to see the cliffs by moonlight, Con. Come on. I'll go with you. We'll kept it a secret. You go out by yourself, and I'll wait a minute and come after you and nobody will see."

Matt knew he was supposed to think of something now, but he didn't know what. Emily was not getting out of the car nor even looking up at him, in spite of the fact that he was holding her door open and had even unsnapped her seatbelt for her. "M&M, all your girlfriends are here," he coaxed. "People to talk to."

"Oh, Matt, where am I going to sleep tonight? And the rest of my life?"

It was probably not the time for a raunchy joke. Matt said carefully, "You can stay with us. That's what my mother thinks you should do."

Emily read between the lines on that one. "What do your father and grandfather think?" she asked.

"They think you have to make up with your family and keep the peace." Although after that little scene in the driveway, Matt didn't see much hope for peace any time soon in the Edmundson family. "Let's stop worrying for a few hours now and just dance," he suggested, bending down into the enormous old station wagon like a contortionist. He jiggled her hand and made their two arms dance together, hoping Emily would laugh.

She didn't. But at least she got out of the car, and Matt was relieved. It would all be okay. They'd dance, and Emily would talk with her girlfriends and feel better. They'd work something out; he knew they would. Matt had the kind of life where everything always worked out.

But Emily got out because she realized Matt could never understand. That was the thing with happy families. Good people came out of happy families, people who cared and wanted to help, but what could happy families really grasp about rotten miserable families?

Emily's mother did not like her. Period.

Emily's father preferred the television. Period.

I'm sixteen, Emily thought. Almost seventeen. Could I live on my own? People did in the olden days. Laura Ingalls had married Almanzo by now, hadn't she? Didn't they already have their first homestead by now? So what's the matter with me that I'm afraid to start my own home, instead of pretending that getting my father a beer is a home?

Emily and the boy she loved walked up the gravel path from the parking lot to the ballroom. Through the great glass walls they could see everybody dancing. It was like a film: sparkling, gaudy, whirling, and bright.

A film of happiness and rhythm.

A film of laughter and love.

Emily thought, Will I be the only one out of step?

She looked at Matt's watch. It was nine thirty. Sometime in the next three or four hours, she had to decide what she was going to do.

She could not go home with Matt.

She loved Matt. He loved her. She loved Matt's family. They loved her right back. But to move in with her boyfriend's family — well, that was a step Emily was not ready to take. That was much more than shelter for a night. That was proclaiming to the world, and to Matt, and to herself, that she and Matt were hand in hand for good.

Emily didn't know that.

She couldn't even begin to think like that. Living together? Marriage? Children?

Emily had one plan only: to get through the summer and have a good senior year. That was as far as Emily could think.

So Matt was out.

She held his hand. Hers was cool, and he suspected nothing of her turmoil because to him she seemed calm and poised. They arrived in the ballroom just as Con was following Mike, Beth Rose, and Gary out. "Hey Con!" Matt yelled and they slapped palms and backs.

Con told Matt to come up the mountainside to Two Cliffs in the dark..

Matt shook his head, grinning. "If I came alone," he said, "definitely. But right now I gotta dance with M&M."

Emily wondered whether she was just a good excuse or whether he really felt that way — "I gotta dance with M&M."

Another difference between boys and girls: girls always thought about every sentence, thought about it to death. Boys never thought at all.

"Dance later," Con said. "The dance will last forever anyhow. Come on up the trail with us. It isn't pitch dark. There's almost a full moon. Practically as much light outside as there is in here."

Matt just grinned and shook his head again.

Matt had had two jelly doughnuts and a lemon-filled doughnut not half an hour earlier, but he was starved, completely starved. What he really wanted was a quart of chocolate milk, but he would have to settle for Coke. He coaxed Emily to go with him across the dance floor to get something decent to eat, something cold to drink.

Emily thought, I don't have my purse!

How do I survive without my purse?

What's in my purse anyway? I can't remember. I only know that I never travel without my purse, and now my purse is gone forever in my father's house, and I don't have it.

Matt thought, oh good, they have real food. Roast beef and turkey slices and hard rolls and lettuce and sliced tomatoes. I won't starve.

Matt was always worried about starving. He didn't care about the weather, or the condition of his shoes or clothing, or whether he'd done his homework or anything like that. He just wanted to be absolutely sure there would be plenty to eat.

Matt chose a hard roll without seeds, slathered it with mustard and mayonnaise and put together a sandwich so thick nobody else in the room could ever have gotten a mouth around it.

Emily began to giggle. "I may have to

start calling you Jaws. Look at that mouth open up for that food."

"What can I say? I'm a shark. All appetite." He grinned, pulling back his lips to show every one of his teeth. His goofy, all-American look was the least sharklike in the United States. Emily laughed and kissed his mayonnaisy lips.

For herself she took a single carrot stick.

Across the room she saw Anne. Oh, Anne! she thought. If there was one person in this room who would know pain, it was Anne. Emily handed Matt her half-bitten carrot stick and ran over to Anne.

Matt ate the carrot, not being a picky sort when it came to food, and fixed himself a second sandwich to carry around, because once M&M and Anne started talking, hours could pass. A person didn't want to starve all those hours.

They slipped between two enormous hemlocks: black instead of green in the night. The boys laughed when the feathery tips brushed their faces and sleeves, but all Beth Rose could think was that she was going to get tree sap on her beautiful dress and in her hair. I already lost a hunk of hair to the door hinge! she thought. Now I have to get sap in it? Gary, why can't you be romantic? Now if you'd suggested that just the two of us should go drift off behind the hemlocks . . . but no, we have to take Mike and Con with us.

Actually, it was Mike and Con taking *them*.

Con was upset about Anne going to Emily instead of to him. Well, if you're upset, you two-year-old, Beth Rose thought, there's a very simple solution. You go back to Anne.

She staggered after the boys. Had she been a swearing person, she would certainly have chosen this moment. Sworn at her boyfriend, her shoes, and herself for being a wimp and submitting to this.

Mike was whispering so loudly that any hotel employee could have heard him a mile off. However, all hotel employees, being in their right minds, were indoors. Nobody knew that Mike was telling them all to run fast over the open space to the start of the trail.

Open space, Beth Rose thought irritably.

It was a croquet court. How civilized that sounded, how British. If it were a slow Sunday afternoon, she in her flowery frock and Gary in his suit — no, Gary would never play croquet. Gary might rotate tires or go fishing, but play croquet, forget it.

Gary grabbed her hand to make her go faster. Her shoes were almost flat, but not quite: the heels were an inch or so in diameter, shaped rather like squashed horseshoes. It was half the reason Beth bought them: those nutty little heels. Now they caught in the turf of the croquet court. She could just imagine the way the grass would look by day, with holes stabbed all through the pretty green surface.

She was not running fast enough for the boys, so Mike grabbed her other hand and they hauled her along.

"Pick up your feet, will ya?" Mike said.

Beth Rose was actually an acceptably good athlete and had played junior varsity field hockey. But then she had worn proper shoes and could see where she was going.

In spite of the fact that she *wanted* the manager to catch them, she was afraid that he *would*, and so when they reached the safety of the trail, her heart felt more safe instead of less.

"Awright," Con muttered. He punched Mike, and Mike punched Gary, and Gary squeezed Beth's hand.

Boys, Beth Rose thought. She wanted to find out what Emily was saying to Anne instead.

"I'll lead the way," Con said eagerly and off he went, becoming a shadow among shadows.

Beth Rose was disgusted to find the trail went up.

"What did you think?" Mike demanded. "This is a mountain. Of course the trail goes up."

"It also comes down," she pointed out. "It depends on which way you're headed."

Mike neglected to hold the narrow branch of a tree. He ducked under it, but Beth didn't see it, and it snapped back against her arm. Her arms were bare and it hurt. She said nothing. The trail was not exactly a croquet court. It was rocky and roots poked up out of it, and it tilted unexpectedly, and it was impossible to get a grip on the surface when her shoes were slick for dancing.

Gary said, "I feel as if I'm carrying you."

"You practically are," Beth said. "I don't have the right shoes on. I thought we were going to the Last Dance, not the last mountain expedition."

"Look out," Con warned, "the trail dips."

Beth Rose prepared herself for a slant.

There was not a slant.

There was a drop-off.

The boys shouted happily, pretending to be diving into deep cold water.

"This is ridiculous," Beth Rose said. "I'm going back."

"Aw come on," Gary said. "Where's your spirit of adventure?" He took her waist in both hands, said, "Now!" and she half jumped and he half lifted, and she was down with the boys.

It was the last part of the trail to go downhill. Now it was not simply up, it was practically vertical. Beth Rose was panting.

"We're at the edge!" Mike cried.

The moon was ahead of them, partly hidden by the trees that grew twisted by wind that whipped around the two cliffs. Moonlight shone on the first cliff, still way above them, and silhouetted the far-off second cliff.

All was black, silver, and grey: like pearls and ice.

Rushing River Inn lay directly below them, casting enormous rectangles of light out of its windows and over the trees and shrubs, making spooky deep shadows that led into the woods. The music from the dance band rose faintly. She could not see the ballroom, but in the dining room that was off limits to the teenagers she could see a group of party-goers all leaning toward the middle of the table, the way people do when a joke hits the punch line and they laugh together.

The wind lifted her hair.

Her skirt was filled with wind and became a balloon beneath her and then sank down again.

She took a step toward Gary.

"Not that way!" he said, grabbing her.

She had been looking so far out she had forgotten to look down. The cliff was only a few feet from her slippered toes. "Ooh," Beth Rose gasped.

"Pay attention," Mike said. "You wanna fall down there?" He tossed a pebble. For a moment it was framed in the gray sky in the moonlight, and the four of them stood still, listening for it to hit bottom. But they never heard anything. It's so far down the sound doesn't carry, Beth Rose thought, and she shuddered, backing up against Gary. In these slippery shoes, she was going to be in trouble if she got too near that pebbly edge.

But when she moved toward him, he had gone on.

"Hurry up, Beth Rose!" Gary said.

"I'll give her a hand, I'm closer," Con said, in a voice so irritated she wanted to push him over the cliff.

"I can do it myself," she said, gritting her teeth.

Con shrugged so elaborately she could see it in the dark.

"Hey, look at this, will you!" Mike cried, and the boys raced on.

A pebble shot from beneath Con's heavy shoes and hit her ankle.

Beth Rose came to her senses.

Gary says jump, and I jump.

Gary says hike, and I hike.

Well, I'm through. It's ridiculous. Next time he says, "I'm bored, lady, let's go for a walk in the woods," I'll say, "We can do that tomorrow, when I'm in jeans and hiking boots. Tonight we're dancing."

Normal people say that.

Kip always says what she's thinking.

Beth Rose grabbed the trees as she walked, hauling herself from safety zone to safety zone.

But then, she reflected, Kip wasn't exactly shining in the boyfriend department. Maybe saying what you were thinking wasn't the right thing to do. Maybe you had to lie. Beth Rose despised people who had to lie.

I've been lying, she thought. I've never

really said to Gary, I hate this, don't ruin my day with this kind of thing.

Okay. I'm going to strive to be more like Kip. Honesty and leadership.

Oh, right. It's me.

Well, it could be. I bet you can learn that just the way you learn algebra.

Of course, I'm not so good at algebra.

Beth Rose's foot came down on the trail, but the trail was not there.

Her foot kept going down.

Her lungs went into a spasm of fear and her heart leaped up to fill the space.

She tightened her grip on the tree she was holding, but the tree was rotten and the branch broke off in her hand.

Her fingers tightened around the punky wood, her nails digging through the bark.

And she fell.

And there was nothing in front of her but space.

Kip said, "Listen, are you supposed to be working or something?"

"Mmmm hmmmm."

"Maybe you should get to work then."

"I don't know, Kip, the old work ethic feels pretty thin right now. Let's just keep going."

"This is as far as I go," Kip said.

Lee was incredibly disappointed. He had no idea he was going to be that disappointed. "Ever?" he said.

Kip thought. "Certainly not *ever*. It would be a little hard to have kids unless I do."

"Kids!" gasped Lee, clutching his chest and heart. "Kids! That takes stuff like marriage and money."

"You got it." Given what Anne had just gone through, Kip was more sure of that one than ever.

Kip hopped right down off the table. "You'd better go to work," she said.

"Are you mad at me?" Lee asked anxiously.

"No. No — I'm — uh — well —"

Lee flipped on the lights.

He caught Kip taking a deep breath, her tongue touching her lip, her face set in self-control.

"Yeah," Lee Hamilton said. "Me, too."

Gary said, "Where's Beth Rose?"

"Dragging her feet somewhere," Mike said.

Gary said, "Beth? Bethie? Where are you?"

"She's right here," Mike said crossly.

"Where?" Gary asked.

There was a half minute, perhaps, while they swerved in circles and reached their hands out into darkest shadows, and muttered, "Beth? Beth Rose, where are you?"

And Gary said, "She — she — she couldn't have fallen!"

"We were right at the cliff edge when I talked to her last," Con whispered. Con thought, what if she fell?

Mike said, "Well, she didn't fall. We would have heard her scream."

Gary turned silently and began going back, cursing himself for not having a flashlight, for bringing Beth at all, for not having her hand in his every moment. For another eternal half minute he worked his way down the Two Cliffs path, and then he began yelling, "Beth! Beth Rose! Beth! Beth Rose! Answer me! Where are you?"

Con thought, she could have fallen without screaming. She could have hit her head first.

He thought of her falling, falling, falling, farther than the pebble, her summery dress no parachute. Gravity the king. Hard, hard earth the death.

Con's lips felt like rubber. "Beth!" he screamed. "Beth Rose!"

They got to the open spot by the cliff's edge where they had all looked into the moonlight and stared at the spookiness of Rushing River Inn below. The Inn was unchanged, its lights and music wafting up to them. Nobody heard their screams.

Gary held up a hand for silence. But Beth Rose did not answer.

Gary walked right to the cliff edge and looked down. Too dark to see anything. He knelt in the dirt. But he could not tell if anything had happened there.

He muttered, "She must have gone back to the Inn. She must have."

Beth Rose? The most considerate girl on earth? The girl who agreed to everything, who liked everything easy and smooth? Not even letting him know what she was doing? Walking on her own through the woods she had barely staggered up?

She fell, Gary thought. She fell, and it's my fault.

He was running then, running down the path, the branches smacking his face, running to look for his girl.

Lee Hamilton could not get Kip out of his mind.

Mr. Martin said, "Lee?"

He jumped a foot.

"Yes, sir?"

"Am I perhaps paying you money?"

"Uh. Yes."

"Are you perhaps considering the possibility of working in order to receive that money?"

"Uh. Sure. Yes. Sir."

Mr. Martin smiled. "How decent of you, Lee. And here I thought teenage boys today thought exclusively of girls."

Lee blushed. He had never blushed in his entire life before.

Mr. Martin said, "Try being a waiter, Lee. You can get into it if you really try."

Lee nodded.

Out in the ballroom he became a waiter again, but a slow one.

She wasn't there.

Neither was her "boyfriend." The one who didn't even like her.

Lee circled the entire ballroom.

No Kip, no boyfriend.

He thought, they made up. Well, that's that. My first true love was certainly brief. An hour. And I only admitted it on minute fifty-eight.

I don't think I'm off to an impressive start.

Emily held Anne so hard Anne knew Emily needed her. It was a pretty nice feeling: being needed. Anne had needed help herself for so long that to be a tower of strength to somebody else was a pretty terrific thing.

But Matt was there, chewing alternately on a sandwich in his left hand and another in his right. He looked like a fast food restaurant ad. Anne figured any problem Emily had was with Matt so she wasn't sure how to begin talking. "You were so late!" she tried. "Did your car break down?"

"My car?" Matt said huffily. He was very proud of his cars. "Break down? Certainly not."

Anne thought of herself and Con. They had hugged like that once, needing each other that painfully. She and Con had not yet learned how to touch each other again. Before, they had had two touching stages: the first, which lasted from eighth grade through tenth, was silly breathy giggly messy kissing. And comfort. And pleasure. But the second was different. It was so unfair! You would think that if you had decided to have a total relationship, you could also get the huggy comfort relationship to go with it — but Anne and Con had not. And now, they could not figure out how to touch at all.

Oh, why did the whole world have problems?

Why couldn't the whole world have terrific families, like Kip's great crowd or Matt's wonderful huggy kissy clan?

The band stopped playing.

There was a moment of utter silence and then before the conversation of the dancers took over, Emily burst into terrible agonizing sobs.

Chapter 9

Afterward, the three boys privately wondered why they behaved the way they did. Why didn't they race into the ballroom and tell all the boys to help search? Certainly every boy there would have been much happier searching the forest in the dark than dancing! Why didn't they grab Mr. Martin, demanding lanterns and search lights and trained dogs? Why didn't they call the rescue squad, the police, the fire department? Anybody at all?

But Gary didn't, Con didn't, and Mike didn't.

Mike was appalled by the snide things he had been saying to Beth Rose along the way. As if frozen in time, Mike's muscles reminded him that his *hand* had gone to help Beth Rose, but not his heart. He had just yanked her along. He'd been thinking contemptuously: girls. dances. Kip. Stupid high heels.

Mike thought: Kip would never fall. She'd be too well organized. Kip would note the precise distance between her feet and the cliff edge for exactly the right safety margin, and when she went back to the Inn, she'd notify the authorities that the railing had fallen down. Next week, she'd call them to be sure they had fixed it.

When Mike had that thought, he expected to be angered all over again at Kip. But he wasn't. He missed her. He missed her sense, her calm, her ability to make a decision and act on it.

If Beth Rose fell . . . Mike thought. If she fell . . . it's my fault.

Con had decided not to worry about Beth Rose. During the climb, he knew perfectly well she was having a hard time, and he preferred not to think about her or her difficulties.

Racing down the mountain, roots catching at his feet, hemlock branches slapping his face, and oak leaves turning into slippery ski slopes beneath his shoes, Con thought — *this is how I treat Anne.*

Practically from the night she told me about the baby I decided not to think about it. I decided she was on her own.

But people aren't on their own.

Sometimes they need you.

He thought of himself running around with Molly while Anne sat alone at Aunt Madge's, watching rented movies on the VCR because she hated to appear in public, and because he hated to appear with her.

For a moment he thought he could not handle the shame.

He had run away from Anne once before and managed to crawl back.

Con did not see how he could repeat that performance.

But if he found Beth Rose . . . if he rescued Beth Rose . . . it would be like an offering.

He would be able to say to Anne: Here, I'm not so bad. I'm shaping up, as a matter of fact. See how I saved your friend?

So Con never thought of calling for help because he needed to rescue Beth Rose himself. Con decided right away to return to the croquet courts, take the lower path to the base of the mountain, and try to find where she had fallen through.

That it was dark, that he was talking about dozens of acres of thick woods, he did not pause to consider.

Gary didn't think at all.

He was falling inside himself: feeling the weightlessness, the horror, the plunge. He was torn by treetops — soft green leaves that looked like featherbeds became stabbing spears to kill Beth Rose.

He thought his girlfriend had not screamed because the wind was knocked out of her, or maybe because, as he was now, she was frozen by her own fear of falling.

And perhaps she didn't scream simply because she couldn't be that disruptive. Beth

Rose hated to be a nuisance. Beth Rose hated to speak up.

Oh, Bethie! Gary thought. You didn't speak up. You didn't scream up! -And if you're dead, it's my fault. You expected me to know, and deep down I really did know. But I want you to talk out loud. I want you to say what you mean, say what you want!

You never do, Beth. You expect me to mind read.

Gary thought: I can't mind read if you're dead.

And then he thought, I dragged her up here.

I did read her mind. I did know she just wanted to stay inside and dance.

If she fell. . . .

Con said, "The lower path! We'll find her down there!" He led the way through thick shrubs and underbrush.

Gary did not want to find Beth Rose "down there."

But it had to be him and not Con or Mike who found her, because she was his girl.

So he ran with Con in the dark, yelling Beth's name, wondering if he would see Beth's billowing summery skirt, like a sign, a flag to mark where she hit bottom.

Anne took Emily into the girls' room.

Where would the female of the species be without girls' rooms? thought Anne. A girl can always kill time in there.

The lounge included a daybed, in the same maroon color as the flocked wallpaper. Anne and Emily sat on it, leaning on each other, and Emily wept. "I'm so sorry," Emily sobbed. "I shouldn't be crying."

Anne smiled. "Listen. I cried for nine months. I guess you rate a single evening. Tears aren't so bad. They don't arrest you for it, anyhow." They clung to each other.

Emily said, "Anne, you just wouldn't believe what happened to me tonight."

Anne felt as if Emily could not have a problem that Anne could not understand. She'd been through so much and been through it, essentially, alone. Oh, her parents and her grandmother had stood by her — but very uncomfortably, and very reluctantly. And Con, well, if you stretched a point, you could pretend he'd stood by her. And Beth Rose's Aunt Madge had provided a bedroom, and meals, and cozy forgiving talks.

But that was the thing of Aunt Madge.

She was busy forgiving Anne for being bad.

I made an error in judgment, Anne thought, and I made it over and over again. But I wasn't bad.

I was alone, she thought.

Anne would never, never be so dumb as to say she was glad all the last nine months had happened to her. But she was stronger for it, and she was glad to be stronger.

Strength turned out not to be muscles flexing, but a kind of peace. Anne settled into the maroon upholstery and leaned back against the silvery weeping willows and dancing birds of the wallpaper and knew that whatever life dealt her, she could take it.

Of course, this time she would deal her own hand a bit more carefully!

"So," Anne said comfortably, "so tell me what happened."

Emily was a puddle of emotion, sobbing, using up all available Kleenex and then hopping up every few minutes to get toilet paper to use instead to sop up all her tears. Anne had forgotten (so soon!) what it was like to cry your way through an entire box of Kleenex! She listened to the story with appropriate shudders and gasps of understanding.

"First things first," Anne said firmly. "The whole thing with Christopher was probably jangled nerves, but not necessarily. Christopher is a creep. Don't you remember that Saturday night of the Autumn Leaves Dance? How he got drunk and practically attacked the band and the police were called and Molly had to drive him home? Anyway, a guy that big and that strong, the only reasonable thing is to be afraid if you're afraid."

The girls both giggled.

"Matt would have trouble understanding that sentence," Emily said.

"So would Con!" Anne said. "But girls wouldn't. If you're afraid, it's reasonable to be afraid, and that's that. But that's not really the point, Emily. That was just the icing on the cake. The real problem is your parents."

"It's odd to think of the problem as a cake," Emily said. "I mean, I know what you're saying, the icing on the cake. But Christopher wasn't exactly sweet frosting, and my parents aren't exactly chocolate cake, either."

Anne said, "Okay, so I don't have the perfect metaphor at hand. What can I say? I missed a lot of school this year." She hugged Emily again. "You make it sound as if your parents just aren't worth living with. Is that true? Because if they really are not worth living with, there's no reason to try to make things smooth again."

Emily tried to look down into her childhood as if it were a well, and she could see the bottom of it. "I always had nutritious meals," she said slowly, "and my mother picked me up at school if it was raining, and when I wanted music lessons they bought me a flute. But . . . they weren't really interested in me. Weren't interested in each other, either. I don't actually know what they do like. That's awful, isn't it? Imagine being their age and not knowing what you like in life."

The girls talked of their parents, and other people's parents, and grown-ups in general. Anne's home life had been immeasurably better than Emily's, and yet she had always been something of a trophy for her parents: the perfect daughter to dress in the perfect fashions.

The girls sat in silence for quite a while, each looking back at her errors in life. Emily had no real mistakes that she knew of — other than to be born into an unloving family. And who had control over that?

I have control now, thought Emily. The choice is mine now. But I don't have the slightest idea what choice to make!

Molly had not bargained for such a steep treacherous trail up toward Two Cliffs. Having staggered across the soft thick cushion of the croquet courts, she had expected to find easy going on the path. Instead it was clear she was going to break an ankle.

She stood in the trees for a moment trying to decide what to do. She wanted to follow Con. She wanted to press her advantage, but she did not want to ruin her clothes, break a bone, or make an idiot of herself.

She lit a cigarette and smoked it to help herself think.

Molly found everything about smoking very soothing. It gave you something to do, it calmed you down, and it took up time. She ignored all the realistic warnings about smoking.

She flicked the match into the bushes and after an interval tossed the half-smoked cigarette in after it.

She faintly heard the boys yelling at Beth Rose.

Molly would never put herself in the position of being a pain. What could be worse than boys who were sorry you were along? Although in Molly's opinion, having Beth Rose along automatically meant you were sorry about it. She could not imagine what anybody, least of all Gary, saw in such a namby-pamby as Beth.

All right.

She'd go back to the dance.

No point in throwing her energy into something pointless.

She had another cigarette first, though, because it was nice to be able to smoke (Rushing River Inn's lovely rooms were marred by large red and white No Smoking signs) and because she wasn't sure yet what she'd do once she got back to the ballroom.

Pammy really and truly wanted that VCR.

Her parents said they already subscribed to cable TV and HomeMovies, and there was no need for a VCR.

Pammy felt there was a deep imperative need, and that without a VCR she was going to die.

She was putting all her energy into this questionnaire. She was the only one to care this much, so she figured she had the best chance of winning it. She had most of the questions answered. She knew now that Douglas was the one who did not like chocolate. Her whole opinion of Douglas was changed now, although Douglas did not seem to care very much about this, and now Pammy was trying to find out who had skied in six countries. She had asked every single person who could possibly afford to live that kind of life. None of them admitted to skiing in any country except the United States, and several hadn't skied there, either.

Pammy's appetite was whetted by this.

It meant that somebody at this dance had a lot more money and a lot more style than Pammy would ever have dreamed. She was now asking the unlikely ones. She tried Kip, who with her four little brothers lived in an apartment, not a house, and certainly didn't dress as if she went skiing abroad. Kip just looked annoyed and said, "No, I don't even have a passport." Pammy asked Evelyn, a nervous girl if there ever was one, and Evelyn said her idea of thrills and chills in winter was to look out the window at the snow. Evelyn's date laughed. Pammy said, "So who can I ask? I've asked everybody."

"Try the girls' room," Evelyn said. "The interesting people always hang out in there."

Pammy had never known that. She rushed to the girls' room to see if somebody interesting was hanging out there.

It was Anne and Emily sitting together on the couch.

Well, definitely Anne had not spent the winter skiing in Switzerland. And Emily? Dubiously, Pammy said, "Emily, are you the one who went skiing in six countries?"

Emily stared at her for a moment. Then she said, "No. I've only been skiing in five."

"Oh, wow!" Pammy cried. "Maybe it's a

misprint! Maybe it's really you! Did you write that down on your questionnaire? Did you, Em?"

Emily rolled her eyes. "I was kidding, Pammy. I've never been skiing anywhere."

Pammy flung herself down on the couch with them. "How am I ever going to win this VCR?" she cried. "I just can't find out the last few questions!"

"What do you have so far?" Anne asked, looking over Pammy's answers.

"Let us copy Pammy's answers," said Emily, giggling. "Then we'll be just as far along for a fraction of the effort."

Anne thought that Pammy was a very lucky person. She had no idea that she had interrupted anything, or that she was the least bit unwelcome. Pammy was happy and ignorant. Kind of a nice way to be, actually. It spared you an awful lot of worry. Look at Emily — not telling Christopher where to get off because she was afraid it would be rude. Pammy would never think of that. Pammy would just say, "Christopher, stop your stupid car and let me out, you creep."

I have to be more like Pammy, Anne thought.

She hid a giggle. Con would hate that.

But did she care any more?

Did Con mean anything to her now, other than some very mixed memories?

It sounded like a record or a movie.

Mixed reviews.

Anne said, "You don't have Gary's name

down here for anything, Pammy. He's kind of a mysterious person, don't you think? Ask Gary if he's an answer."

Pammy looked pouty. She said, "Gary took off with — " she caught herself.

"Right," said Anne. "With Con and Mike. Go for it, Pammy. One of those three is sure to have done something on this question-naire!"

"But do you know for sure?" Pammy asked anxiously. "Has Gary ever said any-thing about skiing abroad?"

"Pammy, Gary never says anything pe-riod. You have to drag it out of him. Maybe Beth Rose knows."

"And maybe not," said Emily. "I think in that relationship, Gary dictates and Beth Rose obeys." She felt overwhelmingly glad to have Matt. She wanted Pammy to leave so she could tell Anne that Matt had sug-gested she could live at his house, and what did Anne think of that? But Pammy stayed, and stayed, and Anne, not one to surrender an opportunity handed to her like that, copied down Pammy's questionnaire answers on her own paper. Pammy said, "Well, okay, you can have my answers, but if you win, Anne. . ."

Anne giggled. "I'll give you half the VCR."

Lee found Kip.
Alone.
He had, until this moment in his life, found

a girl standing all alone to be frightening. He would never consider walking up to a girl who was all alone. She might draw some kind of conclusion from it.

Kip alone, though. She was different.

"Hi," he said to her.

She was startled, and for an instant her expression was nothing but surprise. Then her face softened, and her chin lowered. Turning slightly, she smiled at him. No words, just a smile.

She's glad to see me, Lee thought.

There was no sign of the so-called boyfriend.

Just to be sure, Lee asked, "So where is he?"

Kip shrugged her eyebrows. He loved how she did that. Very economical of movement. No shoulders in her shrug — the so-called boyfriend wasn't worth that much. She said, "I'm told he went for a hike up Two Cliffs trail."

"Oh yeah, I heard some of the boys saying that they wanted to do that."

"Is it safe?"

It was Lee's turn to shrug eyebrows. "It's safe as long as you stay on the trail."

Kip giggled. "I guess that's true of life in general. Now listen, I heard Mr. Martin yelling at you just as I slipped out of the kitchen; for once my timing was excellent. Aren't you supposed to be working?"

"I am working. I'm checking hither and

yon for chaos and mess that I can clean up."
He shaded his eyes and stared into the dark
shadows as if searching for icebergs at sea.

They flirted.

They knew nothing about each other.

They didn't particularly want to.

Kip just didn't want to start the whole
thing — the "How many brothers and sisters
do you have?" and "Did you always live
here?" and "Are you getting good grades at
school?" and "Do you like to sail?"

Boring.

Kip wanted to stay on the surface, gliding
along, batting eyelashes, and trading silly
remarks. Dancing. Laughing.

She knew from Mike that when she got
serious, she got too serious. And since Lee
was a boy she really *wanted* to get serious
about, well then, she could not get serious
at all.

Now that's weird, Kip thought.

That's a truly weird thought.

But correct. I have only to ask Mike, and
he will say, Go for it, Kip. Be light-hearted
for a change. Don't organize the evening,
don't organize his life, don't organize his job.
This Lee wants to get in trouble with Mr.
Martin, let him, it's his job, you're not in
charge.

"Shall we dance?" Lee asked.

Kip choked back a suggestion that he
should be working.

The rule is — just dance, she told herself.
Don't organize.

So they danced. For at least thirty seconds Kip forgot about being in charge and just enjoyed Lee. Then she couldn't stand it.

"Listen, I can't stand it," she said.

Lee let go of her like a burning torch in his fingers.

"Not you!" Kip said, taking him back again. "You just don't know me. Lee. I'm very driven. I like things to go the way they ought to. You ought to be working. You'll have to ask me out for a date so we can go dancing when you're not working."

Lee laughed.

What a wonderful change from the girls he knew at school. He could never tell what they were thinking, which always made him nervous, which always made him run, which meant he never *would* understand what a girl was thinking.

He said, "I don't suppose you know what you're doing next Saturday night."

Kip said, "I am the type of person who always knows what she is doing next Saturday night."

Lee thought, my kind of person.

At that point Kip, who never forgot anything, forgot she had come to this dance with Mike. She gave Lee a tremendous hug, and Lee being a wrestler gave her a tremendous one right back, and they began making plans for next Saturday night.

Lee was looking at Kip's hair: her dark hair, and the way the lights made it gleam like gold, and he looked beyond her, and out into the darkness of the forest and mountain, and there was gold there, too.

At first he thought it was a reflection, and then he thought —

Hanging onto Kip's arm he walked swiftly to the door of the ballroom and out into the fresh air. Gold?

Lee sniffed.

Kip whispered, *"Fire."*

Chapter 10

Kip had but one thought: was the fire a sufficient threat to call the fire department?

But while Lee was saying, "We'd better check it out first. Maybe we can put it out ourselves," Kip was realizing that it had not rained in some time, that this fire was on the rim of a very dry forest, and that there was a steady evening breeze off the mountain.

Her mind flipped through the possibilities of putting it out themselves: there was an underground sprinkler system: she had seen it working earlier in the day. So there would be outdoor water faucets somewhere, but hoses might be stowed anyplace, since they obviously weren't normally used. Finding them would take valuable minutes. There were fire extinguishers inside, but ripping them off the walls would cause needless panic. There was Mr. Martin, but Kip's opinion of his ability to handle a crisis was not high.

She had cataloged in her mind where the telephones were early on in the evening.

While Mike was being annoying, and wishing he hadn't come, and hoping his buddies like Gary would show up soon, Kip had taken in everything. She had a mind for detail. Just as she had known the questionnaire might not work well, because its sponsors hadn't thought it out very clearly, Kip had absorbed without really looking for them the important things: phones, womens' room, soda supply.

She had also glanced at the speedometer on the car when they were driving up to Mount Snow, curling down the narrow tree-lined roads with their occasional vistas of beauty: Rushing River Inn was four miles from the main road. The fastest any fire volunteers could get there was probably a good fifteen minutes.

A fire in a high wind could eat an acre in that time: attack the very Inn itself.

But the first worry was not the Inn: sprinkling the ground to keep the grass lovely had probably also kept the grounds damp enough for protection as long as the fire was still small.

But how small was it?

Very smoky: a few knee-high flames, but in these first few minutes it did not really appear very threatening.

All these thoughts had raced through her mind in only a few seconds.

"You run and estimate the size of the fire," Kip ordered Lee. "Come tell me. I'll be in the main kitchen."

She did not give him the reasons she was going to the main kitchen; it would waste his time and hers. She simply began running, ducking back through the ballroom and out the side door, down the halls, through the side kitchen where she and Lee had had their first kiss, and burst into the main kitchen. She was right. The place was full of cooks and waiters and busboys slowly shutting down, as the formal dining service drew to a close for the evening.

In a sharp voice that cut through the music of the rock station they had playing and the sound of steak on an indoor grill, she said to them, "There's a fire in the brush by the croquet court."

Startled, they looked up to see a pretty brown-haired teenager in a dancing dress.

"This outside door is closest," she said, gesturing to the door with its huge red EXIT sign. Flinging the door open, Kip began pointing at each person in the kitchen. "You! Find the outdoor faucet and hook up a hose to it. You Get that big bucket under the sink! Carry it out to dump on the fire! We may be able to put it out before it spreads! You! Call the fire department. Tell them to come into the lower parking lot. You!"

And just as the teenagers had obeyed her when she stopped them from swimming in the pool two hours earlier, the kitchen help obeyed her now.

It didn't occur to any of them not to.

Kip had such an air of authority that even

the assistant cook stirring a sauce that would burn if he didn't keep tending it just moved the sauce onto a cold burner and ran to obey his orders.

"You!" Kip said to a busboy. "Round up the waiters without any fanfare and get them out there to put out the fire."

"Right," said the busboy, turning on his heel and heading for the dining room.

"You!" Kip said to the chef. "Get that fire extinguisher. You! Get blankets from the linen closet in the hall. Maybe the fire can be extinguished by smothering it."

Kip had not spent a minute and a half saying this.

Now she was out the door herself to get her people organized at the fire's edge.

Gary and Mike and Con searched fruitlessly among the trees. The steep sides of Mount Snow rose above them, and this was no open ski trail, but a dense wilderness of vines and undergrowth, ragged rock edges and crawling clinging tree branches.

"Beth Rose! Beth! Beth!"

But no one answered their yells, and the dark closed in on them like the arms of the leafy trees.

Gary tried to tell himself that if she had fallen into this it would have cushioned her like a net beneath a circus act.

If she fell? he thought. Who am I kidding? *If*.

He tried to look up the mountain and locate

the trail's edge where Beth had gone over, but of course it was impossible. Not only was it too dark to see anything, but the trees growing higher up leaned over him, sheltering him to the point that he thought in a rainstorm he could probably stay dry down here.

And dry was the word.

Underfoot everything his shoe touched crunched like breakfast cereal. Good weather for a forest fire, he thought, and once more he shouted for her, crying, "Beth Rose! Bethie!"

Nobody answered.

He could hear Con shouting, too, beating at underbrush as if fighting through a jungle after the enemy. Gary's head felt thick. He saw a square of pale light ahead of him and thought — *it's her dress.* He stumbled toward it, muttering her name, gasping for breath, blundering into unseen fallen logs and stepping into a quagmire of wet soft earth where an unexpected spring had soaked the ground.

But it was not Beth Rose, or anybody else.

It was simply an opening in the forest ceiling and moonlight pouring down, reflecting limply on the huge leaves of some evil-looking cabbagelike weed.

It was pointless.

They could find nobody, see nothing in the thick woods by night.

Mike was the first to give up.

"Beth Rose! Beth!" came Gary's voice, despairing, raw.

Standing on the path, staring into the nothingness of a forest at night, Mike thought, She must have broken her neck. Hit her skull maybe. Or else she'd moan, or answer us, or —

There was a moment of silence in which none of them was shouting Beth's name.

In the silence Mike could hear Kip.

He couldn't make out her words, but he could hear the authoritative ring of her shout.

Giving marching orders to somebody, that was for sure! A lot of somebodies.

It was enough to make a guy surrender. Could that girl not get along for an hour on her own without subjecting everybody to a military drill? Kip seemed to have a whole army at her disposal right now. Out of doors? It couldn't be the VCR prize and the questionnaire she was marshaling them all to solve. What on earth could they —

But of course.

It would be Kip who found Beth Rose. Mike could not imagine how Kip would manage this, but she managed everything else.

"Gary," he said. Horror thickened his throat and it came out a whisper. He tried to stay mad at Kip for getting involved, but horror over what condition Beth Rose might be in covered his anger. Because why would Kip need all those people except to move a body out of a terrible spot?

"Gary!" he tried again.

"You found her?" Gary's voice was raw from shouting.

Mike couldn't see him. He wondered briefly what they would do if all of them got lost down here. "I think Kip did. Higher on the mountain. Come back to the path, Gary. We've got to head toward the Inn."

The fire had found a dead bush among the thick pretty hemlocks, and the bush went up like a torch and was consumed so quickly that Lee, the only witness, was not sure he had really seen it. It almost exploded, and its sparks leaped across the grass, and its flames circled the hemlocks and captured dead leaves and the smallest trees on the forest rim.

And even as he turned to run for the phones, and Kip flung open the kitchen door and ran with the first bucket of water to the fire, the fire crawled up another tree and licked branches that reached into the woods.

Molly stared at the kids in the ballroom.

Oh, it reminded her of so many other dances.

As always, the girls seemed to be at one event, and the boys seemed to be at another one entirely.

Girls had spent hours, weeks even, getting ready for this. They had shopped for dresses, made hair appointments, worried about the color of their shoes dyed to match their dresses.

Boys, however, had simply shown up. As usual there were a dozen boys who simply refused to dance at all, even slow dances, so their dates had the questionable privilege of being at a dance where they never got out on the floor. One of those girls was Roxanne, a wonderful gymnast, a terrific jazz dancer, who looked incredible in a tight shimmery short dress made to show off long legs and graceful moves. Her date was so unwilling to dance that he wouldn't even leave the tables where the food was spread.

Roxanne had begun dancing alone, and the rest of the girls in that position had joined her. This seemed to make the boys very happy: no longer guilty about not dancing, they could stand with a bunch of other boys and talk about what they would do on Sunday, which would be a good day, as opposed to Saturday night, which was a dance and therefore boring.

Molly gave some thought as to which group she would join.

The boys?

Molly was always ready to join boys.

But Molly was always ready to dance, too, and like the girls on the dance floor, she lacked a partner.

Molly's feet tapped. Molly's hips swayed. Molly's shoulders moved, and her hair swung lightly with the music. It was the girls she joined.

She lost herself in the dance.

Hypnotized by her own rhythms, Molly stamped and whirled and slid and reached. Half the time she had her eyes closed. They danced fast and hard, and the band, thrilled that finally somebody was out there living it up, played faster and harder and they spun like cars around a race track, endlessly circling, and loving every minute.

A hose was found down by the rose garden. The waiter assigned to that chore unscrewed the hose and carried the whole awkward roll of it up the path and over the croquet court.

The fire actually seemed to know that trees arched above it: that if it could just shift a few yards into the woods, it could climb — climb an entire mountain! Swallow a whole resort!

The wind played in the leaves as if teasing the fire to join its dance, high up there, out of reach, out of control.

The people below prayed for the wind to drop.

If anything, the wind picked up, and fire grew gold fingers, orange at the tips, like a witch's hands.

Swirling as the wind swirled, the fire went west, stretching for the forest. It consumed everything in its reach. It cooked. It grilled. It baked.

It spread.

Lee and the busboy dropped two heavy

wool blankets down where the fire was low, not raging. He wasn't afraid of it, yet.

He had a sense that it was a tie score so far: Kip's team could win at this stage.

The chef assigned to call the fire department raced across the lawn to report to Kip that they were on their way.

Two waiters turned on the ground sprinklers to keep the Inn side of the fire wet and safe.

Lee was standing right over one sprinkler when it went on. A gentle spray of water climbed up his legs and filled his shoes. Somehow it was an all too familiar feeling.

Second time tonight I've been drenched, he thought. He turned to share the joke with Kip, but she was far too busy to notice or to care.

Lee thought, This woman is amazing. I have never seen authority and leadership like this.

Fearless, too.

She gave orders calmly, so that while the waiters jumped into activity, they were also steadied by Kip's purpose; nobody was frightened, nobody was wasting time, nobody except me is just standing here.

Kip said, "Lee, the hose isn't going to do it, and there's only the one water hook-up here. We've got to organize a bucket brigade from the kitchen." She turned to the rest. "You! You! You!" And beckoning them to come after her, she ran back to the kitchen and they followed, Lee among them.

Lee thought he had not met a girl before who could do this.

In fact, he didn't know if he'd met anybody before who could.

Marshaling her workers like an army, he thought. She should go to the Naval Academy, or West Point. She has what it takes.

He started to tell her that he had decided on the perfect future for her, but it was definitely the wrong time. Kip simply put a spaghetti cooker in his hands and a lobster cooker in the next guy's arms.

It would be a long brigade.

There was a long, long stretch of wet grass to hand the buckets down.

Kip put the assistant cook in charge of that and sent Lee to the ballroom to get the rest of the kids.

"Me?" Lee asked dubiously. He didn't know these kids, the band was playing very loudly, everybody was happily dancing — how would he break into this and —

Kip shrugged and ran to get them herself.

The important thing was to cause no panic, but to get them working quickly — get the fire stopped.

She was in the ballroom in ten seconds and stopped the band short in one more. She simply held one flat hand up to them and took away the mike in the singer's hand.

Nobody argued with Kip.

But then, nobody ever had.

Not successfully anyway.

*　*　*

Fire.

The word was both terrifying and exciting.

Fire.

There were those who shrank and those who jumped up.

Fire.

Matt, working on this third enormous sandwich, was one who was rather delighted. From the time he was a toddler, he had always wanted to be a fireman. Matt was first through the doors, and the sight of the fire stopped him short.

He had expected some little piddly grass fire: a little smoke, a few charred embers.

This fire — it was a real fire.

Flames taller than he was.

All the colors of fire: hot red, orange, yellow, gold, even white.

The colors of destruction and death.

Matt began running again almost the same moment he stopped, with the result that he stumbled and Kip caught up to him. "Bucket brigade," she gasped. "You be on the fire end. At this stage I think we can douse the actual fire."

Whew, Matt thought.

He was not at all sure they could put the fire out. If he had been in charge he would have opted to wet down the surrounding area, and hope the fire would burn itself out once it used up what it was eating now.

But he was not in charge. Kip was, and he obeyed her.

In the girls' room Pammy gave up and wandered off. Anne and Emily sighed simultaneously and rolled their eyes at each other.

"I'm grateful to her, though," Emily said.

"Really? Why?"

"Well, she made it all normal again. I was feeling as if I had fallen off the edge, and nothing about life was average, and everything in life was overwhelming. But life is really just old Pammy being a pain, and running out of Kleenex, and wondering how Matt is doing."

Anne grinned.

They fixed each other's hair, taking a serene pleasure in making their exteriors smooth, no matter how chaotic their insides might be.

The door opened and they winced, expecting to be interrupted again by a Pammy type, and feeling, unfairly, that they should be allowed to have the girls' room to themselves for an hour or two of peace.

But it wasn't a Pammy type.

Not at all.

Gary got up to the fire first, and Kip stuck a scrub bucket in his hand and a spaghetti pot in Con's.

Gary was a relatively relaxed person, but having to search for the body of his girlfriend — and now to find instead an empty scrub bucket in his hands and a fire raging where he had expected to see Beth's body on a stretcher — Gary just stood there.

"Run the bucket back to the beginning of the line, Gary," Kip said.

The next bucket was passed down, flung on the fire by Matt, and tossed to Gary, so that now he held two of them.

Gary stared at the buckets, and then at Kip.

Irritated by his slowness, Kip said, "Move it, Gary. The wind is picking up. Either we get the fire now, or it gets away from us." She gave him a gentle push toward the Inn.

"Kip, Beth Rose is missing. I think she might have fallen off the cliff path."

Lee, in line now next to Matt, saw that Gary said this as if expecting Kip to solve it. Gary, who had defeated him in wrestling matches, standing there asking Kip what to do?

"*Might* have?" Kip repeated. "Did she scream? Did you hear her fall?"

Lee marveled that Kip could switch gears from the fire to interrogate Gary and find out the precise situation he was in.

"No," Gary said. "She just all of a sudden wasn't there."

Kip shook her head firmly. "I'm sure Beth Rose is just sitting in your car, or else in the girls' room, or even dancing with somebody else, Gary. Check it out in that order and once you've found her come back here to fight the fire." She relieved him of his buckets and forgot him. "You!" she said, handing the buckets to a waiter.

It was not, however, a waiter.

It was Mr. Martin, the manager.

He had been sitting happily in the resort dining hall, talking with a bunch of people having dinner after a wedding rehearsal. One of the guys was a mountain climber and had some great stories to tell. It was only when the bride-to-be mentioned that Rushing River Inn no longer seemed to have any waiters that Mr. Martin realized something was amiss.

We walked swiftly to the kitchen, annoyance building up quickly, and found the kitchen filled with teenagers filling every available container with water.

His hands went cold.

If Kip had ordered him to carry a bucket, it would have slipped out of his hands.

But two things he saw instantly: first, that the fire was not a threat to the Inn itself, not now anyway; and second, that the brown-haired girl who had cleared things up at the pool was now in control of the fire.

He blinked, and stepped back inside. He called the emergency number himself to be sure that had been done — and it had, they told him. They had just gotten a few crew, and the trucks were leaving now. Then he walked back to the wedding party and asked each man to take up a fire extinguisher.

"Hey," said the bride indignantly. "Aren't you an equal opportunity fire fighter?"

But Mr. Martin had no time to worry about that: he just wanted the people who could carry those heavy things the most easily, and he didn't want any bulky, flimsy dresses catching fire.

For the first time in his hotel-managing life he ignored his guests and ran back to the fire, to have a sixteen-year-old girl hand him a bucket and tell him to stand in line.

Chapter 11

Gary had difficulty obeying his wrestling coach and got into heavy arguments when his father gave him orders and spent a good many hours resisting his teachers, and he was not always the most obedient employee.

But he never thought twice about following Kip's instructions.

It was Kip. She knew what she was doing.

Stumbling through the mass of teenagers who were now pouring out of the ballroom and crossing the croquet lawn to join in the firefight, Gary raced down hill to his car. He took a short cut through the formal rose garden and paid the price with badly scratched hands.

Be in the car, be in the car! prayed Gary.

Be mad at me, be as mad as you want, Beth! Just be in the car. Not at the bottom of a cliff.

But she was not sitting there pouting.

Gary turned, gasping for breath and headed uphill again. The slope seemed a lot steeper than when he had escorted the fragile Anne up it a few hours ago. He was more winded than he wanted to admit. The gravel slipped under his shoes, and he momentarily lost his balance, reminding him horribly of Beth Rose's fall.

Con took the next two buckets. The wind that whipped the fire along whipped through Con's dark hair and lifted it from his forehead. He was sure Kip was right. Beth Rose was, after all, much too careful to get any-place near the edge. They hadn't heard her scream because she had gone back to the dance. They had flung themselves into a panic over nothing.

Half laughing, Con said to Kip, "I'll feel like such a jerk if all along Beth Rose had just been fixing her hair in the girls' room with Anne." He had a charming smile, and he used it, sharing the joke with Kip.

Kip was much too strung out to worry about how her words sounded. She only knew that she had been wanting to tell Con Winters off since the day Anne had decided to leave high school. "You *are* a jerk, Con," Kip said. "It won't hurt you to feel like one."

One by one the fire extinguishers were lugged to the scene, but the fire was so hot that no one could get very close, and the streams of chemicals put out by the extinguishers accomplished little.

The wind picked up instead of dying down. People kept shifting from one side of the fire to another to keep out of the heat and away from the reaching flames. Kip moved all girls to the kitchen end of the line because their flaring dresses were too likely to catch sparks.

Nobody seemed to care about clothes. Dresses girls had spent a month searching for were wet, smoke-stained, and torn, but the girls just grabbed the next bucket and passed it on. The boys' shoes were soaked, and their trousers were covered with soot, but they just kept at it.

Kip forgot that she was even at a dance, let alone that her lovely outfit was destroyed.

The waiters had rounded up two more hoses, screwed them together, and run them to another faucet on the far side of the Inn. So now they had more water, but the pressure was low, and the water that was just fine for somebody's shower after a golf game was not an effective weapon against fire.

"Change tactics," Kip said. "We can't put this out after all. We'll have to contain the fire until the fire department gets here."

She put them all to wetting down everything in a desperate effort to block the fire from spreading.

The wind rose, and the leaves rustled, and the kids threw water.

If the fire gets away from us, Kip thought, it goes up the mountain. And how will anybody fights the fire up among the rocks and cliffs and tangles of wood?

And the fire spread and pushed her back

as it had pushed the waiter back. And, Kip thought, we're going to lose.

Molly stared at the fire.

She felt her tiny purse, hanging by a leather strand at her side, and through the thin supple leather she felt the pack of cigarettes.

She knew she had not put out the cigarette when she tossed it away.

It had been on purpose.

She disliked the idea of having to be careful.

She disliked being neat on homework assignments, and she disliked paying attention to whether or not a new blouse should be washed only in cold water, and she disliked being told she could not smoke in a particular room.

She liked flicking a cigarette away.

It was the same sort of gesture she used driving away: too much pressure on the accelerator, which made the tires scream.

A flick.

She stared at the fire. Girls unwilling to risk their gowns stood with her, on the terrace, watching the effort.

Most of them kicked off their silly heels, hiked up their skirts, and raced to the kitchens for help.

Oh, they'll save the day, Molly thought. Kip's in charge. That means it will work out. And then Kip will be a hero, and everybody will have a story to tell for years to come, and the boys will love it, and the party will last til dawn.

I actually did them all a favor.

But still, she did not have quite enough guts to just watch the fire, and she slithered away from them all, taking refuge, as so many generations had done before her, in the women's room.

The women's room, however, was chaos.

Just as Emily and Anne returned to the subject of exactly where was Emily going to live now, a body leaned against the door, pushing it open by that alone, and almost fell into the lounge.

"Bethie!" Anne shrieked, jumping up off the daybed. "*What happened to you?* You look as if you fell off a cliff."

Beth Rose did not laugh. Her lovely dress was torn. The soft papery texture had been no match for the wilderness. Her red hair was standing up, thick with leaves and twigs. There was blood on her cheek, and she cradled her arm at her side because it hurt so much.

"Oh, no," Emily gasped, "you *did* fall off a cliff!"

Mike watched Kip.

Her filmy white lace blouse was torn and hung at the shoulders. The low back had a tear in it that could never be repaired. The wild hot pink and yellow skirt had a great green grass stain where Kip had fallen on the wet croquet court. The heel on her left shoe had snapped off, so that when she ran she was lopsided.

Her hair —

Her hair had been singed.

In horror Mike leaped forward and dragged her back from the fire. "Kip!" he said. "You're going to catch fire yourself! A few feet of brush is not worth getting burned!"

"It's winning," Kip said, meaning the fire.

"It's moving out into the woods," Mike agreed. He tried to comfort her. "But you're holding it. The fire department can't take much longer."

Kip was so hot from the fire she looked as if she had scarlet fever.

He touched her cheek, but she didn't notice.

He thought, We came as *just friends*. She didn't want to be just friends. She wanted me to love her.

Her dress was too wet to catch fire, but she was so close to the flames he had the sensation she would go up like the trees: become a living torch.

Maybe I do love her, he thought. All I can think about is Kip getting hurt. I don't care about forest fires, and I know if Kip said Beth Rose is all right, then Beth Rose is all right.

Mike said, "Please move back, Kip." He was terribly worried about her getting burned.

Kip muttered, "I don't know anything

about fires, that's the thing, Mike. I can't tell what I'm doing right and what I'm doing wrong. I don't know what to press on with and what to quit."

"Quit risking your life," Mike said.

She paid no attention to him.

Mike did not notice one of the waiters paying a lot of attention. He didn't see the waiter at all. He just took Kip's waist and dragged her back anyhow. Being bigger and stronger was an asset now and then. Kip resisted him. "This time," Mike said in her ear, "I know I'm the one who's right."

The heat from the fire hurt.

They all had to move back.

The waiter Mike had not noticed said, "Mike, keep moving. You're not safe, yet." He took Kip's other arm and both boys stepped backward with her.

And below them on the mountain road, strong and reassuring, came the welcome sound of sirens.

"No, I didn't fall off the cliff," Beth Rose said, while Emily used paper towels to clean up her skinned elbow. "I just fell down. I *thought* I was falling off the cliff. It was pretty scary. But I hit bottom pretty fast."

She tried to giggle, but nothing came out.

Anne said, "I just can't believe this dance. I get shoved in the pool and have to be blow-dried, and you fall down a mountain and have to be dry-cleaned."

Beth Rose began to cry. "I was such a

dope," she said. "I went along with Gary because I'm so afraid of losing him that I just agree with anything he suggests. Even if I hate what he wants to do, even if there's no reason for me to do it — I still do it!"

"Well, you lived to tell the tale," Emily said practically. "Although your dress didn't. Your dress is finished."

"What will my parents say?" Beth Rose moaned. She tried to see all of herself in the mirrors over the sinks. "At least the blood is just from my elbow. Who would have thought elbows bled so much? And I have no idea how I got elbow blood on my cheek. It is humanly impossible to touch your cheek with your elbow."

Emily had no purse with her. She could not get out her comb and brush and fix Beth's hair. She could only stand there mopping away with her wet paper towel.

I want somebody to comfort *me*! Emily thought.

I don't want to comfort other people!

I'm the one who needs help here!

Beth Rose went and got dramatic and now everybody will gather round *her*!

I want them to gather round *me*!

Emily was ashamed of her own selfishness. She tried to choke it back. She tried to worry that Gary would be irritated at Beth Rose for walking away without telling him. It took earthquakes to impress Gary Anthony. If Gary even knew by now that Beth Rose wasn't with him, Emily would be impressed.

And if Gary *cared*, Emily would really be impressed.

There isn't a boy in the world who really cares, Emily thought, down as low as she had been all night.

Now it seemed to her that she had not abandoned Matt in order to sit in here weeping with Anne, but that Matt had abandoned her, and she had been forced to sit in here.

The fire department took charge with such speed that Kip felt like a slow-motion film. Suddenly there were real hoses, and men wearing suitable uniforms that resisted fire, talking to each other on hand radios and bringing out the special jeeps and engines that were used to fight brush fires.

The firemen escorted the kids back to the ballroom where they would be out of the way, and all talk turned to clothes: whose dress was ruined, whose suit was destroyed, whose shoes were ready for the dump.

The kids were laughing and excited and having an absolutely wonderful time.

Kip thought, in some strange way, everybody loves a disaster. They get to sacrifice. They get to do their best. They get to fling themselves into it.

She walked away from the fire with Mike at her side.

She was looking for Lee, though.

He was right there, and he was grinning at her.

* * *

Lee had never had to make a decision regarding a girl before in his life. Simply by avoiding girls, he had managed to be sure the problem never arose. Now here was Kip, with whom he had fallen totally, irretrievably in love, and her so-called boyfriend was back again. Next to her. Arm at her waist. Obviously impressed with her.

Kip deserved admiration. Lee agreed with that.

But Lee didn't want the so-called boyfriend admiring Kip!

Hey, buddy, it's my turn, Lee thought. Move out.

But of course the so-called boyfriend did not move out: he moved in closer.

Lee thought about this, and he decided that he didn't like it, and he wasn't going to stand for it. When Kip turned and smiled at him, he grinned back. She looked terrible. Her hair was clotted to her head. If she had started the evening with any makeup, she certainly had none left now. A huge soot mark on her cheek obviously annoyed her and she had rubbed it with her hand and spread it over most of her face. The lovely lace blouse Lee had admired an hour before was no longer white and no longer in one piece. And the wild, crazy skirt was filthy.

Lee said, "You were wonderful, Kip." He gave her a hug, which involved inserting his right arm between Mike and Kip's waist, and elbowing Mike away literally. Mike let it happen only because he didn't know what was happening, and when Mike said, "Hey, what — ?" Lee simply kept on hugging. Then he moved into kissing.

Kip said, "I'm too dirty, don't kiss me."

Lee said, "Lady, when you find out how dirty you are, you're really going to be in for a shock, so I want to get all my kissing in now before you decide to go home for a bath."

"Home for a bath!" Kip cried. "It's that bad? I look that awful?"

"You look perfect," Lee said. "Just dirty."

Lee chose to pretend that Mike was not there at all. When Kip stopped hugging him, and started to look down at her clothes and put a hand to her hair, Lee pulled her back to his chest and kissed her again. He still didn't look at Mike, and said, "Come on. We'll rent a guest room, and you can have a shower."

"Hey!" said Mike. "Hey, what do you mean by *that*? Hey!"

He sounded like a jerk, saying "hey" so often, but Lee knew that Mike couldn't think of anything else under the circumstances. Lee intended to be sure that Mike didn't come up with anything else, either.

Mike got in Lee's path, and said, "Who the hell are you?"

Lee smiled at him. "I'm her new boyfriend. A guy decides to hike up the mountain to see Two Cliffs, he's taking a much bigger risk than just falling off the mountain, see. He risks losing his girl."

* * *

Molly swung into the bathroom. Nervous, strung-out, she was already reaching for a cigarette to calm herself down again when she practically tripped over Anne, Emily, and Beth Rose.

What a trio, Molly thought. I can't stand any of them.

But then, Molly was not particularly fond of any collection of girls.

She lit the cigarette and blew smoke at them just to be sure they didn't give her a hard time back.

"You look a little worse for wear, Beth," Molly said, laughing. "Didn't Gary tell you you're supposed to *climb* the mountain, not sled down in your new dress?"

Anne debated what penalty she would pay if she just shoved Molly through the wall. Beth Rose thought an excellent final chapter for her ruined dress would be to strangle Molly with it.

As for Emily, she had reached her limit.

For the second time at Rushing River Inn, Emily burst into agonized sobs, flinging herself down on the daybed and burying her head in the one lone pillow.

"What's with her?" Molly asked, waving her cigarette at Emily.

"She has no home," Anne said. "Her parents threw her out. She doesn't know where to live."

Beth Rose gasped. "How horrible! Oh, Anne, what's wrong with our town that so many people have family problems!"

Molly snorted. "It's nationwide, Beth Rose. You're just insulated if you think the rest of us don't have problems."

"At least the rest of us aren't out *starting* problems," Anne said. Perhaps Two Cliffs had a use after all. Perhaps she could get together a happy-go-lucky group to lose Molly on one of those cliffs.

Anne and Beth sat on the daybed on either side of Emily and tried to hug her. Molly rolled her eyes and smoked on. Molly said, "What's the point in having a boyfriend if you don't use him now and then? That Matt is a cute kid, Emily. Just move in."

"It isn't that simple," Anne said.

Molly raised eyebrows at Anne. "Simple?" she said. "Why, Anne Stephens, you're the most simple-minded of us all. Getting pregnant! Anybody with a room temperature I.Q. knows how to avoid that. Who are you to say what's simple?"

Emily sat up. "I say we kill her," she said to Anne and Beth Rose.

Beth Rose said, "No, if I go to prison I want it to be for something that matters."

Anne, Emily, and Beth Rose laughed together and blew pretend cigarette smoke at Molly, and tapped pretend ends of non-existent cigarettes into invisible ashtrays and then blew more pretend smoke in Molly's face.

The door to the girls' room was flung open with tremendous force.

Molly, standing with her back to it, was

caught by the door and thrown into Emily's lap.

"It had to be *my* lap," Emily said.

"At least she dropped her cigarette first," Beth Rose said, giggling. "Molly has such good manners."

The girls looked up to see who had to use the bathroom so urgently, and it was Gary.

Chapter 12

Kip touched the white lace of her lovely filmy blouse. In a maidenly way it was the sexiest thing she had ever owned. Sweet but sensual, covering all, yet hinting of what was beneath. And it was ruined. Where it wasn't torn, it was smoke-stained. She swallowed. Her mother had let her spend much more than budgeted because the blouse was perfect, and because, as her mother said, Kip could wear it for years, to all sorts of things: her cousin's wedding, the summer theater series, the evening in the city. All coming up within the month.

And the skirt, too — the swishing exciting skirt in its wonderful hot splashes of color — it, too, was dead.

Kip's chin began to tremble. Partly for the lovely clothes that had made her feel so special, that were supposed to turn this last dance into one where Mike would love her once more — and partly for what her mother would say to her when she got home. Actually her mother did not ever yell at Kip: she would look at Kip with intense deep disappointment, so that Kip would feel she had just let down generations of family by ruining her blouse.

"Don't cry," Mike said.

Kip reserved crying for when she was home alone. But she was exhausted, and wet, and shivering, and filthy . . . and now the fire didn't seem half as important as the shredded white lace sleeve.

She bit her lip hard, but the tears welled up anyway.

And then the unbelievable happened. The sort of thing that happened to sweet romantic-type girls, like Beth Rose, or Anne.

Two boys (count them, Kip, she thought, count them, two!) hugged her to make her feel better.

Believe me, Kip thought, I feel better. What is a mere forest fire and a little smoke compared to having two boys worried about me?

Lee was in the best position, as he had his arm around her anyway. He tightened his arm, and pulled her in against his chest and said, "Half the problem is you're soaked. And the wind is blowing and you're freezing."

"You're not exactly dry yourself," Kip said.

"I know. The sprinklers sprinkled my legs instead of the croquet court."

"I'm dry," Mike said. "Come on inside with

me, Kip, and we'll find a blanket or something."

"*I* know where the blankets are," Lee said, not letting go of Kip at all.

Kip's teeth began to chatter. Both the boys demanded the privilege of finding a blanket to wrap around her.

This is the life, Kip thought. Boys wanting to coddle you. Where have I been for sixteen years? She began laughing. She put a kiss on Lee's cheek and Mike said, "Hey!" so she also kissed Mike, and now Lee said, "Hey!"

"If I could only be dishonest," Kip said, "I'd be so much better at flirting."

"You aren't flirting, you're freezing," Lee said.

"I am flirting," Kip said, "this is called flirting. Normally a person wants at least to be *clean* while flirting. And probably she wants to have brushed her hair in the last century, and maybe eaten sometime in the last decade. *Then* she can flirt. But I, because I am tough, I can flirt even in this condition."

Lee and Mike looked at each other while Kip giggled.

Lee — who had never considered love at all until tonight — knew now that he was the kind of guy who was going to fall in love once and stay in love forever. He knew that for sure, and he knew Kip was the girl. He knew it the way he knew few things: it was just a matter of explaining it to Kip, and they would both know.

Mike, however, was remembering what fun Kip had been in the beginning. All winter long, it seemed to him now, they had laughed together just like this and tickled each other with silly remarks and silly fingers. He remembered how he had always felt so darn good when he left her house. So good that he just had to telephone Kip once he got home to hear her voice again. Her lovely authoritative voice: the one that didn't fool around, and didn't play games, but just spoke up, and made him feel terrific.

I made a mistake, Mike thought.

She annoyed me, and I decided to throw her away.

What, did I think she was garbage or something? This terrific funny great person who can lead an army or a dance, who can laugh off ruined clothes, and hug me till I think I'm the god of love?

Kip was so dirty that he shuddered to think how she would react once she saw herself in a mirror. He wanted to protect her from that, because in some way she was also beautiful to him. She who had saved the evening, saved the forest, and by doing that, saved their love.

Mike thought, it's just a matter of getting her away from this waiter guy, and she'll remember how it was between us. He resented fiercely the way Lee's arm was centered on Kip's body, and the way she was leaning in Lee's direction instead of his.

He thought, I could tell her I love her. She

likes that word. Her L word. I could use it. Not in front of this guy Lee, of course. But later. When I've got her alone.

So Mike turned Lee into the errand boy — the waiter — that Lee really was. He said, "Lee, I'll run ahead and get blankets, you bring her inside to meet me."

The fire chief said, "Mr. Martin, you are a lucky man. Those kids did a great job. If they hadn't gone to work on this fire as efficiently as they did, you'd have lost a mountain here." They stared at the site of the fire, lit now by the searchlights from the fire trucks: blackened, steaming, ugly proof that disaster had touched gentle Rushing River Inn.

Mr. Martin said, "Those kids probably also *started* the fire. What could have started a fire there except a cigarette? And who would be wandering around out here but kids?"

Gary picked himself up, pulled Molly to her feet, mumbled an apology to her for knocking her over, and sat down next to Beth Rose. By now the daybed was getting very crowded. Gary said, "You're all right." He wanted to run his hands over her, feeling for broken bones and bruises, but being in the women's room, supervised by Anne and Emily and Molly, made it very difficult to act normally. Not that there had been anything normal about this terrible night. Gary suppressed a desire to look around. He had never been in a women's bathroom before. His first thought was that it didn't appear to be a bathroom at all, but a bedroom. Complete with bed. He didn't know what to think about that at all.

Beth Rose started to apologize for letting him worry about her, but Emily jabbed Beth in the ribs.

"I felt that jab all the way through Beth Rose," Gary said. "What are you telling her, Em? Tell me, too."

He was so exhausted he could hardly move his lips, and the words came out thick and slow. "I guess mountain climbing is pretty strenuous, huh?" Emily said. "You sound as if you've been mountain climbing for years now, Gary, not just an hour or so."

"It feels like I've been searching for Beth for years now, not just an hour or so." He sat up. "I'm sorry," he said to Beth Rose. "I really am sorry. It just sounded like fun, and so I wanted to do it. Walk up Two Cliffs, I mean. I knew you didn't want to, but you're easy to drag along, you know, Bethie." And as always in their conversations, Gary managed, however gently, to put the blame right back on Beth. "A person should stand up for herself and not let herself be dragged along," he said reprovingly.

What Beth Rose really wanted to do was kiss Gary, but she restrained herself. If she did, once again Gary would have dragged her along. She said, "I realized that halfway up the mountain, Gary. So I simply left. I came back to the dance because dancing is what I came here for."

Dancing was what they had all come for, on this hot June Saturday night. It was hard to remember that this even was a dance. To Emily it was a family disaster, and a scary ride, and a moment with Matt, and some weeping with Anne. A problem not straightened out at all because there hadn't been time. To Beth Rose it had been a ridiculous hike at the wrong time in the wrong clothes. For Anne it had been a very unexpected swim in a cold pool.

"Do you realize," Anne said, "that not one of us has danced a single dance yet? And Saturday night is half over." She began thinking of Con again. Why do I always go back to him in my thoughts? Anne asked herself. He doesn't appear to be worth it. And yet if my thoughts came in neat little indented paragraphs, there wouldn't be a single paragraph without a mention of Con.

Anne looked down at her own dress. Bought by her grandmother, soaked by Con, dried by Kip, and untouched since. She wanted to dance in it. She wanted to dance with Con. She wanted the warmth of Con's body against her, and the heat from his hands, and the look in his eyes, and touch of his lips. You're pitiful, she said to herself. Always looking for romance. What did you find last time you looked for romance, huh, lady? Ask yourself that!

Gary took Beth Rose's hands in his and

turned them over. One palm was scraped raw where she had fallen onto rocks. "Oh, no! You did that on Two Cliffs trail, didn't you?" he mumbled. "I'm sorry, Bethie, I — "

"It's just a matter of being grown-up," Beth Rose said. "I never have been. I let you be the grown-up while I stayed the little girl. You want to hike up a mountain while I'm wearing an evening gown? Yes, Gary, yes, if that's what you want, I'd love to, too," she imitated herself. She smiled at him ruefully. "So it's really my own fault, Gary."

Even as she said it, she knew she had let Gary have his way yet again. She had let it be her fault instead of his. But if for once I admit it's my fault for being weak, she thought, maybe I can be stronger next time around. Because one thing I do know: I want to be with Gary. So I'd better figure out how to pull it off.

Gary looked at the raw flesh of her hand and said nothing. Eventually he heaved a huge sigh. Whether it was a sigh of relief that Beth Rose was all right, or exhaustion from the evening's panic, they could not tell.

Molly, whom they had all forgotten, said sarcastically, "So this is what the best couples talk about. I'm so impressed. It's so fascinating." She blew cigarette smoke in front of her and pretended to be massively bored.

Beth Rose said, "Molly, could you just flush yourself down the toilet or something?"

Gary began to laugh. He pulled Beth to her feet and kissed her and hugged her and said,

"That was good, Beth. You should speak your mind more often. I'm in favor of it. Come on. Let's dance."

He opened the women's room door to escort Beth Rose out, only to find on the other side Matt's fist raised to knock. His face an inch from Matt's knuckles, Gary said, "Oh, hi, Matt, how's the fire?"

"Out," said Matt. "Uh. Gary? Uh. What are you doing in the women's bathroom?"

"He has serious problems," Molly said.

"Nah," Gary said. "All my serious problems are solved now, huh, Beth?" Gary grinned at Beth, grinned at Matt, and even grinned at Molly. Then he said, "Kip get the fire out?"

"Nope. Just held it. Fire trucks got here, though, and they've got a couple of pumpers so they had the water to put the fire out pretty fast. They'll be here for a while, I guess, making sure they got it all. Then they're going to start asking questions. See who started the fire."

"*Who started the fire?*" repeated Gary, absolutely shocked. "*You mean it was arson?*" He had been so frightened by the idea of Beth dying that the fire had stunned him, and he had not really thought about the fire as a living creature that somebody had started. Now that Beth was okay, and he was okay, Gary could think. But this thought had never crossed his mind.

Anne, Emily, and Beth Rose knew nothing of the fire at all. They had spent the whole time in the women's room talking. So Matt had to bring them up to date, with all the details of the bucket brigade, and Kip's leadership, and the height of the flames, and so forth.

"I can't stand it," Beth Rose moaned. "All our lives people will talk about the great fire we put out at the Last Dance. Everybody will share memories of what they did to help, and everybody will have souvenirs or scars or something, and I'll have to admit I was sitting in the bathroom the whole time."

They all laughed. It did sound ridiculous.

Matt sat down on the daybed where Beth Rose and Gary had been a moment ago and leaned on Emily. "You smell great," he told her. He had found fighting the fire incredibly exciting and had loved the smell, and the sound, and the sight of that fire: loved the war of it, the battling between man and nature. But he loved equally the peace of this strange little room, with its old-fashioned colors and designs and this peculiar little bed, the likes of which they certainly did not have in the men's room. And he definitely loved being next to Emily again.

"What perfume is that?" Anne asked, trying to identify it.

"Obsession," Emily said.

They all laughed. "The perfect name," Matt said kissing her. "Because I am definitely obsessed."

"Not to mention filthy," Emily said. "This fire was definitely not the cleansing sort."

"Wait'll you see Kip," Matt said. "She doesn't even have a dress left!"

They stayed in the lounge: Gary and Beth Rose leaning on each other, Matt and Emily hugging, and Anne alone.

Caught in their own thoughts, they forgot there was another person in the women's room: a girl who quietly backed out of sight, putting out her cigarette in a toilet before sliding into the baby-changing room where nobody would notice her.

Arson?

The fire department was going to question people?

For arson?

Molly was furious. Arson was where you meant to destroy something. Molly had simply had a cigarette, and it wasn't her fault the leaves were dry. They weren't going to find out who had had that cigarette, that was for sure, and if they managed to question her, well she would just manage to be casual, because she certainly had not committed any crimes; it was not a crime to slip out doors and have a cigarette while you waited.

Con Winters was one of the few kids who did not leave the scene of the fire when they were told to. He retreated back against the wall of the Inn, where he stood with a couple of assistant cooks and watched the firemen at work.

In its raging splendor, the fire had a certain beauty, but now as the firemen doused it, it became merely a nuisance that crackled and spat. And then it was gone. It left behind a terrible acrid smell, and when the wind blew back toward the Inn, Con choked.

You are a jerk, Con. It won't hurt you to feel like one.

Kip's words rang in Con's head over and over again.

Is that what the school thought? That he was a jerk?

Did they all think that Anne was a fool to bother with him? Did they all really know about Molly, and was he kidding himself that he'd kept it a secret?

Like everybody else, Con now had wet shoes, and inside the shoes his socks were wet, too, and he scrunched his toes miserably, wanting to take the socks off and get dry and comfortable again.

I am a jerk, he thought.

That's what every guy wants to know, isn't it? Handsome, athletic, smart, charming, articulate, the whole nine yards.

But basically just another jerk.

The firemen knelt by the bushes, looking for evidence of how the fire started. Con wished he had a chore like that to keep his mind occupied. Like everybody else in the high school, Con felt that Kip had a handle on life. So if Kip said he was a jerk, that wrapped it up. He was, indeed, a jerk.

He thought he might lean against the wall of the Inn forever, with that smell in his nostrils and that wind in his hair.

But he saw Molly leaving. Walking toward the parking lot and the car in which she had come alone.

Molly . . . who had said in the ballroom that she would join him on Two Cliffs trail. That suggestion had made Con really race up the trail, which had made it that much harder for Beth Rose to keep up, and impossible for Molly to follow. Molly never did anything that would cost her. But the fire had started right at the base of the trail. Where Molly would have stood making the decision whether or not to come up after Con. And Molly smoked. Incessantly. It had always annoyed Con because he found it a repulsive habit, and besides when he kissed her he was kissing cigarette taste. Molly never used ashtrays. She flicked the cigarette out the car window or onto the sidewalk. It was Con's shoe that ground it out if they were walking together.

No, Con thought. She wouldn't —

But of course, she would.

Molly didn't care.

Right now, was she leaving early because nobody had danced with her? Because she had not succeeded in getting Con away from Anne? Or was Molly leaving early because it would be dangerous to stay late?

Con tried to remember what cigarette brand she smoked but couldn't. Molly kept to the bushes as she moved toward her car and nobody but Con saw her. She took a shortcut downhill which led her by the pool.

In the moonlight trees reflected blackly in the water.

I didn't push Anne in the water! Con thought suddenly. I was nowhere near Anne. But I was so furious when she accused me of shoving her in, I forgot that maybe somebody else shoved her in! And who would do that? Molly. Only Molly.

You are a jerk, Con. It won't hurt you to feel like one.

Oh, Kip, he thought. I feel like one. I promise you. I really feel like one. But what do I do about it? Tell me that, Kip. Give me a few lessons in that, Kip.

Pammy was delighted to have everybody back in the ballroom again and readily available for questioning. "Oh, I just can't stand it!" she cried. "I know who was born in Beverly Hills. I know who has a peacock for a pet. I know who here does not like chocolate. But who was born on an ocean liner and who has been skiing in six countries? Somebody admit it! Somebody here is fascinating and won't tell! That's not fair! If you were going to keep it a secret, you shouldn't have come to the dance."

She got no answers.

"Pammy, get lost," everybody else said.

They wanted to compare notes on what they had done to save the forest. The girls with damaged dresses wanted to see what could be fixed, and the boys with ruined shoes wanted to go barefoot. But most of all, everybody was absolutely starved. Totally, completely starved. They descended on the remaining food like animals and consumed everything in sight and demanded more. Of course, there was nobody available to supply anything more. The kids debated the wisdom of simply going into the kitchens — which several of the girls knew intimately now, having filled an awful lot of pots of water from those sinks — and taking food.

Pammy wailed, "But I want to win that VCR!"

"You will, you will," one of the girls said. "You'll win by default, Pammy, because nobody else has bothered. You'll have the most answers even if you don't have all the answers. Now pay attention to the important things, Pammy, like the fact that there is no more soda. None! And we are all dying of thirst and smoke damage!"

Mike pushed through looking for blankets.

Lee followed with Kip.

Two things immediately happened: half the kids wanted to hug Kip and tell her how wonderful she was, and the other half recognized Lee as a Rushing River Inn waiter, and wanted him to get to work and supply them with soda. It was a situation where everybody but Lee got what they wanted.

Mike returned with the blanket, the kids separated Lee from Kip, Mike wrapped Kip in the blanket, and Mr. Martin appeared, ordering Lee to get refreshments not only for the dancers but also for the firemen.

Lee seriously considered quitting on the spot.

Mike was going to get Kip unless he, Lee, stuck around.

But if Lee quit on the spot, Kip would have no use for him. He knew her well enough already to know that Kip did not approve of quitters.

So Lee, furious but helpless, went back to serving.

And Mike, having won that round, stayed with Kip.

Chapter 13

"I don't believe we've ever had a party in a women's bathroom before," Matt said, grinning.

"I suggest we adjourn to the ballroom," Beth Rose said. "There's so much to do. Ruined dresses to inspect, fire damage to repair, stories to hear."

"Food to eat," Gary said, "soda to drink, potato chips to crunch."

Gary took Beth's arm and together they walked out of the women's room.

How romantic they looked! Beth's heavy red hair pressed against Gary's thick dark hair, and the skirt tangling between them, and then puffing out behind. The room was much emptier without them: as though love had walked out and just left the other three there, killing time.

Anne's throat hurt. Con, she thought. *Oh, Con.*

Emily touched the little silver knots that dotted the pale green dress, and caressed the silver rope that hung at her waist. She stared at her pink-polished toes and the thin silver strap of her dancing shoes. I just want to be a girl at a dance, Emily thought, not a girl without a family. I don't want my heart to be heavy. I just want my feet to be light.

Apparently Matt felt lighthearted, because he put one arm around Anne's waist, and the other around her own, and tried to get the girls to stand with him. He said, "I can beat old Gary. I can have one beautiful girl per side."

Emily could not even stand, let alone dance.

She literally felt heavy. It was as though all her problems really did weigh something, and they really were on her shoulders. Unless somebody had a winch to haul her up, Emily could not possibly get to her feet. Gary and Beth Rose might just as well have carried the laughter away when they left. Sure enough, Beth's musical giggle wafted down the hall toward their ears. A sound Emily might never make again.

"Matt, I just don't — I just can't — I still — "

She put her head on his shoulder. She could smell the smoke on him.

Once more she felt as if she were doing something wrong. I have troubles, Emily thought, real troubles, and yet I feel pushy for wanting to talk about them. I ought to deal with my own dumb problems in my head, and let everybody else have the stage. Never complain. Always be the one to laugh, always be good company, never be rude.

How did I learn that, in a family where all my mother and father ever do is complain?

Now I'm going to walk out there into the ballroom and be polite again. Have a soda, dip my potato chip in sour cream, and giggle about this fire I didn't see, don't care about, and hate the smell of.

She was immensely tired. Maybe this really *was* the last dance. Maybe she would never conquer this heavy sick feeling. Matt wanted her to dance and forget her parents. As if it didn't matter.

But they were her parents. It would always matter.

Perhaps she could just sleep for several weeks, and when she woke up it would all have solved itself. Sleeping Beauty had the right idea. Lie there on your pedestal and let somebody else deal with the wickedness abroad.

Sleep, Emily thought. It's a nice enough idea, but in what house? What room? What family?

She began to cry again. Matt sighed, as though Emily's tears were a burden to him. And, of course, they were.

Emily tried to stop crying.

Another, softer hand rested on hers. It was Anne, touching her across Matt's lap.

"Live with me," Anne said. "I want you. We have a large house, you know. And a guest room. And my father's abroad again, so we're kind of at loose ends. We need somebody else." Anne's smile was both sad and eager. "We need another topic, too, Emily. If my mom and grandmother could talk about you and your problems, instead of me and my problems — oh, wow, what a difference it would make!"

Live with Anne Stephens.

Emily tried to imagine it.

Matt, however, did not think much of the idea. "You mean you want Em around in order to make life easier for you?" he demanded.

"Matt," Anne said softly. "I know what it's like to hurt all over. I know what it's like to look into the next few months and wonder if you can live through them. And people helped me, Matt. They made life easier for me. Isn't that what friends are for?"

Matt could only wish that right now he was with friends like Gary and Mike and Con. Girls were always getting deep and intense and exhausting. What if M&M came to live with him and wanted to talk like this all the time? Matt liked to talk about antique cars and baseball. All this talk of hurt and the meaning of friendship. . . . "She could stay with us," Matt said uneasily.

Anne patted his hand, too. "She could," Anne agreed. "But I don't think you want to find yourselves in the mess I've been in."

"Hey," Matt said indignantly, "if you think that I — "

Anne kept patting. "No, I don't," she said. "I'm just telling you that my house is a better place for Emily than your house. That way she can keep dating you like a normal person, and have a normal life."

Actually that sounded pretty darn good. Matt wanted to date like a normal person. Coping with Emily's family problems sounded as if it would consist of sitting and moping, sitting and worrying, sitting and talking deep depressing stuff for hours.

"Anyway," Anne said, "I have a little sorting out of my own to do. Emily and I can sit up every night and counsel each other."

Matt could think of nothing worse, but Emily and Anne began jabbering across him, planning the living arrangements, and the studying, and the talking, and the phone calls.

He waited. Emily's voice, which started low and sad, began to rise. Matt didn't really listen to the words but just the tune, ready to start dancing when the pitch of her voice reached its usual happy level.

"The guest room is boring," Anne said. "We'll have to decorate it. It's got vanilla colored walls without a single picture, and plain Colonial curtains without any trim, and the carpet is a dull speckled greyish color. Mother has this ugly throw on the bed that somebody gave her: big sprawling roses in pink and yellow and red, and the leaves are lime green. You won't even be able to sleep until you cover it with a blanket. Then we'll put up rock star posters and stuff."

Emily's mother never paid attention to Emily's room. She certainly never cleaned it; that was Emily's job. But neither would she allow Emily to spend any money on it. There was never another coat of paint, never a suggestion that they could replace the old tired bedspread this year.

Emily loved the advertising in *Seventeen*: her walls were papered with cutout perfume ads or jeans ads. But if Emily were to Scotch-tape sexy record jackets on the walls or cents-off coupons for detergent, it was all the same to her mother.

Emily had always wanted a mother who cared: a mother who said, "Absolutely not! I refuse to allow those things on your walls!" or else a mother who said, "Listen, darling, let's do your room all over this year. Yellow, do you think? Or do you like mauve?"

To think that Anne's first consideration was making the room pretty for Emily's sake! Emily's own mother had never cared whether Emily liked her room or not. In fact, at this point, her own mother didn't seem to care if Emily even *had* a room or not.

"Your mother won't mind?" Emily asked anxiously. "She'll think it's all right for me to stay a while? Anne, I don't even know how long! It could be months, it could be — I mean, I just don't know anything! I don't even have my clothes. I don't have anything!" Emily started to cry again, and Matt got agitated, and shifted all over the daybed with nervousness. Emily fought back her tears.

"Are you kidding? She'll be thrilled," Anne said. "First of all, decorating a room is something she knows how to do. My mother will be so happy to be back where she knows what she's doing."

Matt, being a boy and slightly thick, said, "Oh, what's she been doing lately that she doesn't know how to do?"

"Having her first grandchild," Anne said.

Matt decided to shut up.

Emily thought that surfing must be like this. At last you could stand up on the board! The wave carried you, and the sun smiled on you, and the water cooled you, and you skimmed toward the shore. Emily was heading for the shore; she was not going to drown after all.

At first when you knew Anne, you knew only her beauty and perfection and it sort of tired you out. You felt unequal to it. But later you found out there was this really neat girl inside all that beauty. Living with Anne would be pretty wonderful. Her parents would be kind, nobody would raise a voice or a hand against Emily, and she would have somebody to talk to! It sounded much too good to be true. "Maybe we should call your mother up and ask her," Emily said nervously.

Matt liked that. Get this straightened out, stop crying, go back with other normal people and maybe have something to eat. "Well, then," he said, "let's go. Phone is in the hall."

"Next to the food, huh?" Anne teased. She stood up and shook out the folds of her dress and ran her fingers through her lovely sleek blonde hair. Matt did not notice her. He was watching Emily. He loves her, Anne thought. He really does. I wonder if he's ever said so. Is there a single boy here who's ever actually used that old L word?

This time Emily cooperated when Matt wanted her to stand up. She looked nervously in the mirrors to see what damage all this crying had done to her. Matt could not stop touching her. He tucked her hair back behind her ears, and adjusted the long earrings so they fell straight, and he ran his finger down the long back zipper of the dress he had picked out, and fiddled with the tiny silver knots. "You look pretty good, M&M."

That's it, Anne thought. That's as close to the old L word as Matt is going to come, if I know boys. All he can tell her is, she looks pretty good.

Matt and Emily kissed each other: not the kind of kiss Anne had ever done with Con. They pursed their lips and they tilted ever so slightly toward each other until their lips touched. After a moment of frozen kiss, they tilted until their faces were squashed together. Then Matt grinned and Emily giggled, and they moved apart and did it again. Anne wanted Con to kiss her like that.

Not a kiss that was a prelude to sex, but a kiss that meant — here I am! and I think you're cute and funny and neat to be around! I know what I'd like to do with Con, thought Anne. Be friends again. But I don't think he can.

Anne remembered Molly. The girl didn't seem to be in the bathroom anymore. It would be hard to miss her, in that short purple slab of a dress she had on. Probably went to find Con, Anne thought. And this time it was Anne who felt tired: so tired she did not see how she could walk after Matt and Emily. They would be in love, walking together just as Beth Rose and Gary had, and she, Anne, would be alone. Better get used to it, girl, Anne thought. Because this is your last dance.

With Con, anyhow.

Because Gary came for Beth Rose, and Matt came for Emily, but nobody came for me. No Con finished fire fighting and came searching for me.

For a moment she thought she, too, would break down and cry, but she got past it, and then Matt remembered her, and put his arm around her, too. The three of them paraded down the hall toward the phone (and the food) and Anne managed to laugh with them.

She and Emily would go home together, and they would get their acts together, and figure out what they were going to do with their lives.

And it would be good enough.

Con thought, I am such a little kid.

I haven't grown up at all.

I mean, you would think becoming a father and all that would have matured me at least a little tiny bit.

But no.

Here I am, still the little kid, still an annoying, noisy, stupid, aggravating little kid.

Con was grinning.

He couldn't wipe the grin off his face.

All the action was behind him, between the mountain and the Inn, where the firetrucks and the smoke and the frantic manager were making a racket. All the kids were either watching that, or inside watching each other. But me, Con Winters thought, I am watching Molly.

He had not been this happy in months.

Just thinking about it made him feel absolutely terrific.

He ran after Molly.

Pammy congratulated Kip on an excellent job of fire fighting. Then she got to the important part. "Listen, Kip, I have two questions. Were you born on an ocean liner and have you skied in six countries?"

Mike, not letting go of Kip at all because Lee was circling the place, had forgotten all about the VCR questionnaire. He stared at Pammy wondering if she had lost her mind.

Girls were peculiar creatures, definitely, but what kind of questions were those?

"Pammy," he said wearily, "do you mind? I gotta get Kip to the girls' room for repairs."

Kip said, "Ocean liner, Pammy, that's me."

Pammy crowed like a rooster.

Mike thought, Girls are so weird. He said, "What are you talking about?"

"I was born on an ocean liner, of course," said his girlfriend.

"*You*?" Mike repeated. "Go on."

Kip glared at him. She had always had a short temper, and here it came again. "What's the matter, Michael?" she said. "You don't think anything interesting could ever have happened to me?"

Somehow Pammy had gotten between Mike and Kip.

Mike tried to maneuver around Pammy, but Pammy's elbows and pencil were in the way and before he knew it, Lee was back, saying, "You were born on an ocean liner? Tell me about it! That sounds like a great story."

"Oh, it is," Kip said, and she walked away with Lee.

"Goodie, goodie, goodie," crowed Pammy. "I've got everything but this last one! Oh, I'm going to win that VCR, I know I am, I can start renting my movies right now! Mike, how many countries have you been skiing in?"

The band began playing again, and everybody was sort of surprised. They had been too busy thinking fire to think dance. The girls instantly changed gear and wanted to begin dancing again. The boys still thought there was plenty to say about the fire and there was no reason to ruin a perfectly wonderful night by going and dancing.

Beth Rose shrieked, "Kip! Your dress! Your hair! Your face! Are you all right! Oh, no! Oh, Kip, what'll we do?"

Kip was one of the few girls in the ballroom who often forgot about looks. She had a tendency to check herself at home before she left for school and not remember anything like hair or lipstick again till the following morning. She knew her blouse was torn, and her skirt ruined, but she hadn't really thought of her hair yet, or her face, or her hands and arms.

"Thank you, Beth Rose," Lee said acidly. "She was fine till you started screaming."

"Fine?" Beth Rose repeated. "She may be *your* definition of fine, but she's my definition of very bad shape. Come with me, Kip."

Gary was sick and tired of the women's room. He just wanted to be with Beth Rose. Why did she have to go and rescue Kip, who even filthy and torn looked completely in control? Gary moaned, "That women's room has seen more action tonight than it usually does in a year," he said. "Come on, Bethie, stay with me. Kip — "

He almost said, "Kip can take care of herself," which was certainly true. But that remark would not earn him any points. As it was Beth Rose glared at him. "I did what you wanted earlier in the evening," she said acidly, "and now — "

Gary nodded twenty times. "Right. Right. Now we'll do what you want. You set up housekeeping in the women's room and notify me when you're done. Right. Good idea. Go with it."

He and Beth Rose laughed, and he didn't kiss her, because there were too many guys around, but he grinned at her and knew that they were still friends.

Gary wondered briefly what had happened to Con.

Con had a habit of disappearing when the going got rough.

Gary readily understood.

Girls could put a lot of pressure on you.

But still. Anne. Con should either go with her or not go with her.

Anne was looking down. Gary couldn't stand people being depressed. He said, "Anne, still the evening star. Shall we dance?"

"Actually," Anne said, "I think we shall eat first. Then we shall dance."

"You understand the call of the empty stomach. I like that in a girl." Gary flirted with her easily, not having to pay attention to it, because it was second nature to him. And he knew Anne didn't care one way or another about him. They filled paper plates with goodies and drank large sodas too quickly and leaned against a wall with Matt and Emily.

Molly was right by the pool when she heard Con calling her.

She turned and saw him framed against the hillside: the black of the grass at night, and the silvery sky in the moonlight. He was taller than she was, and now he loomed up like an Olympic athlete, bounding gracefully toward her.

I won, Molly thought.

He wants me.

Triumph ran through her, and victorious laughter bubbled up and she wanted to yell, Come look at this, Anne. You think you're so great, Anne? Well, look who he wants! Not you, you ice maiden with your perfect elegant hair! But me. Me. Molly Elmer Nelmes!

She tilted her body sensuously and waited for Con.

Kip found herself hustled down the hall by Beth Rose, and she was of two minds about this. If she really looked that ghastly, she wanted to be cleaned up. But she didn't care nearly as much about her looks as she cared about Mike and Lee. Mike actually had seemed interested in her again, as though it were not, after all, the last dance — but a reprieve. In Mike's eyes and in his embrace Kip had felt his original crush on her returning: he had seemed glad to be near her, and proud of her, and excited by her. And Lee — he was definitely without question glad to be near her and excited by her.

Kip muttered, "Beth, can it wait?"

"Can what wait?"

"How awful I look."

The girls stopped walking and Beth Rose looked intently into Kip's eyes. Kip whispered, so Lee couldn't hear, "I mean, I'd rather spend the time with him unless it's Disaster City."

It was definitely Disaster City.

It was Disaster Nation, as far as Beth Rose could see.

On the other hand, Lee was no disaster. Lee was cute and built and interested in Kip, and a person could not discount that just to wash her face. So Beth Rose said, "What do you think we should do about her dress, Lee?"

"What can you do?" Lee said practically. "You don't have another one hanging around, do you?"

"Good point," Beth Rose said. "Let's — uh — let's all go into the women's room and wash her face and stuff and then we'll just go back to the dance — and uh — dance!"

"All?" Lee repeated. "All go into the girls' room? I'm not the right gender, in case you haven't noticed."

In Lee's case, it was very easy to notice. A wrestler like Gary? You didn't overlook that kind of thing, not if, like Beth Rose, you found boys the most interesting scenery on earth. She said, "Oh, I've been hanging out

there for hours, and so have Matt and Gary.
You'll feel right at home."

"Uh. I don't think so." Lee looked as
though he might cut and run, which was
definitely not what the girls had in mind for
him. Hastily Beth Rose said, "Okay, okay.
You wait here. We'll take exactly two
minutes. Don't go anywhere."

Lee used his two minutes to find a sheet.
It was white and it had lace trim; it was used
in one of the suites upstairs. But it would
make a great toga for Kip. When the girls
came out again, the soot was gone from Kip's
face and her hair no longer had half-burned
leaves in it, and her hands were clean. Her
dress was still the complete shambles it had
been. Lee said, "I have a toga for you. Here."
He held up the lovely white sheet.

Beth Rose and Kip exchanged glances and
grinned behind the protection of the sheet.
Beth Rose nodded and Kip nodded back at
her. Beth Rose and Lee wrapped Kip in the
sheet draping it tightly. Beth Rose said,
"We don't need this old sleeve; it's torn to
shreds anyway," and she ripped it off the rest
of the way, so that now, in her white sheet,
Kip had one bare shoulder and one bare arm.

Lee grinned from ear to ear.

Beth Rose looked at the other two and
thought, Togas are pretty sexy.

Then she thought, Lee is pretty sexy!

And then, because every girl loves a romance, whether its hers or not, Beth Rose
thought, This is a perfect dance.

*   *   *

Con just kept right on running. It made him feel terrific and incredibly strong, like a race horse going for the jump. Molly was in the perfect position, about a foot from the pool's edge. He stuck out a hand, palm first, like stopping traffic, and as Molly cooed hello, Con pushed her into the pool. He kept running, taking an enormous leap over the corner of the pool and landing safely on the tiles. Behind him the water rose in a huge splash and Molly's scream turned into a gurgle as she went under. Con plowed to a stop in front of the thick bushes. He turned around to make sure Molly could swim, and she could, so he squatted down and said to her, "Molly, old girl. So far tonight you've shoved Anne in the water and you've started a forest fire. I think it's time to cut your losses and drive on home."

Chapter 14

The first fire truck to arrive was the first to leave.

Gary and Beth Rose were dancing as it swung slowly down the mountain road and back toward town. Beth Rose's eyes were closed, and she was barely even swaying. Gary simply shifted his weight from left to right and stared over her red hair and into the black night beyond the windows.

He kept reliving the falling sensation he had had inside back during those horrible moments when he really thought Beth had fallen off the cliff. It seemed silly now. Why, like Kip, had he not known right away that Beth had just joined the dance? He would have preferred to sit and let the falling feeling go away, instead of standing here halfway imitating it.

But Beth Rose wanted to dance, and he wanted her to have her way for a change, so he danced.

He thought about the following day, and

what he was doing then. A bunch of his friends who would never come to a dance, not if they were paid a salary to do it, were going to a car race. Gary loved races of any kind: men, horses, cars, dogs — he didn't care. He would never consider taking Beth Rose, or even telling her about it. It was not her kind of thing, and he just wanted to be with the guys there, anyhow. He wished he could give Beth Rose a slot: say, Tuesdays and Saturdays, leaving the rest for himself and his buddies. But girls didn't do that, not happily, anyway, so Gary accepted the compromise. It was not in him to waste time arguing either with himself or with Beth Rose.

Con opened the door to the ballroom.

More than one girl looked up to admire him.

He had a slouching sort of arrogance, like a rock star who couldn't be bothered with his fans, who knows they will come back to him no matter how rude he is.

"Con's back," Gary murmured to Beth, because she had been terribly worried. She said that if Con abandoned Anne one more time, Anne woud lose it. Gary didn't think for one minute that Anne would lose it. Con might. From guilt. But not Anne. Anne was much stronger. That was why Con needed her, in Gary's opinion: Con was the kind of boy who was only half there without his girlfriend.

Beth opened her eyes and followed Con's progress. The dance floor was crowded now, and Con threaded between couples. It was slow going. Or perhaps Con had to go slowly to get his courage up to face Anne, with whom he had not spent one minute so far this evening.

Either Matt and Emily had adopted Anne, or else Anne had adopted them.

Beth Rose was finding it difficult to tell the strong ones from the fading ones. "Do you ever think you have something completely psyched out," she asked Gary, "only to find you don't understand anything at all?"

Gary laughed. "All the time." He followed Beth Rose's eyes. "But if you're thinking of Con, that's pretty easy to understand."

"Oh, good. Tell me."

"He just didn't want to deal with it. He had a choice and Anne didn't."

"But he's going to deal with it now," Beth Rose said. She wondered why she was standing up for Con. In many ways she despised Con. Yet in the end she always wanted him to be okay.

"No," Gary said firmly. "*It*, meaning a pregnant girlfriend, *it* no longer exists. He'll never have to deal with *it*. He just has to deal with tonight."

Beth Rose wanted terribly to join the others. She wanted to hear how Con dealt with tonight, and whether he mentioned *it* and whether Anne forgave him. But she didn't want to admit to Gary that parts of her heart were dying out here away from the real action.

Gary began laughing. "You can't even wrench your eyes off them," he teased.

"I can so. I'm not paying the least bit of attention."

Beth Rose had to laugh at herself even as she pretended.

Gary said, "Hey, I'm gallant. I'll escort you back to the scene."

"Oh, goodie. Do it quickly; we're going to miss the opening act."

Mr. Martin said, "Lee, I realize this is a very stressful evening. I realize you are saving the girl who saved the Inn. However, I really must request you to get to work."

Kip said, "He's working quite hard right now, Mr. Martin. I'm having a hard time keeping my toga up."

"Uh-huh," Mr. Martin said dryly. "Lee, the task at hand, please, is once more to replenish the food supply for these starving animals, otherwise known as teenagers."

Lee sighed.

Kip said, "Saturday night, then, Lee."

He could hardly bear to let go of her hand. And next Saturday night seemed a hundred years away. But her eyes were fixed on him, bright piercing eyes, as excited about next Saturday as he was, and Lee thought: Mike is out. I'm in. That's that.

He went to work.

Mr. Martin asked Kip if she knew how the

fire started. Of course she didn't, and they talked of the fire a little, but Kip was bored talking to Mr. Martin. She began sliding away from him and back to the dance, so she could show off her toga and hear more compliments and maybe flirt with Mike again.

Two boys, Kip thought. This is me. I know this is me because I looked in the mirror. Furthermore, it's me in a mess. Me totally bedraggled.

And I have two boys.

There's a message in that, but I don't know what it is.

Touching Lee excited Kip, but knowing Mike was interested again excited her more. She wanted to tell the world that two boys were fascinated by her, but she wanted to keep it in her heart, all private and cozy and perfect.

She was also starving.

Holding her toga around her, Kip went to the food table to figure out how to eat while holding her clothes up.

Mike was there before she had even found the kind of roll she liked. He put mayonnaise on the roll for her and mustard on the other side. He remembers I hate butter, Kip thought. Mike put roast beef and ham in the same sandwich. "No," Kip said firmly, "you were doing great till you mixed meats. Back up. Dump the ham."

Mike dumped the ham. He said, "Coke?"

She nodded.

He got her a glass of Coke.

She could not hold the Coke, eat the sandwich, and still keep her toga up. Mike alternated holding the Coke and the sandwich for her. He said, "I'd hold the sheet instead, but you seem to have a pretty steady grip on that."

Kip could think of nothing to say, so she just drank more Coke.

"That guy Lee asked you out?" Mike asked after she finished the glass of soda.

"Yes."

"What'd you say?"

Kip pulled her toga a little tighter around her shoulders. "Does it matter to you, Mike? You said you were just coming to this dance as a favor to me. You said we were just coming as friends."

Mike hated this kind of thing.

He *hated* having to let go of any part of himself and admit anything. But with Kip you never had a choice. He drew in a deep breath. "It matters to me."

Kip nodded for a while. Mike didn't know what the nodding meant. He was surprised how much he cared. He didn't know if it felt good to care that much again, or bad. He just wanted her to say —

She can't say yes to me, Mike thought. I haven't asked her anything. That guy Lee is the one who asked her out. Mike said, "Uh. Next Saturday night. Uh. You want to go to a movie?"

"Next Saturday I'm going to the country fair with Lee. We're taking my little brothers for the day, and then we're going to send them on home and spend the evening at the fair on our own."

Mike swallowed. "Sounds like a nice day," he said. He thought, Great. Now I have to bid, like an auction. He said, "How about tomorrow? Sunday afternoon." He couldn't think of anything they could do. He said, "We could go swimming. First swim of the summer." Where? he thought. Great. Now I have to get up early tomorrow morning and figure out who has a pool.

But Kip didn't answer him. She just kept looking at nothing in particular.

"How about it?" Mike asked. His stomach hurt. And not because he needed food. He wanted her to say yes.

He realized suddenly that one reason he had broken off with Kip was because it had been terrific. Mike didn't want to want a girl so much. He wanted to want a girl *occasionally*.

"Why?" Kip said bluntly. She was always blunt.

It was easier to be "just friends" than to be head over heels in love.

He almost walked **away**.

He almost abandoned her instead of admitting how he felt.

He said, "Because I love you."

"This was a great dance," sighed one of the boys, happily examining his completely ruined clothes and sniffing the acrid smell of smoke in them.

"That's because you never danced," his girlfriend said, who was not nearly as pleased with the dance as he was.

"Think of the cost of this dance," Pammy said, shaking her head. "We're talking millions here. Add up the ruined dresses, the ruined shoes and stockings, and hairdos and all."

"That's true," Jimmy agreed. "We're probably a disaster. We should apply to the federal government for special funds to get new clothes and hairdos again."

The boys teased him. "Oh, *you* need a new *hairdo*, Jimmy?"

Nothing ever bothered Jimmy. He just laughed.

Roxanne, whose beautiful gown had been torn when she slipped in the muddy croquet court and fell on her own water bucket, said, "You know what my mother is going to say about this?"

"What?" Although they could well imagine what *their* mothers were going to say!

"She'll say, Roxanne, that is the *last* Last Dance you'll ever attend!"

Emily was at peace.

She knew it was a temporary peace.

She knew that out there, beyond the dance, were two angry parents. No home. A place for a night or a week at Anne's, but not a lifetime. She knew that she would have to go home to get her clothes, if nothing more. She did not know if her parents would offer her a truce, or if she would accept.

But she knew she had friends, and that Matt loved her, and that Anne had come through for her, the way other people had come through for Anne. I can make it, Emily thought. I'm strong, like Anne. This isn't what I wanted, in fact, this is exactly what I did *not* want out of life. But it's here, and I'm going to deal with it, and I'm going to be okay.

"We've got every answer except who skied in six countries," Anne said. "I think whoever has been abroad so much didn't come to the dance after all." You would have thought Anne had nothing on her mind but the VCR questionnaire. Emily stared out into the ballroom, wondering who else out there was knee-deep in pain, or possibly deeper than that: maybe drowning in it. But having a good time in spite of that, Emily thought.

Or faking it.

Emily was not faking it.

She turned to Matt, and kissed him lightly, to reassure herself that he was there. And he was.

Beth Rose was relieved. She hadn't missed a thing. They were killing time talking about dumb stuff, like the questionnaire, instead of real stuff, like whether Anne and Con would go together again. There was a bench against

the wall, a rather long one, on which three
or four could easily fit. Gary plopped down
in the middle and sprawled on it. The band
was playing a hard, fast rock piece. Beth
Rose moved in front of Gary and kept on
dancing from the waist down.

Con just stood awkwardly opposite Anne,
as if he had come with somebody else and
didn't know Anne particularly well.

Gary said, "Well, Annie, old girl, actually,
I just happen to know who skied in six
countries."

"You do!" Pammy cried, whose ears picked
up anything at all to do with winning the
VCR.

Gary beckoned to Anne. She moved closer.
Gary sat up and patted his knee. Anne
perched way out on the very tip of the knee.
Gary, grinning, tugged her back against his
chest. Then he brushed away her golden hair
so he could whisper in her ear.

Con watched without expression.

Beth Rose kept dancing.

Anne sat on Gary's knees as if she were
sitting on a counter somewhere. She made a
fist, rested her chin on that, and rested her
elbow on her own knee.

Gary made a big production out of whispering the answer in Anne's ear. Very loudly he
whispered, "I made it up."

Pammy was outraged. She almost broke
her pencil in half.

"See, I've always wanted to be a con
artist," Gary explained. "I love to say out-

rageous things and see if anybody believes me. At the restaurant when I wait tables people from out of town ask me if I'm in school. I say, Yes, I'm putting myself through medical school, or Yes, I'm an apprentice in music box repair." Gary smiled happily. "They always believe me," he said proudly.

"What's so funny about that?" Pammy demanded. "After going to all this effort to fill out our questionnaires, everybody is snagged on number seventeen because number seventeen is a big dumb fib."

"Yeah, but it's a big dumb fib that worked," Gary said, grinning.

Pammy glared at him.

"Aw come on, Pammy," Gary said. "You've been happy all night tracking down the skier. Admit it. You had a terrific time and all because of me."

Pammy snorted and walked away.

Anne's large eyes were fixed on Con's. Her head was tilted in their old trick: they used to match tilts, so that their eyes were always even. Con hadn't thought of that in months. By the time he remembered their habit, Anne had given up and looked away.

Con loved how her fist was tucked under her chin. How her smooth gold hair fell to cover her face. But it was Gary's lap she sat on, and Gary didn't appreciate what he had. Gary actually preferred boring old Beth Rose.

Anne, hidden by her hair, struggled with tears. Why was she on Gary's lap? Oh, Gary

242

was nice enough, but it was Con she wanted.

And Con, Anne thought, who doesn't really exist. I made him up. I constructed the Con I want as if he were made out of Legos.

She made herself think of Emily instead, of how she and Emily would talk into the night, and share the things Anne had nobody to share with, and talk of the things that hurt Emily too much to say to anybody else.

The band broke off playing and the DJ's voice rang out. "Ladies and gentlemen, we have a winner! We can finally give away this beautiful VCR!"

Pammy jumped up onto the little stage, kissed the DJ, patted the VCR on its little display table, and grabbed the mike herself. "I just want to say thank you to everybody here. I just loved talking to all of you and I learned such interesting things tonight! Don't you just love all that we've learned about each other tonight? Aren't we just having the best time?"

Luckily the DJ took the mike back.

Anne slid off Gary's knee and on to the far end of the bench. "Well, pooh," she said. "None of us gets the VCR."

Emily giggled. "Strong language there, lady. *Well, pooh?* Where have you been that you picked up such questionable language? I am shocked."

Beth Rose was tired of spying on Anne when she had a romance of her own to attend to. She bowed in front of Gary, extending her hand graciously. "I would like to dance with my favorite con artist. Tell me, did you prefer the slopes in Switzerland or Tibet?"

Gary leaped up, and danced her backward until they were right in front of the band, getting their ears blasted out. Speech was impossible, but the dancing was perfect. They went wild, writhing and stomping and twisting to the music, hardly looking at each other, but aware of nobody else.

The L word, Kip Elliott thought.

Aaaah, they're collecting the wrong questionnaire. Nobody cares who was born on an ocean liner, and nobody cares who won't eat chocolate. The thing the girls want to know is: who said the L word?

Mike said it to me, Kip thought. She was staggered. She could hardly look at him, but she need not have worried. Mike could hardly look at her, either. They were definitely the twitchiest couple in the ballroom.

Two boys, Kip thought. One of them I know that I am going to be in love with shortly, if I'm not already, and in the kitchen, he as good as told me he's in love with me! The other one I used to love, and I don't tonight, but I could fall back in love with him pretty quickly.

Is it possible to love two boys at once?

Is it possible for me, inside me, Kip thought, to love two people?

And just as important, is it possible for

two boys to allow themselves to love the same girl?

Kip thought, now there is a challenge for the well-organized woman.

Kip thought, I think I am looking forward to summer.

Anne sat still. She didn't look at Con. His face would be closed up anyhow, and it wouldn't tilt to match hers, and he would be a stranger to her, as their own baby would always be a stranger to both of them, and she would start to cry, and he would leave her and go to Molly.

Con said, "Miss Stephens?"

She stared at his waist which was directly in front of her face.

"Excuse me, Miss Stephens, I realize you hardly know me, but I'd like to become better acquainted."

Anne tilted her head way back until she could see his face. It was expressionless as always. And handsome, handsome, handsome. Her hair fell backward like silk. She could feel it against her bare neck.

Con said, "Tomorrow's the first day of summer vacation." He seemed to be very nervous. "Maybe we could have a first date, too. Something casual. You know. Just trying to get to know each other."

Anne turned her head sideways and looked up at him out of the corner of her eye. "I haven't been dating much lately."

Con licked his lips. "I don't want to rush

you. I thought we'd start slow. Nothing emotional. Not even a kiss."

"I'm not such good company these days," Anne said.

Con located her hands. One was still tucked beneath her chin, and she was half sitting on the other. "A person can learn how," Con said. He very slowly tilted his head, turning it away at the same time, so now they were both staring at each other from the corners of their eyes, at angles so great it was hard to focus.

Anne said, "I need to talk. Heavy things. Important things. Things I couldn't seem to discuss with — with — with my — old boyfriend."

Con shrugged. "He's gone now."

Anne's hands in his were very hot and very dry. He sat down next to her. Anne whispered, "I can't even hold hands very well. I'm sort of at the end of my rope."

Conrad Winters bent over very slowly and took the laces out of his shoes. The laces made thin whipping sounds as they came out of the holes. Con held the cords in his hand. He knotted them together and then made knots at each end. "Maybe," he said softly, handing her one end, "maybe if you hold your knot, and I hold my knot, we can keep each other up."

Not from guilt, Anne thought. And not because Molly bores him. Not because his parents said he should.

Con is here because he wants to be with me.

Anne took the knot.

Con turned his wrist, looping the lace around his wrist until he had a bracelet, and her hand, holding her knot, was pulled in close.

"I'm sorry, okay?" Con said, so softly she could hardly hear him. "I should have gone to see you more. I should have called more and written more. But I did volunteer to get married, and you said that would be the stupidest thing we could do at our age, and I was so glad you said that, but I was so mad at the same time! I didn't want you to say I was the stupidest thing in your life."

"I didn't want you to volunteer!" Anne said. "I don't want somebody to *volunteer* to marry me, like I'm a charity case, or a soup kitchen! I wanted you to *want* to marry me." Her hand was getting a cramp, hanging onto the knot. "But mostly I couldn't stand it that we even had to think about it. I wanted to be a happy kid. Not a pregnant woman. I wanted to be worrying about math tests instead of a baby. Oh, Con — I — "

Con said, sucking in a deep breath, "Miss Stephens, I thought we were going to be mere acquaintances for a while. We seem to be losing control."

Anne began to laugh. It was a real laugh, a laugh that came from inside and welled up and overflowed. She let go of the knot and put her palms on Con's cheeks and pressed his face together until Con's lips were all bunched up. She did not kiss him. She let go and took up the knot again, unraveling the cord from Con's wrist. She slid back from him until the lace was stretched out taut and they were a good four feet apart. "Mr. Winters," she said, "let us definitely *not* lose control again."

Con grinned. He said, "Maybe we could sort of pass kisses down the rope. You know, the way little kids try to send messages down fake intercoms? Two paper cups and a string?"

Anne, whom he had adored since junior high, tossed her yellow hair and her eyes teased and her lips curved into a smile.

"Aaah, it's quicker to use the wind," said Anne, and she blew him a kiss, and he caught it.

It was midnight.
The Last Dance was over.
Summer had begun.

point

Other books you will enjoy, about real kids like you!

point ® THRILLERS

☐ MC44330-5	**The Accident** Diane Hoh	$2.95
☐ MC43115-3	**April Fools** Richie Tankersley Cusick	$2.95
☐ MC44236-8	**The Baby-sitter** R.L. Stine	$3.25
☐ MC44332-1	**The Baby-sitter II** R.L. Stine	$3.25
☐ MC43278-8	**Beach Party** R.L. Stine	$2.95
☐ MC43125-0	**Blind Date** R.L. Stine	$3.25
☐ MC43279-6	**The Boyfriend** R.L. Stine	$3.25
☐ MC44316-X	**The Cheerleader** Caroline B. Cooney	$2.95
☐ MC45401-3	**The Fever** Diane Hoh	$3.25
☐ MC43291-5	**Final Exam** A. Bates	$2.95
☐ MC41641-3	**The Fire** Caroline B. Cooney	$2.95
☐ MC43806-9	**The Fog** Caroline B. Cooney	$2.95
☐ MC43050-5	**Funhouse** Diane Hoh	$3.25
☐ MC44333-X	**The Girlfriend** R.L. Stine	$3.25
☐ MC45385-8	**Hit and Run** R.L. Stine	$3.25
☐ MC44904-4	**The Invitation** Diane Hoh	$2.95
☐ MC43203-6	**The Lifeguard** Richie Tankersley Cusick	$2.95
☐ MC45246-0	**Mirror, Mirror** D.E. Athkins	$3.25
☐ MC44582-0	**Mother's Helper** A. Bates	$2.95
☐ MC44768-8	**My Secret Admirer** Carol Ellis	$2.95
☐ MC44238-4	**Party Line** A. Bates	$2.95
☐ MC44237-6	**Prom Dress** Lael Littke	$2.95
☐ MC44884-6	**The Return of the Vampire** Caroline B. Cooney	$2.95
☐ MC44941-9	**Sister Dearest** D.E. Athkins	$2.95
☐ MC43014-9	**Slumber Party** Christopher Pike	$3.25
☐ MC41640-5	**The Snow** Caroline B. Cooney	$3.25
☐ MC43280-X	**The Snowman** R.L. Stine	$3.25
☐ MC43114-5	**Teacher's Pet** Richie Tankersley Cusick	$2.95
☐ MC43742-9	**Thirteen** Edited by T. Pines	$3.50
☐ MC44235-X	**Trick or Treat** Richie Tankersley Cusick	$2.95
☐ MC43139-0	**Twisted** R.L. Stine	$3.25
☐ MC45063-8	**The Waitress** Sinclair Smith	$2.95
☐ MC44256-2	**Weekend** Christopher Pike	$2.95
☐ MC44916-8	**The Window** Carol Ellis	$2.95

Available wherever you buy books, or use this order form.

Scholastic Inc., P.O. Box 7502, 2931 East McCarty Street, Jefferson City, MO 65102

Please send me the books I have checked above. I am enclosing $_____ (please add $2.00 to cover shipping and handling). Send check or money order — no cash or C.O.D.s please.

Name _____

Address_____

City_____ State/Zip_____
Please allow four to six weeks for delivery. Offer good in the U.S. only. Sorry, mail orders are not available to residents of Canada. Prices subject to change. PT991